TOUR to DIE FOR

Also by Michelle Chouinard

The Serial Killer Guide to San Francisco

A Tour to Die For

A Serial Killer Guide to San Francisco Mystery

MICHELLE CHOUINARD

MINOTAUR BOOKS
NEW YORK

This is a work of fiction. All of the characters, organizations, and events portrayed in this novel are either products of the author's imagination or are used fictitiously.

First published in the United States by Minotaur Books, an imprint of St. Martin's Publishing Group

EU Representative: Macmillan Publishers Ireland Ltd, 1st Floor, The Liffey Trust Centre, 117–126 Sheriff Street Upper, Dublin 1, DO1 YC43

A TOUR TO DIE FOR. Copyright © 2025 by M. M. Chouinard. All rights reserved. Printed in the United States of America. For information, address St. Martin's Publishing Group, 120 Broadway, New York, NY 10271.

www.minotaurbooks.com

Designed by Meryl Sussman Levavi

Interior art: trolley © Allied Computer Graphics/Shutterstock; pickax © Love Employee/Shutterstock; knife: pink.mousy/Shutterstock

Library of Congress Cataloging-in-Publication Data

Names: Chouinard, Michelle author
Title: A tour to die for / Michelle Chouinard.
Description: First edition. | New York : Minotaur Books, 2025. | Series: The serial killer guide to San Francisco mysteries ; 2
Identifiers: LCCN 2025013709 | ISBN 9781250910011 (trade paperback) | ISBN 9781250420657 (hardcover) | ISBN 9781250910028 (ebook)
Subjects: LCGFT: Detective and mystery fiction | Novels
Classification: LCC PS3603.H687 T68 2025 | DDC 813/.6—dc23/eng/20250514
LC record available at https://lccn.loc.gov/2025013709

The publisher of this book does not authorize the use or reproduction of any part of this book in any manner for the purpose of training artificial intelligence technologies or systems. The publisher of this book expressly reserves this book from the Text and Data Mining exception in accordance with Article 4(3) of the European Union Digital Single Market Directive 2019/790.

Our books may be purchased in bulk for specialty retail/wholesale, literacy, corporate/premium, educational, and subscription box use. Please contact MacmillanSpecialMarkets@macmillan.com.

First Edition: 2025

10 9 8 7 6 5 4 3 2 1

For Lynnette & Maddie, for making it all happen

A Tour to Die For

SF KILLER CRIME TOURS

The Barbary Coast

The Barbary Coast is San Francisco's loving nickname for her original waterfront, the one that lined the shores of Yerba Buena Cove before it was filled in to accommodate a burgeoning population. The name comes from North Africa's Barbary Coast, where pirates from the Berber tribe were infamous for kidnapping merchant ships and holding them for ransom. And while that reference feels charmingly oxymoronic in light of San Francisco's current flower-power-hippie-liberal-environmentalist reputation, it's actually charmingly understated in light of San Francisco's dramatic history.

Most cities grow slowly, over hundreds of years. Paris and London, founded in 259 BCE and 43 CE, respectively, both clocked in between 20,000 and 25,000 inhabitants in 1000 CE. Even relatively recent cities like New York and Boston, founded in 1624 and 1630, didn't reach 25,000 inhabitants until 1776 and 1800. But when James W. Marshall discovered gold at Sutter's Mill in 1848, San Francisco exploded from a sleepy trading post of 800 to a teeming metropolis of 25,000 in less than two years.

Ships filled with men who came to make their fortune in gold mining found themselves without sufficient crew to leave again, and were abandoned in the water. Housing, which already consisted largely of tents and shanties, was completely overwhelmed; men paid upward of $400 in 2025 dollars to sleep in a chair for eight hours, and crowded conditions led to disease and fire. Skyrocketing demand for goods and nonexistent supply chains led to skyrocketed prices: a dozen eggs cost the equivalent of at least $400, a loaf of bread at least $20 (ten times what it would cost in New York), and the cheapest of blankets $1,500. The meager twelve-man police force and limited government infrastructure were swamped beyond hope, and vigilantes tsunamied into the void in an attempt to deal with the criminals, only to morph into criminals themselves. Because when thousands of men are looking to get rich quick and have no check on their baser impulses, all hell inevitably breaks loose.

So step back through time on this tour of San Francisco's Gold Rush, when the West was truly wild and the waterfront had no limitations: drinking, gambling, brothels, opium dens, lawlessness, protection rackets, theft.

And, of course—murder.

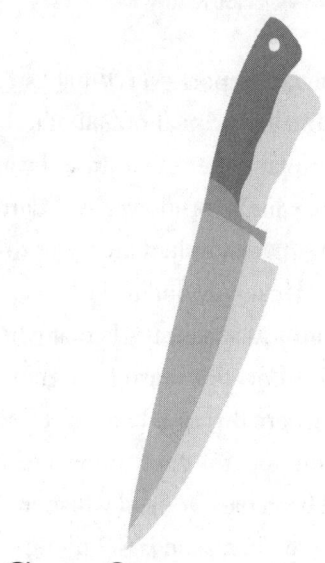

Chapter One

"Okay, everybody, huddle in close to me so everybody can hear safely." I gestured toward myself to make sure all the guests stepped onto the sidewalk. I loved the atmosphere added to my Barbary Coast tour by the dual siren songs of night life and neon, but the last thing I needed was a guest turned into street pizza by downtown's Friday-evening traffic.

A late-fifties woman who'd previously identified herself as Lorraine took the opportunity to sidle up to me, flipping her oversized glasses into her cloud of honey-blonde hair as she leaned over her venti-Starbucks-something to whisper at me. "Hey there. Are you the one that's related to—"

I threw up a hand to stop her, softening the gesture with a smile. If I'd thought solving the original murders attributed to my grandfather, dubbed Overkill Bill by the media, along with a pair of recent copycat murders, would stem the flow of questions that inevitably came when I led one of my true-crime tours, I'd been sorely mistaken. The questions hadn't slowed; they'd intensified, despite a change in focus. "It *is* true. That's the reason I started SF Killer Crime Tours' companion podcast, to report everything as I investigated the murders. And I'd love to talk to you about all of it, but I know some of the guests have dinner plans after the tour, so I want to keep us on schedule."

Lorraine's cornflower eyes darted around to the other tour guests; if her expression had anything to say about it, they'd have been vaporized instantly out of existence. "My friend told me you finished up her tour at a speakeasy. Is that where we're going today?"

Ah—Lorraine wasn't as ignorant as she let on. "That's a bit far from where this tour ends, but we'll be right by a café if that works?"

The hopeful glint in her eye faded along with whatever visions she'd been harboring of whispered illicit code words and dirty martinis served in mason jars. I plumped my smile up as though taking her silence for agreement, then launched into the next part of my spiel.

"This is the Old Ship Saloon, one of my favorite stops on the tour because it's a dramatic example of the sort of lawlessness that marked early San Francisco. We just saw Hotaling Place, which marked the location of San Francisco's original waterfront—that means this area where we're standing was once underwater." I glanced around to make sure everyone could hear me. "Ships continually crammed into the cove, filled with men looking to make their fortunes mining gold. When those men dissolved into the hills, they left behind ships without adequate crew to sail off again, so many ships were abandoned where they stood. When abandoned wood abounds, fire follows, and several conflagrations swept through the area, depositing massive amounts of detritus into the shallow waters. Men wheelbarrowed in sand to cover the gaps, and the cove gradually filled in, burying hundreds of ships under these streets. They remain there to this day, and the Old Ship Saloon is built over one of them."

I scanned their expressions. As if controlled by a single brain, they stared down at the base of the redbrick building, picturing the ship buried below.

"Her name was *Arkansas*, and she was damaged when she ran into rocks over on Alcatraz Island. She had to be towed the rest of the way into the cove, and because she was too damaged to ever sail again, was turned into a storehouse. Shortly after, Joe Anthony turned her into a saloon by cutting a doorway in her hull and placing a sign outside that purportedly advertised 'Gude, bad, and indif'rent spirits sold here!'"

Smiles broke out at the Wild West ingenuity.

"But the Old Ship Alehouse, as it was called then, was far more than a saloon. It was one of the most notorious Shanghaiing dens in San Francisco."

"What's Shanghaiing?" Lorraine asked, her annoyance at my earlier sidestepping temporarily forgotten.

"I mentioned many ships were abandoned when their crew ran off to find their fortunes—but some ship captains weren't willing to say goodbye to their ships. So they paid 'crimps' to kidnap new crew members for them." I leaned in as their eyes widened. "The crimps would lead unsuspecting men to saloons like the Old Ship Alehouse, where the bartender would give them a 'Mickey Finn'—a dose of opium in their drink. Once they lost consciousness, they were dumped down a trapdoor, and when they woke again—*if* they woke again—they were out at sea, forced to man the ship. San Francisco was so notorious for this, the term 'Shanghaiing' was coined here."

"But why is it called 'Shanghaiing'?" Lorraine persisted.

"Because Shanghai was one of the ships' primary destinations, and it was especially difficult to find sailors willing to go so far a distance." Lorraine's face cleared, so I continued. "As this part of San Francisco was filled in, a boardinghouse was built over the *Arkansas*. But the alehouse remained and the Shanghaiing continued until a 1906 federal law ended the practice, leaving the saloon to make money only from serving drinks. It's been here since, and the bones of the *Arkansas* are still located below."

As countless of my tour groups had done before them, they again stared at the base of the building, x-raying the layers of brick and cement for evidence of the structure. I gave their imaginations a minute to soak it all in, then signaled to Ryan Navarro, my employee and tour coconspirator, that it was time to move to the next stop.

• • •

But Lorraine wasn't done with me yet. As we passed Jack Kerouac Alley on our way toward Broadway, she pointed a French-manicured finger toward City Lights Bookstore. "Didn't I hear in your podcast that you're writing a book about the Overkill Bill murders?"

I threw a passive-aggressive glare at Ryan's back. He'd added that little nugget of information to the end of each podcast episode without my knowledge, and since I hate the sound of my own voice, I didn't find out until it was too late. "Um. I'm, um, yes I am," I sputtered.

In light of the promise Ryan made to our listeners, I had no choice but to put together a book proposal once I'd identified the killers in both the original Overkill Bill murders and the copycats. Then, much to my extreme shock and consternation, I'd almost immediately found an agent who wanted to represent it and a publisher who wanted to buy it.

"Boo-ya! I tolllllld you soooo," my business partner and bestie Heather Chen had crooned, swiveling her neon-pink chair away from her neon-orange desk as I stared open-jawed once the acquisition call ended. Heather's tall, lithe, and naturally elegant appearance belies her unexpected way with words—a way eerily reminiscent of the one Animal had with his drum set on *The Muppet Show*.

"Actually, *we* told you so," Ryan had grumbled from his own desk, a bare-bones utilitarian model he selected himself.

"True." Heather sent a single nod toward Ryan. "But she's been ignoring *my* good advice for far longer than she's been ignoring *yours*. After forty years of friendship, you'd think she'd've learned to listen to me."

"Damn," I'd said, still wading through the emotionally viscous implications of the call. "If someone wants to publish the book, that means I actually have to write it."

Heather and Ryan both shifted their attention fully to me, softening.

"You can do this," Heather said. "You're gonna kick the crap outta that book."

"Yeah," Ryan agreed. "You do a great job with the blog."

I nodded absently. Because we all knew the problem wasn't the writing per se—I'd loved writing since the day I had, at age two, picked up a crayon and insisted my mother teach me how to write my name. I'd started journaling not long after I started kindergarten, jotting down deep insights like *I love ice cream* that evolved over time to encompass emotional angst, spontaneous topical essays, and, once I found out my grandfather had been convicted as a serial killer, reports on whatever bits and pieces of information I cobbled together about his crimes and those of other killers. Fueled by my desire to know whether or not my grandfather had truly been guilty, I majored in journalism at Cal, and had even taken a stab at freelance journalism before getting pregnant with the love of my life, my daughter Morgan. Putting words on paper was not my problem.

The problem was my father. He'd never speak to me again if I wrote the book.

Heather scooched her chair closer and laid a hand on my arm. "You can't worry about your father, Capri."

"Yeah," Ryan chimed in. "He'll get over it eventually. Time heals all wounds."

I barked a terrified laugh. "In my father's world, all time does is distill down the bitter essence of a grudge. And he's been holding on to that one since before I was born."

From the day a nasty schoolyard bully shattered the innocence of my youth by telling me my grandfather was a killer, my father had made it abundantly clear that he would not allow either the names Overkill Bill or William Sanzio to be uttered under his roof. I've never been good at listening when people forbid me to do things, so my father's kibosh ensured that my interest in my grandfather's fate morphed into a low-key obsession. Luckily, I also have a strong self-preservation instinct, so I kept that obsession out of my father's line of sight. But when an Overkill Bill copycat murdered my ex-mother-in-law, I had to clear my daughter and myself as suspects, which meant I had to dig into that murky past. In the process I discovered an ugly truth my father wanted hidden, and he hadn't spoken to me since; writing the Overkill Bill book would throw a permanent dead bolt over that slammed-shut door. Still, I couldn't turn my back on my responsibility to tell the Overkill Bill victims' stories, either. So my adult conscience had been engaged in an epic battle with my frightened inner child since the day I signed the book contract, resulting in a mental block I couldn't shake and an in-progress manuscript that wasn't nearly as in-progress as it needed to be.

"When's the book coming out?" Lorraine asked, eyes shining with excitement.

"My, uh, my publisher hasn't set a date yet," I mumbled, then hurried to turn onto Broadway by way of subject change.

I perched on a spot across from the Beat Museum and waited for the group to catch up. While Ryan wrangled the stragglers up to me, I watched the waiting faces absorb the bawdy neon signs lining the wide street. Humans are remarkably predictable creatures, and over the years I'd memorized their reactions and used them to punctuate each tour's talking points. Sure enough, whispers broke out as the majority of eyes landed on the scantily clad neon blonde proclaiming "Topless Entertainment."

I dove in. "This is Broadway, one of the main arteries that run through North Beach, and one of the areas that defined the Barbary Coast as an adult playground dedicated to gambling, drinking, and prostitution. This spot is an interesting illustration of the push and pull between the San Franciscans who tried to keep order and those who tried to thwart it—what is now the Beat Museum was the sight of San Francisco's first jail, built in 1851, now memorialized by a plaque in the sidewalk. Law enforcement was badly outnumbered then and remained so for some time. Even twenty years later the much-improved force had only one policeman per fifteen hundred residents while the standard in cities like New York was one per five hundred residents."

I paused as all eyes turned toward the museum, seeking out the yellow-gold glint of the landmark plaque set into the pavement.

"As law enforcement caught up to the needs of the city, the Barbary Coast stopped being quite so Barbary, but this area of North Beach continued to be the red-light district into the 1970s and '80s. Now it's more of an artists' haven than anything else, although as you can see, adult entertainment is still liberally represented." I paused again, this time for the normal smattering of nervous smiles and tittered laughter.

But it didn't come. Instead, the guests' eyes widened, and one jumped in with a question. "If this is the main part of the North Beach red-light district, is this where Overkill Bill came to select his victims?"

I froze—this was new. This wasn't a side question about my relation to Overkill Bill that I could delay and revisit after the tour. This, I realized, was actually relevant to the tour itself. Given Lorraine's questions about my book, I should have seen it coming—and I couldn't see any way to sidestep the issue.

I swallowed hard, composed my face back into professional-guide mode, and nodded. "It is. All three of the sex workers Overkill Bill murdered worked this strip of North Beach."

"Because your grandfather had relations with each of them, right?"

I homed in on the man asking the question. Medium height,

prematurely receding hairline, glasses too small for his face. "That's right, yes."

"And the prostitute who identified him as Overkill Bill, she saw him in a streetlight." A mid-twenties blonde with one arm tentacled around her tall, muscular boyfriend's waist waved her free hand toward the posts. "Was that one of these streetlights here?"

"I, uh, I'm not certain where exactly that identification took place," I said. "But yes, I believe it was on Broadway."

As the group's collective gaze flicked up and down the street, picturing the partially lit murderer speaking to his victim, I tried to regain control of the situation. "For our last stop—"

But a scream rent the air, cutting me off.

I whipped around—the cry had come from Lorraine. Her well-manicured fingers were now plastered across her mouth, her venti-Starbucks-something splashed across the pavement in front of her. As I rushed to her side, one of her hands shot out, pointing toward a building down a side street.

"Someone's attacking that woman!"

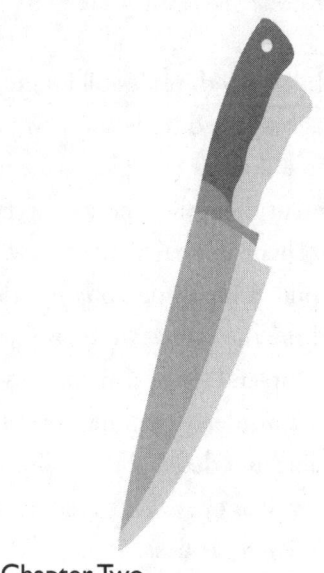

Chapter Two

In my decade of giving true-crime tours, I've become adept at dealing with unexpected situations. When I had a woman collapse on the considerable hills in Chinatown, I learned to put steepness ratings in my tour descriptions. After my first random cloudburst, I learned to always track nearby venues where I could temporarily stash twenty people. I even once had a rabid raccoon jump out of a dumpster and attack a guest in the Tenderloin—and learned that day never to cross Ryan, because while he looks like a typical tech geek, he has hidden ninja skills that can turn a backpack into a lethal weapon. It took more than a screaming guest to put either of us off our game.

"Who's attacking what woman?" I asked. "Where?"

"Right there." Lorraine started forward toward the apartment buildings lining the side street, her still-extended hand leading the way. "The white house, with the lit window."

Several of the building-in-question's windows were lit, but her gaze lasered on the one directly over the building's garage door.

"What exactly did you see?" I signaled to Ryan I'd be right back, and he turned to the rest of the gaping group.

She stopped, voice still frantic. "A woman. Her hands waving and her face screwed up like she was having some sort of argument with someone. Then two gloved hands shot out around her neck. She clawed at them like she was trying to get them off of her, and then they yanked her back out of view."

I pulled my phone out and dialed 911. Once the dispatcher assured me the police were on their way, I escorted Lorraine back to the group and asked if anyone else had seen anything. When nobody had, I considered sending Ryan to the final stop while I waited with Lorraine, but decided the police might want to interview everyone—the way their eyes were glued to Lorraine and to the house, I doubted they'd go, regardless.

The police pulled up fifteen minutes later, lights flashing, and we watched two burly officers disappear into the building. After fifteen more minutes of passersby shooting resentful glares as they ping-ponged around us, the two officers reappeared and strode toward us.

I met them in the middle. "I'm Capri Sanzio, I made the call. What's happening?"

The officers exchanged a glance, professionally wooden with lashings of skepticism. "You made the call? What exactly did you see?"

I explained, then gestured Lorraine over to repeat what she'd seen.

"Can you describe the woman you saw?" the taller of the two officers, whose nameplate identified him as H. Robles, asked when she finished.

"She was a white woman with wavy, reddish-brown hair," Lorraine answered.

"What color were her eyes?" Robles asked.

"I couldn't tell."

"You saw the expression on her face, but not her eye color?" Robles asked.

Lorraine bristled. "She was agitated. Her posture and her gestures weren't ambiguous."

"What did her attacker look like?"

"I couldn't see him." Lorraine's weight shifted between her feet. "I only saw his hands."

"How do you know it was a 'him,' then?" Robles asked.

"I don't." Lorraine's arms crossed over her chest. "But from the angle of the hands, the attacker was taller, and he was clearly stronger. That makes it far more likely to be a man."

I tensed as the officers exchanged another glance. That was the downside of Murderino membership—a little knowledge can make you think you know more than you actually do.

"You're sure it happened in that window, not in any other?" Robles pointed back.

"Yes, because of the sunflower picture on the wall."

Robles exchanged yet a third glance with his fellow officer, then cleared his throat. "Have you been drinking tonight, ma'am?"

Lorraine's mouth dropped open. "I—what—no—"

"Are you on any sort of medication?" Robles asked.

"No, of course not—" Lorraine took a step toward Robles, eyes flashing.

My arm snaked out to intercept her. "Officers, what's going on? Weren't you able to check inside the apartment?"

Robles's gaze shifted toward me. "The landlady let us in to do a welfare check. There's nobody home."

"But"—I pointed up—"the light's on. Did the landlady hear any sort of argument?"

"People often leave their lights on when they're not home as a theft deterrent. And no, she didn't hear anything." His eyes swung back to Lorraine. "We take false reports very seriously. When we waste time following up on something that never happened, resources are channeled away from people who need us. We'll give you a warning this time," he said, looking between us both, "but if it happens again, we'll have to charge you."

The threat had the desired effect—Lorraine shrank back a step, and her mouth snapped shut.

The stubborn part of my brain rebelled against the officer's accusation, but the rest reminded me I'd known Lorraine for all of an hour and a half—for all I knew, this was her idea of a prank. The wise thing to do was pour oil on the troubled waters, so I put a confused-slash-conciliatory expression on my face. "Thank you for your time, Officers. I'm not sure exactly what happened, and we appreciate you checking it out."

Robles's eyes swept my face, probably looking for sass. But I learned long ago not to sass people who carry guns, so he found nary a drop. Satisfied, he turned back toward his car, dismissing the pair of us.

• • •

I waited until the officers drove away before turning back to the group, then activated both my outdoor voice and Jedi-mind-trick skills to convey that nothing of consequence had happened.

"The police have assured us everything is fine and we can continue with the tour. Our last stop is Washington Square, where you can find a number of restaurants or can continue up to Coit Tower if you'd like to see the night views from Telegraph Hill."

As the group headed up Columbus, I surreptitiously studied Lorraine with Robles's questions in mind. I hadn't smelled any alcohol on her, or noticed any sort of intoxicated behavior—if anything, her eyes when she'd asked about Overkill Bill had been a little *too* sharp. But that didn't necessarily mean she'd actually seen an attack. Had she misinterpreted something innocent? Someone practicing a play, or doing some sort of contemporary dance? Every contemporary dance piece *I'd* ever seen certainly looked like the dancer was fighting desperately for life.

But the officers hadn't said the resident was fine—they'd said *nobody was home at all.* There should have been nothing for her to misinterpret. Maybe she was the type who craved drama, or was an uber-zealous true-crime junkie? That would fit with the questions she'd been asking; true-crime fans sometimes stanned strange things, hence the popularity of "murderabilia" on sites like eBay. And since her initial questions about Overkill Bill hadn't gotten her anywhere, maybe she'd escalated to garner my attention. I couldn't be sure.

I tried to shake off my doubts as I delivered my spiel about the historical significance of Washington Square park, including an explanation of why the statue located there is of Benjamin Franklin, not George Washington. The guests listened with polite but distracted attention, and once I announced the official end of the tour, they crowded around Lorraine and me asking for details about what she'd seen.

So I pulled out my best trick for ending a lingering tour—tip envelopes. The gesture had the desired effect; those who wanted to tip were distracted from their questions to dig into their purses and pockets, and those who didn't want to disappeared faster than California's water supply. As everyone scrambled for money or refuge, I pulled Lorraine away for a private conversation.

"I just want to touch base with you," I said. "Are you okay?"

Her eyes bounced across my face. "I'm not crazy, I swear. No mental illness in my family, not even depression."

I nodded. "On a scale of one to ten, how sure are you about what you saw?"

Her posture straightened. "Twelve. Maybe the police went to the wrong apartment, I don't know. But *something* happened."

I nodded again. I was usually able to get a good read on people, but in Lorraine's case I couldn't seem to separate the pain-in-the-ass-tour-guest vibe from a potentially-unstable-liar situation. That meant I had to choose my action based on a different criterion: if Lorraine was wrong or manipulating me, it would put me in an awkward position to insist the house be checked again, but if she was right, a young woman was in trouble. And prioritizing a woman's safety over my potential embarrassment was a no-brainer.

I took out my phone and closed my eyes for a moment, swearing mentally at the universe for putting me in this position.

Then I pulled up my contact for Homicide Inspector Dan Petito.

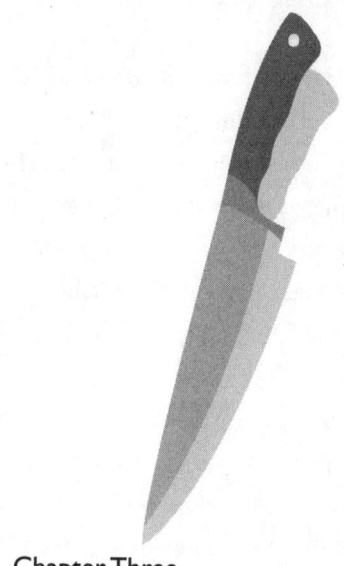

Chapter Three

But my finger hovered over Petito's contact, refusing to tap connect. Because my history with Petito was complicated—very complicated.

We'd met when my ex-mother-in-law Sylvia Clement turned up murdered by the Overkill Bill copycat. When Petito came to inform Sylvia's husband Philip of her murder, only to have the door answered by Overkill Bill's granddaughter, he'd been surprised (to say the least). When he then discovered Sylvia had just cut off my daughter Morgan's tuition, I catapulted to the top of the suspect list, with Morgan just below me. I've always been a protective mama bear, and in this case "protective" meant hell-bent on finding the real killer so neither of us ended up on death row. Unfortunately, Petito and I hadn't seen eye to eye on some of my decisions along the way. To my mind, I'd merely followed up leads that would have been difficult for him to investigate; to his mind, I withheld evidence and obstructed justice. When I nearly got myself killed in the process, he let me know I'd been reckless, irresponsible, and a pain in his ass.

So you can imagine my surprise when he asked me out on a date. Since then I'd spent more than a few weeks overthinking whether it was a good idea to go out with a man who'd almost put me in jail, and who'd found himself elbow-deep in my familial dirty laundry. Add on his busy homicide-detective schedule, the time it took to put the pieces of my life back together, and the holiday season, and we'd rung in a new year before finally setting up dinner at Damiano's the following night. I was girlishly excited about the prospect of getting to know him better—but because the universe was a tricky little bitch who didn't want me to have nice things, I now needed to call in a favor Petito didn't owe me, for a person neither he nor I knew.

I glanced one last time back in the general direction of the purported attack before potentially destroying my first date in years over a hallucination, then took a deep breath and tapped the contact.

He picked up after the second ring. "Capri. Please tell me you didn't just test positive for Covid and have to cancel tomorrow."

The anxious edge to his voice made me smile—until I remembered why I was calling, and my stomached flip-flopped like a fish in a boat.

"Um, no." I turned my back to Lorraine to hide the blush I could feel creeping across my cheeks. "I have a bit of a situation." I explained to him what happened. "Officer Robles said nobody was home, but I'm worried. I don't suppose you know him, or that you could just . . ." The sentence petered out as I realized I had no clue what politics existed between patrolmen and inspectors, and thus how big an ask this really was.

His voice switched into efficient-cop mode. "Robles. I can do a quick check-in with him."

"I'd appreciate that. It's gonna bug me until I know the resident is okay," I said.

"No problem. Hopefully I'll have some answers for you by tomorrow night."

After reluctantly ending the conversation, I hurried back over to Lorraine.

"Good news. I was able to reach the detective and he's looking into it," I said. "He'll report back to me by tomorrow night."

"Tomorrow *night*?" Lorraine's brow tightened. "That woman's in trouble *now*. God only knows what could happen to her by then!"

My emotions split in two. On the one hand, I shared her impatience to be sure the mystery woman was okay. On the other, I'd just gone out on a huge limb for her, and a little bit of gratitude would've been nice. Since she was a guest and I was running a business, I mushed the halves together into professional peacemaking. "If he finds something out sooner, I'm sure he'll let me know. Let me verify your number so I can call you right away once he does."

• • •

Once I managed to talk Lorraine down, Ryan and I headed back to the Hub, our loving nickname for the office that SF Killer Crime Tours operates out of.

"O-M-G, what exactly happened?" Heather sprang up and ran over to me as I walked through the door.

I tossed my bag onto my mahogany desk and sank down into my comfy office chair as I gave her an encapsulated version. She pulled her chair over, large brown eyes wide as she listened.

"Lorraine was adamant," I finished. "So I called Petito."

Her expression shifted to horror. "You didn't."

I bristled. "I did. I couldn't do nothing when someone may be hurt."

She beamed at me. "See, that's why I love you."

"Because I'm not okay with a woman being possibly murdered in plain sight?" I asked. "That seems like pretty much the lowest rung someone should have to pass."

"Do you pass a rung or step up one?" Ryan asked.

We ignored him. "No," Heather said. "I love you because you

care so much you're willing to blow up your date with Captain Hottie over it."

I rubbed my hand over my brow. "First, he's an inspector, not a captain. Second, thanks for the vote of confidence."

"Or, wait." She leaned forward and stabbed a finger at me. "Is this your way of sabotaging it so you don't have to go?"

"That tracks." Ryan nodded.

I glared at them in turn. "Why would I want to sabotage the date?"

"Oh, I don't know," Heather said. "Maybe because you haven't had sex with anyone in ten years and you aren't sure if your vagina works anymore?"

That's Heather in a nutshell: bull's-eye insight paired with sledgehammer subtlety. While she'd been forcing me to face ugly realities since kindergarten, her reign of terror specifically over my romantic life started in the seventh grade when she helped me get over my crush on Armando Corbin by convincing me to ask him out. He'd turned me down instantly, with no attempt to even cushion the blow. I'd walked back to Heather's side in a daze of humiliation amplified by the revealing expression on her face.

"You knew he was going to say no?" I'd asked.

She'd nodded. "I did."

My hands flew to my hips. "Then why did you tell me to ask him out?"

She grasped my hand with a conciliatory squeeze. "You've been mooning over him for weeks even though he has shown less than zero interest. This way you know for sure and can move on with your life."

I'll never forget standing there flabbergasted as the realization that she was one hundred percent correct smacked me right between the lobes of my brain. Because while my feelings were of course hurt by the rejection, within just a few days I was able to put a period on that particular sentence rather than continue to spin my wheels, and my newly unencumbered heart was prepped and ready to go when I met the guy who'd become my first boyfriend a couple months later.

As much as I hated to admit it, she was right now, too, and not just because of my vagina's potential 404 status—her proclamation set my mind racing down a paranoid path I'd been trying very hard to avoid. "My time and energy have gone into building up SF Killer Crime Tours for the past ten years, and I was ridiculously faithful to Todd for the fifteen before that. The last time I had sex with someone else was literally back in a different millennium. Cell phones and texting hadn't been invented, and the internet was still dial-up."

Heather nodded sagely. "And the intervening years have birthed *He's Just Not That Into You*, the third-date rule, and a web of other unspoken expectations."

I winced. "And speaking of birthing, the last time a stranger saw me naked I'd been in my high-and-tight twenties, before my body grew, delivered, and breastfed an entire human being."

Heather waved a hand in my direction. "You still look gorgeous. You've got amazing boobs."

"Should I be hearing this?" Ryan mumbled, fidgeting in his chair.

But I was too far gone down the spiral of my own discomfort to consider his. "Back then women were considered racy if they did more than a little gentle trim on their bathing-suit region, while now you're a horrifying troll if you have as much as a five-o'clock shadow—" I threw up a hand and attempted to short-circuit the panic attack creeping up my chest. "Please let's turn the topic back to Lorraine. Are there any other implications here we need to think about?"

"Like what?" Ryan asked. "It's not our fault if one of our guests witnessed a crime."

"Of course not. But we don't want people to think our tours are unsafe. San Francisco has already been labeled since the pandemic as having more crime than it actually does, even though we're below average in violent crime rates compared to other cities."

Heather snorted a laugh. "You're worried that true-crime fans will be put off by someone witnessing a crime on one of our tours? Hell, I'm kinda sad I didn't think to do something like this myself, for promotional purposes. We need to lean into it for our brand."

"Turn it to our advantage." Ryan flipped a pen over his knuckles. "Like how the Mandarin word for 'crisis' also means 'opportunity.'"

"That's not actually true," Heather said. "Don't get me started on how JFK screwed us on that one. But your underlying point is sound. We aren't just a true-crime tour company anymore, we also now have a successful first season of a podcast. We need to be thinking about what's next, and I think 'next' just fell into our lap."

A blinding pain sheared from my right eye to the back of my skull. "I'm not sure that's a good idea until we know more. For all we know, Lorraine was hallucinating or lying."

"Even if she's lying, it's an interesting story—there's no non-nefarious reason to lie about something like that, and either way someone's gonna end up in handcuffs." Heather tilted her head at me. "I'm surprised at you. You just said yourself you weren't going to be able to relax until you were sure the resident of that apartment is okay."

I glanced down at my laptop. Making sure the woman was okay was one thing, but the thought of podcasting about it activated the same tug of resistance I'd been struggling with when trying to write the Overkill Bill book. I'd been champing at *that* bit since I was eight, and I'd wanted to be an investigative journalist for most of my life. Why was I freezing up now?

Since no answers presented themselves, I glommed on to the one concrete concern I could identify. "I just think we need to be circumspect until we know what's going on. Real people are involved here. Let's take a moment before we blow up their privacy."

Heather nodded, but her expression stayed somber. "But we can't wait forever. We need new content if we want to keep people interested in the podcast. And your book advance took care of Morgan's tuition this quarter, but fall will be here before you know it."

"What we need is an Overkill Bill tour." Ryan stared at me pointedly. "The guest questions tonight made that clear."

My chest constricted so hard I could barely draw breath. I rubbed my temples until the spasm subsided, then stood and gathered the documents I needed for the following day. "Speaking of which, I need to get home and actually write that book. But you're right, I at least need answers for myself, and the more I think about it the more it bothers me that the cops found nothing to confirm Lorraine's story. As soon as I get home I'll pull up her reservation info and see what I can find out about her."

Heather's grin showed she knew she'd won. "Keep me updated. And tomorrow after your date, call me the instant you get back home with all the deets." The grin broadened still farther. "Unless you bring him home with you. Then text me on the DL once you finish."

I reached for a witty response to ninja-star her with, but the mental image of Petito in my bedroom kneecapped my brain's ability to process anything else. All I could do was wave a hand to block out her lascivious smirk as the door swung in place behind me.

• • •

As I threw together a quick chicken piccata, I knew I should be focusing on figuring out the first chapter of my Overkill Bill book. But the resistance kicked back in, now buttressed by my worries about what Lorraine had—or hadn't—seen, and I shifted to generating explanations. While I couldn't one hundred percent rule out some form of intoxication, my experience of people who were drunk, stoned, tripping, or otherwise in an altered state didn't track with what I'd witnessed of Lorraine. I also couldn't believe she'd just observed and misinterpreted something harmless—because if so, where had the residents disappeared to? That left two possibilities: either she'd really seen a woman attacked or she was lying. I had to consider both possibilities and Petito was looking into the first for me, so I shifted to the second. But would someone really lie about something like that?

The true-crime portion of my brain churned out a stream of possibilities, each chilling my blood a little more. People used all sorts of ruses to get others in vulnerable positions. I'd heard of faked purse snatchings designed to distract so a pickpocket would have free range in a crowd of tourists. I'd heard of killers who used female partners who pretended to be lost so they could kidnap their victims. It was possible, and I needed to at least see if I could identify any obvious reason why she'd lie.

I pasted Lorraine's name, address, and phone number into Google, and was once again blown away by what a truly terrifying place the internet is, especially if you have a less-than-common name like Lorraine Kostricka—within seconds I knew more about Lorraine than I did about some of my relatives. She was a non-local local, meaning a Northern Californian who lived two hours away in a town called Roseville. She was also a fifth-grade teacher, something I found initially reassuring since teachers have regular background checks as a condition of employment. But as I continued to search, I discovered that the house located at her address was a large new McMansion-style home that, despite being located in a much more affordable area than San Francisco, was valued by Zillow at close to two million dollars. I double-checked the value—she'd told me she was single, and I was fairly certain elementary school teachers didn't make the sort of salaries that could afford a home like that.

I dug in, looking for a simple explanation. According to the Zillow listing, she'd purchased the home only three years ago; maybe she'd received a huge divorce settlement or some such. A little more digging took me to the public record of her divorce proceedings—which occurred twenty years before, too far in the past to be relevant. I dug still deeper and found her previous address, wondering if that house had been huge, too—but it listed at less than half the value of her current one.

I leaned back and tried to generate non-criminal reasons for her sudden leap in economic status. Maybe Lorraine had won the lottery, or maybe she had a side hustle? But I couldn't find anything legitimate, not even a sideline for Mary Kay. Still, there was a limit to how deep I could dig since, unlike the police or private detectives, I didn't have access to databases that would give me detailed information about her financial activities. So I sent a quick text to Petito telling him what I'd found. Then I resigned myself to waiting and tried to stem the flow of criminal-underworld theories spewing from my brain by focusing on the Overkill Bill book.

After an unproductive hour fighting with my own brain, I gave up and got ready for bed. Thankfully, as I went through my nighttime routine, I came up with a better way of distracting my brain—the image Heather had planted in my head of Petito sharing my bedroom sent me smiling off to dreamland faster than I'd fallen asleep in months.

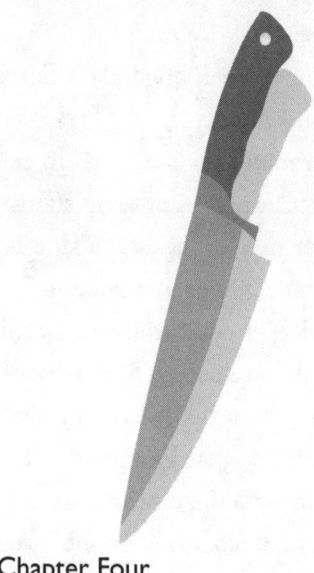

Chapter Four

But despite falling asleep quickly, I was plagued by disconcerting dreams. I was back on my Barbary Coast tour, and after describing the original jail, I fell down a trapdoor set into the sidewalk, landing in an underground cage. I woke with a start, heart pounding, and the panic left behind a niggling sense of dread. To assuage it, I grabbed my phone before I even got out of bed, hoping for a text or message from Petito telling me he'd found the occupant of the apartment from last night alive and well.

There was a text and a voicemail, but neither were from Petito. The text was from Morgan, asking me to call when I had a chance; she didn't pick up when I did so. The voicemail was from the *San Francisco Chronicle*, wanting details about the attempted murder my tour guest had witnessed the night before.

I did a double take and listened to the message again, wondering if I was in some sort of caffeine-deprived state of delusion. How could they possibly have found out about something so random so quickly? But they had, and when I pulled up the *Chronicle*'s site, there was a brief article about what Lorraine had witnessed along with a note that the situation was still developing.

My dread megaphoned into full-blown anxiety, and I hurried to put a call through to her. "Did you see the piece in the *Chronicle*?" I asked after initial greetings. "How did they track you down?"

"They didn't," she answered. "I called them last night when I got back to the hotel."

That stopped me short. "*You* called *them*?"

Her tone rose. "Yes, I called them. The police didn't believe us and by the time your detective contact gets back to us, that poor woman could be dead, dismembered, and decaying. I needed someone who'd help."

I paused for a moment, considering the implications of this revelation. Because surely someone who was lying about what they'd seen wouldn't go to the press about it?

But the true-crime lobe of my brain disagreed. *Unless they needed someone to pay attention to their story*, it shot back. *Like Sherri Papini.*

Sherri Papini—a housewife who got busted for abandoning her family, then returning and claiming she'd been kidnapped in order to cover up what she'd done.

Maybe Lorraine needed to create an ironclad alibi for some reason, to distract from something else? Or maybe she wanted attention focused on that apartment for some reason?

I shook my head to clear it—either Lorraine was gaslighting me or the universe was, and either way I wasn't going to stand for it. Even if I was at risk of getting tangled up in someone's marionette strings, the only way I could protect myself from whoever had the nefarious motives in this scenario was to figure out what exactly was behind all this.

"Tell you what," I told her. "I have a tour I need to lead this morning, but as soon as I'm finished, I'll go over there myself and see what I can do."

Lorraine exhaled relief. "I'd so appreciate that. Will you call me after you do?"

I assured her that I would.

● ● ●

After brewing a travel mug of coffee, I held my nose and gulped down a bowl of heart-healthy oatmeal. Every few years some article convinces me that oatmeal will Rotoclear my arteries, but as soon as I take my first bite, I remember eating oatmeal feels like chewing someone else's vomit. I have no idea why my brain periodically erases this knowledge, but I suspect it's the same underlying process that makes women forget how painful childbirth is so they'll continue to create new humans. Unfortunately, since I do most of my shopping at Costco, I always end up with a bag of steel-cut oats big enough to last me until the apocalypse.

The upside was, the low-glycemic-index breakfast, paired with copious caffeine, fueled me well through my Murder in the Castro tour, which again was peppered by a slew of Overkill Bill questions from the guests and unsubtle eye-daggers from Ryan. I made my escape over to North Beach as quickly as I could and got lucky with an open meter just a few blocks away from the apartment building. I sent a grateful prayer to whatever higher power watched over parking meters, then trotted down the street scouring the environs as I went, searching for any clue to what had really happened the night before.

I'm always surprised at how different things look in the day versus the dark. The previous evening, neon and nightlife had dominated, giving the area a dance-hall-type energy that hinted at the seedier elements of its past. But during the day the feel was more home-neighborhood focused; signs from restaurants and boutiques now shone out of their previous shadows, the apartments hovering atop them popped colorfully rather than fading into gray, and whiffs of coffee replaced the occasional blasts of cigarette and marijuana smoke. I identified the building in question without any trouble; it was the only one on the block with a garage door that opened into the alley. The window seemed higher than I remembered, but the sunflower picture Lorraine had pointed out was unmistakable.

Before crossing toward it, I stood at the approximate spot where Lorraine had claimed to see the attack. Sure enough, the angle captured the sunflower picture and would have shown someone standing near the wall—but anybody in the room facing that person wouldn't have been visible. I approached, continuing to monitor the angle of the window. The alley was narrow enough that I had to be standing directly across from it to see fully into the room, and no angle allowed me to see below chest height of anyone inside.

A panel of three buzzers hung on the side of the porch, reflecting the three apartments inside. I pushed the button marked A, but got no answer. Same for B, but when I pushed C, labeled REYNALDA HARRIS, PROPERTY MANAGER, a voice crackled over the line.

"Heylo?"

"Hi," I said into the speaker, quickly calculating which approach would make a property manager most likely to talk to me. "My name's Capri Sanzio. I'm following up on the incident that happened with the first-floor apartment last night."

"I already talked to the police. You with the paper? I told the guy that called from the *Chronicle* I'm not talking to nobody."

I recalibrated—if she didn't want to talk to the *Chronicle*, she probably wasn't itching to hear her name on a podcast. "I'm the one who called the police last night."

That perked her up. "You the one said they saw Leeya get attacked?"

I explained who I was. "Nobody's answering in the other apartments. I don't suppose you've seen the tenant since last night?"

There was a brief pause. "Hang on a minute."

The static went silent, leaving me confused. After a minute, the slap of flip-flops Doppler-effected me and the security door flew open—revealing an eighty-something Black woman engulfed by what appeared to be a pink blanket but on further inspection turned out to be an oversized track suit. The gray bunny slippers sticking out of each leg were at odds with her severe bun, pulled so tight a sympathy headache tugged at my temples. Her sharp eyes peered out at the street, then she took a step back.

"Come on in here."

I slipped into the entry enclave and she closed the door behind me, amplifying the television noise leaking from her apartment door.

She held up her telephone. "I texted her last night but got wrapped up in my stories and didn't realize I never heard back." She rapped the leftmost of the three internal doors. "Leeya? You home?"

My stomach flipped and I chided myself—there were a thousand nonlethal reasons why someone wouldn't respond to their property manager right away. "Is she usually home on Saturdays?"

"She comes and goes whenever. You know how artists be, working when the muse strikes. Mostly out of her studio in the Mission 'cause I told her I can't have her making noise all hours in the garage." She grimaced at her phone. "Normally she answers right away."

"Can you call her right now?" I asked.

"None a these kids answer calls." But she tapped anyway, and *Leeya Styles Apartment A* appeared in gigantic font on her screen.

Voicemail picked up. Reynalda ended the call and her grimace deepened. "Told you."

"When was the last time you saw her?"

"In person, day before yesterday, I think? But I heard the garage door open around two p.m. yesterday."

"And she's the only one who uses the garage?"

"Yep. She pays extra 'cause she needs a truck to haul the junk she uses for her art."

I thought back to the night before. "Could we check inside?"

She stared at the door and shook her head. "Cops doing a welfare check is one thing, no way I'm gonna get in trouble for that. But going in on my own? Uh-uh. My luck, her boyfriend just took her somewhere for the weekend or something, and I'd end up fired."

"Does he do that often? Can we call him maybe?"

She shrugged. "Don't know what they do. And I don't know his name or number."

"But you're sure she has a boyfriend?"

The hand not holding her phone perched onto her hip. "I'm not *blind*. Tall guy, black hair. But where I came up, we mind our business. Don't know nothing I don't need to know."

That sent my mental brows up. Because the way she kept staring at the door suggested she wanted in as much as I did—I just hadn't found the right approach. "Do you have an emergency contact for her? Can we call *them*?"

She tilted her head. "I suppose that *is* the point of an emergency contact."

"Absolutely." I hurried to assure her before she could think herself out of it. "And if something's wrong, you don't want to be blamed for *not* letting her emergency contact know."

She pointed a finger at me. "You're exactly right. 'Cause when someone claims they saw somebody get attacked, that's an emergency in my book."

"One hundred percent." I nodded vigorously.

"Wait here." A blast of dramatic sobbing from her TV poured down her stairs when the door opened. Once it closed again, I was left in blessed near-silence until she reappeared, this time with an open folder.

She tapped, and a string of huge numbers danced across her

phone display. The call went to voicemail. "Hello, I'm looking for Quinn Shovani. I'm calling about Leeya Styles. The cops were here looking for her, and we just want to make sure she's okay. Can you call me back when you get a chance?" She recited a number, then hung up.

"Quinn Shovani," I repeated. "Could that be the boyfriend?"

She shrugged again, still staring at the door. "The form just says 'friend.'"

I fished one of my business cards out of my bag. "If you hear anything, could you let me know? I'm not going to sleep well until I know Leeya's okay."

"I will." Reynalda scoured my face. "Last night I assumed some junkie musta had a hallucination, but you seem pretty normal. I don't like that she hasn't texted me back. Hang on." She tapped the number from my card into her phone, and I felt my messenger bag buzz. "Now you have my number. Call me if *you* find anything out."

I thanked her, let myself out, and hurried around the corner—and as soon as I was out of sight I furiously tapped Quinn Shovani's number into my phone, praying I hadn't scrambled any of the digits as I'd been mentally rehearsing them.

Chapter Five

But as I tapped on the contact I'd created for Quinn, a voice in the back of my mind tapped me on the shoulder.

You stole that number from Reynalda, it said. *If you put that call through, you're violating two people's privacy.*

I winced, both at the undeniable truth and the oddly familiar judgmental ring to it.

Don't stick your nose in where it doesn't belong. This has nothing to do with you, little girl.

Recognition flooded me. Those were the words my father had used when he'd tried to convince me I had no business poking my nose into the Overkill Bill case. He'd been traumatized when William Sanzio came under suspicion for murder, and me digging into the case had opened old wounds—for all of us in the family. I'd explained that the truth was the only way for us to heal, but he didn't agree, and apparently my falling-out with him had internalized an invasive specter of his objections into my head, determined to undermine any true-crime activity I engaged in, be it book, podcast, or investigator format.

But now that I'd identified the voice, the rest of my brain could fight back against it. *That's what journalists do*, it proclaimed with a resounding echo. *They investigate, even when people don't want them to. Especially when people don't want them to.*

You're not a journalist, the voice lobbed. *You have no right to mess with people's lives just because your ego wants to know whether or not Lorraine is playing you.*

"I have a degree in journalism and I helped solve two murder cases," I fired back out loud. "And a young woman may be in trouble."

But despite my bravado, the doubt had seeped in, tainting my thoughts and paralyzing my decisions. Was this just a case of ego? Was I just selfishly wanting to be relevant without caring whose life I plowed into? Because as much as I wanted to ignore my father's voice, he'd taught me one undeniable thing during the Overkill Bill case: no matter how long gone the past was, there was always someone who would be hurt by digging around in it. How much more true was that of the present?

"No," I said aloud. "If someone's in trouble and I walk away, I'll never forgive myself."

An elderly woman walking her dog pointedly avoided eye contact with me and crossed the street.

I snapped my mouth shut and tapped through the call to Quinn before I could second-guess my second-guessing. "Hello?" a young, out-of-breath woman answered.

"Hi. My name's Capri Sanzio. I'm looking for Quinn Shovani?"

"Did you just call a few minutes ago?" she asked.

"I—not exactly—"

"Hold on a minute." Something thunked—she must have thrown down the phone. I waited, listening for any clue to what was happening amid the background noise. Nothing, then crinkling, then another thunk as she picked the phone back up. "Sorry about that, I was in the middle of bringing in my groceries. When you called earlier I was driving and couldn't pick up. What did you say your name was again?"

My mouth opened to explain that it wasn't me who'd called, but I realized I couldn't risk losing my shot. "Capri Sanzio. I'm calling about Leeya Styles."

She paused. "Why are you calling *me* about Leeya?"

The question had an undertone I couldn't quite put my finger on, and since I had no idea what I was dealing with, possible responses bottlenecked in my brain. I finally opted for simple and straightforward. "Her building manager had your number listed as her emergency contact. I'm trying to locate her." Afraid she'd think I was a collection agent, I hurriedly recounted what happened the night before.

"Oh, God," Quinn said.

The hair on my arms stood up. "What's wrong?"

"I—the thing is—" After another pause, she seemed to collect herself. "What exactly did your tour guest see?"

I gave her as much detail as I had. "So you haven't heard from Leeya?"

"Not for over a month." Her voice tightened. "Can I call you right back? I'm going to call her."

"Yes, of course."

I'd reached my car, so I climbed inside to wait for her to call back. She did almost immediately.

"She's not picking up," Quinn said. "I sent a text, too, and she didn't answer that, either."

I swore internally. "Would you be willing to give me her phone number?"

"No," she said. "I don't know who you are, or if you're telling me the truth."

Fair enough. "How about this. Can you contact her boyfriend and give him my number?"

"How do you know she has a boyfriend?" The words were bullets.

"The building manager mentioned she had a boyfriend, but didn't have his number."

Her tone relaxed, but only slightly. "I'll do what I can."

"I'd appreciate that," I said. "And if you'd rather talk directly to the police about it all, I spoke with Dan Petito in the—" I caught myself, because the word "homicide" would only freak her out. "With Inspector Dan Petito."

She took down his name and number. "Thank you. I appreciate your concern for Leeya, and your sensitivity. I'll get back with you or Inspector Petito as soon as I find something out."

• • •

I let traffic whiz past me as I sat in my car, feeling apprehensive and anxious—the conversation with Quinn had shaken my Spidey senses awake like an early-morning earthquake. Why hadn't someone who was close enough to this Leeya to be listed as her emergency contact spoken to her in a month? And Quinn's "Oh, God" felt like she'd expected bad news—that might be coincidental, but my brain responded to coincidences with the same unrepentant intolerance it used for lack of caffeine.

Still, I realized, I now had a foundation—however small—that I could work from. I knew the resident of the apartment was an artist named Leeya Styles, and that meant I could now see if Lorraine was able to identify her. If Lorraine was just dramatically creating an alibi or some such, she'd have no idea what the actual tenant looked like. And if she'd seen someone else—like some cat-burglar couple who'd broken into Leeya's apartment and aborted the burglary when the cops pulled up—whoever she'd seen wouldn't match up with Leeya.

I needed to find a picture and put together a mini lineup.

I pulled up Instagram and plugged in Leeya's name. Over a dozen Leeya Styleses came up, but luckily only one was an artist from San

Francisco. Her profile picture was of a cresting ocean-wave sculpture that had a strange feel to it, and when I clicked on it, I realized that was because it was a conglomeration of white, clear, and blue trash, including bottles, bags, and plastic packaging. Intrigued, I made a mental note to return to her art—I had a sense it was telling me something important about her—but continued scrolling for a picture of her.

Several spots down I found one of her holding up a sculpture, this one a cricket made out of what appeared to be pieces of metal, captioned *I think I'll call him Jiminy*. Smiling, I pinched to enlarge it. Her brunette hair had red highlights that flirted with the line between mahogany and chestnut and contrasted with her creamy peach skin in a way that suggested she'd just stepped out of a Renaissance painting. She was undeniably beautiful, but in an understated way that defied explanation; each individual feature was a little too *something*—too big, too small, too wide, too sharp—but somehow the combined imperfections created a harmonious whole. The same principle was reflected in her sculpture, I realized. Conglomerations of flawed items that came together to create new, compelling entities.

I quickly cross-checked her account with Lorraine's to see if they knew each other, but I couldn't find any overlap—so no obvious connection, at least.

Excited to finally have a concrete plan, I revved up the car and hurried home to finish the job. In my years scouring true-crime cases, I'd learned that asking witnesses to pick out suspects was fraught with pitfalls. Memory is a tricky thing, and even the way a question was worded could influence what people remembered. Accordingly, lineups had to be carefully constructed to be sure a witness's identification wasn't influenced by accidental word choice or a salient characteristic. As I planned out how to do that effectively, a devious idea occurred to me—a little trick I could insert to be double sure about Lorraine's identification.

After fortifying myself with a huge cup of my favorite Arabica coffee, I scoured the internet for other white women with similar hair, skin, and eye color. Once I had enough, I used my minimal photoshopping skills to remove the backgrounds and make their shirts all the same color. Once they were ready to go I used a random number generator—Morgan had told me more than once how important random assignment was in all aspects of experimental design—to determine which order to place them into a document. Once I finished, I emailed Lorraine with an update and the photo lineup and asked her to pick out the woman she'd seen in the window.

Then I sat back to wait.

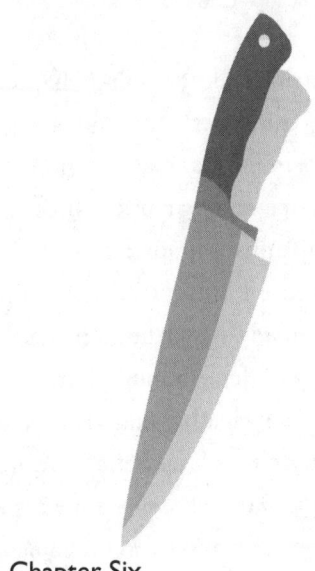

Chapter Six

While I waited for Lorraine to get back to me about the lineup, I needed something to keep me from obsessing about my rapidly impending date with Petito. I'm not normally neurotic about my appearance; on the scale of earth-muffin natural to glamour-gal gorgeous, I'd place myself at yoga-mom yummy. Professional-but-comfortable is the watchword for my job, and while I don't want to look like I just crawled out of bed, I'm not willing to preen for more than ten minutes a day, even for a date. I'd planned ahead with a red wrap dress to play up my just-a-hair-too-generous curves, matching red lipstick to play up my black curls, and a simple swipe of black mascara to help pop my blue eyes. But the downside of preplanning was it left my brain to roam free-range, so I dove into the Overkill Bill manuscript with both feet, effectively penning my lurking insecurities inside my mental roost.

I hit the ground running with a prologue presenting each of the three women Overkill Bill had murdered, touching on their backgrounds and personalities so I could make sure they were forefront in the readers' minds as they read the rest of the book. Then

I transitioned into a first chapter, which gave a very brief history of my grandfather's life, including his emigration from a tumultuous village in the Campania region of Italy, where an overwhelming mafia presence and corrupt police made America seem like a haven of opportunity and justice.

Before I knew it I'd written three more chapters and it was time to get ready. My date prep went smoothly, with just enough nervous energy to deposit me at Damiano's several minutes before the date's start time. Heather had instructed me to show up ten minutes *late*, so I wouldn't look pathetic or overeager, but no matter how much she and the internet assured me a successful romance in 2025 required mastery of complex mind games, I just couldn't get on board. I was who I was, and if he didn't like that, there was an expiration date on it all anyway—especially since my relationship with Petito had started off with us locking horns at every stage of a homicide investigation. The ship had sailed on me being something I wasn't.

His deep cerulean eyes jumped out from amid the tables of patrons quietly enjoying their upscale Italian meals. A smile slid over his face, popping his dimple and sending jolts of electricity into my hips. It'd been several weeks since I'd seen him, and already I'd started to forget just how powerful his understated good looks were. He was tall but not too tall, muscular without being full-on cut, broad-shouldered without being a billboard. The gray slowly spreading through his short black hair added a touch of weathered character, as did the web of lines creasing the corners of his eyes and cheeks.

He rose as the hostess escorted me over, then pulled out a chair for me. I smiled and held my breath as I sat. I've never gotten used to having chairs pulled out for me; I always worry I'll sit down too quickly and the chair won't be under me yet, or too slowly and the chair will reverse-kneecap me, plummeting me down gracelessly onto my butt. Luckily, all my parts cooperated, and I breathed a sigh of relief. "I hope I didn't keep you waiting long."

He recognized the snark, and smiled wider. "That's what I get for not picking you up."

I gave what I hoped was a flirty eye roll. "You're still not over that?"

"What can I say, I was raised a certain way. Times may have changed, but my mother's voice in my head hasn't."

I gave an exaggerated eyebrow pop. "So you hear voices. Tell me more about that."

He shook a narrow-eyed smile at me. "I've met your father. I know you've got a voice or two of your own up there."

My earlier inner struggle came flooding back. "I hope your mother's is more forgiving than my father's."

"Hope springs eternal," he said as the waiter appeared with menus.

After the waiter described the chef's specials and left us to ruminate, Petito asked, "Have you eaten here before?"

My eyes flashed up to read his face, because, was he kidding? Damiano's was my grandfather's alibi during the time his third purported murder took place—we both knew that's why Petito had picked it. "You know it's changed ownership at least three times since the sixties."

His crooked smile popped his dimple. "And if I know you the way I think I do, you found a way to eat here probably within days of moving out of your father's house."

So he thought he knew me, did he? "Ha. You're wrong."

The dimple faded. "This is your first time, then?"

I took a sip of water before answering. "When my senior prom date asked me where I wanted to have dinner, I picked here. So I was *still living* in my father's house the first time I ate here."

Petito's laughter rumbled out deep and rich, and he leaned back in his chair. "I stand corrected. And here I was thinking I knew better than to underestimate you."

The words, combined with the sparkle in his eye, turned my knees weak, and I had to grab myself by the mental lapels and remind myself

I was a forty-nine-year-old woman rather than a goofy teenager filled with raging hormones. I covered by glancing around the room, taking in the black-and-charcoal walls, sleek oak tables, and minimal settings. "Back then it was filled with cream and gold decor, with aggressively padded armchairs."

He mirrored my glance. "Have you seen the movie *The Menu*?" he said, voice low.

"Yes!" I widened my eyes conspiratorially. "I was just thinking that. If the chef comes out to announces each course, I'm outta here."

The waiter appeared as if from nowhere, forcing us to sit up straight like teenagers who'd just been told to leave enough room for Jesus. But once we finished and he stepped away, Petito laid a protective hand on his knife and shot a look at the back of the waiter's head. I stifled my laugh and shook my head in mock chastisement.

His dimple popped out again. "I don't know about you, but I hate 'safe' first-date chitchat, so I say we jump directly into politics and religion."

"Oh, very convenient." I waved a finger at him. "You know all my dirty laundry already, and I know next to nothing about you. To even the playing field, I think you should tell me the most embarrassing thing that ever happened to you."

"Right for the jugular." He smoothed the tablecloth on either side of his plate. "Hmm, let's see. I could tell you about the time my partner almost shot me because he mistook me for the suspect we were pursuing."

I tilted my head. "That sounds more embarrassing for him than for you. Unless you needed to change uniform after?"

"Not quite, but not far off." He also pretended to consider. "How about a little family history, then? I promise something in there will count as embarrassing."

"Hit me with it."

We slipped into easy conversation that centered largely around his childhood. Like me, he was a San Francisco native, although he'd grown up in Bernal Heights while I'd been across town in the Sunset District. He had four sisters, all older, and a father who'd also been a cop.

"Was he a homicide inspector, too?" I asked.

"No." A shadow crossed his face, but he didn't elaborate. "Mom was a court reporter."

I chased the shadow. "They must have been proud that you also chose law enforcement."

He half smiled. "You have quite a talent for cutting to the heart of the matter. Not a bad trait for an up-and-coming investigative podcaster. How's the book coming, by the way?"

His talent was apparently for evading questions he didn't want to answer. But this was a first date, and if I wanted there to be a second one, I figured it was wise to play nice. "I have a proposal, a publisher, and an ending. I did most of the sorting out when I recorded the podcast. When I get past my father's disapproving face, the writing goes quickly and well."

Our entrees arrived, and we slipped into early adulthood. We'd both gone to Cal, five years apart. While I'd married and had a child after, he'd gone to the police academy.

"My marriage didn't happen until a few years later," he said as our waiter slipped chocolate torte in front of us. "But it followed pretty much the same timeline as yours in terms of implosion."

Despite his light tone, another shadow bled over his face. Sure enough, he shifted the subject. "One thing I don't know much about is the tour-guide business. Sounds like it involves far more drama than I realized. How often does one of your guests claim to witness a homicide?" He reached over and stroked my hand with his thumb.

I forced myself to concentrate despite the zings racing up my arm with each swipe. "Believe it or not, this is the first time. The crazy I usually get involves either guys with octopus hands, people who get a little too excited by murder, or people who want to buttress their self-esteem by showing they know more than I do."

"Sounds like our professions overlap more than I realized."

"You struggle with octopus-handed suspects?" I deadpanned.

"More than you might think. But I was referring to suspects who're overexcited about murder and convinced they know more than I do."

"In my case, the joke's on them. The more I can learn about a site, the better. If someone points me in the direction of new details, that makes the next iteration of the tour better." I shrugged. "Nothing I love more than a geeky research deep dive."

"Another way our work overlaps. Which reminds me, I talked to Officer Robles after I got off the phone with you." He took a bite of chocolate torte.

My own fork froze midair. "What did he say?"

"Swore up and down there was nobody in the apartment. Even linked me to the upload from his body-worn camera."

"I don't suppose I could see that cam footage?" I asked.

A ghost smile flicked over his face. "I can let you see his incident report."

Yeah, I hadn't really thought the video would wash. "I'll take it."

He pulled out his phone and tapped at it. "There. He checked each room, including closets and under the bed, and the garage."

My head flew up. "Was her truck there?"

"Yes, but you know how little that means."

I did. Parking in San Francisco was only slightly easier than putting out a building fire by spitting on it, so even locals who owned cars walked, ride-shared, or used public transport regularly.

He grinned. "Then Robles went out to talk to you and Lorraine."

The implication of his grin hit me: he'd seen Robles's conversation with me on the footage. My mind flew back as I prayed I hadn't said or done anything too annoying.

He read the expression on my face. "You did a good job of de-escalating the situation, actually."

I reached for my water glass to put out the fire that'd burst out on my cheeks. "What about Lorraine? Have you found out anything about her finances?"

"I did a quick check. On the surface everything seems aboveboard, but I agree with you. The value of that home raises red flags for me. Especially since I found a robbery three blocks away at the same time Lorraine spotted the attack."

That dialed my Spidey senses up to four-alarm. "So you think Lorraine may have been creating a distraction?"

He tapped his fork on his plate. "It's possible. As soon as we've identified the offenders, I'll be able to look for possible connections."

The waiter apparated again. "Can I get you anything else?"

Petito checked my head shake. "No, thanks. Just the bill."

"Well." I sighed and told him about my conversations with Reynalda and Quinn. "Something feels off, but I'm not sure what else to do."

He slipped a credit card into the black folder the waiter slipped onto the table. "I agree with you, it seems strange. I'll drive by myself tomorrow and double-check on it."

"Thanks. I'd appreciate that."

• • •

We slipped back into chitchat as he finished paying for the meal. Then he stood, pulled out my chair, and helped me on with my coat.

"Can I walk you to your car?" he asked.

"I insist. I've already had quite enough drama for one weekend." I tossed my head, hoping that a little sass would convince him, and maybe myself, that I was breezy and calm. Because, up until a literal moment before, I had been. The night had been easy and fun, like we'd known each other for years—apparently being investigated for murder is an excellent ice-breaker. But with my car only a three-minute walk away, I had a limited array of potential scenarios barreling down at me very, very quickly.

When I'd mentioned to Heather how I wouldn't have to face this choice right away, smiling smugly thanks to my recent, internet-obtained knowledge of the third-date rule, she glared at me the exact same way she had when we were thirteen and I told her my mother said I was too young to shave my legs.

When I told her as much, she said, "And how did *that* situation end?"

"With me sitting on the edge of the bathtub with your Lady Schick."

"And you've been thanking me ever since."

"One hundred percent," I replied. "But how does that relate to the third-date rule?"

"In both cases, you've aged out." She slashed a finger up and down the length of our bodies. "We're sidling up to fifty, blushing virgins no more. Every day another piece of us wrinkles or cellulites or droops a little more. We don't have time to play. If the opportunity to have sex with Captain Hottie presents itself, carpe diem. Tempus fugit. All the Latin sayings."

But she knew it wasn't that simple—I'd never been the sort to just scratch an itch. I wanted to feel a connection with a guy in order to sleep with him, and if I felt a connection with him, I was going to want to explore a future with him. Having sex too quickly was like playing rugby on a newly planted lawn—emotional intimacy had to take root before you got physical or you'd be forever mired in booty-call mud. Still, I didn't want him to think I was playing games if I didn't invite him to my house, or that I'd friend-zoned him five minutes into the date—and I had zero idea how to handle the situation tactfully.

As the restaurant door swung closed behind us, Petito slipped his hand into mine. Liquefaction shot up my arms, then down my spine. Suddenly I wasn't worried about how to say no, I was worried my peripheral nervous system would throw me into some very impetuous decisions.

"I had a really nice time tonight," he said as we approached the garage.

"It *was* nice," I replied, happy for the distraction. "You're quite charming when you aren't looking to arrest me for murder."

He laughed. "And you're a lot more fun when I don't have to wonder what desk you've broken into or what crime scene you've crashed each time you leave a voicemail."

My eyes snapped to his—after my mother-in-law had been murdered, the first thing I'd done was break into her desk looking for clues. "You knew I picked the lock on the desk?"

"Not for certain, until now."

I narrowed my eyes at him as we reached my car. "Tricky. I have to watch you every minute."

He took my other hand in his and stepped closer to me. "Do you have any idea how cute you are when you throw me that nasty glare?"

I narrowed my eyes harder. "It's not supposed to be cute. It's supposed to be a warning."

"Then you're doing it wrong. Because I find it very, very sexy." He leaned forward toward me.

My breath caught as his lips brushed mine, warm and soft. When my own parted in response, he slipped his hand around my waist and gently pulled me toward him. He tasted like chocolate and red wine and late mornings spent lingering in bed.

I stepped back from the kiss with a little sigh, reminding myself I was firmly against spending the night with him after only one date.

"I'd like to see you again." He smiled, then slipped his hand away from my waist. "Maybe next week?"

"I'd like that."

"Great, I'll call you." He lifted one of my hands to his lips, then reached for my car door.

He watched as I belted in and reversed out of the spot, then waved as I turned toward the exit. I caught a last glimpse of him in my rearview, blue eyes bright even in the dark light.

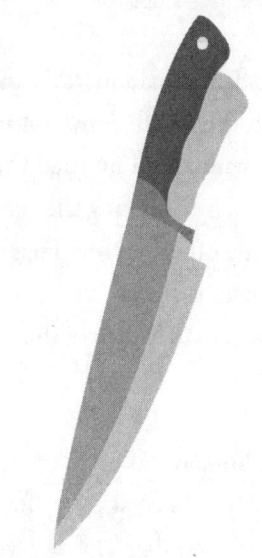

Chapter Seven

I was out of the garage and around the corner before I realized *he* hadn't given *me* the chance to *not* ask him back to my house.

When the realization finally hit, a chorus line of emotions high-kicked their way through my head. Relief did a quaint glissade along the back, because I still hadn't figured out how to turn him down without turning him off. But confusion, indignation, and worry dominated the front with raucous grand jetés—because *why* hadn't he tried to sleep with me?

"No," I said out loud, short-sheeting my dysfunctional thoughts. "I refuse to be that girl. He's probably just a gentleman, and when I didn't put out any overt signals, he backed off. Or maybe he *also* thinks emotional intimacy is more important than physical intimacy."

Heather popped in my head, face screwed up into a *yeah right* expression, and sniped: *Because that's what guys do—they turn down sex until they're emotionally connected.*

I shoved the vision aside and made my way from the garage to the kitchen while reminding myself what I'd've told Morgan if I heard her saying these things to herself. "What he thinks doesn't matter,"

I proclaimed aloud. "My time should be spent deciding how *I* want to proceed with *him*, not in obsessing about how *he* wants to proceed with *me*." I nodded firmly at my reflection in my oven door as I passed, punctuating the sentiment so it would stick. Then I tromped into my office, texting Heather on the way that I was home safely and the date had gone well, then pulled out all my notes and got to work on the next chapter of the Overkill Bill book.

• • •

The human brain is an amazing thing, especially when sublimating thoughts about sex. By the time fatigue set in at two in the morning, I'd finished three more chapters of the book, enough to send some pages to my mother to read—I'd promised her I'd let her look it over before anyone else did. After emailing it off to her, I dragged myself to bed and fell asleep reliving the memory of Petito's kiss.

When my alarm went off telling me it was time to prep for my Sunday-morning Alcatraz tour, I forced my body into the shower, but my brain remained curled up in bed. Thankful that I knew my tours inside and out, I chugged my coffee, grabbed my messenger bag, and hurried out the door and down to the ferry, praying the caffeine would kick in before I reached the island. On the way I sent out another round of messages asking if anybody'd heard from Leeya, but my notifications remained silent.

Heather called within minutes of when she knew I'd be boarding the ferry.

"Hey, girl," she purred. "I'm guessing the reason you didn't call me first thing this morning is you were too consumed by the afterglow. But now I want *all* the deets."

I braced myself for her disappointment and put on a cheerful tone. "He gave me a very gentlemanly kiss, then asked when he could see me again."

"What?" She sounded like a child who'd just been told Santa Claus didn't exist. "Why didn't you call me last night, then?"

"Because I needed to write. But now that I have you, I need to update you on the situation with Lorraine." I quickly recapped what I'd learned the day before.

"Any word back about the lineup?"

"Not yet."

"Yeah, well, if the *Chronicle*'s breathing down your neck, you got no time to waste."

I assured her that if I didn't hear anything by the time I finished my tour I'd call her again, then deboarded onto Alcatraz and spent the next few hours weaving tales of the murderers that once populated the federal penitentiary.

Thankfully, I didn't have to hunt her down—as I made my way back to the ferry, my phone alerted me that I'd received an email from Lorraine. She said she'd gone cross-eyed trying to determine which of the pictures were the right woman, and while she'd been able to easily eliminate most of them, she couldn't decide whether number five or twelve was the woman she'd seen in the window.

My pulse blew into the stratosphere—because numbers five and twelve *both* were Leeya Styles. In an attempt to give her as strict a test as possible, I'd included two correct pictures on purpose, each from a different angle and with a different hairstyle. Picking one right picture out of twelve would be nearly impossible if she hadn't actually seen Leeya, and picking only the right two was astronomically unlikely. That eliminated a number of avenues and left only two possible explanations: either Lorraine had really seen Leeya be attacked, or she'd known Leeya lived in that house before the evening of my tour. Either way, something shady was happening, and that meant I needed to figure out what was going on as soon as possible.

My phone rang, jolting my attention back down.

"Ms. Sanzio?" Reynalda's smoky voice said when I answered.

"Is everything okay?"

"Better than okay. Last night when I was getting ready for bed, I heard the garage door open around eleven, and saw Leeya's truck pull out. It was too late to call you then, but I wanted to let you know she's alive and well."

My brain slammed up against the information, combining it with Lorraine's identification of Leeya. "Are you sure?"

"Positive. I looked out my front window when I heard the rumble. It was our garage, and Leeya's red truck pulled out."

"Could somebody else have been driving it?"

"Her windows are partly tinted, and it was dark, so I suppose so. But I don't see how. They'd have to be able to get into her apartment *and* the truck, and her doors are locked."

"I see," I said. "Thanks for letting me know."

"No problem. Stop by and say hi next time you're nearby. Anybody who goes out of their way to make sure a stranger's okay is good people in my book."

I told her I would, then hung up, my heart banging out a furious rhythm against my chest. If Leeya was alive, that exponentially increased the likelihood that Lorraine was screwing with me. And if someone was gonna screw with me, they'd *damned well* better at least buy me dinner first. I stabbed at the phone to pull up Lorraine's contact.

Another call came through, flashing the name *Quinn Shovani* on my screen.

I tapped to connect. "Hello, Quinn?"

"Ms. Sanzio?" A sob broke up her words. "They found a dead woman behind the dumpster outside of Leeya's studio. They called Leeya's mother to identify her."

SF KILLER CRIME TOURS

The Mission District

San Francisco's Mission District is named for the oldest building in San Francisco, Mission San Francisco de Asís—now known as Mission Dolores—one of twenty-one missions built by the Spanish in Alta California. The district boasts a thriving arts community and an assortment of colorful murals; it's often warmer and sunnier than other parts of San Francisco because its location insulates it from the fog and wind common in the rest of the city. For this reason, it throws some of San Francisco's best festivals, including one honoring Día de los Muertos, or Day of the Dead—particularly appropriate since the Mission is home to the site of San Francisco's first serial killings.

The Emmanuel Baptist Church had problems from the start. The church's two inaugural pastors killed themselves using gruesome methods: the first slashed his throat with his razor while the second shot himself in the head. The church's third pastor, Isaac Milton Kalloch, found a different sort of trouble: on April 23, 1880, he was charged with shooting Charles de Young, co-owner of the San Francisco Chronicle. Charles de Young was out on bail at the time for attempting to kill Kalloch's father, a motivation that slots Kalloch's alleged attack firmly into San Francisco's legacy of vigilante justice. Unfortunately for de Young, his attacker was a better shot than he himself was, and de Young died as a result of his wounds. Kalloch was acquitted by a jury for the murder, but the church's reputation took a hit just the same, and it quietly moved to a new location on Bartlett Street.

Unfortunately, the bad luck tagged along. On Saturday, April 13, 1895, the Easter decorating committee found Minnie Williams murdered and mutilated in a storeroom. A search of the premises uncovered a second body, that of Blanche Lamont, at the top of the church's bell tower; she'd been strangled eleven days before and was in an advanced state of decomposition. Theodore Durrant, a student at Cooper Medical College and superintendent of the church's Sunday school, had been courting both women and was believed to have made lewd propositions to several others. He'd also been spotted entering the church with Lamont the day she went missing, and was seen fighting with Minnie outside it the day before she was found murdered. He was immediately arrested, and the press dubbed him the San Francisco Ripper, recalling the mutilation of London's Whitechapel murders just seven years before. After a jury found him guilty, he was hanged in San Quentin state prison on January 7, 1896.

Not surprisingly, area residents clamored to have the church torn down. Today the site houses the Mission Center of the City College of San Francisco, but the legacy of evil may still linger—if you're in the area late at night, stop and listen for the moans of the murdered women, crying out from where the belfry once loomed over the neighborhood.

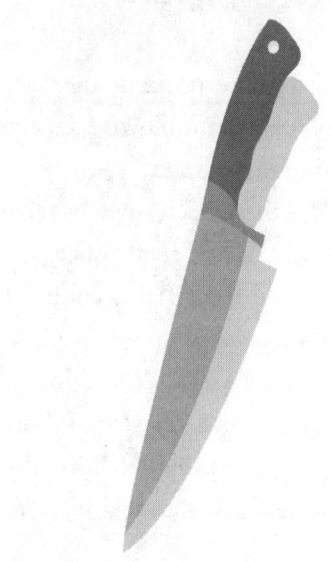

Chapter Eight

The ferry ride back from Alcatraz never felt longer as I paced the perimeter of the ship feeling helpless, unable to do anything that didn't involve my phone. So I left messages for Lorraine and Petito with what little I knew, updated Heather, then spent the rest of the ride wrangling what-ifs. Did this mean Lorraine was telling the truth about what she saw? But if so, how had Reynalda seen Leeya alive the day before? Had she been mistaken, had someone managed to get access to Leeya's apartment and her truck? I needed information: first and foremost, if the dead woman was Leeya, and if so, when exactly she'd been killed.

When the ship finally docked, I dashed out to my car, then flew up Market to the Mission. Quinn's apartment turned out to be a studio in a well-kept redbrick building, and she was waiting for my knock. Eyes widened by shock and arms wrapped around her chest, Quinn silently led me through her entryway-slash-kitchen into her spartan living space. The few items she did have were beautiful, a quality over quantity situation, and favored relaxing blues and greens that sent me subliminally to the seaside. Her gray leggings and slate-blue tunic fit the backdrop, and her chin-length black waves had a windblown feel, accented by the hint of lavender that followed in her wake.

"Has there been any news? You said they were talking to Leeya's mother?" I asked gently once perched on her blue couch.

She nodded. "Trisha confirmed the woman they found is Leeya." Her throat closed up on the last word.

My heart sank. "What happened to her?"

"They wouldn't say, but she saw marks around Leeya's neck like she was strangled." She jutted her head at me. "Google said you're not just a tour guide. You also have an investigative podcast."

I winced at how sketchy that sounded. "One season, about my grandfather."

She held my eyes. "So the police would have to tell *you* what happened."

My emotions did a U-turn—she wasn't seeing sketchy, she was seeing opportunity. I knew the smart thing to do was step through the door she was opening and stomp directly on the imposter syndrome camping out in my brain disguised as my father's voice. Successful-Tour-Guide Capri would have done exactly that—seizing opportunity when it appeared and working out details later was how I'd built my business. So, if this was a next step I was seriously considering, I needed Investigative-Journalist Capri to get on board with that strategy lickety-split.

You're screwing with people's lives, my father's voice rumbled.

I pushed his voice down with one mental hand and shoved Investigative-Journalist Capri over the threshold with the other. "I can try. But the police don't have to tell anyone anything, including journalists."

Her jaw tensed. "Your client saw hands reach out and grab Leeya's neck, and now she turned up strangled. They have to tell you *something*."

I shook my head gently to soften what I was about to say. "That doesn't seem to be relevant. Leeya's building manager said she was alive last night."

Her brows flicked together, then straightened again. "Okay, so her killer failed Friday, then finished what they started last night."

My heart wanted to jump on the bandwagon, but my head had gone a thousand rounds on this already. "Nobody came out of the building while we were all standing there."

"They must have gone out the back way. Her apartment opens to a shared courtyard behind the building. It has a little pathway that wraps around out to the street."

I did a literal double take between Quinn's face and the direction of North Beach. How had I not thought of that? Hidden courtyards and alleyways were almost as abundant in San Francisco as recycling bins and oat milk. I tapped at my phone and pulled up Leeya's address on Google Maps, then zoomed down on her block. "Show me."

Quinn leaned over and pointed to the right spot. "Here. It's just a few doors down."

I followed her finger. A rectangular courtyard sat behind Leeya's building, with a covered path to the northeast that branched off and ended in a doorway three doors down from Leeya's. My hope for an easy explanation deflated. "That's just a few yards from where we were standing, and I was on high alert. No couples came out of the buildings, and nobody carrying anything bulky. They couldn't have abducted her out."

Quinn glanced around the walls and ceiling of the room, looking for alternate explanations. When she didn't find any, fresh tears formed in her eyes and fell down each cheek. "It—it can't be a coincidence. Please, can't you at least try to talk to the police?"

The quiver in her voice pulled me back to our previous conversation. "If you want my help, I need you to come clean. Yesterday when I told you something might have happened to Leeya, you said 'Oh, God,' like you'd been afraid of that. Why?"

She paused, then gave a shuddering sigh. "Leeya and I had a falling-out. That's why we hadn't talked in a month. Her boyfriend, Zach, came on to me. I told her what happened and she didn't take it well."

My mind instantly flew to the purportedly male hands around Leeya's neck. "You think he attacked her when she confronted him?"

"That's what's confusing. She didn't believe me. She flat-out called me a liar."

I grimaced and sucked air through clenched teeth. It was an impossible catch-22, having your friend's boyfriend make a move on you. If you didn't tell your friend, you'd be hiding something crucial from them. But if you did tell them—well, "killing the messenger" was likely to be an understatement.

She nodded at my expression. "You get it. I tried to reason with her, because why would I lie about something like that? We'd been friends for a decade, since we met at Cal. We were roommates up until two years ago."

"What did she say?"

"That I must have misinterpreted something he did because I had a crush on him."

I watched her carefully. "Did you have a crush on him?"

"No way." She slashed the air in front of me. "Zach's a self-absorbed douche and she knew I thought she deserved better. When I reminded her of that, she asked me to leave. So I did, hoping she'd come to her senses. But she didn't call, and she didn't answer *my* calls. And it sucked, you know? Because he was the asshole, but somehow the stink stuck to me."

I nodded. "I'm still not clear on why you said 'Oh, God' like that."

Her hands slid across her chest and she rubbed her upper arms. "It—it's hard to put into words. Part of it was worry she'd confronted him and it hadn't gone well. But also, she was willing to give up her best friend for this man who wasn't a good guy, you know?" Her eyes searched my face for understanding. "I'm not making any sense."

But she was. Her worries tapped directly into something I'd worked to instill in Morgan since her preschool days, via my father's favorite expression: You lie down with dogs, you get fleas.

Quinn nodded vigorously. "Yes. Like, if he'd come on to her best friend, what other things is he capable of? And what other lies or compromises was she willing to put up with to keep from losing him?"

"Did he hang with a bad crowd?" I scanned her face for any signs of overacting.

She gurgled out a laugh. "Not on the face of it. He works for a children's charity."

"Was he violent?"

She rubbed her upper arms again. "I never saw him hit her, but he had a temper. I watched him tell off a waitress once to the point that she was in tears. Out of nowhere." She snapped her fingers.

"Right," I said. "We definitely need to tell the police about this."

She nodded, still clutching at her arms. "Yes, but that's not all. I think something else may have been wrong, too."

"What do you mean?"

"The night before Zach hit on me, Leeya seemed distracted. I asked her what was bothering her, but her mom was there and Leeya didn't want to talk in front of her."

I continued to watch her carefully. "Do you have any guesses what it might have been?"

She shook her head. "I've been wracking my brain."

I pulled out my phone. "Can you give me Zach's full name and number? And her mother's?"

As she dictated and I tapped, questions flew through my mind like a cauldron of rabid bats. "You said they found Leeya at her art studio. Where is that?"

"It's a shared space called Liminal Studios over in DoReMi, not far from here. I can give you the address."

"Right." The acronym sparked a vague memory. DoReMi referred to an artists' community that had sprung up amid the intersection of the Dogpatch, Potrero Hill, and Mission District neighborhoods due to zoning that limited use and dropped rental prices, making it more accessible to artists and galleries. "Is that how she made a living, with her art?"

"Mainly." She bobbed her head at me. "She also does some freelance graphic design work to help pay the bills, but in the last year her sculpture has really taken off, so she's been able to cut way back."

I was impressed—making a living as an artist, especially in an expensive city like San Francisco, was less common than the type of miracles that qualified people for sainthood. "How did that work? Did she sell through galleries?"

"Mostly pop-up galleries around the city. They allow—allowed," she said, her eyes filling with tears, "a lot of flexibility and relatively tight control over supply and demand. Really easy for her to create exclusive buzz."

"Pop-up. So no permanent location?" I asked.

She shook her head. "I think the longest one she had went for two weeks, but usually it's just for a weekend."

"Are you an artist, too?" I glanced around.

She shook her head. "I preserve other people's art. I'm a special collections librarian over at the Bancroft."

I popped my brows appreciatively. The Bancroft Library had been one of my favorite places when I was a student at UC Berkeley; in addition to being gorgeous inside, it housed one of the country's best collections of rare manuscripts and materials. "Do you know of anybody else besides Zach who Leeya may have been having an issue with?"

She seemed surprised by the idea. "No, not really. She had friction here and there with her mother and sister, but nothing out of the ordinary."

"What kind of friction?"

She shrugged. "I'm an only child so the sister part of it was always weird to me. But as far as her mother, well, after Leeya's father died, Leeya had to be the more responsible one. Her mother's the free-spirit type. Does what she wants when she wants, thanks to a small nest egg Leeya's father left for each of them in trust, and the insurance settlement. Kept bees for a while. Made artisan soap for a while. Nothing ever sticks for long, and she only ever loses money."

That helped explain how a twenty-something artist could afford not just an apartment with a garage in the city, but an artist's studio as well. "That must have been quite a trust."

She shrugged again, more tensely this time. "It's the sort of settlement where they aren't rich, but if they're smart they'll never be unhoused, if you know what I mean. Leeya's and Jenna's—Jenna's her sister—trusts were set up to pay for any schooling they wanted, with the rest doled out in chunks on a yearly basis until they turn thirty. Leeya went to a financial advisor, who helped her to reinvest as much as she could, I guess like a retirement fund or something. And she took graphic design along with her art degree so she'd have a fallback to pay bills. Her goal was to have a strong financial foundation before she turned thirty next year."

"Got it," I said. "And her mother's money was set up the same way?"

Quinn's eyes raked the ceiling. "I know it was different somehow, but I was never clear on the details. I just know Leeya was always worried her mother was running out of money."

A text came through my phone from Petito: *Got your message. Checking out the crime scene now.*

I started to text that I'd meet him there, but quickly deleted. Because if he texted back that I shouldn't come and I went anyway, that would be flat-out ignoring him, and if there was one thing my rusty self knew about the world of investigative journalism, it was that seeking forgiveness got you a helluva lot farther than asking permission.

I stood up. "The detective I know is heading over to the crime scene right now. I'll go over and see what I can find out."

She also stood, fingers clutching her arms so hard I could see white depressions in her skin. "I really appreciate it. She was my best friend for so long, and—" Her throat seized up, and tears flooded her cheeks again.

"I know." I reached out and gave her forearm a gentle squeeze. "I'll do everything I can to find out what happened, I promise."

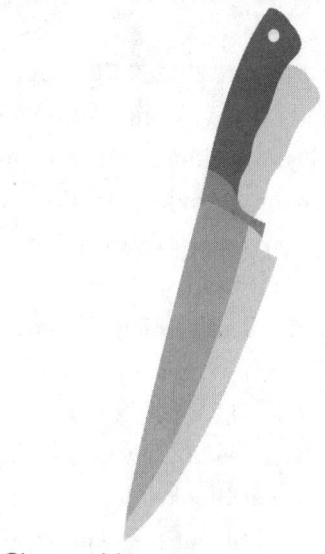

Chapter Nine

I jotted notes into my phone at every stoplight as I hurried to the crime scene, processing what Quinn had told me while making sure I wouldn't forget details. The biggest revelation was Zach, Leeya's boyfriend—if he'd hit on Leeya's best friend and had a temper, who knew what else he might do? Of course, Quinn might be lying about the whole situation. But if she was, that meant there was something she wanted to hide, and either way, something potentially dangerous was going on. The other issue that leaped out at me was the question of Leeya's mother's financial status—the first and foremost rule in any investigation was to follow the money, and if Leeya's mother needed it, that might be important. I made a note to find out who inherited from Leeya.

Liminal Studios turned out to be located in a tan building with red garage doors, probably previous apartments converted to its current purpose. A small parking lot separated the building from the one next to it, with four parking spots and three large dumpsters mostly blocked from sight by police cars, a CSI van, and several uniformed bodies. I lifted my phone over my head for a better view and snapped several pictures; one of the uniformed bodies narrowed his eyes at me, and I could feel him deciding if it was worth the effort to tell me to stop. I ignored him soundly, reminding myself I had every journalistic right in the world to be there.

You're a freelancer who only has a podcast, my father's voice jabbed through my head.

Hey, I silently rebutted, *I'm also writing a book.*

That's right, Heather's voice chimed in my head unexpectedly. *So go ask the cop for details about what happened.*

I started to nod my grateful agreement to my internalized friend, but realized I looked like I'd lost my mind. So I shook my head instead to clear out the expanding Greek chorus and forced my feet forward toward the officer.

"Capri?" Petito's voice, tinged with incredulity, stopped me in my tracks.

I turned and watched as he and Sergeant Kumar, the middle-aged woman detective who'd played good cop during the Overkill Bill copycat murder investigation, strode toward me away from their sidewalk-parked car.

My glance slid over the slightly amused expression on Kumar's face to the suspicious one on his. "I was in the neighborhood, so I figured I'd just meet you here," I said.

He surveyed my face more closely than I liked. "You were in the neighborhood?"

"Quinn Shovani, Leeya's friend, lives in the Mission. She's looking for answers." I forced myself to stay concise. I'd learned in my previous "professional" conversations with Petito that less was more—he could sniff out the tiniest implications faster than a bloodhound hunting a rabbit.

A string of competing emotions played out over Petito's face, and Kumar's amusement deepened. I braced for the inevitable response inviting me to spend my day elsewhere.

His face landed on *I'll deal with this later*. "Wait here. We'll see what we can find out."

I nodded silently, afraid anything I said would change his mind.

Once they'd safely ducked under the caution tape to liaise with the cabal of law enforcement professionals huddled by the dumpster, I returned to photographing the crime scene. But try as I might, I couldn't find an angle that revealed Leeya's position. A CSI team was processing a red pickup parked next to the dumpsters—that must have been Leeya's. One other car, a blue Hyundai, was parked in the slot across from it; since the traumatized blonde talking with a pair of officers gestured at it periodically, I assumed she owned it, and that she was the one who'd found Leeya. I snapped a shot of her and her vehicle, then stretched up to my tippy-toes with craned arms to get a picture of the pickup's bed; it turned out to be empty except for a couple of tarps and bungee cords.

I switched focus to the buildings themselves, lining up which windows had a view of the lot. The ones that did were high up, nearly impossible to accidentally observe anything happening by the dumpsters. I scanned for cameras, but there were none in the lot; the only one pointed at the building's entry. Not surprising, since limited resources would be pointed at watching for break-ins, not dumpster diving.

Petito reappeared and ducked back under the tape. "I just talked to Inspector Laskin. At seven forty-five this morning, Ellen Trott"—his head jutted toward the blonde—"parked in the lot, intending to go inside Liminal. She walked to the dumpster to throw away the bag from her McDonald's breakfast and noticed feet in between the dumpsters. She's sure they weren't there when she left last night."

"Did she check to see if Leeya was dead at that point?" I asked.

His jaw tightened. "The position of the body didn't leave much doubt."

A man in a brown overcoat who looked like he'd be happier selling me a used car ducked under the crime-scene tape. "Enjoy," he called to Petito with a smirk.

Petito raised a hand in acknowledgment, but continued to talk to me. "I told Laskin we'd like to take over the investigation, given I've already reviewed Friday's incident report and talked with Robles."

I watched Laskin climb into his vehicle. "He's okay with that?"

Petito's single dimple briefly flashed. "Contrary to what you see on TV, we're more than happy to let someone take a new case off our overloaded plates."

I hadn't considered that, but it made sense. "Can I see Leeya?"

His face shifted in surprise, then slid to professionally blank. "You know I can't let you into a crime scene."

I bristled and, calling up Heather's voice in my head for backup, stood up straighter. "I'm here in my capacity as a journalist."

His jaw flexed before he spoke. "Capri. I initially looked into this because of your situation, but now I'm officially heading the investigation. I realize you're invested in this—"

I cut him off. "I'm not just interested on a personal level. Quinn asked me to look into this because of my investigative history."

"I'm not sure one season of a podcast with a personal focus counts as an investigative history." His eyes narrowed as he watched my face. "How did she know about the podcast?"

Self-esteem, it turns out, is a strangely vicarious thing. While I'd been second-guessing my ability to investigate this situation to the point where my father's voice in my head was haunting my every move, the moment Petito so much as questioned me, every cell in my brain rose up in protest.

I resisted the urge to throw my hands on my hips. "She googled me when I called about Leeya. And I do have a degree in journalism—*and* I used to freelance back in the day."

His glance bounced to where Kumar was talking with the CSIs, then the rest of the crime scene, then back to me.

I gagged my father's skeptical voice in the back of my head and jumped on the pause. "I've already established contact with the victim's inner circle. I can even tell you who her boyfriend is." I rattled off the name and number Quinn had given me, told him Zach had hit on Quinn, and followed up with the news that Reynalda had heard Quinn's garage door open the night before. "I can help."

He considered me another moment before responding, worry flashing across his face. "Let me be sure I'm clear on this. You're now investigating Leeya's death for your investigative true-crime podcast? As a journalist?"

Despite feeling certain I was being lured into a trap, I didn't have time to mull over the implications for my potential career or our potential relationship—Leeya was dead and Quinn needed answers, and I'd promised I would help. "Correct. I told you I was considering expanding the podcast, and I can't turn my back on Quinn if she wants my help."

He gave a sharp nod, but a hint of the worry remained in his eyes. "If you're approaching this as a journalist, I'll treat you like one. Do you have a press credential from the SFPD?"

"Um," I said. "No."

"Apply for one. They probably won't give it to you since you're relatively inexperienced, but you can make an argument that you've helped us solve two cases recently."

I tapped what he was saying into my note-taking app. "Got it."

"And, just like with any other journalist, I can't let you physically on the scene even if you do have one. I'll have to hold back information just like I would with them."

I nodded, ignored the pinpricks stabbing my chest, and barreled onward. "Can you tell me how she died?"

"The medical examiner won't be able to say for sure until the autopsy."

"Leeya's mother said there were bruises on her neck like she'd been strangled."

His eyes narrowed again. "I need a verbal assurance that whatever I tell you goes no further without explicit confirmation from me that it's on the record."

I raised my hand with three fingers up, then realized that the Boy Scout salute might not have quite the same implications it used to. "Promise," I said.

"Leeya has trauma to the neck, but we aren't certain that's what caused her death. Especially because there are complicating factors."

He turned his phone around so I could see the screen. Leeya was lying on her right side in an awkward fetal position: knees pulled up to her chest, elbows resting on them, hands tucked under her neck but poking out from it. Her eyes were closed and her head sagged down over her shoulder, splaying her red-brown hair like a fan over the pavement.

I tilted my head and considered the photo. "Did she curl up to protect herself from her attacker?"

Petito shook his head. "The contusions are on the front of the neck."

"Maybe she broke away and the attacker smashed her in the head or something?"

"It's possible, that's why we need the autopsy. She may have other contusions or lacerations we can't see, or that haven't developed yet."

"Could she have been killed somewhere else and dumped here?" I asked.

Petito's professionally blank face returned. "Lividity is consistent with her current position."

So she'd been in that position when she died, or placed in it very shortly after. I scanned the picture again and pointed toward her ears.

"Those earrings look like real gold. I'm guessing that leaves out robbery as a potential motive for her death?"

Petito nodded. "She's also still wearing several rings and a necklace made of gold and gemstones. And her purse and phone are in the car."

I gestured toward the entryway camera. "In the car—so she never made it inside?"

He shook his head. "Laskin already had the building manager check the footage."

My mind raced. "Then either someone was waiting for her out here or they arrived with her. Any idea about the time of death?"

"The ME estimates she's been dead about twelve to eighteen hours."

"That's broad," I said.

"He can't say even that with certainty until he takes a closer look."

That put her death between ten the night before and four in the morning. "Reynalda said Leeya left the house around eleven last night, so that's consistent." My mind flew back to my conversation with Quinn. "How old are the bruises on her neck? Could they have happened Friday?"

He shook his head. "Only a few hours old, not a few days."

"Then her attacker must have tried again, and this time succeeded."

His face stayed blank. "If Lorraine actually saw something Friday night."

The hand I'd been holding back flew to my hip. "She identified Leeya out of my photo lineup, so I know it's relevant somehow."

He went rigid. "She did what with your what?"

Dammit. I hadn't told him about that part.

I cleared my throat to buy myself a few seconds. "I was trying to figure out if Lorraine was lying about what she saw, so when I found out who lived in the apartment, I put together a photo lineup and emailed it to her." As I explained exactly how I'd done it, his jaw flexed dangerously.

"Now her memory is tainted." His voice was steely. "We'll have no way of verifying the identification."

"I was careful—" I started to object.

He cut me off. "For any investigation to be prosecutable, we have to follow very specific procedures. And she may be playing you regardless. If Lorraine *is* involved in this somehow, she could very well know what Leeya looked like. Even if she didn't, she could have looked Leeya up the same way you did."

"I didn't tell her Leeya's name—" But even as I said it, I knew I wasn't the only possible source of the information. I mentally face-palmed, then tried to shift back to more solid ground. "There are other reasons to think what happened Friday is relevant. Quinn told me there's a covered alley that leads out of the back courtyard. I didn't see any pairs of people come out, so her attacker didn't leave with her then, but maybe he left alone and came back later. I wouldn't have noticed a single person."

"Why wasn't Leeya in the apartment when Robles checked, then?" He raised a hand to stall my objection. "I happen to agree that Friday's incident is related—just not necessarily the way you think."

I ran with his attempt to de-escalate. "Maybe she or the attacker went upstairs to the second-floor apartment? Maybe the second-floor tenant was the attacker, or maybe Leeya just happened to go up and visit them and didn't realize the police had come?"

He nodded. "I'm following up with the other tenants."

"The building manager's about a hundred years old and a hundred pounds dripping wet, but she might have a partner or something who lives there with her that could . . ."

He raised a hand in another "stop" gesture. "Tell me what you're thinking."

There was a warning in his tone that activated my stubborn

streak—I had a right to do this, dammit, and I didn't need his permission. "I'm thinking I need to call Reynalda and tell her what's going on."

"And ask her about the other tenant while you're at it?"

My second hand jumped to my hip, phone still in it. "Yes, actually. Because that's what investigative journalists do. They investigate. And they don't need permission from the police to do it."

I watched the muscles at his temple twitch as he realized the situation he'd backed himself into. His eyes softened, and he took a step closer to me. "All I'm asking is, if you're going to do this, work *with* me, not *against* me. Make good choices."

"Cross my heart and hope to die." I ran a finger over my chest.

He gave another curt nod, then stalked off.

And I hauled ass away before it occurred to him that his definition of a "good choice" wasn't very likely to match up with mine.

Chapter Ten

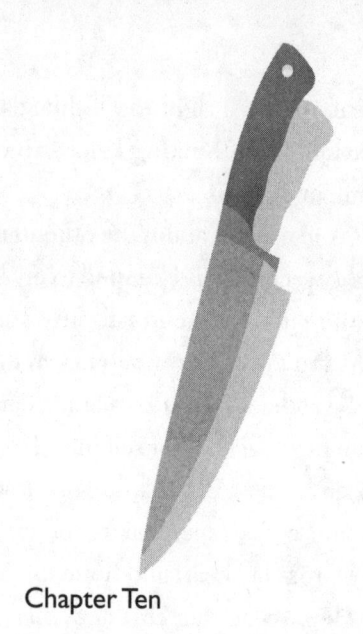

As I hurried away from Liminal Studios, the scene with Petito replayed itself in my head to the soundtrack of my father's chuckle. Apparently when Petito wasn't in front of me to immediately fight against, my bravado faded into the background, and while I'd need to sort that out with my therapist eventually, for the moment I needed to focus on my next steps. As much as I wanted to push back against my photo lineup faux pas, as a mature adult, if I was seriously considering pursuing investigative podcasting, I needed to take responsibility for my action and assess how to do better in the future. Petito was right that I didn't know the full ins and outs of correct identification, there was no getting around that.

But if that was such a huge factor here, why didn't Robles or Petito do the identification themselves, the remaining petulant adolescent portion of my brain objected.

Because resources are limited, the true-crime lobe answered back. The police didn't have infinite manpower, despite near-infinite calls they had to respond to every day. A woman claiming without proof to have witnessed something odd was not going to be a top priority. And that meant I'd needed to take the lead on the situation, and if push came to shove I'd do it again—with a little more wisdom behind my methodology next time.

As I reached my car I shifted mental gears—I couldn't do anything about that now regardless, and I needed to decide who to talk to first: Leeya's boyfriend Zach, Leeya's mother Trisha, or Reynalda. While Quinn's story about Zach made him my number one suspect, the smart thing would be to get a better understanding of Leeya's life before approaching him so I could pick up on any inconsistencies. Talking to her mother was the best way to do that, but since she'd just finished identifying Leeya, she could probably use a minute to recover before I showed up asking questions. That left me with Reynalda, and the drive would give me about fifteen minutes to plot my way into Leeya's apartment. So I updated Quinn via text at stoplights between wracking my brain for a strategy.

Once I reached Leeya's house, I checked the second-floor apartment before hitting up Reynalda, but the mysterious tenant still wasn't home. Then I braced myself, buzzed Reynalda, and prepared to break the news as gently as I was able.

"The police called and told me," she said before I'd finished saying hello. "I'll be right down."

Petito must have called her the moment I'd walked away from the crime scene. Well played, Petito. Well played.

She opened the door a moment later looking ashen and dazed. "I don't understand how that's possible?"

"That's what I'd like to figure out," I said to Reynalda. "So I was wondering if I could ask you a few more questions."

Her head bobbed up and down. "Whatever you need."

"The tenant in the second-floor apartment isn't home. Can you tell me anything about them?"

"Khalil Jackson. He's a security guard over at Saks Union Square. Works swing shift and sometimes additional midnight shifts. Usually has Sunday dinner with his mama." Her eyes lit up with clear appreciation.

I checked the time. It was two thirty, but if Sunday dinner at his mother's house was like my mother's house, "dinner" started in the early afternoon, and you were expected to arrive not much past noon. "So he'd've been working Friday night?"

"Yep. And he's working lots of extra hours lately, too, to help with her medical bills."

I ran with a hunch I hoped would crowbar me into Reynalda's personal life. "Sounds like he's a good son. I wish I got to see my daughter every weekend." I saw Morgan twice a week on average, but wasn't one to let an overadherence to truth stand in the way of solving a murder.

Her smile was wistful. "Hardest part of being a parent is letting 'em go."

"Don't I know it." I rolled my eyes. "Sounds like you've got one of your own?"

"My son Trevon. Every time I tell him I wish he'd come around more, he tells me I need to get a life." She made a *psh* sound and flapped her hand. "My life is just fine, I got no problem living alone. Don't mean he can't come eat a home-cooked meal now and again. Last time I saw him was October."

I nodded earnestly, mentally checking off her living-arrangement status. "My daughter constantly tries to fix me up."

"Ha," she barked. "Trevon knows better than that. Last thing I need in my life is a man. More trouble than they worth."

"I hear you." I laughed in mock agreement and put a mental tick next to her relationship status. "Anyway, I forgot what time you said you saw Leeya's truck leave last night."

"Eleven." She cocked her head at me. "Police asked if I was sure. But I knew because I always tape *SNL* and watch it right before bed."

Whatever Leeya's reasons for the late hour, it fit the timeline. Even if she had gone to some party or such first, that didn't mean she stayed for long. One way or the other, something had drawn her to her studio, and she'd had a run-in with her killer. "You said you didn't hear any sort of fight on Friday night. But have you heard any sort of altercation any other time?"

"Never. But it'd have to be a pretty loud one to get all the way up to my floor."

I put on a confused grimace. "But you asked her not to work here because of the noise?"

"That was for Khalil. He has to sleep whenever he can."

That made sense for an off-shifter, and left me with only one last tack. I took a big mental breath and dove in. "It's just so weird that Lorraine thought she saw someone attacking Leeya only to have her show up dead two days later." I left the implication dangling like a cat toy on a wand.

She batted right at it. "You're right. Never had trouble out of her, now two things in one weekend."

I nodded.

Reynalda nodded.

So much for subtlety. "If the fight Friday had something to do with her death, there might be some clue about what happened in her apartment."

She shook her head. "The cops went through and found nothing."

"But you were only looking for Leeya, right? To see if she was in there, but not really more than that?"

Doubt crept into her eyes and they slid to Leeya's door. "I'd'a noticed if there were any signs of a fight. She kept a clean house."

I pursed my brow hard. "So difficult to say when nobody knew what was going on."

Her eyes stayed glued to Leeya's door, but she didn't move.

All I had left was my ton of bricks. "The thing is, now that she's dead there's nothing illegal about you going in there. You'll actually *have* to go in anyway to deal with the apartment."

Her brows rose and she took a half step toward the door. "That's true. And I really should make sure there's nothing dangerous in there, like a curling iron left on or something, since she's not coming back."

I nodded vigorously. "Old house like this, even too many things plugged into an outlet could burn down the place. Then you'd catch a ration of trouble."

She pirouetted back up her stairs. "Wait right there," she tossed at me over her shoulder.

• • •

I fought the temptation to high-five myself right in the entryway as I waited for Reynalda's return. She reappeared clutching a cascade of keys, thumbing through the forest of fobs to find Leeya's. She located it, slipped it into the lock, and without a second's hesitation plowed into the apartment.

A surreal mix of recognition and novelty swept over me as I crossed the threshold into Leeya's living room. I'd seen it before as a backdrop for several of her pictures on Instagram, but to be there live and in three dimensions felt like standing in front of the Eiffel Tower after staring at it in movies your whole life. I soaked it in, trying to get a feel for who Leeya was from the surroundings—if I was going to help find out who killed her, I needed to form a picture of who she was. Against the blank, undeveloped Polaroid of never having met her, the apartment gave an oddly museum-esque feel, like if I so much as brushed up against anything, alarms would go off and security guards would cart me off. Luckily, Reynalda was right that she was a neat person, and only a few errant objects dotted the room's surfaces—a coastered mug on the end table, a few pieces of mail on the coffee table. The colors—muted yellows, oranges, and browns—along with the warm residual scents of spice and citrus created a warm, homey feel that suggested a confident, happy resident. I pulled out my phone and clicked several pictures, including a close-up of the mail, two bills and a supermarket circular.

"You've been in here since she moved in, right?" I asked Reynalda.

Her nose scrunched like she was smelling something bad. "Just a couple times when something needed fixing that I could manage with help from YouTube."

I raised my brows to compliment her skill. "So would you know if anything was out of place?"

Her lips pursed toward her nose as she considered. "Can't be sure, but nothing's jumping out at me."

When I nodded, she passed between the nonfunctioning fireplace and the brown-striped couch, bookended by two sculptures of cats made from an assortment of wire hangers and paper clips, to the hall that led off the right side of the back wall. Like many San Francisco apartments made from sliced-up single-family dwellings, the floor plan was shotgun-style, with the rooms branching one after the other off a single hall that ran the length of the building. The next room on the left was a streamlined kitchen with a dining area at the far end, along with a second door that led back into the hall. The cabinets and counters were old but not shabby, decorated with kitschy fifties-esque plaques espousing the virtues of coffee. I scanned the single dirty bowl in the sink and tried not to picture her last meal, from the look of it either a red-sauce pasta or tomato-based soup whose residue had dried out and cracked. The dining area contained a simple white table, along with a statue of a mother and child made from pieces of antique toys.

I snapped my pictures. "Everything normal in here?"

"Far as I can tell."

We exited through the dining-portion door and backtracked to the first room on the right, a bathroom decorated in greens and blues.

The room was clean, with few items out on the sink. After snapping a picture of each wall, I grabbed a tissue from the box perched atop the toilet and used it to open the medicine cabinet. The contents were fairly standard—Band-Aids, Neosporin, Advil, NyQuil—and the only prescription I could see was a dial pack of birth control pills. I hesitated, then grabbed the pack and, carefully keeping the entire thing covered with the tissue, clicked open the container. The last pill had been taken on a Monday—that meant she'd missed at least the last six of her pills, if not more. I snapped a picture of the pack, then returned it to its place.

Attached to the bathroom was Leeya's bedroom, decorated primarily in burgundy with jolts of teal. I'd never have thought to put those two colors together, but here they created a sense of youthful sophistication. The bed was quasi-made-up, covers only pulled into place in a way that would never pass military muster. Pillows tumbled onto one another, and a blouse of some sort lay tossed across the armchair in the corner. This room's sculpture was a pair of embracing lovers made from antique postcards and costume jewelry.

"Looks the same as I saw it last time," Reynalda said.

I strode over to her nightstand and used the same tissue to pull out the drawer, desperately hoping for a journal or some such inside. Instead I found a Kindle, two paperback books, and a lip balm. Something tugged at me; Leeya loved coffee and reading, and while I knew that applied to lots of people, everything about this apartment made me feel I would have liked her.

The final room, a small space probably originally intended as a nursery, contained a desk and two bookshelves. A laptop sat next to a vertical filing frame; a potted boat lily with purple-edged leaves complemented the aubergine accents in the cream room.

"She wasn't afraid of color," I said, using the tissue to open the drawers of the desk.

Reynalda's eyes widened. "Not really my style, but you gotta admire it."

The office supplies inside the middle drawer were relatively neat, as were the files in the side drawers. I briefly considered riffling through them, but Reynalda's sharp glances warned me that would be one step too far. Still, I couldn't resist snaking a hand forward to the two folders slanted in the vertical file as I straightened back up. The first was labeled THOMAS, NELSON and seemed to be a basic file outlining the client's needs and desires for his website, along with a smattering of notes about Leeya's design ideas. The second, labeled MARCUS, KODY, had a paper-clipped sticky note on the outside declaring in large, bloodred block letters that the account was unpaid.

"You find something?" Reynalda asked, and sidled up to peer over my shoulder.

"An unpaid account." I flipped through the file, taking pictures of each page as I went.

"You think someone would kill her rather than pay their bill?" Her voice was skeptical.

"Extreme, I agree. But we can't rule anything out yet." I flipped the file closed again and slipped it back between the silver prongs.

Reynalda stepped out to the end of the hallway and pointed to a staircase tucked out of sight. "Garage is down there."

I followed her down and the feeling of connection grew stronger in the space, which mirrored my own garage at home. I loved the extra industrial sink and long counter in mine, and while I used it less these days, I had fond memories of confections stacked precariously in preparation for Morgan's bake sales. Rather than cupcakes, Leeya's counter was dotted with containers of art supplies; I only recognized a few of them, like the one marked Gesso. My working-class upbringing had taught me to pinch a penny until it shrieked, so the extra pantry shelf space and second freezer spoke to my bulk-buying soul, even if the metal shelves next to her washer/dryer duo were stacked with what looked like random pieces of junk. Based on the sculptures I'd seen above, what I perceived as junk was the treasure she used to create her art. I snapped a series of pics.

"What are you hoping to do with those pictures?" Reynalda shifted back toward the stairs, telegraphing to me my time was up.

"If I'm honest, I have no idea." As I followed her out, another something tugged at me, this one more ominous; I ran my mental eye over the house's contents, but couldn't figure out what was causing it. "I'm not even sure what exactly I was hoping to find in here. Maybe a spot of blood Officer Robles missed, or two telltale wineglasses together on the coffee table? Mainly I just want to have a record of how it all looks in case the family comes tomorrow and changes it."

She nodded, and we reached the main floor again. "Do you mind if I take a quick look at the courtyard, and the alley that exits around the building?" I asked.

"Sure."

She took me out through the back door, then led me to the exit, but the up-close and personal didn't give me any more insight than I already had from my trip through Google Maps. "Does this door open from the outside?"

"If you have the key."

I gazed up. Unless someone was literally hanging out of the window, they wouldn't be able to see down into the narrow courtyard.

"Thank you," I said when we'd finished, and assured her I'd keep her informed about anything I found.

But as I made my way back to the car, the feeling I was missing something obvious kept taunting me, just out of my mental reach.

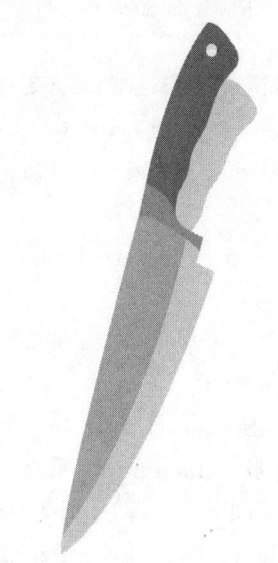

Chapter Eleven

To fight off the sense I was missing something, I turned my attention to the next concrete actions I could take. I called Leeya's mother; when she didn't answer, I drove by her house. Nobody was home, and visions of her identifying Leeya at the morgue or giving a statement down at the homicide division flashed through my mind. Zach Haines also didn't answer my call, but since I didn't know where he lived, I couldn't go see him. I needed to make a stop by the Hub anyway, so I headed back, checking the pictures I'd taken of Kody Marcus's file—Leeya's past-due account was another important lead I needed to follow up on.

When I pushed through the door of the Hub, Heather swiveled to greet me, her head cocked to the side and her expression grave. "What did you find out?"

I gave them a quick run-through of everything that had happened, throwing up my hands as I finished. "Nothing fits or makes sense, but it just feels like too big a coincidence. And I feel like I'm missing something, but I can't figure out what."

"*Way* too big a coincidence." Heather held up a slip of paper and leaned toward me, watching my face. "And the *Chronicle* agrees. They've called twice, like we're stupid enough to give up our scoop to them. And on that note, we need to drop something on the pod ASAP."

I groaned internally as I took the messages, little daggers stabbing at my stomach.

It's not your place, little girl, the voice rumbled.

"Quinn asked me to look into everything," I said, ostensibly to Heather rather than the ghost of my father. "I have a responsibility to help. But I'm not sure we can drop an episode just yet. These are real people who lost a real loved one, and I know firsthand how badly being at the center of a murder investigation can mess with a family, even after decades. I need to talk to her mother before I make any decisions."

Heather's chest expanded as she took a careful, measured breath. "I get that your father isn't happy about the Overkill Bill book. But those victims deserve justice, and so does Leeya. And it's way better that someone who actually cares look into it all rather than news vampires looking for bloodsucking clickbait. Don't let your father hijack your shine."

Did she have a psychic stethoscope stuck to my skull? "Father or no, I've got to figure out which lines I'm willing to cross as an investigative podcaster and which I'm not."

Ryan chimed in. "Someone saw or knows something, even if they don't know it's important. You need to get the word out into the true-crime community, and fast."

He wasn't wrong, even if it made my throat tighten. "I need to at least talk to her mother first, and I need to make sure I go in with a plan so I don't do any damage I can't repair."

"Totally admirable." Heather's face turned contemplative. "So let's shift gears. What you need is a good old-fashioned gabfest to get your thoughts in order."

The knives in my stomach partially retreated. "Let's do it."

Heather pulled her legs up into a cross-legged position under her, then grabbed her coffee. "Okay, let me make sure I'm getting this right. Leeya left around eleven last night and ended up at her studio. So whoever killed her either met her there or came with her."

I nodded. "They might also have staked out her studio. It seems strange she'd willingly meet with someone who had already tried to hurt her."

Heather nodded in agreement. "Plus, if they came with her, how did they get away?"

"Not hard to call an Uber or a Waymo," Ryan said.

"But both of those would leave a record of the ride," Heather said. "And I *know* I asked you to never mention the word 'Waymo' in this office again."

I tried to forestall what I knew was about to happen—San Francisco's driverless taxis were a rancorous bugaboo for Heather, while Ryan was the overzealous TikToker who couldn't resist dancing on her perilous ledge—but was too slow.

"Like it or not, this is a perfect example of why you can't stick your head in the sand when it comes to technological progress," he crooned.

She death-ray-glared him. "You may have already sold your soul to our artificial-intelligence overlords, but I remain committed to resistance. Those kids that were nearly hurt—"

"That wasn't Waymo, that was a different company—"

"Okay, true, but I was behind one the other day that did a random three-point turn out of nowhere, then turned around and kept on the way it was originally headed. How does that happen?" She clapped out each of the words. "How?"

I threw up a hand. "As much as I love these Luddite-versus-hacker cage matches, I forgot my popcorn at home today. So let's get back to the point at hand: you could easily walk a few blocks, then grab a ride from there. You wouldn't have to go far before it would get hard to trace back specifically to the crime scene with all the ride-share activity on a Saturday night." I grabbed my phone. "I'll ask Petito about it, and about security camera footage of anyone walking down that street."

Heather sent a last mini-glare at Ryan, then turned to me. "Let's talk suspects. What Zach did to Quinn rubs me the wrong way."

"Quinn might be lying," Ryan said, energized by the Waymo scrapping. "Maybe *she* came on to *him*."

Heather spun back to him. "And then killed Leeya *why*? For ending their friendship? That's mad dramatic, don't you think?"

"As of right now, they're both on the suspect list." I stepped in to parry. "There's also the problem-client folder I found on Leeya's desk. I need to track him down."

Heather nodded. "Definitely. Who else?"

"What about the landlady?" Ryan asked. "In mystery novels, the killer always turns out to be some side character you think isn't even involved."

"She's in her seventies and tiny to boot. No way she'd be able to strangle someone young and strong like Leeya. And she has no significant other to help."

"You said she has a son," Heather said. "Maybe her son didn't like Leeya for some reason."

"Maybe he came on to Leeya and she rejected him?" Ryan asked. "He could have found out where she spends her time from his mother."

"Reynalda claimed he hasn't been around for a while. But if he did something to Leeya and she's covering for him, that would explain where everybody suddenly disappeared to when the police showed up Friday." I jotted it down in my notebook.

"That's the sixty-four-thousand-dollar question." Heather grabbed a pen and flipped it over her knuckles. "Where did Leeya and whoever owned the hands disappear to when the police showed up?"

I told them about the courtyard exit. "I didn't know who I was looking for, so if she went out that way, I wouldn't have seen her."

"So, two possibilities at least," Heather said.

I grimaced. "I need to find someone who's talked to Leeya more recently than Quinn. I need to get hold of her mother and Zach." I grabbed the phone and tapped Leeya's mother's contact again.

Heather popped her legs back out from under her and shifted forward. "Hey, I have an idea. Why don't I come with you when you talk to Leeya's mother? I could convince her—"

I cut her off. "You have many superpowers, but diplomacy isn't one of them. And the point isn't to talk her into doing something she's not comfortable with, the point is to help if we can."

As Heather began grumbling her dissent, Leeya's mother answered the phone, and I scrambled to introduce myself. Through a torrent of intermittent sobs, Trisha agreed to meet with me if I could come over before she was due at the funeral home.

"Gotta run." I snatched up my coat, then put up a hand when Heather tried to follow. "Don't you have your True-Crime Chinatown tour in an hour, anyway?"

"Yeah, sure, fine," she grumbled, and turned back to her computer. "Call me the moment you leave her house."

● ● ●

As I made my way to Leeya's mother's house, my phone rang. When I saw Morgan's name flash on the display, I hurried to put the call through, remembering her earlier text.

"Hey, Mom," she crooned with an annoyingly adolescent tease in her voice. "How'd the date go?"

I squeezed my eyes shut against the wave of *Freaky Friday* surreality that washed over me. Objectively it wasn't strange that my daughter would question me about my dating life, given that she's a fully adult twenty-four-year-old who studies human behavior via forensic psychology in graduate school. But none of my few dates over the last decade had been serious enough to justify putting them on her radar, so I had zero experience broaching the subject with her.

I laughed away the awkward. "How's everything with The Chateau?"

Her sigh held an undertone I couldn't quite pin down. "Stressful. Some days I wish Grandma hadn't left it to us."

My brows creased. My mother-in-law Sylvia was descended from Jacques Reynard, who'd made his fortune selling overpriced pickaxes to men on quixotic quests for gold in the California hills, and her Pac Heights mini-mansion was part of her birthright from Reynard's line. As such, she believed it should stay in the hands of Reynard's descendants, so had left it to Todd and Morgan rather than her husband Philip. Since Philip now resided across the bay regardless, Todd and Morgan had moved in, but because of the financial shenanigans Sylvia had enmeshed herself in before her murder, the house was mortgaged to its multimillion-dollar hilt. The only way they could pay the mortgage was to rent out rooms to people Morgan knew and trusted from school. The whole thing gave me hives—I'd learned over my five decades on the planet that things rarely went smoothly, especially when Todd was added into the mix. His *the bigger the risk, the bigger the reward* approach to business ventures had cost me more nights' sleep than I could count.

"We're thinking we'll simplify it all by leaving the three guest bedrooms decorated as is and rent them out as furnished," she continued.

I cast my mind quickly over the rooms. "You should move the heirloom pieces to your room or the attic. Renters aren't known for being careful."

"Good point."

"You also want to factor in maintenance when you're figuring out how much you need to charge each boarder," I said.

"Maintenance?" Alarm crept into her voice.

"With seven people using the kitchen, appliances will wear out and dishes will get broken. Paint and floors will get scuffed and scratched, and someone will shove something down the disposal that they shouldn't. And you should budget a regular deep clean by professionals, given your grandmother's decorating scheme." Sylvia's entire house had been decorated in shades of off-white. Some rooms with hints of sage, some with hints of lavender—but all undeniable, unrepentant dirt magnets.

"I never even thought of that." The alarm grew. "And there's no way I want to have to oversee when people clean what, especially with busy students."

We continued on, working through all the implications of turning the private residence into a business venture as I navigated around double-parked cars and darting scooters. By the time we touched on the importance of insurance and properly worded leases, I'd nearly arrived at my destination. "Okay, honey, I need to start looking for parking. Love you."

"Okay, Mom. Thanks for walking me through all of this."

The odd undertone from the beginning of our conversation was back. "Is everything okay, honey?"

She sighed. "It's fine. I'm sure it's nothing."

I put on my most soothing mom voice. "Tell me."

"It's just that Dad hasn't been around much, and when he is, it seems like something's weighing on his mind."

A knot formed in my stomach—the description sounded uncomfortably similar to how he behaved when he was having money troubles. But I couldn't let Morgan worry about it, so I cleared my throat and put on a light tone. "It's probably some new girl he's seeing or something. I'll talk to him and make sure everything's okay."

"You're probably right." She sighed, then switched into her singsong tease. "Say hi to your new boyfriend for me . . ."

I matched the teasing tone. "Hey, when do you think you're gonna start giving me grandchildren?"

Her tone sobered up. "Gotta go, talk to you tomorrow."

I laughed as she hung up, then set all my attention on scoping out a parking spot somewhere in the vicinity of Leeya's mom's house.

Chapter Twelve

Trisha's house was dark gray and blocky, with a huge extended bay window on the second floor that looked out over Aquatic Park to Alcatraz. When she answered the door, Leeya's chocolate, almond-shaped eyes stared out of Trisha's face, here lined with wrinkles and ringed with red. She also had Leeya's high cheekbones, but her hair was enhanced with red highlights that shifted her to a brash auburn.

"Trisha Schlesinger? I'm Capri Sanzio. Thanks so much for meeting me."

"Just Trisha, please." As she stepped back to lead me through her entryway and up the stairs to her main floor, I did a quick Terminator-style scan of both her and the environs. Hers divulged quality clothes from mid-range designers and the sort of layered haircut that required frequent touch-ups to look natural and effortless; the house yielded modern design choices in a nearly open floor plan—sleek, gray-on-gray vibe throughout, Scandinavian-modern furniture in shades of brown that pulled from the deco-design parquet hardwood floors—but with enough scuffs and chips to show it hadn't been redone in the last few years. My conclusion: well-off but not rich, right in line with the picture Quinn had painted about her financial status.

A man in khakis and a slate-blue polo shirt rose from the couch and approached me, hand out. His salt-and-pepper hair leaned more toward salt than I would have predicted from the moderate web of lines across his forehead; they pulled me toward early fifties while the hair tugged at early sixties. His brown eyes also were ringed with red. "I'm Roger Prentiss, Trish's fiancé. Thank you for coming."

Trisha pointed to one end of the brown leather couch, then perched herself on the other end while Roger took the armchair next to us. "This can't be happening." She pulled a tissue from a box on the coffee table. "If I hadn't seen her with my own eyes—" Her throat seized up.

My own throat tightened sympathetically. Identifying my mother-in-law's body had been one of the worst moments of my life; I couldn't imagine how I'd have felt if it had been Morgan. I leaned over and put my hand on her forearm. "I'm so sorry."

She hunched over, head in her hands, and her body shook. After a long moment she clutched at my hand and raised her eyes to meet mine with haunted desperation. "Quinn said you're a private investigator. We'll pay whatever your rate is. We have to find the monster who did this to my baby. The police—" Her throat seized again.

My stomach clenched. "I think there's been a miscommunication. I'm not a licensed PI. Quinn's thinking of my true-crime investigative reporting."

She tensed, and leaned slightly away from me. "Investigative reporting?"

Dammit—I needed her to *not* think I was paparazzi. "I've worked on two investigations in the course of researching my podcast, and uncovered evidence that helped the police." Her eyes widened when I said the word "podcast." "Don't worry, the podcast isn't why I'm here. My only concern is with Leeya."

A fire blazed into her teary eyes. "Oh, a podcast is *exactly* what we need. That Detective Laskin couldn't have been worse—he wouldn't tell me a single thing, just said to come home and wait. Wait for what? Their failure to take your call seriously Friday night has already cost my daughter her life. I'm damned well going to make sure they don't shove her into some cold-case cabinet to be forgotten."

Heather's voice in my head whispered to me that I should lean into this, tell her how much our podcast could help. But the line between encouraging Trisha to confide in me and slagging off the police was thinner than a nineties heroin-chic model, and I didn't at all care for walking it. "Another inspector, Dan Petito, just took over Leeya's case. I've worked with him before, and I'm sure he'll do everything he can to find Leeya's killer."

Her face screwed up like she'd taken a sip of sour milk. "I don't understand. I thought you were here to *help* us."

I raised my hands to reassure her. "I am. In fact, I have some questions about Leeya, if that's okay."

The tantrum warning signs receded. "What can I tell you?"

"Do you know of anyone who might have wanted to hurt Leeya?"

She pushed the tissue up to her nose, and her eyes filled. "Everybody loved Leeya. This must have been random violence."

I nodded, fairly sure challenging her objectivity wasn't the best approach. "Were the two of you close?"

Tears overflowed onto her cheeks. "I'm close to both my girls, of course, but Julia was my baby. Your youngest is always special."

My brain stuttered over the names for a moment, but finally kicked in. "Leeya's short for Julia?"

"She always said 'Julia' was an 'old-lady' name." She rolled her eyes as she put air quotes around the phrase.

I could relate. "Capri" was my attempt to squeeze some brand of normalcy out of "Capricorn," the name my mother saddled me with due to her lingering obsession with the Summer of Love. "When was the last time you heard from Leeya?"

"Thursday afternoon." A shadow crossed her face. "We talked on the phone."

"Did something happen when you talked? Was she upset?"

"No, nothing like that." She waved her tissue-clutching hand. "I told her about a gorgeous dress I'd found for a holiday party. She told me about the piece she was working on."

"What was it?" I asked, figuring it might be a clue.

"A leopard, I think? Or, no, that was last month. Something to do with umbrellas." She waved the hand again.

My mind screeched on her lack of details. "I saw some of her sculptures on Instagram. She makes them with found objects, right?"

Trisha gave a shuddering nod. "She just loved diving through junk. The older and grimier the better."

Try as I might, I couldn't figure out what to say to that. "Did she mention Zach at all?"

"Not that I remember." She seemed confused.

"It's just that Quinn mentioned Leeya'd been having a problem with her boyfriend?"

Trisha's head jutted backward. "Between Leeya and Zach? Not as far as I know."

Huh. Either Quinn had been lying, or Leeya hadn't ever mentioned the situation to her mother. Which, if they were as close as Trisha claimed, seemed odd. "Did you like Zach?"

A smile lit up Trisha's face. "He's so sweet, and respectful. He works for the Anything-Your-Heart-Desires Foundation, the one that does special things for kids. I couldn't wait for them to get engaged." Her expression crumpled as her new reality hit again. She picked up her phone off the coffee table. "He's going to be just devastated. I've called him several times, but he's not answering. He works a lot of weekends."

"I've called him several times, too. I'll keep trying," I said. "What about her other relationships? Any fights with friends or family or business associates?"

Her eyes filled again. "Not that I know of."

"There was that client," Roger interjected.

Trisha shot him a confused stare.

"The one who didn't want to pay her, remember? She called me for advice."

"Oh, right. I'd completely forgotten about that." The tissue hand flopped through the air. "But that couldn't be enough to *kill* someone over."

"What exactly happened?" I asked.

"She had a client who wouldn't pay, and she'd never really dealt with that before. She asked me what she should do. I suggested she hire a collection agency, since the amount wasn't large enough to sue over."

"And did she?" I asked.

"I'm not certain," he said, sending a questioning look at Trisha. "She never told me what she decided."

"How long ago was this?" I asked.

"A couple of weeks, I think."

"You didn't follow up?" I watched his face.

"I didn't want to overstep." He shifted in his seat and sent another quick glance at Trisha. "Leeya wasn't my biggest fan when we started dating. It was a big step for her to trust me enough to make the call."

Trisha laid a hand atop his, then met my eyes. "You know how it is with stepparents. But Leeya admired Roger's canny business sense."

"What business are you in?" I asked.

His smile was modest. "I'm in the business of businesses. I really love swooping in and saving a business that's struggling. Once it's successful, I look for another challenge."

I didn't care for the vagueness of that. "Anything I might have heard of?"

"Currently a bakery in North Beach. Holy Cannoli." He pulled a card out of his pocket and passed it to me. "I've spent the last year and a half instituting changes. Now it's thriving, so much so I'm now looking to launch a chain of them across the state."

I glanced down at the card. The name stirred a memory, but I'd never been inside of it; my family has been loyal to our bakery since before I could walk. "Do you remember the problem client's name?"

He shook his head. "She didn't give me specifics."

I nodded, glad I'd stumbled on the Kody Marcus file I'd found on her desk. I shifted gears. "Can you give me a list of Leeya's other friends so I can talk to them?"

"Quinn was really Leeya's only close friend. Leeya has always been a solitary girl." Trisha stopped, eyes filling again. "If anything was going on, Quinn would have known about it."

"Was she close with her sister?" I asked, keeping my voice gentle.

"Oh, yes." She waved the tissue through the air again. "They love each other deeply. Losing their father so young bonded them."

My heart panged—the family had already seen more than its share of pain. "Can I talk to her?"

"Certainly." She rattled off Jenna's name and number to me. "I'll let her know to expect a call from you."

I took a mental deep breath before I continued—they weren't going to like this next part. "The police are going to want to know what everyone in her inner circle was doing on Saturday night and Sunday morning."

Her hand made a fist around the tissue. "Oh, that horrible detective wasted no time asking me for my *alibi*." She stabbed a finger at the air in front of her. "I carried that girl for *nine months*, then went through twenty-seven straight hours of hard labor to give birth to her. It took me two months to heal from my episiotomy. I'm her *mother*."

The true-crime lobe of my brain automatically churned out a torrent of cases where women had killed their own children—*Diane Downs, Susan Smith, Andrea Yates*—but I had a feeling they wouldn't be a welcome contribution to the conversation. "He'd lose his job if he didn't ask everyone. Hopefully you both had alibis?"

Her eyes flicked over my face. "I was at my friend's daughter's bachelorette party until about two in the morning. When I got back, Roger was asleep—"

"I remember you getting into bed, though. Just after two."

She smiled a teary smile and squeezed his hand. "And he brought me breakfast in bed around, what, ten?"

"Bloody Mary and toast," he explained. "Hair of the dog."

I turned to Roger. "What did you do while Trisha was at the party?"

"I went to Martuni's for a few drinks with a couple of old friends," he said. "I got back about an hour before Trisha did."

My phone vibrated; I pulled it out of my bag. Todd—why was my ex-husband calling me? I slipped it back in and stood up. "Right. I have a few people I need to talk to, Zach and Jenna, and I need to hunt down Leeya's deadbeat client. I'll let you know what I find out."

Trisha and Roger rose to walk me out. "How quickly can you get a podcast out about this?" Trisha asked. "I'm sure this was some sort of random attack, and we need to reach anybody who was in the area and saw something as soon as possible."

I winced internally—I'd prepared myself for someone who *didn't* want publicity, not somebody who wanted publicity *instantly*. "I'd like to talk to both Jenna and Zach first, so I can get a clearer idea about what exactly we want to say."

She grimaced. "But we need to—"

Roger interrupted her with a gentle hand on her arm. "Honey, she's the professional." He turned to me. "What can we do to help?"

I nodded at him gratefully. "Just think back for any other issues going on in Leeya's life. Anything strange, no matter how small."

"We'll do our best," Trisha said as her eyes filled up again.

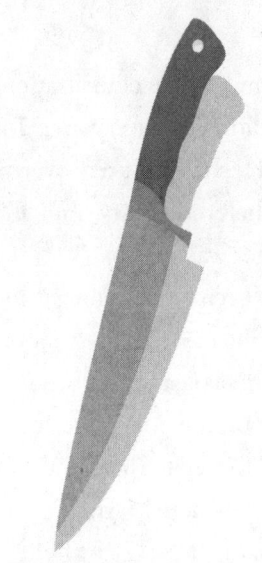

Chapter Thirteen

As soon as I got back out to my car, I put a call through to Leeya's sister Jenna. When she didn't answer I left her a message, then called Petito to update him on what I'd just learned. I figured I'd get his voicemail, too, but to my surprise he picked up on the third ring.

"Hey, you."

The hint of warm intimacy to his voice made a flush start at the small of my back and crawl up my spine. "Hey, you. I just finished talking to Reynalda Harris and Trisha Schlesinger."

His voice abruptly shifted to briskly professional. "What did you find out?"

I summarized the conversations but skipped a description of the sojourn I'd taken through Leeya's apartment, figuring what Petito didn't know couldn't hurt me. "So I'm thinking I need to find out more about Reynalda's son, and the second-floor tenant. And I'm struggling to account for the divide between what Quinn told me and what Leeya's mother told me—Trisha wasn't aware of any issue with Zach, or with Quinn. So somebody's lying, or Trisha's deluded about how close she and Leeya were."

"Who do you find more credible?"

I considered. "I suppose both could have reason to lie. And both seemed genuinely upset, although Sylvia's murder taught me how good people can be at faking emotions."

"True. And motivations can be hard to differentiate. Someone who's scared of going to jail for a crime they didn't commit can show behaviors that read like guilt. The range of normal human behavior is far wider than you think. When a loved one dies, some people fall apart instantly while others show no emotion at all."

I held my mental breath—if Petito was gonna give me a primer on how detectives read people, I was gonna soak it up like water in the Mojave Desert. "So how can you ever judge whether people are being genuine?"

"Part is experience. The more people you deal with, the more you start to recognize patterns and can detect when something's off. But mostly you have to establish a baseline."

"A baseline?"

"Yes. Watch how they behave when they're relatively comfortable. Make chitchat about coffee, the weather, sports, whatever the person of interest doesn't need to lie about, and watch how they behave. Do they bounce their leg up and down or are they still? Do they stare at the ceiling when they talk, or keep eye contact? Then, when you ask the key questions, you monitor them for any changes."

"I think I read something about how people look to the left when they're lying?"

"Complete BS. Some people look left when they're lying, some people look right. Some people keep eye contact, some people break it. The only way to know which your suspect does is by establishing your baseline."

My mind flashed back to my own time as a suspect for my mother-in-law's murder. "What did you figure out about me?"

He snorted. "You wore your thoughts right on your sleeve, for the most part. I just had to figure out if you were an innocent woman or a psychopath who did a great imitation of one."

I was so intrigued I overlooked the assault on my character. "So how *do* you tell the difference between a psychopath and a non-psychopath?"

"Find a pressure point. Something you push that makes your suspect drop their act, even if just for a split second. For you it was easy—any mention of your daughter spun you right out."

Painful, but fair. "So now the only question is how I'm going to be able to manage as an investigative journalist if I don't have a poker face."

"Oh, I never said you didn't have a poker face—I said you wore your thoughts on your sleeve *for the most part*. When you want to, you know how to shut down behind a mask. So you just need to pull that out when you're talking to people and you'll be more than fine."

I thought back to my years dealing with my father, having to hide my interest in my grandfather and whether or not he was a serial killer. I'd learned early and well that I couldn't let my father know what I was really thinking, and apparently that skill had leaked into other areas. "Huh. Interesting. Thank you."

He cleared his throat. "Why do I feel like I'm going to regret telling you that?"

I saw no reason to linger on the point. "Anyway, the summary is I have two main potential leads, the boyfriend and the deadbeat client, and two tangential possibilities in Reynalda's son and the second-floor tenant. I'm assuming the story Trisha and Roger told me matches what they told Detective Laskin? And I suppose it's too soon for you to have any information about who inherits Leeya's money?"

"We're looking into all persons of interest."

My jaw dropped. "Oh, come on. I just shared everything I've learned with you, and you're going to tell me nothing?"

"Capri, that's not how this works. We're not dishing over coffee, this is a murder investigation."

My hackles rose. "That's exactly how this works. The police work with journalists all the time exchanging information."

"Journalists we have established professional histories with. This is—different."

It *was* different, on so many levels, but his tone set off my stubborn streak and dug it down deep. "So why did I agree to keep everything off record until you say otherwise? Everyone has to start somewhere."

I could swear I heard profanity under his breath—then he sighed. "We're checking everyone's alibis, including the tenant's and the boyfriend's. He was supposedly at a hockey game with friends down in San Jose last night, and they supposedly went out drinking after. But we did reach Leeya's lawyers. She left a significant amount to a trio of charities, and set the rest up in a trust similar to the one her father set up for her, leaving her money to her mother on a very controlled schedule."

"Controlled enough that it cuts down on motive?"

"I've seen five dollars be motive for murder. But the way Leeya structured the trust, it wouldn't be a luxurious living, no. Not even if she moved out of the Bay Area."

I considered that; Trisha had expensive tastes, and every little bit helped. "Got it. Oh, and if you happen to stumble on any information about Kody Marcus, I'd love to hear about that, too, since I was kind enough to tip you off to the deadbeat-client situation."

"Kody Marcus?" Petito asked, his tone razor-sharp.

Shit, shit, shit. I'd only mentioned that Roger told me about the deadbeat client, not, for obvious reasons, that I'd found a potential identity for said client in Leeya's office. Now there was no way I could explain without coming clean. I rubbed my temple, trying to figure out how to shave off the nasty corners. "Um, right. Kody Marcus.

There was a folder on Leeya's office desk with 'Kody Marcus' and 'unpaid' in red, so I figured that might be the problem client."

The line went ominously quiet. My heart slowed to a near stop.

"A folder on Leeya's office desk," Petito finally said. "I don't suppose Reynalda Harris just happened to notice that and mentioned it during your conversation?"

The memory of his tight jaw and steely gaze roared into my mind's eye. "Um, well, no. While I was there, Reynalda decided to check Leeya's apartment, and I, um, went with her."

He took a slow, deep breath, probably while counting to ten. "And I'm sure you had nothing to do with Reynalda's choice to go in."

I cleared my throat and reminded myself I'd done nothing wrong. "We were both concerned about Leeya. It's too coincidental for her to show up dead after what happened on Friday."

His voice turned so cold it gave my soul frostbite. "So you figured you'd go right in and contaminate a crime scene."

My hackles leaped up onto their tippy-toes. "Crime scene? Liminal Studios' parking lot is the crime scene, not Leeya's apartment." But even as I objected, the true-crime portion of my brain tapped me on my shoulder, reminding me that—

"There can be more than one crime scene for a given homicide," Petito said. "Particularly when we don't know exactly how a crime was committed."

"But—" I sputtered, about to argue that the apartment hadn't been cordoned off by the police. But, that true-crime lobe reminded me, I hadn't given them a chance—I'd headed straight there. "Shit."

"Couldn't have expressed it better myself," Petito said. "Now I need you to tell me exactly where you went and what you touched while you were in there, since the CSI team is going to find your DNA and fingerprints."

"We didn't touch any—" I started automatically, wiping my now-sweating palms on my jeans, then stopped when I remembered that wasn't true.

He homed right in on it. "What did you touch?"

I squeezed my eyes shut to put myself back in the apartment. "I used a tissue to open her medicine cabinet. I did the same with the drawer of her nightstand and desk, and opened them from the bottom. The only thing I touched without a tissue was the Kody Marcus file on her desktop."

"And it never occurred to you that the tissue would remove any extant prints on the surfaces?" His voice wasn't icy any longer—it was balls-to-the-wall angry.

"What I *know* is when a CSI team goes into a crime scene the size of an apartment, they don't have the time or resources to indiscriminately fingerprint every surface in the place. They choose based on what's logically related to the crime. And since, according to both you and Robles, no crime took place there, I had no reason to think there was an issue. Even if you did backtrack to what Lorraine saw, the attack took place in the living room, not her bathroom or bedroom. You'd never have fingerprinted a damned thing in there, regardless."

"And the folder on her desk?" he snapped. "You can't possibly claim we wouldn't consider her business dealings relevant to the investigation."

"And *you* can't claim you don't know fingerprints can't be wiped off paper even if someone else touches it. The oils soak in. Me touching that folder and the contents—which I did very carefully—will have no impact on your ability to figure out if someone else touched it."

His voice tightened. "I need your assurance you won't do anything like this again."

My jaw dropped. "Would you ask another journalist not to examine a murder victim's apartment if the opportunity arose and the apartment wasn't cordoned off?"

"I'd bring another journalist up on charges for interfering in a police investigation."

Like hell he would—I'd legally done nothing wrong and he damn well knew it. "In that case, you know where to find me."

And with that, I hung up.

• • •

I stared down at the phone, pulse thumping, righteous indignation amplifying as I ran through the content of the conversation. But then doubt raised its head and peered out—had I stepped over a line? Should I have known better?

I shook my head at myself and shoved the phone into my bag—I couldn't allow my imposter syndrome and insecurity to make me second-guess myself. Everyone had been assuring me since Friday night that nothing had happened in Leeya's apartment, and since she'd been killed at her studio, there was no reason for me to think there was an issue going in. And despite that, I'd still been careful about what I'd touched. No, Petito knew as well as I did that any investigative reporter would have jumped at that apartment like a mob of starving kangaroos on a pile of whatever kangaroos eat. If I was serious about being a journalist, risking the ire of the police was something I was going to have to get used to.

But a pang of sadness I hadn't anticipated stabbed at my chest. I really liked Petito, and putting our fledgling relationship at risk didn't make my heart happy.

Still, I'd already done the repress-my-personality-for-the-sake-of-marriage thing, and I knew exactly where that road dead-ended. I wasn't interested in visiting that particular muck-infested swamp again.

Deep from inside my bag, my phone rang. I dug it out to find a picture of my ex-husband Todd: speak of the muck-infested swamp and he shall appear.

My thumb reached over to reject the call. It wasn't a good time to talk to him, considering my conversation with Petito had left a black cloud of grumpy hanging over me that would severely impact my willingness to put up with any level of crap.

On second thought—that might be the exact *right* mood for dealing with Todd.

I tapped to accept the call.

"Hey, Capri!"

His upbeat tone put me on guard. "What's up?"

"Nothing much. I was just wondering if I could take you out to dinner tonight."

My stomach plunged into the heel of my left foot. Todd and I had always prioritized maintaining a positive relationship so we could co-parent effectively, but since Morgan was now an adult, there were only two possible reasons he could want to take me to dinner—and since he knew I'd rather make out with a rabid grizzly bear than rekindle our relationship, that left only one. "Are you in trouble?"

"Wow, Capri." His tone shifted to injured. "Is that really where your mind jumps when I ask you to have dinner? Can't I just want to have a nice talk with the mother of my child?"

"No. What's wrong?"

He sighed. "It's no big deal, Capri. I just thought dinner would be nice. How about I swing by your place, or you come over to The Chateau and see all the changes we've made?"

My free hand clenched into a fist so tight my nails dug into my palm. "I don't have time for this, Todd. Cut to the chase."

His voice went back into upbeat mode, giving me distinct used-car-salesman vibes. "Sounds like this isn't a good time. Tomorrow's your day off, right? I'm free all day, I can meet whenever works for you."

I didn't even try to hide my frustrated groan. Whatever the problem was, it wasn't going to go away, and the last thing I needed was to toss and turn all night obsessing about what brand of detonation was awaiting me. "Fine, I'll meet you tonight at Salerno's at seven. Your treat."

"Great! See you then." He hung up, smart enough to run while the running was good.

I stared down at the phone again, this time resisting the urge to throw it out the window and drive over it repeatedly. After giving myself a few long seconds to imagine Todd's picture on the screen cracking and flying apart, I forced myself to get my act together. Because as good as it felt to stew in my own annoyance, it wasn't helping anything—I needed to put on my big-girl panties and point them toward something useful.

Shaking my head at how inadvertently X-rated that thought sounded, I tapped at the phone to pull up Zachary Haines's contact. There was a reason the significant other was always the primary suspect in a murder investigation—they were closer to the victim than anyone else. Whether he was the murderer or not, it was vital I talk to him.

Yet again he didn't answer.

Having hit three brick walls in a row, the stubborn-as-a-rock troll that lived under the bridge of my personality reared up and chose violence. *How dare Zach thwart your attempt to sublimate the frustration you're feeling toward Todd and Petito into next-action steps?* the troll roared at me. *Are you gonna let him get away with that?*

I shook my head in frenetic denial: I most certainly would *not* let him get away with it. I was frustrated and I had time on my hands, and those two things together meant I'd damn well track him down if I had to scour every inch of the internet on my hands and knees to do it.

With aggressive taps, I located Zach's Instagram account. His feed had the professionally curated feel of someone savvy enough to understand the implications of what they put out into the world: no beer-bong keg-stand rowdiness, just shots of lattes and laptops, gorgeous bay hikes, and events making kids' dreams come true. I clicked onto his stories, saying a little prayer that he'd put something up recently enough that I'd be able to track him down.

Apparently someone upstairs was listening—because all his story panels advertised an Anything-Your-Heart-Desires fundraising event happening at that very moment, a power-walk challenge smack-dab in the middle of Golden Gate Park. He wasn't likely to be there—Petito had mentioned they'd already tracked him down so he'd been informed of his girlfriend's death—but the other workers there would know how I could find him.

I threw my car into drive and floored it.

SF KILLER CRIME TOURS

Golden Gate Park

Golden Gate Park is not only San Francisco's biggest park, it parallels the history of the city itself. Built in 1870 when the area was nothing but windswept sand dunes, the initial emphasis was on introducing plant species that would stabilize the landscape. The park then went on to hold California's first international exhibition, provide a refugee space for victims rendered homeless by the 1906 earthquake, give birth to the Summer of Love, and somberly display a memorial to those decimated by AIDS in the 1980s and 1990s. It boasts museums, gardens, bison, windmills, a stadium, polo fields, lakes, and music festivals.

And, of course, it played a role in some of San Francisco's most brutal murders.

One of the grizzliest involved Anthony Sully, a former police officer in nearby Millbrae who quit the force after developing a cocaine habit and a fondness for "escort services" that progressed to torture and murder. Over the course of six months he killed five women and one man, beating, stabbing, and shooting them in a secluded Burlingame warehouse; in May of 1983 he stuffed three of those victims into fifty-five gallon metal drums, covered them with cement, and dumped them near a path in Golden Gate Park. He claimed he dumped the drums in such an obvious place so he could bask in the press coverage when they were discovered; unfortunately for him, police also discovered his fingerprints on the barrels, which led to his arrest and conviction.

But what may be the strangest murder to take place here occurred two years prior, on February 8, 1981, when a good Samaritan notified the police that they'd found a blood-splattered backpack in the park. Police searched the area and found a dead man in a sleeping bag along with corn cobs and a mutilated chicken—but minus his own head. His fingerprints identified him as LeRoy Carter Jr., a Vietnam vet with PTSD who'd fallen on hard times. Because of the corn and the chicken, police consulted an expert in Santeria; the expert declared Carter had been the victim of an elaborate human-sacrifice ritual, and claimed the perpetrator would need to keep the head for forty-two days, then return it to the site of the murder in order to complete the ritual. The homicide inspectors were understandably skeptical, and chose to direct their resources to other avenues of investigation.

Forty-two days after Carter's body was discovered, his head appeared in the previously well-searched greenery near the murder site.

To this day, his murder remains unsolved.

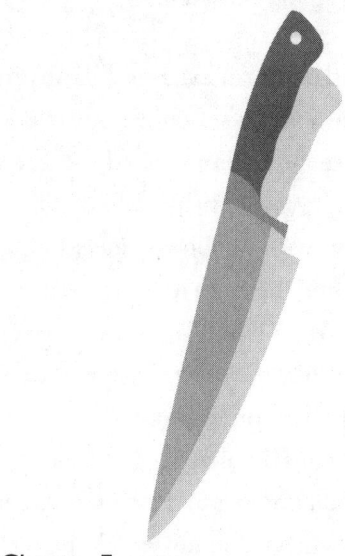

Chapter Fourteen

I gritted my teeth and raced toward the park, mentally calculating the fastest way to the event's finish location, sending up a prayer I could get there before the fast-approaching power-walk deadline. Finding a parking space in Golden Gate Park was an oddly feast-or-famine crapshoot determined by a lengthy algebra equation of events and visiting exhibits—some days parking spots stretched out in an endless buffet, while on others it could take hours to drive a few feet, let alone find a place to park. If the Anything-Your-Heart-Desires event was a huge bash, I was likely sunk.

Luck was with me, and I was able to park relatively close. As I dashed past the row of food trucks perched behind the concourse, my stomach sent up a screech of protest—I hadn't eaten anything since I'd left the house that morning—but I only had fifteen official minutes left, so I pushed the lure of soft-serve ice cream and arroz con pollo out of my mind, swearing to my stomach I'd make everything good once I had at least a lead on Zach from a colleague.

Once around the neoclassical band shell, I scanned the crowd. Most participants had already passed the finish line and were huddled around bottles of Evian and vegan protein bars, reliving the tribulations of their journeys. I didn't expect Zach to be there himself, since he'd just been told his girlfriend had been murdered, but figured someone would be able to help me find him. I sussed out a sprinkle of red shirts printed with rainbow comets topped with event-staff lanyards, then measured the faces to find whoever was closest in age to early-thirties Zach. Most looked closer to my age than his, except for a few who looked like they were in grammar school—probably high schoolers doing community service hours for their college applications. Every year high schoolers looked younger and younger, a phenomenon I'm sure had nothing to do with me getting older.

Then, what to my wondering eyes, I was stunned to spot the man himself. Wholesomely handsome with spiky black hair and deep brown eyes that perfectly matched those on his Instagram account, he was furiously stacking protein bars on one of the food tables. As I strode over to him, I reminded myself that different people grieve in different ways; for some people, working might help them through the first hours of denial and pain.

I kept my voice low and gentle. "Zach?"

His head swiveled toward me. He looked dazed, like he was thinking about something else, and the smile he put on wasn't convincing. "Hey, you made good time! Congrats!"

Good time? From what I could tell, I'd've been one of the last people to cross the finish line. Either the exclamation was the organization's version of a participation trophy or Zach was a little out of it—my annoyance with him faded in the face of his upset. "Thanks, but I'm not one of the participants."

"Oh." The plastered smile flaked off. "How can I help you?"

I'd spent the ride over coming up with creative ways to get people to give me Zach's address (e.g., pretending to be the aunt who couldn't find his address in my phone while declaring "In my day, phones only did one thing, they called people!"), but hadn't expected to come face-to-face with him. I delayed, hoping to mentally shake myself enough to dislodge a credible approach, by gesturing away from the half circle of tables. "Can we speak privately for a moment?"

He dropped the empty box under the table, then led me several feet away to the staircase that sprawled around the bandstand. "This is about Leeya, isn't it?"

Okay, one problem solved. "Yes."

He stuffed his hands into his armpits. "Are you with the police? I told the detective I'd come sign the statement when I finished here."

I searched for a way around my disadvantage—I had no idea what the police had told him, or what he did or shouldn't know. "I'm not with the police. Leeya's mother asked for my help figuring out who hurt Leeya."

"*Nobody* wanted to hurt Leeya. I told her about a million times it wasn't safe for her to go to that studio by herself in the middle of the night, but she never listened. There's nothing I can tell you that will help, and we're shorthanded today or I wouldn't still be here. So if you don't mind—" He took a step back toward the ring of tables.

I had to act quickly, or he'd be gone. "Did you come on to Quinn?" I blurted.

He snapped back toward me. "What did you say?"

"Quinn Shovani. Did you come on to her?"

"Are you seriously asking if I cheated on my girlfriend when I just found out she was *murdered*?"

The righteous indignation grated my nerves like a zester across a lemon. I'd been in his situation not that long ago, and I'd managed to understand that sensitive questions had to be asked. Was he just an egocentric ass, or was this a front he was putting up to hide something?

"Very seriously," I said. "On behalf of the woman who just found out her *daughter* was murdered."

The words hit, and his face rearranged itself into a mask of empathy—with little flashes of anger leaking out. "I'm sure she's devastated. But she has no reason to think I'd ever harm Leeya."

"I never said you did. I asked if you came on to Quinn." I crossed my arms loosely over my chest and planted my feet.

He snorted. "*She* came on to *me*. When I turned her down, she ran to Leeya to get ahead of it before I could tell her so it would look like I was the liar. Now she's trying the same thing with you."

"But it didn't work," I said.

"No, it didn't." He glanced around. "And that pissed Quinn off, big-time. So if you're looking for someone who wanted to hurt Leeya, maybe start there."

Thanks to Ryan's prediction, I was ready for this. "So why, when I asked you who might have wanted to hurt Leeya, didn't you tell me about Quinn? Why did you say nobody wanted to hurt her?"

He waved dismissively. "It didn't occur to me it could be relevant."

I gave him my best *come on now* glare. "Their friendship ended when she tried to break you and Leeya up, but you don't think that created bad blood?"

He gave a jerky shrug. "Why would you kill someone when the friendship was already over? Look, you've met Quinn, right? And you know what Leeya looked like? Why would anyone smash hamburger when they can have steak?"

The oxygen rushed out of my bloodstream, causing angry stars to burst around my peripheral vision.

He must have read my distaste on my face. "That came out wrong. I just mean, why would I risk throwing away something so amazing? And the proof of the pudding is that Leeya stopped being friends with her."

The correct expression is "the proof of the pudding is in the taste," my newly reawakened bridge troll shot back, begging for a fight. It was one of those little pet peeves I generally didn't hold against people since I knew it made me come off as a complete lunatic, but in this case, I took joy in adding it to the list of strikes against Zachary Haines.

Still, I took a deep breath to redirect myself. "Is there anything else you didn't mention because you didn't think it was relevant?"

His taut posture relaxed slightly as he rubbed his chin and searched the sky. "I mean, if you're going to that level, I guess her mom and her had mad tension a lot of the time." His eyes widened. "And she legit hated Roger."

"Her mother's boyfriend?" I watched his face carefully. "How so?"

He shrugged. "Leeya didn't approve of Roger's history."

He paused, clearly enjoying making me follow up. But if that's what it took, I had all day and all night. "His history?"

He looked me up and down with a smirk. "Wait. You're here hassling *me* and you don't even know Roger was a hustler?"

My mind screeched to a halt. "Roger was a sex worker?"

He winced. "Thanks for the visual. Hustler as in con man. Scammer." The smirk returned. "Or, I guess for your generation, *a swindling scalawag*."

Oh, every minute I spent with this little punk made me fall deeper in love. "What made her think he was a con man?"

"Leeya looked into every man her mother dated as soon as she knew their name." He wagged his head. "Found out quick he'd spent time in jail."

"And she told her mother?"

He tucked his hands back into his armpits. "Not that it did any good."

The ironic parallels to her situation with Quinn leaped out at me. "Her mother didn't believe her?"

He gave an incredulous snort. "Her mother knew already. Told Leeya that everybody makes mistakes and he'd learned from his.

Claimed Leeya's 'whole problem' was she needed to unclench and trust people more." He made air quotes around the words.

"So Leeya backed off?"

"Yes and no. She didn't buy that Roger was a reformed man, but she was over it."

"Over what?"

"Over trying to protect her mother. I told her, why are you wasting your time? If your mom wants to screw up her life, that's her right. So Leeya was civil to him, but then I'd catch her chanting some poem to herself about being smart enough to know you can't change anything."

I overlooked the bastardization since he'd captured the gist. "What about her clients, were any of them unsatisfied? Or how about professional jealousy? Someone upset by her success?"

He shook his head. "Not that she mentioned to me. She always went out of her way to help people."

"Zach?" A woman's voice called from behind me. "Is everything okay?"

I turned. A sixty-something cloud of beehived blonde-gray hair stared at me like her cat had just puked me up.

"Yep, no problem. Thanks, Pauline." Zach gave her a tight, lips-pressed-together smile.

She glared at me again. "We could use your help breaking everything down."

I can take a hint when it smashes into me like a truncheon. "I should let you get back to work." I fished out a card. "If you think of anything else that might help, please let me know. I'm so sorry for your loss."

As I started back across the concourse I felt an almost instant contrast with my thinking before, like when you step outside a movie theater to find the bright blue sky you left two hours before now gray and stormy. Everything looked shadier, and something wasn't sitting quite right. I tried to identify the underlying reason while I procured and chowed down on my self-promised soft-serve cone, hoping the combination of whole-fat cream and copious sugar would jolt my system into a revelation.

Miraculously, it worked. By the time I reached my car, the odd discomfort crystallized into a concrete question: In what scenario did a woman talk to a stepfather she didn't trust about a problematic client, but completely fail to mention said client to the boyfriend she supposedly loved?

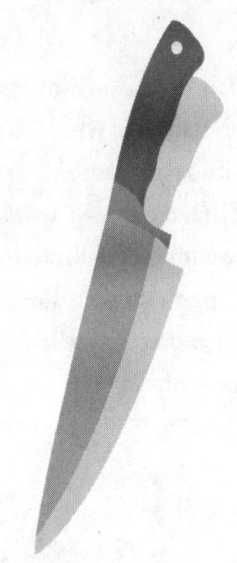

Chapter Fifteen

As I drove home, that strange contradiction—why Leeya had gone to someone she didn't trust for advice rather than her boyfriend—called up a passel of reinforcements. As I wrestled with everything I'd been told about Leeya, trying to flap my mental Polaroid of who she was into focus, my mind bounced from conversation to conversation, snagging on a myriad of details that clouded up the swirls again. I struggled to corral it all into some logical structure, jotting notes into my Moleskine at each stoplight.

I started with the contradictions surrounding Zach himself. According to Leeya's mother, Zach was a great guy; according to her best friend, Zach was a cheating scumbag. According to Zach, Quinn was the one who'd betrayed Leeya, not him. According to Leeya's mother, Quinn was one of the few people Leeya trusted—but Leeya hadn't believed her about Zach. Given Leeya's disbelief, I'd normally weight the evidence toward Quinn being the liar.

Except for two inconvenient truths I couldn't avoid. One, pretty much everything else Quinn told me had turned out to be true. She'd mentioned tension both between Leeya and her mother and between

Leeya and her sister. Trisha had claimed Leeya was close to both of them, but that simply didn't fit with how out of touch Trisha was with Leeya's life. Trisha hadn't known much about Leeya's art projects, or her break with Quinn—and Roger had to remind her about the problem-client call. That meant either Trisha was oblivious, or she was lying. What Quinn had told me about Trisha's expensive tastes and Leeya's fiscal responsibility had also turned out to be true, verified both by my own observations and Petito's information. And as anathema a thought as it was to most people, the annals of true crime were replete with parents who'd killed their own children.

What I needed was someone to break the tie—and sister Jenna was the next closest person to Leeya. I jotted down a note at the next light to make talking with her a top priority.

That brought me back to the other inconvenient truth on Quinn's side: Leeya's failure to go to Zach about her deadbeat client. There were only two reasons I could think of why she wouldn't have. The first was that there was some sort of breach in their relationship. My mind flashed back to the unused birth control pills, something that suggested she hadn't been having sex lately. If Leeya had changed her mind about believing Quinn, she might have confronted Zach, and his temper might have gotten the best of him. Or, if Zach's temper was a problem, Leeya might have been worried Zach would overreact and take the problem client into his own hands. Either way, the lapse signaled some lack of trust between Leeya and Zach—and that fit with what Quinn had told me, not with what Trisha had.

I threw a mental hand up in the air—maybe the smarter way to go about this was to start with the things everybody agreed on. But as far as I could see, there was only one thing—that Leeya's relationship with Roger had been problematic. My brain was more than happy to latch onto Roger's con-artist past like a terrier on a juicy bone—it was an awfully big thing to ignore. If my brain kept wanting to fixate on it, maybe Leeya's had, too, even if she'd been playing nice with Roger for her mother's sake. Maybe she'd kept digging and discovered something Trisha *didn't* know, and word had gotten back to Roger?

For me to judge how likely that was, I needed to know exactly what brand of malfeasance Roger had engaged in—there was a big difference between bad investments, armed robbery, and some form of aggravated assault. I grabbed my phone at the next stoplight and tapped out a text to Petito, summarizing what Zach had said and asking him to look into Roger Prentiss's background.

He sent me back a thumbs-up.

With a Herculean effort I ignored the passive-aggressive emoji, sublimating my emotions into calling Leeya's sister Jenna again while the light was still red. Again she didn't answer.

I tapped my nails on the page of my Moleskine, and my mind flipped to Lorraine. On the one hand, she'd been proven right—it was too much of a coincidence that Leeya was now dead given what she'd claimed to see, and that seemed to put her in the clear. But I could hear Petito's remonstration that a good detective—or investigator—had to be open to all options, and my brain leaped to cooperate. I had to consider that it wasn't a coincidence at all—that Lorraine was involved somehow, and had lied about seeing someone attack Leeya. But what possible motive could she have for that?

A distraction, the Agatha Christie–loving portion of my brain whispered. *Very Queen of Crime to throw in a red herring that made it look like something bad had happened before it really did, to distract from the actual murder.* Maybe this was some attempt to fool the police into thinking Leeya had been killed Friday night instead of Saturday? Maybe that's why she'd been so insistent about going to the press to make sure someone paid attention?

The more I thought about it, the less paranoid and more possible it all seemed, and I grabbed my phone again at the next stoplight. When Lorraine didn't answer, my first thought was she was dodging my call—until the more sensible part of my brain reminded me that her getaway weekend would be likely wrapping up and she was more than likely driving home.

I heaved a frustrated sigh. Lorraine wasn't answering and Jenna wasn't answering and it would be far easier for Petito to pull up Roger's past than for me. That left me with only one lead to follow while I waited: Kody Marcus, Leeya's deadbeat client. I had a couple of hours before my unwilling dinner with Todd, more than enough time to make a strong start tracking him down before I was due at Salerno's.

As I pulled up to my garage, Morgan's face popped up on my phone again—for the second time that day. I hurried to connect the call.

"Hey, Mom. I was wondering if you have any time to stop by this week? I can't move some of this furniture on my own."

That stopped me cold. I'm no slouch, but if you have a choice between asking my six-foot ex-husband and five-eight me to move furniture, I'm not the obvious choice. "That sounds like a job for your father."

"He hasn't been around much, and I need to get it done before Wednesday." The worried edge was back in her voice.

Oh, I didn't care for *that* one bit. Combined with his cryptic desire to have dinner with me, this didn't bode well.

But I didn't need to pile my own worry on top of Morgan's. "Sure, honey, I can come do that. You have classes Monday, right? So would Tuesday work?"

"Sure, that works. Thanks, Mom," she said absently, then hung up.

• • •

Once I made myself a steaming cup of caffeine and slunk into the psychological security of my office, I pulled up the pictures I'd taken of Kody Marcus's file. Right off the bat my heart soared—his phone number and address were buried inside, and I was more than willing to accept the gift from the universe. But I'd learned the hard way that going into interviews blind is not wise, so figured I'd better do some further research before calling him directly.

The notes Leeya had taken for his project indicated he was an author who was self-publishing a sci-fi novel, something that fell under the descriptor of "space opera." He'd come to her for a graphic design package that included a book cover, promotional materials, and a revamp for his website. He'd paid half of the money up front, with the rest due at the time of delivery of the finalized designs. I scanned the notes she'd jotted down about the plot of his book, but found my eyes glazing over after just a few sentences. Somebody with a five-consonant name hated somebody with a five-vowel name and wanted to blow up their planet; allies were recruited and there was some sort of sneak attack, at which point everything began to run together like a sidewalk chalk drawing in a rainstorm.

Leeya must have understood it far better than I did because she'd created a cover that made me want to pick up the book, even knowing the synopsis had sent my brain off to sleepy-land. I pulled up the sample website and again found myself engaged enough to consider giving the synopsis a second shot. She was a talented artist, that much was certain.

I returned to the file. She'd printed out hard copies of emails and text exchanges, adding notes to the margins as she went. She'd delivered everything, including the website, and sent him a form for his feedback so she could make any needed tweaks. He hadn't filled it out, but instead sent an email:

Leeya—
I've had a chance to review the materials you sent over, and they just won't work. They aren't at all like we discussed. I'm going to have to hire someone else to do the work, and since I now have such a limited time to get it done, I'm going to have to pay someone extra to get it

finished in time for my publication date. For that reason, I need the money I paid you refunded to me as soon as possible. Please credit it directly back to my card ASAP.

Leeya responded, explaining that if he didn't want to move forward he didn't have to pay the outstanding balance, but the deposit he'd made couldn't be refunded since it paid for the time she'd invested in the design process. She reminded him this was both stated in the contract he'd signed and explained during his consultation with her. A flurried exchange ensued—he objected, she re-explained, he became insistent. She sent what she clearly intended to be a final email telling him the debate was over, then went into his website to remove her design and restore the previous one.

Except that she couldn't get in any longer—he'd locked her out. So she checked the Amazon listing for his book and discovered he'd used her "completely unacceptable" cover design for his book, now uploaded for preorder.

She sent another email to him telling him that if he was going to use her designs, he'd have to pay the remainder of the money he owed her. He responded saying that since she wouldn't refund the money he'd paid to her, he had the right to use the designs. Things spiraled out of control from there, and her notes showed that about a week before her death she'd contacted a collection agency, Golden State Collections.

I did a quick search for the company's number and put through a call. When someone named Gwen picked up, I launched into a nasal voice that channeled every underpaid corporate employee I'd ever dealt with, in a panicked voice just slow enough to be understood. "Hi, my name is Mavis Crepila, and I work for Leeya Styles. I was supposed to create a whole thing in our system about the delinquent account you guys are collecting for us, but I totally forgot and I can't find where I wrote all the notes down and I'm so fired if I don't fix this. Is there any way I can get the details from you?"

The woman sounded amused. "As long as you have the account number and your identifier."

"Okay, phew." I blew out a breath and laughed. "I have that right here." I read off the numbers Leeya had jotted into the margins.

Keys clacked in the background. I far preferred that to being put on hold; I'm not sure I even believe in the existence of hell, but if it exists, an eternity of Muzak you can't turn off is certainly its soundtrack.

"Got it," she finally said. "Oh—*this* guy."

That was disturbing in exactly the right sort of way. "You remember him?"

"I sure as hell do. Guy was pissed with a capital P when he got our letter, and called up and threatened my coworker Casey. Told her that if he got bad credit because of this, he was going to kill himself and leave a note for his children that it was Casey's fault."

"Whoa," I said, not needing to fake the reaction. "That's above and beyond."

"Right? Talk about sick. Casey went directly to our boss, wanting to call the police."

"Did they do it?"

"Yeah, right. He said that if he called the police every time someone started in with threats, they'd have to assign an officer permanently to our office. But it shook Casey enough that she quit, and that put the fear of God into the higher-ups that we were all gonna go. So they finally agreed that we didn't have to give our real names when we answer the phone."

"So you're not really Gwen?" I laughed.

"Nope, and I'm not gonna tell you my real name so don't ask." She laughed back.

"Not a problem. When did all this happen? We didn't create the account all that long ago."

"It happened Wednesday, and Casey quit Thursday."

I continued to chat as she walked me through all of the steps that had been taken with respect to Kody Marcus's case, but nothing more of interest had occurred. I thanked her, hung up, then tapped my pen on my notes as I considered my next step.

If Kody Marcus was the sort of jerk who tried to weasel out of paying for work he'd commissioned and who had no qualms about threats and intimidation to get his way, was he also the sort who'd follow through on those threats? He'd threatened a stranger two days before someone's hands had been spotted around Leeya's neck—had he shown up at her apartment and attacked when she refused to drop the collections case? Had my call to the police interrupted him, and forced him to try again Saturday night when she went to her studio late at night?

I needed to have a little chat with Kody Marcus, but I only had half an hour left before I was due at dinner with Todd, and that was barely enough time to drive over to Marcus's house and back. So, with an annoyed grunt, I grabbed my coat and headed down to my car, taking far too much pleasure in grumbling curses under my breath that blamed Todd for all my life's problems.

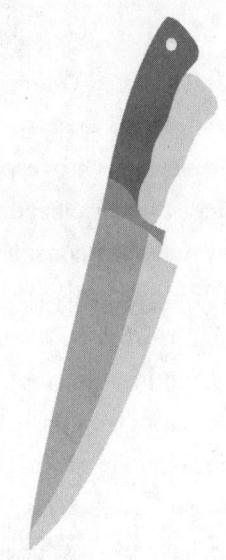

Chapter Sixteen

Salerno's is one of my happy places. From the outside, it looks like exactly the sort of hole-in-the-wall that will send you to the ER, with odds split between a raging case of food poisoning and a fierce bout of tetanus. From the inside you'd likely be convinced you'd stepped back into a 1950s-sitcom Italian-restaurant cliché. But people from the neighborhood know that behind the peeling-paint door and underneath the half-burned-out neon signs resides the best pizza on the West Coast—or the East Coast, for that matter. Heather swears up and down that the restaurant's owner, Gianna, keeps it looking that way on purpose, so tourists won't swamp the small restaurant and her pies will be saved for those she adores.

After taking my habitual moment to innervate my soul with the scents of tomatoes and basil and bubbling cheese, I scanned the room for a table and nearly choked on my own tongue: Todd was waving at me from a booth. Todd was notoriously late, so much so that when we were married I'd taken to setting all the clocks in the house fifteen minutes early and lying to him about event start times. Since I was five minutes early, Todd must have been at least ten minutes early, so

I peered back out the door to be sure four horsemen weren't bearing down on me.

He stood to hug me while bestowing his most charming smile upon me, then gave me a quick buss on the cheek. I sat across from him, scanning his face for any clue as to what brand of disaster was about to befall me.

"Thanks so much for meeting me," he said. "How has your day been so far?"

I stared him dead in the eyes. "It's been the kind of day that obliterates my ability to tolerate BS. What's going on, Todd?"

His smile teetered for a moment before crumpling, then he sagged back against the booth bench. "Look, don't get upset, okay?"

Little yellow starbursts ringed the periphery of my vision—those words triggered me in a way that made PTSD feel quaint. I'd heard them when he forgot to pick Morgan up from preschool until three hours past pickup time. I'd heard them every time he forgot to transfer funds while on his research trips, leaving me to make a week's worth of dinners out of a single Costco rotisserie chicken. And I'd heard them when I found a pair of panties that most definitely did not belong to me in his suitcase after a business trip to Monaco.

The cumulative trauma must have shown on my face because he jumped in before I had a chance to speak. "Morgan's fine. I'm fine. Everything's fine."

I gripped the Naugahyde bench and tried to take a deep breath. "Just. Tell. Me."

"Okay, so." The charming smile slid partially back onto his face. "You know I've been working on a couple of business ventures."

I nodded, but said nothing.

"I don't want to bore you with the details, but there have been complications. And sometimes you have to speculate to accumulate—"

I cut him off. "You need money."

"Not from you," he hurried to assure me, both palms up. "That's not what this is about. I know you're working hard just to pull together money for Morgan's tuition. But there's a way you can help me without giving me a penny."

For reasons that likely sprang from the deepest core of my lizard-brain instincts, those words turned my blood to ice. "How?"

"Just put my name back on the house. I'll take it from there."

The bench under me turned to marshmallow, and I clutched harder to prevent myself being sucked down into the void. Several months ago, when Todd had been in the midst of researching safaris for his luxury travel business, he'd signed our house over to me. Since I paid the mortgage single-handedly anyway and needed to be able to deal with any decisions regarding the house quickly, I hadn't looked that particular gift horse in the mouth. Now I sensed a flock of Greek soldiers were about to stream out of its nostrils, and I had to fight back my instinct to shut him down instantly. The more wizened portion of my brain knew Todd rarely gave up on an intended goal, instead manipulating and scheming until he got what he wanted. The only way to defend against this newly impending doom was to understand and defuse it.

"Tell me why," I said, playing on his hope I'd say yes.

He rolled his eyes. "Oh, it's complicated and boring."

"I myself am complicated and boring," I quipped, eyes still narrowed. "So hit me with it."

My film-quote sass missed the mark, and he reached over to give my hand a consoling pat. "You're not complicated and boring."

"I know I'm not," I grumbled. "It's a play on the line from *Beetlejuice*."

His brow pursed at me.

"Winona Ryder's character says 'I myself am strange and unusual.' It establishes why she can see the ghosts. It's my way of saying I have the needed mental capacity to process whatever situation you've gotten yourself into. So let's have it."

He shifted in his seat. "There's nothing specific. I just need flexibility to pursue opportunities as they come."

Before I could decide if that statement was more chilling as truth or deflection, Salerno's owner, Gianna, whose chic elegance fit the restaurant's kitschy decor exactly the same way an elephant fits into a gopher hole, stopped at our table. Much to her credit she only glanced between the two of us once before plastering an *I see absolutely nothing weird about the two of you back eating together after ten years* expression on her face.

"Salerno's special?" Todd asked with a smile, invoking what he knew to be my favorite meal on the planet.

"I'll have the eggplant parm," I shot back.

Gianna did a quick about-face. Todd's smile dented downward. My eyes stayed firmly affixed to him. "Are you in trouble, Todd?"

One hand flicked back through his thick brown hair. "You know that Mom left the house mortgaged to the hilt, and it's inevitable Morgan and I will have *some* situation arise."

I leaned back against the bench. He was, unfortunately, falling into my trap—I knew he was lying, and I knew this would force his hand. "Ah. So, you're saying you want to put the one house up to secure the other?"

His face lit up. "Yes."

"That's an easy answer, then," I responded. "No."

"But—"

"The best thing I can do for Morgan is make sure that she has some form of inheritance waiting for her. If The Chateau venture goes south and you two lose it, she'll still have a place to live and bring up her own kids regardless."

Blotches of red flecked up his neck, a reaction I'd last seen when he realized he couldn't talk me out of a divorce. I'm not proud that I enjoyed watching him realize he'd backed himself into a corner, but I undeniably did.

He gave me a plaintive look. "You know I'd never do anything to hurt our daughter, don't you?"

"Not willingly, no."

"Then I'm asking you to trust me."

I barely kept myself from barking out a laugh. Trust him? The man who'd cheated on me repeatedly, who always managed to be out of the country when some crisis happened with our daughter, and who, when faced with the murder of his own mother and potential incarceration of his daughter, had delayed coming to our aid and lied about where he'd been to boot?

I grabbed my jacket and slid toward the open end of the booth. "Hard pass."

The blotches grew and sprouted into anger on his face. "I don't appreciate the rudeness, Capri. Didn't we promise each other we'd always co-parent in a mutually respectful way, for Morgan's sake?"

My jaw dropped. "*I* don't appreciate *you* invoking our daughter to manipulate me. Because whatever this is actually about, it's absolutely *not* about co-parenting our *adult* daughter."

He drew himself up with righteous indignation. "Everything I do in this life is for Morgan. My financial success is her financial success."

I opened my mouth to call him on that steaming pile of bull, but snapped it back shut again. Going down that path wouldn't help. As I put on my jacket, I took time to choose my words carefully. "If you want me to consider putting your name back on the house, you need to tell me the truth about why. When you're ready, you know where to find me."

I turned, gestured my apology to Gianna as I passed, and pushed through the door without a backward glance.

• • •

Once I was around the corner and sure Todd hadn't run after me, I pulled out my phone and called Heather. My ice-queen impersonation with Todd had been a show, and I was shook—Todd had never before tried to use Morgan to manipulate me, and his willingness to stoop to this new level was frightening.

"Strange things are afoot at the Circle K," she said once I'd recounted it all to her. "But his failure to adult adequately does not constitute an emergency on your part."

"Except Morgan needs his backing to make The Chateau work. If he goes down, she goes down with him."

"You've taught her to make responsible choices."

"When she has all the information, yes. But I've been very careful to never trash Todd to her. She knows the basics of why our marriage ended, but not the details, and not the litany of times I've had to cover for him. I didn't want to be the one to tarnish his shining armor. Every daughter deserves to have a father they can look up to."

Heather made a strange sound somewhere between a cough and a laugh.

"What was that?" I asked.

She cleared her throat. "You know I love you, right?"

"Oh, geez. Funny how you always say that to me right before you're about to piss me off."

"Then I'll jump right in. By their mid-twenties, most girls have long since realized their fathers aren't perfect. You just want Morgan to have the relationship with her father *you* were never able to have with *yours*."

"Ouch." I winced. "Gun to a knife fight."

"You know I'm right."

My heart sank into my stomach. "I'm going to have to warn her, aren't I?"

"Ye-ep."

"How, exactly? Just sit her down and say, 'Hey, honey, you know how your grandmother took an unconventional approach to money and finance? Turns out, that's a Clement family trait, so you might want to watch your back and hope your own relevant genome favors the Sanzio side of the family'?"

"Give or take."

I dropped my head into one of my hands. "Can't I just do the sex talk again?"

"Might not be a bad idea to add that on, you could probably learn a lot from her. I just found out yesterday there's something called a Diva Cup the kids are using these days."

"I'm supposed to help her move furniture Tuesday. I guess I better talk to her then. This isn't a conversation we should have over the phone."

Heather's voice softened. "You want me to come with you?"

The crazy part was, I really did. "You're the best."

"Don't you ever forget it."

Now that I had a plan in place for dealing with that, I couldn't avoid turning back to the other issue looming over me—Leeya's murder. Since my evening had just opened up, I could try to contact Leeya's sister Jenna or Lorraine-the-alleged-witness again, and maybe even run over and pay a visit to Kody Marcus.

Neither Jenna nor Lorraine picked up my call. In Jenna's case I wasn't overly surprised, since she might not yet recognize my number—but the fact that Lorraine still wasn't answering set off my alarm bells. She hadn't called me back since this morning, after begging me to help her? She wanted action so fast she'd gone to the press, but now she was dodging my calls? That felt shady in a way I didn't care for at all—and exactly what I'd expect from someone who wasn't what they were claiming. Yes, I'd found her on the internet, but how did I know she'd even told me the truth about why she was in town? Maybe the whole girlfriend-getaway thing was a complete fabrication to cover up for whatever wool she was pulling over my eyes—and if so, it was time to shear that sheep to the skin.

I wracked my brain trying to remember which hotel Lorraine had mentioned staying in. It started with a *V* and was near Union Square—her group of friends had been excited about shopping. So I pulled up a Google Earth image and did a quick scan of the area, hoping the name would pop out at me—and two *V* names did: the Vincennes and the Vintage Orchard Inn.

I started with the Vincennes. "Do you have a Lorraine Kostricka staying with you?"

The perky woman who'd answered the phone tapped at some keys. "How do you spell the name?"

I spelled it for her.

"I'm sorry, we don't have anyone by that name. Could she be using another?"

Of course she could, but I had no clue what it might be, so I took my next stab. "She may have checked out earlier today. Could you look that up for me?"

"I'm sorry, madam. I can't give out that information."

Yeah, I'd pretty much figured, but it was worth a try. "I understand. Thank you."

After hanging up, I immediately put a call through to the Vintage Orchard Inn, hoping it would go differently. It didn't. So I called Petito, intending to leave a message asking him if he'd found out any more information about Lorraine—but he answered, and I found myself tongue-tied in light of our earlier spat. Denial had always been a strong tool in my arsenal, so I pretended nothing had happened and lurched right in to why I was calling.

"You're sure it was one of those two hotels?"

"She said it was near Union Square, and it started with a *V*."

"I'll look into it, but most likely she's just on her flight home."

"No flight, she lives in Roseville. That wouldn't take her more than a couple of hours to drive home, and it's been a full day."

He skipped a beat. "You're sure she was going home today?"

"She said they were just here for the weekend. Checkout time is usually before noon, and definitely before eight in the evening."

"Right." He paused again. "I'll call the hotel and I'll try to track her down in Roseville. What contact information did she give you?"

I dictated what I had. "Thank you."

"Do you have any information about her friends?" he asked.

"I don't. She came on the tour alone."

"Right. I'll get back to you as soon as I know something."

Chapter Seventeen

After I hung up with Petito, the next item of business on my list was Kody Marcus, so I pulled up his address and went to pay him a visit. I found a parking space near his subdivided Victorian relatively quickly, but the building was dark. I rang each of the bells anyway, but nobody answered; I called his phone, but he didn't pick up and I didn't hear any ringing off in the distance. So, swearing under my breath, I gave up and went home to write another couple of chapters of the Overkill Bill book. The next day, Monday, was my day off, and I promised myself I'd hunt down Marcus if it killed me.

Normally, waking up on my day off is an almost spiritual experience. I float into consciousness gently reveling in all the things I *don't* have to accomplish that day, then slink out of bed and trot down the hall for coffee. But that Monday a panoply of unresolved anxieties tap-danced across my consciousness at seven in the morning, bolting me up to check the phone I'd left on the pillow beside me in the desperate hope Lorraine or Jenna had called. They hadn't, but a text from Petito asked me to call him when I woke.

He picked right up. "Couple of things. First, I tracked down Lorraine at the Vincennes. They said she checked out, so I had Roseville PD do a welfare check. Nobody home, no car in the driveway. Neighbor said she never parks anywhere else."

"That can't be a coincidence," I said. "The person who may or may not have seen Leeya get attacked Friday night is now nowhere to be found?"

"Agreed, we have to assume this isn't a coincidence. Either Lorraine saw something somebody doesn't want her to remember, or she's involved somehow."

I nodded to myself, brain racing to construct theories that best fit the facts.

He continued. "We're trying to figure out who she was in town with so we can talk to them. I also did some digging on Roger Prentiss. Zach's right, he did a year and a half for fraud. Took people's money to finance a nonexistent start-up. I got the sense there was other shade in his past, but this was all they could pin on him. Released five years ago, and has been a model citizen since."

"Any hints on what the other shade could be?" I asked.

"No, everything else I've been able to find is positive. He volunteers with charities and donates to them. He helped a diner pull itself out of debt both by investing financially and putting in hours to help them reorganize. Now he's doing the same with a bakery called Holy Cannoli. He seems to be doing the exact opposite of what he did before, now using his own money and time to help other people out."

"You sure it's his money?"

"I triple-checked. All aboveboard. With the money he made from the diner, he even managed to pay back the restitution he owed."

For some reason, my mind didn't want to accept Roger's one-eighty. "How often do you see that sort of thing happen? Someone has a history with a type of crime, but then goes straight?"

"It's been known to happen." Someone called to him in the background. "Gotta run. I'll call you back as soon as I have more."

• • •

I paced the bathtub as I showered, so stressed about Lorraine's vaporization into the nether that I forgot whether I'd washed all my relevant parts and had to start again. But even as I soaped and rinsed everything for what might or might not have been the second time, my thoughts played dodgeball with my brain, refusing to pop out useful conclusions. In light of that failure, I doubled down on my promise to myself that I'd track down Kody Marcus and added in Leeya's sister Jenna to the agenda for good measure. After what Petito had shared with me, I also now needed to talk to Roger, but I had a little more digging I wanted to do on that front first.

Once dried and dressed, I headed back over to Marcus's house, putting in another call to Jenna on the way. When she didn't pick up *yet again*, I decided it was time to involve Trisha more directly. Every mother has a full arsenal of guilt in her back pocket, and I wasn't above asking Trisha to deploy hers.

"Jenna's working today," she said when I asked, sounding annoyed. "I told her that her boss would surely let her have a few days off, but she didn't want to ask. She's an administrative assistant to a wedding planner and doesn't want to leave her in the lurch. I'll call her again and make sure she gets back to you."

"That's very considerate of her," I said, careful to stay sympathetic. "And I appreciate your help. Also, while I have you on the phone, there's something else I want to ask you about." I summarized what Zach told me about Leeya's relationship with Roger.

"Oh, that." Her annoyance amplified, but she tried to cover it with a *girls will be girls* lilt. "That was Leeya's way. I know she wanted what was best for me, but sometimes she forgot who the mother was in our relationship. We all have elements of our past we're ashamed of, and Roger told me all about it long before Leeya brought it up. I made it clear to her that he'd been honest with me and she needed to let it go."

"He told you before she did?" I asked.

"Yes, on our second date, actually. He mentioned what he was doing with the bakery, and I asked him if they were looking for more investors. He told me right then and there about his past and explained he's very careful about his work now because of it. He's the only investor now so nobody ever has to worry. Even after our engagement he's refused to take a penny from me, and insisted we draw up a prenuptial agreement. And between the way he's built up his fortune with that bakery and my limited trust, it's far more likely I'd be the gold digger than the other way around." She sniffed.

I was pretty sure that's exactly what most con men wanted you to think—that they were doing you a favor. "I'm sure your house is worth something," I said.

"It's not my house. Leeya and Jenna's father left it to them. I just live in it."

I thanked her for the information and hung up, my mind racing to process everything she'd just told me. If the house was Leeya and Jenna's, it would now belong to Jenna rather than Trisha, giving no additional motive for Trisha or Roger to want Leeya dead. And if Trisha was telling the truth about Roger—and I couldn't see any reason why she'd lie—it seemed highly unlikely Roger was playing her.

And yet, my brain wouldn't let it go. So I fired off a text to Petito summing up the conversation.

That all fits with what we've seen, he texted back.

I glanced up in the rearview and shook my mental finger at myself—why was it so hard for me to believe Roger was a changed man? Wasn't that the goal our justice system was supposed to aspire to, rehabilitation rather than just punishment? But Morgan told me all the time how the human brain uses shortcuts to process information and make decisions—and when you're looking for a criminal and one pops out in front of you, that's a compelling shortcut. But she'd also told me more than once that past behavior was the best predictor of future behavior.

Another text came through from Petito, breaking into my thoughts. *Garcia just mentioned he saw you at Salerno's last night.*

My stomach dropped into the heel of my shoe. I should have realized that dating a homicide inspector meant he had eyes everywhere. And Garcia would have reported the man I was with, too.

Todd said he needed to talk to me, I clarified.

Relieved to hear that, his response came back. *Not that you owe me anything after one date. But I've always been a one-woman-at-a-time kind of guy.*

A warm glow rose up inside of me. *I've never been a play-the-field type myself. I tried once and it didn't go well.*

Sounds like quite a story, he prompted.

I'll tell you over a nice glass of wine sometime.

How about tomorrow night?

The warm glow turned into a smoldering fire. *What time are you free?*

Probably around seven. I'll call you when I know for sure.

A smile slid over my face as the smoldering fire spread through my limbs. I patted myself on the back for prioritizing my personal and professional growth over a romantic prospect—yes, I knew (and had preached to Morgan many times) that you couldn't make your life choices based on fear that the person you were dating wouldn't approve, but that was easier said than done. I gave myself a long minute to revel that my faith in Petito had been well placed, and that he had too much character to be put off by our professional clash.

But, as much as I wanted to sit and daydream about date two, I had things to do and people to track down. Like Kody Marcus.

• • •

This time I had to drive by Marcus's apartment multiple times because the daytime parking situation had notched up to cage-match edition—but repeatedly circumnavigating the tangle of one-way streets turned out to be a blessing in disguise. Amid a post-flirting buzz, I'd figured I'd have no problem figuring out how to trick Marcus into *not* slamming the door in my face, but as it turned out, Past Me vastly overestimated Future Me's trickster capabilities. Thankfully, on my hundredth trip through the urban labyrinth, a twist of fate lent me a helping hand—a blond, shaggy-haired man in sweats who matched the author picture plastered on Marcus's website emerged from the target Victorian and headed off down the street.

In my relieved excitement, I sailed right past him.

I didn't have experience with the logistics of following a pedestrian while driving in a car. There was no way to keep a surreptitious distance behind him, and since San Francisco streets were a whimsical fabric woven with one-way restrictions, the strategy of four-right-turns-bring-you-back-to-the-start was a delirious pipe dream. The path I'd been following while searching for parking involved no fewer than fifteen blocks for a complete loop, and Marcus would certainly be out of sight by the time I completed it again. Taking a random turn was a risk; back in the days before GPS all San Franciscans had mental maps of their relevant one-way webs and could navigate better than bats in a cave, but just like cell phones had rendered us incapable of remembering our own mother's phone numbers, GPS obviated the need to store mental mazes. Since this wasn't an area I spent much time in for my tours, I was flying blind—and not in the cool bat-sonar sort of way.

But I had to act quickly—and the only solution I could come up with was to turn right at the end of the street and immediately double park. I then stared into my rearview waiting for Marcus to appear while praying I could pull off an emergency U-turn without drawing police attention once he did.

Then, as if in alternate answer to my prayer, Marcus turned right, too—and headed toward me. Luckily, double-parked cars are to San Francisco what pigeons are to Venice, so he didn't give me a second glance. I tried to play nonchalant in my driver's seat as he continued past me, then kept on straight at the next crosswalk; I then merged back into traffic and again double-parked a block in front of him. After passing me a second time without noticing, he turned right at the end of the block—the wrong way down a one-way street.

I swore under my breath, then made a legal left onto the street and immediately double-parked yet again, this time watching as he moved away rather than toward me. If he turned down another street, the only option I'd have would be to abandon my double-parked car and follow on foot.

Then, as he reached the halfway mark down the block, he turned and opened a door. I leaned over as far as I could, trying to read the yellow awning above him: Café Papillon.

Even if he was just ordering a coffee to go, that bought me at least five minutes. It took me seven to finally find a spot, and I sprinted the two and a half blocks back to the café, chanting a prayer that he'd still be there. I slowed the last half block so I wouldn't look like the second coming of the Tasmanian Devil when I pushed through the door, then entered.

The café was decorated like a throwback to Hemingway's Paris, with pictures of flappers and young men in suits having lively conversations over wine, coffee, and cigarettes. I bellied up to the order line and nonchalantly peered around the space—sure enough, Marcus sat in a corner, earbuds sticking out of the sides of his head, scowling down at a stack of books perched near his laptop. He looked to be in his early sixties, at least a decade older than the pictures on his website; since the site had been put up literally a few weeks ago, I figured his choice of photo had been based on vanity.

While waiting for my latte, I kept him under surreptitious watch. When a table near him opened up, I sprang forward to set my bag down on it, then pleaded with my brain to come up with some stroke-of-genius strategy for approaching him. But by the time my drink was announced, I had only the teensiest inkling of a ridiculously bad idea and no choice but to go with it.

I walked over to him with a curious, semi-confused expression. "Hello . . . You wouldn't be Kody Marcus, would you?"

He looked up from his computer screen with several emotions duking it out on his face: annoyance at being interrupted, suspicion about how I knew him, and excitement that someone had recognized him. After about ten seconds, his ego won out. "Have we met before?"

"No." I switched to a semi-embarrassed look. "But I recognize you from your website."

He sat a little straighter. "You've read my books?"

I deepened the embarrassment. "No, sorry. Your website was sent to me by a graphic designer as an example of her work. I remember thinking your glasses were a perfect fit for your face. I'm an optician." I patted myself on the mental back for the great detail, and told myself mild flirting never hurt any situation.

"Oh. Well." He studied my face, probably trying to suss out exactly how I felt about Leeya as a graphic designer.

I grimaced. "I liked *your* website, but didn't care much for the designs she did for me. I told her I'd find someone else and ducked out. Cost me a bundle, though."

His face relaxed, and he leaned toward me. "Same thing happened to me. She refused to give me my deposit back, and set a collection agency on me for the rest."

I sent righteous indignation flooding my face. "How is that even possible to go after the rest? The contract says that's why it's divided up the way it is."

He raised a hand. "Preaching to the choir. Now I'm going to have a black mark on my credit because she's shit at her job."

I widened my eyes. "But—didn't you hear the news that somebody killed her?"

His face went blank. "She's dead?"

I eagle-eyed his face for any sign of BS. "Murdered outside her art studio Saturday night. The police called to find out my alibi. Thank goodness I was in Vegas for a bachelorette party. You can't swing a dead cat in Vegas without hitting a security camera."

He let out a low whistle and glanced at his phone. "I was playing poker with some friends."

As I scoured my brain for some way to get more information about "poker with some friends" without blowing my cover, my eyes landed on Marcus's stack of books. He noticed.

"Just some research I'm doing for my next book," he said. "But it's always been a little hobby of mine."

"Gold Rush artifacts? Aren't your books set in the future?"

"I'm working on a new series about aliens that visit Earth during the Gold Rush era here in San Francisco. Sort of like *Wild Wild West* meets *Dune*."

A blood vessel burst in my brain as I tried to cram those two concepts together. "Wow, that sounds innovative. What made you think of that?"

His eyes lit up. "I've always been a bit of an expert on the Gold Rush, and then I saw that movie *Nope* and thought, why wouldn't aliens come looking for precious metals, you know?"

I did not know, not even a little. But I did know what he wanted to hear. "So cool! Because if there's any place on earth where something that weird could've happened, it'd be San Francisco."

His eyes widened as he warmed to the subject. "Especially 'cause really strange things happened here back in the Gold Rush. Like Shanghaiing. Guys called crampers would hustle rubes—"

Crimps, not crampers, my tongue itched to correct.

"—and trick them into getting drinks on these floating bars, ships out cruising the bay, and then the crampers would knock them out."

Floating bars cruising the bay? my brain screeched. *Some were built on ships but they were landlocked.* If I bit my tongue any harder, blood would pour from my mouth.

"Then they'd kidnap them and ship them out and sell them into slavery in China."

A sharp pain stabbed behind my eye. The men weren't sold into slavery *in China*, they were sold into slavery right here in San Francisco and forced to help sail ships *to China*.

But his ego would likely implode if I corrected him, and that wouldn't get me what I wanted. I could only think of one way to survive the conversation with my sanity intact: I was going to have to mess with him.

"That seems like a lot of work, to kidnap someone and send them all the way to China," I said. "Why would they bother?"

His brow furrowed. "Because white men were rare in China."

Nope, I'd been very wrong—messing with him only made it sadder, and now he was veering dangerously close to racism. I had to get off this topic and back to the purpose at hand.

He must have also decided a change in topic would be smart, because he beat me to the punch. "No ring." He pointed to the hand clutching my drink. "I guess you weren't the bride-to-be at the bachelorette party."

Okay, I'd been wrong *twice*—it turned out, mild flirting *could* hurt some situations.

I rolled my eyes. "No. My boyfriend and I are saving up for a wedding, though."

But the light in his eye didn't dim. "He must not appreciate what he has if he hasn't proposed yet."

Oh, geez. This was the guy your mother warned you about, in long, awkward conversations that instructed you to always carry a five-dollar bill and a quarter in your shoe for an emergency taxi and pay phone, respectively. And while pay phones and taxis were almost entirely relics of the past, it turned out creeps never went out of style. Luckily, I'd found out most of what I'd come for, so it was time for me to be on my way.

"I'll pass that message on to him," I said, grabbing my bag. "It was great chatting with you and learning some fun new stuff." Before he could respond, I turned and hurried out of the café.

But as I dashed past the big glass window, I caught him watching me with an expression so malevolent it sent a shiver two-stepping up my spine.

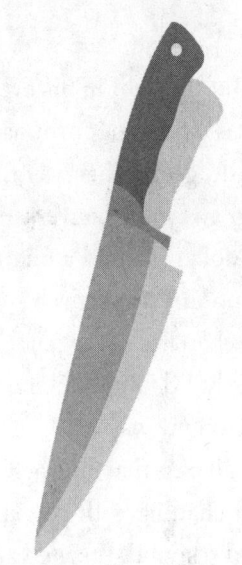

Chapter Eighteen

The ominous feeling of danger was still with me by the time I made it back home. Luckily, Kody Marcus didn't know who I was or where to find me, and I couldn't imagine he'd care enough about a random woman he met in a coffeehouse to come looking for me. But the situation opened up a new possibility—had Kody Marcus shown the same clear lack of post-#MeToo boundaries when it came to Leeya? Had he come on to her, then reacted badly when she refused him? Having a boyfriend wasn't a disqualifying preexisting condition in his book, and I'd read dozens of cases where women had been murdered because they'd rejected the wrong man, and of killing sprees underpinned by the rejection of a woman. The Golden State Killer, for example, who'd been convicted of raping and/or murdering dozens of women, was, some believe, getting back at a girlfriend who'd refused to marry him. Margaret Atwood put it best: men were afraid women would laugh at them; women were afraid men would kill them.

I gave myself a mental shake. Stepping on toes was a necessary side effect of investigating, and if I was committed to this as a serious profession, I'd just have to get used to it and keep on keeping on. I figured I might as well keep the toe-stepping streak alive by calling Roger, but when I did, I got his voicemail.

As I counted up how many people who should have been invested in finding Leeya's killer were dodging my phone calls, my mental bridge troll reared up again, demanding action. Unlike Jenna, Roger was his own boss at work; I wouldn't be putting his livelihood in danger if I tracked him down there. I plugged the name of his bakery into Google and put a call through directly.

"Holy Cannoli." A twenty-something voice answered with a mix of pep and stress, telegraphing that while she was glad for my business, she'd appreciate my alacrity.

I dove to the point. "I'm calling for Roger Prentiss."

"He's in business meetings all day. I can get him a message when he's done. That'll be twenty-nine fifty."

It took several seconds for me to figure out she was multitasking with an in-person customer and wasn't charging me to take a message. "Is there a way to reach him sooner? This is about his fiancée's daughter."

"Oh, I see." Her voice took on a more somber timbre—she'd heard the news. "I'll try, but I can't guarantee. His meetings today are off-site."

I delivered my name and number with as much positivity as I could manage, then resigned myself to sticking Roger's name into Google. I spent the next couple of hours running through a variety of accompanying search terms; when I came up empty, I went to a nationwide paid newspaper search engine to see what I could dig up there. I found a few articles about him, but the details gave me nothing Petito hadn't already shared with me.

My phone rang, pulling me back to the present.

"How's it all going?" Heather asked once I picked up.

"Not well," I grumbled.

Heather clicked her tongue. "Tell me."

I caught her up on how I'd been unable to locate Lorraine, my strange café tête-à-tête with Kody Marcus, and the other sources of my frustration. "I'm running out of avenues to pursue. And then the voices of doubt creep back into my head, telling me I'm not cut out for this investigative-podcast journalist thing."

"Psh," she said eloquently. "That's crap and you know it. You caught not one but *two* killers not too long ago. You think that happens to everyone who decides to look into a cold case? How did you manage it with them?"

"'Caught' is a strong word. But yes, I identified them." I sighed. "And that's the thing. When I was trying to figure out who killed my mother-in-law, I had decades of personal experience with who she was, so when I saw or heard something that didn't fit, it was like a clanging bell going off in my head. But with Leeya, I'm like the proverbial blind men touching an elephant for the first time. Everything everyone tells me seems to contradict someone else, and I can't stitch any of it together into a unified whole."

"But wait." Her voice was patient. "You knew next to nothing about your grandfather, right?"

"I knew a little. And I had access to my grandmother's diaries and scrapbooks."

"Okay, then." She paused, and I heard her take a long sip of whatever she was drinking. "So that's your superpower: connecting to who people are, and letting that tune you in to what does and doesn't fit. That means you just need a way to dive deeper into who Leeya was, something akin to your grandmother's diaries and scrapbooks. Build that foundation so you'll be able to spot what fits and what doesn't."

"Right, but the question is *how*. I didn't find a journal or anything in Leeya's apartment. I guess I can ask Petito if they've found anything like that, but I doubt he'll let me read it." As I navigated to tap out a text to him, I spotted my gallery icon. "I *did* take a bunch of pictures when I was there. I suppose that's as good a place to start as any while I wait."

"It's worth a shot," she said. "At the very least it'll be like a vibe check, since you probably weren't soaking in her essence while you were looking for signs of a struggle. And I'd kinda like a look at those pictures my own self, truth be told. Maybe I can help."

"I'll upload them to the Killer Crimes drive." I reached for my laptop and did the copy-paste, then waited for the little green arrows to finish circling. When they did, I clicked the first file, which started with the last picture I'd taken, and made my way through the pictures of Leeya's garage in tandem with Heather. We glanced over the sink and appliances, then shifted over to the rows and rows of junk on the metal shelves, zooming in and scouring the items.

"Wow, that's an unacceptable amount of crazy," Heather said. "It's like an antique store swallowed a swap meet and vomited it all up into a warehouse."

"True story." I sighed again. "But nothing personal to her. Just stuff she intended to use in her art." I flicked past the last of those pictures, into the ones from her apartment proper.

"Yawn," Heather said when we finished flipping through them all. "We were wrong about this being useful."

"No, I don't think we were," I said. "I'm getting that familiar tingle, like there's something I'm missing, the same one I had when I was there. I think I just need to look through again, maybe from front to back."

"You're on your own. But let me know if you figure out what it is."

"Will do."

I didn't notice anything on my second run-through, or on my third. And I almost gave up, but since I wasn't sure what other action I could take, the stubborn bridge troll insisted I go through a fourth time with a metaphorical fine-toothed comb. Then, as I enlarged each image and went over them inch by inch, I spotted it.

Every part of Leeya's home was composed with an eye to sophisticated visual balance. Every wall, every shelf, even the placement of her furniture was pleasing in a way I couldn't explain if my life depended on it, but which, when violated, clanked on the eye like a toe stubbing a staircase. On the mantel of the converted-to-electric fireplace was an empty spot that made no visual sense; I zoomed in but couldn't see it well because I'd taken the picture from a low angle. Luckily, I'd never been a believer in taking one picture when ten would do, so I had another right after, taken from higher up.

When I zoomed in on this one, I could make out a negative-space outline in the light dust surrounding the spot.

Something had been there until very recently. And that something was now missing.

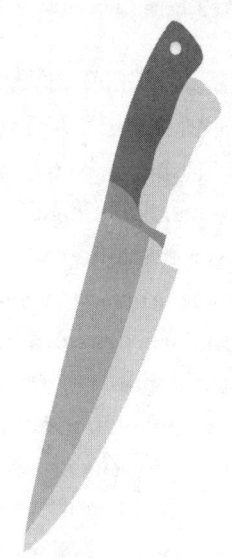

Chapter Nineteen

The missing something on Leeya's mantel sent my pulse off like a jackrabbit bolting from a puma. My gut screamed it had to be relevant, and when I clicked back through the pictures yet again to verify, I couldn't find a single other spot in her home where the decorating wasn't purposeful and balanced.

Still, a voice that sounded like Petito's whispered in the back of my head, *you can't make that leap in logic just yet. Maybe she just pulled the item down and hadn't had a chance to rearrange anything before she was killed. Maybe she'd taken it to her art studio.* And he was right—before I could draw any strong conclusion, I needed to know what the missing item was and if I could find it anywhere else.

I left messages about the missing item for Quinn and Trisha and Jenna and Zach, hoping one of them could tell me what Leeya had kept there. Then, as I tapped my nails on the screen of my phone in frantic frustration, a vague image flitted up from the doldrums of my memory—hadn't I seen a picture of Leeya in front of her fireplace up on her Instagram account? I jetted over to my app, praying my memory wasn't knee-deep in wishful thinking. Sure enough, there was one—and it had only been taken a week earlier. I zoomed in on the spot.

The object was partially blocked and out of focus, and for the life of me I couldn't identify with certainty what it was.

I scrolled furiously through her feed, hoping for another picture in front of the mantel I could use for reference. Finally, two months back, I found one. I zoomed in and this time got a clear shot of the object—but still couldn't figure out what the hell I was looking at.

I squinted and turned my head back and forth, as though my physical movements would allow me to navigate behind the two-dimensional space. Despite my best efforts, the best guess I could come up with was it was some sort of trophy: it consisted of a circular holder, like some sort of shallow bowl sitting on its side, with a miniature pickax and shovel crossed over one another in the center. At first glance there seemed to be words engraved on the miniature tools, but when I zoomed in further, the engraving turned out to be a string of numbers: 81 56 5 48 74 63 10 39 31. The background of the bowl was covered with a tribal-style pattern made up of lines and dots in varying configurations.

I took a screenshot of the zoomed-in picture, then trimmed it down. I texted it to everybody, including Petito and Heather, asking if they recognized the object. As I waited for a reply, I went through all the pictures I'd taken again, carefully scouring every inch to see if the trophy-object-thingamajig appeared elsewhere in the house. With each picture, my gut screamed louder that the missing object must be relevant to her death, and by the time I finished an eye-crossing pixel-by-pixel search of her junk shelves, I was certain she hadn't just moved it to another location.

My phone rang—Quinn was returning my text with a phone call.

"I have no idea what it is," she said after a round of greetings. "But I do remember it. Leeya found it at some swap meet or flea market and was convinced it was something special."

"And when you saw it, it was on the mantel?" I asked.

"Yep, that's why I remember it. Normally she kept that stuff in her studio or the garage, but she said something about that 'spoke to her.'"

My mind flew back to the crowded shelves in her garage. "Spoke to her? Did she say anything more specific?"

"No, and I didn't think to push the issue because abandoned objects have always fascinated her. She spent hours in junk stores picking things up and wondering who'd owned a typewriter or an old-fashioned milk urn."

I could relate—I routinely became obsessed with the history of a building or a statue or a park.

Quinn continued with a sad laugh. "Even down to abandoned paper clips on the sidewalk. She'd wonder if they held together a passport application or a set of divorce papers. That's why she put the objects in her art, to give them a second life. Extend their story."

I let the beauty of that wash over me for a minute, sending my mind back over the statues I'd seen in her house and Instagram account. Now I, too, wanted to know the history of the objects she'd used in them, and I longed for another chance to sit and stare at them. "She must have been a very special person," I said.

"She was." Her throat closed on the words.

I cleared my own. "Do you know if she ever found anything out about it?"

"I don't. That wasn't long before our falling-out."

Since she'd broached the topic, I figured I might as well run with it. "I talked to Zach. He said *you* came on to *him*."

She laughed again, this time bitterly. "Of course he did. I'm sure that's what he told Leeya, too."

I rubbed my temple and switched gears back. "Did she ever put that object anywhere besides the mantel?"

"Not that I'm aware of. Why?"

"There's just an empty gap on the mantel now, so I'm thinking maybe she moved it or used it in a project."

"No way she'd leave an empty gap if she did that." Her voice was stronger now, like she was leaning into the phone. "She'd have rearranged everything literally *as* she was moving the piece. She was a big believer that your surroundings have to be harmonious if you want to stay centered and peaceful. Can you send me the picture you took?"

I tapped through apps to send it to her, then waited until she received it.

"No, no way. She'd never leave it like that. The dust ring alone would have sent her up a wall." She paused a second before continuing. "Someone took it. And she absolutely would have noticed."

• • •

The conversation with Quinn both worried and excited me. It was one thing for my own gut instinct to tell me the missing object was important, but to have that confirmed by someone who knew Leeya well was entirely another. The question was, what did I do with that information? Not much, until I could at least figure out what the damned thing was.

As my brain whirred, my stomach sent out a deeply unflattering growl and I realized it had been hours since I ate. I forced myself to step away from my office to make some fish tacos—my mother'd always sworn up and down that fish was "brain food," and while I'd never believed her, I figured it couldn't hurt. So I chopped veg for a quick pico de gallo, swirled together a smoky cilantro mayonnaise sauce, and sautéed some tilapia to prepare myself for my arduous research journey. Apparently my mother was right, because before half the fish was gurgling happily in my belly, my neural circuitry had a flash of brilliance: I'd do an image search on the object. I abandoned the rest of my tacos and hurried to my office to trim the picture and stick it into Google.

The results I got back were confusing. There were no real matches, although that itself told me something—next to nothing was nonexistent on the interwebs, so Leeya might have been right that it was special. There were a smattering of approximations, mostly logos that showed items crossed over each other in the center: crossed keys, crossed swords, crossed rifles, even the Masons' logo with its ruler and compass. But I continued to scan, and eventually was rewarded with a single image that featured a pickax crossed with a shovel. I clicked on it.

The image belonged to an obscure blog called *Secrets of the Forty-Niners*. At first glance I suspected it was either a gossip site dedicated to our football team or an oblique reference to an obscure sex act I didn't want to know more about—thankfully I didn't have to poke out my own eyes because it turned out to be about conspiracy theories surrounding California's gold and silver rush histories. I clicked on *Start Here* and crossed my fingers I didn't just launch a torrent of malware onto my laptop.

It routed me to a disclaimer:

> The mission of Secrets of the Forty-Niners *is to investigate all possible trails leading to missing or hidden treasure caches. We are agnostic with respect to any given theory or version of a tale; we strive to represent them all. Therefore, the savvy reader must make their own determination regarding which are worth investigating.*

Whoa, pony. That was intense, but after a cousin of mine tried to convince me aliens were living in our sewer system, I'd learned firsthand how frighteningly dedicated such theorists could be. Agnosticism was fine by me.

As I skimmed the blog-post titles, I was swept away on a wave of déjà vu. Once, while channel surfing during a bout of late-night insomnia,

I'd stumbled on a marathon of *The Curse of Oak Island*. Two guys who owned an island off Nova Scotia were searching for treasure, guided by a bunch of theories about who might have left the treasure and why. This included, but was not limited to, Templars, pirates, and Meso-American cultures; I'd been sucked into watching four straight hours in the hopes they'd find something concrete, while shoving Moose Munch down my gullet. While this blog's content was restricted to a different geographic zone, the tone and speculation about stashes of rare metal took me right back to that conspiracy-theory rabbit hole.

I returned to my focus and navigated back to the post with the shovel-and-pickax drawing.

The Min-Pan: Shanghai Surprise

Multiple stories exist regarding this artifact, but they all agree on this set of basic facts: Winston Phelps was one of the few lucky forty-niners who hit a rich vein of gold and amassed a fortune. He managed to keep it private for a time, but some noticed changes to his personal habits that suggested his disposable income had increased. When Phelps realized he was being watched, he hid the bulk of his riches, then created an artifact that encoded the directions for finding his gold and sent it to his brother Raymond back in Boston; he used a code the brothers had created when they were boys so Raymond could retrieve the stash if something happened to Winston.

The purported artifact has been dubbed "The Min-Pan" by hunters because all descriptions agree it resembles a miniature mining pan. All accounts also agree that something was attached inside the pan, but differ on what. Some say it's a skull and crossbones, some a crucifix, but most claim it's a pair of mining tools.

My pulse beat out a tentative pitter-patter. I'm a pragmatic skeptic by nature, but the description was awfully close to the missing object I'd seen on Leeya's mantel. If Leeya had researched the object at all, she'd have come across this same information about it, and she likely would have shared what she found with *someone*. Of course, that didn't mean the stories about the Min-Pan were true—someone might even have created a fake object matching the descriptions to trick people who wanted to believe the tale. But there didn't need to be an actual hidden treasure behind the Min-Pan for someone to have stolen it from Leeya—there only needed to be someone who *believed* there was a treasure attached to it.

And as much as I didn't want to let my bias push me toward assumptions, a hidden treasure chase was exactly the sort of thing that would send a con man salivating.

Several months after receiving the Min-Pan, the Phelps family received notice that Winston was dead, supposedly killed by a runaway carriage. Next to no money or gold was found among his personal belongings. Had someone killed Winston to steal his fortune? Raymond decided he had to go to San Francisco and find out. After a year and a half he managed to save the fare and set off across country.

Raymond sent a letter to his parents letting them know he'd made it safely to San Francisco. But shortly after arriving, he was assaulted and kidnapped by a crimp; he woke to find himself an unwilling crewman on a boat headed for China. What happened after that is less clear, but all sources agree on one thing: by the time the boat landed in China, Raymond was dead. He'd asked another Shanghaied man to get word back to his family if something happened to him, and the Samaritan honored this promise. But the Shanghaied men claimed Raymond had only the clothes on his back—somewhere along the way, the Min-Pan disappeared.

Most sources argue the crimp took and sold all of Raymond's belongings, as was common practice. Since the location of the gold was coded, the crimp wouldn't have known what the Min-Pan was for, and likely believed it was useless. But it's also possible he figured out what he had, and possibly even how to locate the gold.

Other sources believe the Samaritan lied about Raymond's personal effects and kept them for himself. It's even possible Raymond had been ill and told the Samaritan about the Min-Pan on his deathbed so the stash wouldn't be lost forever.

No matter what happened, there have been several reported sightings of the Min-Pan over the years. The most credible is Nolan Pensacola's, whose journal sketch is included here. He claims to have been given the Min-Pan by an old, dying prospector—never identified by name—along with the story of what it was and what it hid.

I fought back a smile at the wording, reading between the lines. The story had all the classic hallmarks of a tall tale—I'd bet my favorite coffee maker Mr. Pensacola had come into possession of the Min-Pan in a less-than-ethical way.

Most speculation revolves around the code. Some say it reveals the exact location of the gold, while others claim it's a riddle that gives clues only.

A final take by naysayers argues the Min-Pan never had anything to do with Winston Phelps. They claim Jimmy Laflin, the notorious crimp who dispatched Raymond, made up the entire story so he could sell the useless object to greedy treasure hunters. They argue there never was any gold, and searching for it is a fool's errand.

I took a deep, pensive breath as I finished the article, then shifted to a series of Google searches using the new information I'd found. I scrabbled through a number of sites and forums of people describing their efforts to find the Min-Pan and speculating about where it was currently located, but couldn't find anything else of interest.

I pulled the picture of the maybe-Min-Pan back up and zeroed in on the numbers engraved into the shovel and pickax: 81 56 5 48 74 on the ax and 63 10 39 31 on the shovel. I cast my mind back to the puzzles I'd done as a child that involved deciphering codes, but couldn't remember much, just that checking which symbols showed up most frequently was a good starting point because they most likely corresponded to the most frequent letters in English: if I remembered correctly, E, A, R, I, O, T. Unfortunately, there weren't enough numbers to be able to differentiate them. If I counted them as individuals rather than pairs, the 3s and 1s were the most frequent, so I played around with substituting Es for them. But the rest of the numbers occurred with almost equal frequency, and despite trying different combinations I couldn't get far.

I tossed down my pen in frustration—what I needed was a crash course on deciphering. But, I realized—*that* was something the interwebs could certainly furnish.

As I cracked my mental knuckles and reached for my keyboard again, my phone chimed a text notification. It was Jenna, Leeya's sister, finally—and she had time to talk to me if I could come over *now*.

Chapter Twenty

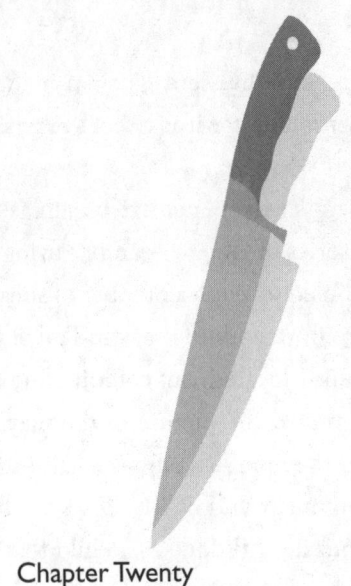

Jenna's apartment wasn't far from Leeya's; in fact, my Barbary Coast tour missed it by a single block. As Jenna silently led me up the internal stairs in her building, I took a stab at predicting her design choices based on the flowing mid-length green velvet dress she wore over her faded jeans. I landed on a confident guess of thrift-store-chic vibes, so I was confused to find most of her interior ready-ordered from IKEA. The only exception was the large framed art photographs that dotted the room; each captured a person or persons in a slightly odd, discomfiting way I couldn't quite put my finger on.

As she plopped onto the couch, I took a moment to examine her more carefully. The resemblance between Jenna and the pictures I'd seen of Leeya was also confusing; the two looked so much alike they were undoubtedly sisters, and yet every single thing about them differed. Where Leeya's brown hair had compelling glints of red highlights, Jenna's was one-dimensional and dull. Her skin was the same creamy peach as Leeya's, but with a smattering of acne that wiped out any Renaissance perfection. And while Leeya's imperfections somehow coalesced into a unique and stunning whole, Jenna's fought each other, pulling attention to all the wrong places in all the wrong order, creating a drab, unbalanced composition.

Her blank expression and puffy eyes passed over me like I was a strange afterthought, and I couldn't decide whether she was dealing with shock or was just stoned and bored. "I told my mother I'd talk with you, but there's not really any point," she said. "I don't know anything about what happened to Leeya. I already told that to the police."

I shrugged off a wave of unexpected antipathy and put on a placating smile. "It's hard to know what might be relevant at this point. For example, I just discovered Leeya had a client who didn't want to pay her for her work. Did she mention that to you?"

"To me?" Jenna slid open a drawer on the credenza next to her chair. She pulled out a cigarette, stuck it into a Holly Golightly cigarette holder, then lit it. "No. Not to me."

I couldn't decide which annoyed me more, the cigarette or the passive-aggressively cryptic answer—both felt like ridiculous affectations. I tried to remind myself that her sister had just died, but my gut wasn't having it—tragedy or no, something inside me just plain didn't like Jenna Styles.

"I ask because your mother said the two of you were close." Maybe not an exact quote, but close enough.

She coughed a smarmy laugh. "My mother is as clueless as someone can be while retaining all their primary senses. Leeya thought she was better than me and made sure I knew it."

The accusation of cluelessness fit what I'd sensed earlier, that Trisha wasn't as knowledgeable about Leeya's life as she wanted to seem. And that gave more credence to Quinn's version of Leeya, but I still felt I was on shaky ground. "Then you're the one I should be talking to. When I asked your mother who might want to hurt Leeya, she claimed everybody adored her."

Jenna took a long puff from the art-deco firestick. "Well. I suppose I both agree and disagree with her."

I took a mental deep breath to keep my temper even—because while I'd been under the impression we were trying to help each other, apparently Jenna's objective was a bout of verbal jousting. Which was fine by me—since Morgan had aged out of adolescence, the opportunities to keep my relevant skills sharp were few and far between, and Jenna's *I'm tantalizingly complicated* bullshit made me itch to slash layers until I reached a raw, bloody center. "Okay. Let's start with why you agree with her."

Jenna waved toward the ceiling. "Because she's right, *everybody* loved Leeya! From the moment she was born Leeya crapped rainbows and pissed champagne. Teachers praised her. Men were obsessed with her. People couldn't buy her art fast enough. The universe laid itself out into one long red carpet for her."

Despite an attempt to keep a bemused expression in place, Jenna's face screwed into a monstruous parody of itself as she finished her snark. *But*, my undergraduate psych-one curriculum reminded me, *jealousy is a secondary emotion*. It masked pain, and that pain was generally caused by insecurity or fear. If I wanted to get anywhere with Jenna, I needed to reach that scared little girl rather than challenge her bad behavior.

I slid on a mask of commiseration. "I have one of those siblings."

For the first time, she engaged with my presence. "A unicorn sister?"

"Brother, in my case. Bolted halfway across country and barely sends my parents a Christmas card, but he can do no wrong." My brother had in fact moved to Texas, but the rest was pure fiction. He and I got along well, so well he'd have no problem with me lying about our relationship for the greater good.

She waved me off. "Same-sex siblings are the *really* ugly situations. Especially when they're the baby of the family."

I popped my brows as I popped out more lies. "Unless your father only ever wanted boys. Even during the pandemic, when I was the one buying their food so they didn't have to wear Clorox-wipes wetsuits while my brother didn't even bother to check in? All I got was crap for getting the wrong mixed-vegetable medley at the grocery store."

Jenna waved her cigarette at me, knocking half an inch of ash onto her hardwood floor. "Oh, same. Leeya rode our mother's ass about everything, from how much money she spent to the men she dated. And still Mother worships her."

I made another mental checkmark in support of Quinn's trustworthiness. "Zach said something about Leeya not caring for Roger," I said. "But I guess that's common for even grown children to object when a parent dates someone other than the other parent."

"Oh, please, our father died when Leeya was seven. She barely remembers him, she just can't keep her nose out of Mother's business. She just loves to put on the self-righteous martyr act whenever Mother asks to borrow money."

I struggled to keep my face neutral. "Your mother borrowed money from Leeya?"

She waved me off. "I'm not saying Leeya was *wrong* that Mother isn't good with money, I'm just saying it's not her place to say so. Mother struggles with schedules, and sometimes she runs out before her next trust payment. She usually pays it back, so I don't understand why this time Leeya said no."

Huh—you'd think Trisha might have mentioned that to me. "I'm guessing your mother didn't take that well?"

She barked a bitter laugh. "Unless calling Leeya a 'controlling tightwad hard-ass' is taking it well."

"Wow," I said, now allowing a bit of the surprise to show through. "How did Leeya respond?"

"Something along the lines of, 'I love you, Mom. But you have to take responsibility for yourself.' Then she left. Mother broke down into tears the second the door closed, and it took me a good hour to get her calm again. But the very next day, she made lasagna for family dinner—Leeya's favorite—to apologize." She took a long, angry draw from the cigarette.

"Did they fight about Leeya's feelings about Roger?" I asked.

"You could say that," she said.

"What would *you* say?"

She shrugged. "Mother put her foot down. It wasn't long after the blowup about the money and I guess it was one step too far. She told Leeya Roger wasn't going anywhere, and that if Leeya didn't like it, she could show herself to the door. I'll never forget the look on Leeya's face." She widened her eyes and dropped the corners of her mouth to show me. "'Jenna,' she said to me, 'tell her she needs to see reason.' But Mother's an adult, and I told Leeya so. She doesn't need Leeya's approval on who she dates."

I detected some sort of discordant note in her voice. "Do you get along with Roger?"

"Me?" She seemed genuinely surprised I would ask. "He's fine. He loves her and makes her happy."

Something about the response struck me as odd. "What about *your* romantic relationships? Did Leeya have opinions about *them*?"

Jenna's eyes flicked away so quickly I almost missed it, then back again. "I haven't had a relationship for the last few years. And yes, she had an opinion about my single status—she claimed it 'hurt her soul' that I hadn't found a partner." She put air quotes around the words.

I winced internally—it was the first indication I'd had that Leeya could be unkind, or at the least, insensitive. That comment reminded me of when my daughter Morgan had her first panic attack and the emergency-room triage nurse told her to calm down; that was the first time I understood why they put glass partitions between them and you, because if there hadn't been one, I'd've leaped over that counter and throttled her while yelling, *Don't you think she* wants *to calm down? What part of "panic attack" do you not understand?* Whether well intended or not, Leeya's comment would have felt similarly condescending.

I switched gears, waving my hand in apology for sidetracking us. "Anyway. You said you also disagreed with your mother about everyone loving Leeya. What did you mean by that?"

"Nobody who's universally loved manages to avoid inspiring envy, do they?" She gave a little head shake to capture the irony.

"Can you think of anyone in particular?" I ignored my own irony.

She stubbed out the remaining quarter inch of her cigarette. "Not specifically."

The boredom on her face made it clear that if she knew more, she wasn't sharing. "What do you think of Zach?"

She reached for the cigarette again, then remembered it was defunct. "What do you mean?"

"Do you like him? Was he good for your sister?"

"He was nice. She seemed happy." She shrugged again. "*I* don't judge."

Uh-huh. "Quinn Shovani says he tried to hit on her."

She pulled another cigarette from the drawer. "I'm not sure I'd trust much of what Quinn Shovani said."

Considering everything Jenna was saying mapped on perfectly to what Quinn had told me, I found that surprising. "Why do you say that?"

"I always got a weird vibe from her. Like she was a little *too* friendly with Leeya, if you know what I mean."

"I'm not sure I do. You mean romantically?"

"More like she wanted to take my place. She liked to say they were as close as sisters." She shrugged, and her face went slack with boredom again.

I pulled out my phone and brought up the picture of the Min-Pan. "Do you remember seeing this at Leeya's apartment?"

She leaned in to peer at the screen. "I think so. Why?"

"What is it?"

She shot me an odd look. "What do you mean?"

"Is it a trophy or something? It must be important to her if it's on the mantel."

Her confusion cleared. "Oh, right, you never actually *knew* Leeya. She picked up strange things like that all the time. God only knows what it was. Why do you ask?"

I watched her carefully as I pulled up the picture of Leeya's mantel with the Min-Pan gone. "It's missing. This picture was taken the day she died."

"Oh, that's easy, then. She must have decided to use it in one of her sculptures." Her pursed brows relaxed and the boredom returned. "Now, if you don't mind, I promised my mother I'd come over when I was done here."

I stood and looped my bag over my shoulder, making a mental note to check with Petito about whether the Min-Pan had been in Leeya's studio. As I did, my eyes happened to land and linger on one of the framed eight-by-ten photographs dotting the room.

Jenna noticed my pause. "Do you like it?"

I considered the embracing lovers. The fact was, I didn't have strong feelings either way, but she was waiting for an answer, so I reached for the sort of analysis I'd heard a thousand times at modern-art museums. "It's an unusual glimpse at a couple's passion. There's something revealing about it, but I'm not sure what. It reminds me of a picture taken by a private investigator who's trying to catch a cheating husband."

Her smile faded. "That's an interesting take."

I'd hit the wrong note, but I wasn't sure why. "Who's the artist?"

She cleared her throat. "I am."

Realization smashed into my temple, and I glanced at the other framed photographs. The strange vibe I'd picked up from them earlier made sense now—they reflected Jenna's view of the world, how she perceived people and situations.

I hurried to spread an enthusiastic smile over my face. "Your mother didn't mention you're an artist, too! Imagine having two talented sisters in the same family."

She said nothing, and her face didn't change.

I scanned again, searching for some positive ground I could land on, and spotted a series of family photos on her mantel. The center picture was of a man in a nineties-grunge haircut holding up a vomit-colored plaid tie in front of a Christmas tree. The angle of the shot was clumsy, as though a child had taken it. "Is that your father?"

She nodded. "About a month before he died. It's one of the few memories I have of him, because I'd picked out the tie. I was so proud that he wore it on his first day back to work."

"You took the picture?"

She nodded. "Digital cameras were still really new, so they didn't have a lot of disk space. Mom didn't want me filling it up, so she deleted most of the ones I took. But Dad made her keep that one." A sadness swept over her eyes, making her look small and alone. "My life has two phases: before and after. Except the 'after' never seems to really begin."

Her emotion sank into me, connecting the dots. Jenna had been Daddy's Little Girl; if he'd lived, it wouldn't have mattered so much that her mother favored Leeya. His death had taken away her only chance at balance. "Like some sort of limbo," I said.

She continued to stare at the picture for a moment, then straightened and composed her face. "Was there anything else you wanted to know?"

I hurried to adjust. "I forgot to ask when you last saw Leeya?"

"Last week, on Monday. She wanted to crow about a gallery exhibit she'd been invited to, so she threw herself a little champagne reception and dinner."

"Did you get the sense anything was wrong that night?"

"Nothing." Her phone rang, and she turned to glance at it on the end of the credenza. "I have to take this. Can you see yourself out?"

• • •

I closed the apartment door behind me, but didn't head for the steps—whoever was on that call, Jenna didn't want me to be in the room when she took it, and that made me all the more eager to hear it. I leaned back toward the door and heard a very faint "Hello," so I stepped closer and placed my ear up against the wood.

Roger Prentiss picked that moment to call me back, blasting my phone's ringtone through the landing.

A vibrant river of profanity flowed through my head as I leaped away from the door. As I reached the stairs, her door opened, and she glared at me. I hurried down out of her sight.

With contrails of four-letter words still fogging my brain, I tapped my phone to pick up the call.

"Mr. Prentiss?"

"Please call me Roger."

"Roger. Thank you for calling me back."

"Anything I can do to help. What did you need?"

"I have a couple of questions I'd like to ask you. I'm not far, I can be at your bakery in about ten minutes—"

"I'm not at the bakery. I'm driving back from some meetings in Monterey and Carmel. Trisha's waiting for me to help her with the funeral arrangements, and the traffic is stopped." His voice took on pangs of frustration and guilt. "I knew I should have canceled the meetings. But she insisted I take them, and since the funeral isn't until Friday and the meetings are at a crucial point for the potential chain—" His voice tightened and broke off.

I jumped to console him. "Don't beat yourself up. I'm sure if she needed you, she would have asked you to stay." I tried to do some quick decision-making. He had to know I'd be asking about his past, so there really wasn't any element of surprise, and seeing his face in person wouldn't be that big a help. "Okay, let's talk now. I'm sorry to have to ask about this, but I've heard from several people that Leeya had an issue with you because of your time in prison."

"She did, and I can't say I blame her. I wouldn't want someone with my past dating *my* mother," he said. "But you also know I came clean with Trisha long before Leeya said anything."

Trisha had already talked to him, then. I reached my car and slid inside. "I don't doubt it. What I need to know is whether Leeya let it go at that point."

He inhaled a deep breath. "If I tell you something, can you keep it between us?"

I crossed my fingers behind my back before realizing he couldn't see me. "Absolutely."

"Trisha doesn't know, but I went to see Leeya after she approached Trisha. I wanted to assure her that I'd learned from my mistakes, but even more important, that I love her mother more than I've ever loved anyone in my life. I'd do anything for her."

He sounded sincere—but then, that's what con men were best at. "Did she believe you?"

"She said she was willing to give me a chance. That's why it meant so much to me when she called to ask my advice about her client."

My mind flew back to Kody Marcus. "I don't suppose she mentioned anything else about him? Like that he made a pass at her or anything?"

"If he did, she didn't mention it to me. I'd've insisted on knowing more if she had."

There was a note of paternal-esque protectiveness in his voice I again found convincing. I switched gears to my next question, tapping at my phone while I did. "I just texted you a picture. Are you able to safely take a look at it?"

"In this stop-and-go? Not a problem. Hang on."

I turned on the seat warmers in my Volt while I waited—the sun had long since set, and the winter chill was kicking my butt. I also checked my notifications and discovered Morgan had texted me while I was talking to Roger.

"Okay, got it." He snatched my attention back from my texts. "It looks like a picture of Leeya's mantel?"

"Yes. Do you have any idea what the round item is on the end, the one with the shovel and pickax crossed over one another?"

"No clue. She always had odds and ends like that hanging around to use in her art." The shrug in his voice suddenly did a U-turn. "Hey, she was killed outside of her studio. Do you think this object is connected to why she was killed? Something she was trying to do with her art?"

"There's a strong chance it's connected," I confirmed, leaving off mention that it likely had more to do with hidden treasure than art. "It's missing."

"Have you mentioned it to Trisha?" he asked.

"I did. She didn't recognize it and hasn't seen it. I'll keep asking around."

"Sounds good. I'll keep an eye out."

I thanked him and hung up, my mind tap-dancing across the conversation as I put a call through to Morgan.

"Everything okay?" I asked when she picked up.

"My friend Shawna wants to come by and look at her potential room tomorrow. Could you come help me move those pieces tonight? I'll even make you dinner."

"You don't have to bribe me." My heart sank down into my ankles—this meant I'd have to talk with her a day sooner than I'd intended about Todd, and I wasn't ready. But fate was determined to rip off this Band-Aid that much faster, and fighting it wasn't going to help. "Oh, by the way, do you mind if I bring along Heather to help? I asked her and forgot to clear it with you."

"The more muscles the merrier," she said.

"Okay, I'll be over as soon as I can."

I immediately called Heather to see if she was available.

"Free as a bird," she said. "Jennifer is having some sort of something and I really can't be bothered. Rose won't mind going alone."

Rose was Heather's partner, and Jennifer was one of Rose's childhood friends. Jennifer didn't approve of Heather's previous marriage to a man, and was a master of that passive-aggressive thing where she observed every rule of polite behavior where Heather was concerned, but at the same time telegraphed how put-upon she was by Heather's existence. Heather being Heather, her response was to purposefully push every one of Jennifer's buttons as often and as hard as she could; Rose had long ago realized that the best option was to keep them apart as much as possible.

"Great. Meet you there."

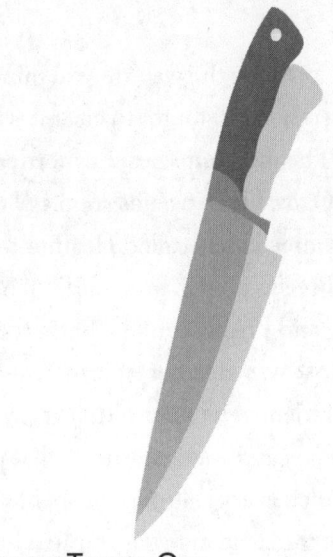

Chapter Twenty-One

Heather pulled up to The Chateau about a minute after I did, just as I'd come up the internal stairs from the garage. I spotted her through a window, carrying a tray of Philz coffees, and opened the front door as she stepped onto the portico.

"I knew there was a reason you're my second-favorite person," I said as I grabbed my mocha and sniffed at the mint mojito she'd brought for Morgan.

"Second-favorite?" Her eyes widened with fake offense. "Who's the first?"

"Me, of course." Morgan popped out of the family room as we crossed the entryway, smile reaching well into her brown eyes, long brown hair tugged back into a ponytail.

"Psh." Heather hooked her into a one-armed hug. "I demand a recount."

"Thanks for coming," she said as she hugged us both in turn.

"Not a problem." I glanced around the house. "What exactly did you need help with?"

"The desk from Grandma's office, and some of the bureaus from the spare rooms."

As we passed into my late ex-mother-in-law's office space, a wave of déjà vu washed over me—I hadn't been in the room since I'd investigated her death. The changes Morgan had made felt strange; shelves that previously held leather-tooled editions and expensive ornaments were now lined with Morgan's text and reference books and file folders. My chest contracted.

Heather set her coffee on one of the shelves and turned to pat the desk. "Where do you want this monster?"

"Over there, I think, with the window behind me. I'm going to put a futon over here along with her armchairs so I have reading space when I need to study."

My soul shrieked at the thought of a futon among Sylvia's nineteenth-century antiques. But if that's what would make Morgan happy, that's what we'd do.

Heather grabbed the corner of the desk and lifted—or tried to. "Holy hernia, Batman. What is this made of, solid iron?"

"It might be." Morgan grimaced.

"I blame myself," I said as I set my own coffee down. "If I hadn't allowed you to pick all of your bedroom furniture from Costco your whole life, you'd know how to navigate real furniture."

After several tries and at least twenty minutes' effort, the three of us together managed to move the desk—barely. The bureaus we had to extract from a different room were lighter, but still required focused effort and left us drained when we were done.

Morgan put her hands on her hips and nodded approval at the arrangement. "Thank you! And now, I promised you dinner."

"I'm craving sushi." Heather pulled out her phone. "Uber Eats can be here in half an hour. And no, don't even think about offering to pay for it. Consider it a little bibbidi-bobbidi-boo, 'cause there's no way I'm gonna let my goddaughter pay when she's working so hard to kick off a new business venture."

"Thanks, Auntie Heather. Can you get some extra in case Dad makes it home for dinner? I told him I was cooking."

Heather shot me a look that Morgan didn't miss. "What's going on?"

I pointedly avoided Heather's eyes. "I need to have a little chat with you."

Morgan put her hands on her hips and glanced at Heather.

Heather grinned and draped an arm over my shoulder. "I'm here to make sure she doesn't chicken out."

Morgan muttered something about being caught in an Abbott and Costello skit and pushed by me into the family room; I hid my surprise that she even knew that reference as Heather and I trailed behind her, furiously berating one another in silent pantomime.

Morgan plopped down into one of the off-white couches. "Let's have it."

I took a deep breath to gird myself. "I'm not quite sure how to tell you this." I paused, picking the right words.

Heather jumped in. "Your father's a deadbeat."

Morgan's head whipped toward her, then back to me. I glared at Heather, and she glared back.

"What's going on, Mom?"

"Look, honey," I said. "You know I have a lot of respect and affection for your father, and I don't believe in trashing him to you."

"But?" she asked, mouth tight.

"Your father makes bad business choices on a regular basis and leaves your mother to clean up his mess," Heather said.

I shot her another glare. This time she refused to make eye contact.

Morgan stared at me. "Is that true?"

I rubbed my forehead. "Yes."

"But how is that possible? We never struggled when I was growing up," Morgan said.

"Because your mom busted her ass to make sure you didn't know what was happening and never felt insecure. And because when your father showed back up, he'd always have some ridiculously expensive guilt gift for you, so you always thought everything was hunky-dory."

I watched Morgan mentally inventory her childhood and adolescence, ticking off iPods, bicycles, and cell phones. "How come you never told me?" she asked me.

"Because your father's not a bad man. He'll just never be a nine-to-five person."

Her eyes narrowed. "So why suddenly tell me now?"

She was a smart cookie, my daughter. "Because your financial future is now intertwined with his. And yesterday he asked me to put his name back on the Hayes Valley house so he can use it for an equity line."

Her eyes widened. "Why?"

I shook my head. "He wouldn't tell me."

Her cheeks flushed red. "He wanted you to sign over the house and he wouldn't tell you *why*?"

I opened my mouth to respond, but my thoughts logjammed in my brain. There was so much she didn't know, and I couldn't tell her most of it. After Sylvia's murder, Petito had shared with me an ominous warning about Todd's potentially unsavory connections, but he hadn't had any concrete evidence. It was one thing for me to keep an extra eye open, but it was a bridge too far to share that with Morgan unless I had solid proof.

Heather jumped in to fill my void. "You've hit on the heart of it, Morgan. Why won't he tell her why? And with your future now wrapped up in his, how could she *not* warn you?"

"But Mom should have told me before I entered into all of this." Morgan waved her hand in a circle around the room.

"I probably should have." I nodded. "But until he asked me about the Hayes Valley house, I didn't think he'd allow his business ventures to interfere with your future, since you said he was just your backup."

"That backup is crucial, Mom. What am I going to do when something goes wrong? You're the one who said it always does." She stared at me like I'd betrayed her.

Something about her expression snapped me out of mama-bear mode and into business-owner mode—I'd apparently erred during her upbringing too far on the side of sugarcoating the risks and responsibilities of running my business, and couldn't let that stand.

"If my business had failed, do you think my father would have bailed me out of it?" I asked. "Only one person was responsible for the success of SF Killer Crime Tours, and because of that I put in maximum effort every day to make sure there was food on our table and a roof over our heads. If you want your business venture to succeed, you're going to have to take the same level of responsibility. I'm here giving you information so you're able to do just that."

She drew back from me as if I'd slapped her. My eyes flitted to Heather's, expecting to see judgment and shock reflected there. Instead, she flashed me a proud smile and a thumbs-up.

Morgan saw, and bristled. "That's not true, you have a partner! Auntie Heather is there backing you up every step of the way!"

Heather shook her head with a warm laugh. "Oh, baby, don't get it twisted. Your mother gave me a job when I didn't have one. She let me in on a great thing she spent years building with her own two hands. She had *my* back, not the other way around."

My phone rang. I slid it out of my bag, but didn't connect the call. "It's Petito, probably about the murder investigation. I can call him back."

Morgan flapped a hand at the phone. "Get it, Mom. It's fine. I need to get my mind off this stuff with Dad for now anyway."

I tapped the screen, grateful that Morgan seemed to be processing it all. "Hello?"

"Capri," Petito said. "I finally heard back from the medical examiner."

His voice was tense in a way I'd never heard before, and since he'd once suspected me of murder, this escalation set off every alarm bell in my head. "What's wrong?"

"Leeya Styles was frozen."

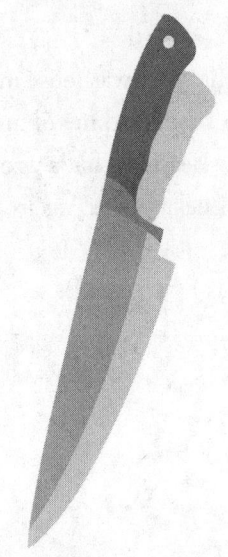

Chapter Twenty-Two

"Leeya was frozen?" I repeated as Petito's words bounced around my brain looking for a safe spot to land. Because as chilly as San Francisco could be, we rarely dipped below freezing. "She froze to death?"

Heather's and Morgan's eyes widened, and they exchanged confused glances.

"No." His voice was now both tense and annoyed. "Cause of death was strangulation. The presence of petechiae on her neck and in the conjunctiva of her eye paired with the bruises on her neck were conclusive. She was frozen *after* she was killed."

The information clicked into place and my mind charged off to the races. "The *killer* froze her? But then why did it take so long to figure that out? Couldn't the ME tell when he touched her outside the studio? Or when he took her temperature?"

"By that time, she was nearly thawed. Her core temperature wasn't far off from what we'd expect to see after a night out in the cold."

"Then why does he think she was frozen at all?"

"Cellular changes. He was suspicious because of the strange positioning and a few other discrepancies, so he did some testing. Freezing damages the cell walls."

"Like why you can't freeze a whole orange, it turns to mush," I said absently, my attention divided by the more important implications. "But if she was frozen, that means she was killed *before* early Sunday morning. Or even before Saturday night, if she had time to thaw out again. When exactly was she frozen?"

"He can't determine that."

"Then it could be Friday night." My mind flew back to Leeya's apartment, and I gasped. "The killer must have stuffed her in the freezer in her garage."

"It's possible." His tone was cautious.

"It's more than *possible*. How long does it take to freeze a body? Even a pot roast takes something like eight hours to freeze completely, and it takes at least a day to defrost a turkey. That means the very earliest someone could have killed her is sometime early Saturday morning."

"Who knew culinary skills were so useful for murder investigations?" Heather said to Morgan.

I shot her a death glare as Petito answered in my ear. "We don't know she was frozen completely. She may have only been put in the freezer for a short time."

My annoyance with Heather transferred to Petito. "Oh, come *on*. What's more likely, that she was attacked Friday, stashed in the freezer, and retrieved later, or that she was attacked Friday, escaped and mysteriously disappeared, then attacked again Saturday and stuck in the freezer for no apparent reason?"

"Capri." His tone softened a notch. "I'm not saying it's less likely. But I have a responsibility to rule nothing out without solid reason for doing so. I have to be open to the fact that she was killed later than Friday night—or earlier."

That stopped me in my tracks. "Earlier than Friday night? How is that possible when Lorraine saw her alive Friday night?"

"You're assuming Lorraine was telling the truth. But even if she was, there's a strong family resemblance between Leeya and both her mother and sister."

"They have similar features, yes, but they're easy to tell apart," I shot back.

"If you haven't met them before? And only saw the person from several hundred yards away, at night, framed in a window for what was likely less than a minute?"

My jaw snapped shut. "So we should show Lorraine pictures of both Jenna and Leeya and see who she identifies—except no, I've already had her pick Leeya out of a lineup of pictures, so she'll be biased toward Leeya's picture, regardless."

"Exactly." His singsong intonation efficiently communicated his *I told you so*. "And the fact we can't locate her also complicates her potential identification."

I winced at the implication—we only had the word of a woman who now wouldn't return my phone calls. Maybe she'd been lying about the whole thing.

He continued. "Has she contacted you, by chance?"

I clenched at my brow, trying to rub away my chagrin. "No."

"That's troubling," he understated.

Heather waved to catch my attention, then pointed at the phone and mouthed something.

What? I mouthed back.

She repeated whatever she'd mouthed, but I still couldn't make it out. I pursed my brow and shook my head.

"Tell him about that weird thing missing from Leeya's apartment," she said aloud.

"Who's there with you?" Petito's voice tightened.

My glare at Heather turned into a death ray. "I'm with Morgan and Heather at The Chateau. We're moving furniture."

"Am I on speakerphone?"

His arctic chill made me shiver; I wrapped myself in an indignant tone. "Of course not, I'd never do that without telling you. But"—I continued without stopping so he wouldn't have time to react—"I may have figured out what that mystery object missing from Leeya's apartment is." I launched into an explanation of what I'd found out.

"You think someone killed Leeya over a hidden stash of gold?" he asked, voice still professionally frozen.

My cheeks flushed. When he said it like that, it sounded ridiculous, and the expression on Morgan's face couldn't have agreed more. Luckily, Heather's eyes had widened with interest, and that propped up my courage. "Stranger things have happened, and people have killed for far less. Maybe someone recognized it and tried to steal it, and she caught them in the act. That would explain what Lorraine saw."

"I can say with certainty we didn't find anything like that at her studio—her only in-progress piece was made entirely out of old board games." One of Petito's fellow detectives called out from the background, telling him they needed to get a move on. "I've got a suspect interview on another case I need to get to, and we need to go back to the drawing board on this one given the ME's new timeline. I'll call you back later tonight, or tomorrow."

The doorbell rang as I ended the call, and Heather sprang up. "Oh, thank God—we're gonna need plenty of food to give us strength to sort through all this."

"How do you manage to make everything about food?" I said.

She sniffed. "Yeah, right, because *I'm* the one who just compared a corpse to a frozen turkey."

• • •

Heather wasn't wrong about the need for food, and in my case, caffeine. I drained two cans of the Diet Coke six-pack Morgan produced as we set the table and laid out the food, trying to sort through everything. So much had happened already over the course of the day and my thoughts had already done several U-turns and about-faces, I needed as much fuel as I could pump into my body if I was going to make any sense of it all.

"So," Heather said once everything was spread out across the dining room table. "We've got two new huge pieces of information we need to incorporate. Let's hear it all." She waved her spider roll at me.

I caught them up on what I'd found out since the last time I talked to Heather, and on the gist of my conversation with Petito.

"The Min-Pan." Heather let the words roll over her tongue as she stared down at the image I'd sent her earlier. "How likely do you think it actually is that she found the real Min-Pan, or that there's any gold attached to it?"

"Doesn't matter," I said as I balanced a fat piece of salmon nigiri. "All that matters is someone *believes* there is. And I know for sure Leeya thought it was something, so who knows how many people she told?"

"So that's another motive to add to the list," Heather said. "Who in her circle would be motivated by that hidden-treasure tale?"

"That's the same as asking who's motivated by money," Morgan said. "Everybody is, to some degree."

I nodded and grabbed my third Diet Coke. "But some people fit that bill better than others. Roger Prentiss has a history of committing illegal acts for money, so that would put him at the top of the list. And Trisha had recently asked to borrow money, and Leeya said no."

"But Lorraine saw a man attacking Leeya, right?" Heather asked.

"The policemen asked that," I said, dunking a salmon-skin roll into my soy sauce. "But I'm not sure it even matters what she said. It's looking more and more like she may not have been telling the truth."

Morgan's face puckered. "I don't understand that part. Why would she be involved?"

"Three things," Heather jumped in, taking advantage of my full mouth. "One, she has a house there's no way she can afford. Two, she went directly to the *Chronicle* when Capri didn't get her the results she wanted. And three, after forcing Capri to do the high jump, she's now dodging Capri's calls. Together, that spells hinky."

"Oh my God." I dropped the rest of my roll onto my plate, freeing up my hands to grab my phone. "Hang on a second."

They waited in intense silence as I reran the initial search I'd done on Lorraine. I clicked on the link I'd been searching for, then turned the phone so they could see: a picture of Lorraine on a class field trip, panning for gold in Jamestown.

"This didn't register with me at the time, because I hadn't noticed the missing Min-Pan yet," I said. "But Lorraine clearly knows a little something about the Gold Rush era."

"Don't all fifth-grade teachers?" Heather said. "I remember us going on one of those cheesy trips when we were about that age. I think it's required for the California state-history curriculum or something. I remember you *loved* it."

"Mom loved something about San Francisco history? Shocker," Morgan deadpanned. "But you're right, I went on one of those when I was in grammar school, too."

I ignored the implied assault on my nerd quotient and shook my head vigorously. "Yes, absolutely that's a thing. But Lorraine's goes above and beyond." I stabbed to pull up another link. "See here? She's part of a nonprofit that liaises with teachers on how to effectively teach about California's Gold Rush history. They run tours and have interactive games and books."

Heather stared at me like I'd lost my mind. "What a monster. Working for a nonprofit to educate kids."

I narrowed my eyes at her. "The point is, she's an expert on Gold Rush history. So she probably knows a lot about Gold Rush artifacts and treasure mythology?" I let my voice land on a sarcastic lilt. "And, I remember her asking me a ton of questions when she was on my tour, but she should have known a lot of the answers."

"Maybe she was testing you, or learning some new facts. I'm just saying, let's not take the train too far down the tracks." She drew an imaginary route with her chopsticks. "But sure, that could answer why she's involved in this, if she or someone she knows found out Leeya had the Min-Pan. Maybe pretending to see the attack was a way to try to gain access to the apartment or something."

"Petito said she might have died before Lorraine supposedly saw the attack," Morgan said.

I ran with her train of thought. "Maybe someone broke in to get it earlier and Leeya ended up dead in the process, and Lorraine's job was to make it look like she was still alive Friday night."

"We need to find out if she has any connection to Leeya," Heather said.

"I did a thorough search when I first vetted her and didn't find any overlap. But that doesn't mean it doesn't exist—Leeya might be a friend of a friend or some such. Petito's looking into it, but I could always try again." I pulled out my Moleskine and made a note.

"Okay," Heather said, stabbing a California roll at me. "So one possibility is Lorraine is involved. Next we need to assume she isn't. You said the police asked if she was sure she'd seen a man?"

I took another gulp of soda. "Yes. She said she inferred it because the hands seemed to come from someone taller than Leeya. But there are other possibilities. Trisha's about the same height as Leeya, but she might have been wearing heels."

"And I can totally see it." Heather dropped the sushi to act out her words. "Trisha snags the Min-Pan, assuming Leeya will never miss one of her pieces of trash. Leeya catches her in the act, and gets upset. Then Trisha's anger at Leeya for not lending her money boils over and she lashes out—and doesn't realize until it's too late that she strangled Leeya to death."

"It's possible," I said. "In fact, you could pretty much insert anybody into that scenario. And we already know Kody Marcus is motivated by money—wait."

"What?" Heather said.

"He had a stack of Gold Rush books when I talked to him in the café. He said they were research for a book, and he certainly didn't know very much about the topic. But what if the research wasn't for a book?"

"If he did his consultation at Leeya's house, he might have seen the Min-Pan on the mantel," Morgan said.

I shivered at the memory of his angry expression. "Definitely wouldn't put it past him to come back and try to steal it, or to hurt her in the process."

"Okay, so that gives us several possibilities. Who's left?" Heather asked.

"Quinn, Zach, and Jenna," I said. "Petito is checking into their financials. I didn't think they were relevant once I found out Leeya left her money in a trust for Trisha, but the Min-Pan changes things. I didn't see any immediate signs of anybody needing money, but you never know who has a gambling addiction, or just can't turn down a potential windfall. But as far as Jenna goes, if she killed her sister, it wasn't for the money."

"Oh, do tell," Heather said.

I dipped another salmon nigiri into my soy sauce. "Jenna hinted *Quinn* was obsessed with Leeya, but she herself was so jealous of her sister I expected it to burst out of her chest at any moment like the creature in *Alien*."

"But that jealousy wouldn't have just started," Morgan said. "If Jenna's the murderer, something must have caused an escalation. Did something happen recently?"

"If anything, I would have thought there was reason for the jealousy to de-escalate," I said. "The fight between Leeya and her mother over money, on top of Leeya's disapproval of Roger, was creating tension that would have given Jenna a way to ingratiate herself with her mother."

Heather shrugged. "But maybe Leeya bragged to her about finding a potential treasure map, and that straw broke the sibling's back. No coincidence the first murder was supposedly between Cain and Abel."

"But if she stole the Min-Pan to find the treasure, how would she have explained showing up with a cache of buried gold? The whole family would have known what she'd done," Morgan said.

"Just keeping Leeya from having it might have been enough." My chopsticks drooped over my plate, and I sighed. "Or, maybe the Min-Pan has nothing to do with the murder at all. Maybe Leeya just took it down to some antiques dealer to have it appraised or something."

"If that's the case, Petito will find some record of that. So let's review the other motives." Heather held up a finger. "One, Roger Prentiss, Leeya's mother's boyfriend. Leeya may have found out something else about his past, and he killed her to keep her quiet about it."

I held up two fingers. "Kody Marcus, Leeya's disgruntled client. He either didn't have money to pay her, or she threatened to sue him for still using her designs. Also, after the way he reacted when I turned down his advances, it could be that he came on to her and didn't like being told no."

Heather wagged her head. "I don't know. He sounds like the sort of douche who pisses himself when someone snaps back."

"You wouldn't think that if you'd seen his face after I rejected him." I slashed the air with my chopsticks. "That'll haunt my nightmares. Then there's Zachary Haines, Leeya's boyfriend. He supposedly came on to Quinn, and Quinn also says he had a bit of a temper. Everything else she told me turned out to be right after I talked to Jenna, so I tend to believe her."

Heather grimaced. "How would that turn into murder, though? Leeya and Zach didn't break up, so why would anybody end up dead?"

"Maybe that's what Lorraine saw," I said. "Maybe Leeya had decided Quinn was telling the truth and decided to break up with him, and he lost it."

Heather waved a finger at me. "I'm sure you can rattle off ten dudes right now who murdered a chick for breaking up with them."

"Sexist much?" Morgan said. "Women are killers, too, you know. What about Jodi Arias? She killed Travis Alexander after he broke up with her."

Heather aimed her unagi at Morgan with a raised eyebrow. "Aww . . . look who's turning into Mama's murder mini-me!"

"Or maybe Jenna's right, and Quinn was obsessed with Leeya somehow," Morgan said, pointedly pondering the array of sushi on her plate. "Maybe she didn't react well when Leeya broke off the friendship."

Heather's eyes went wide. "*Single White Female* syndrome . . ."

I rubbed my eyes with my free hand. "Which means everybody has a motive, and we're no closer to the truth."

"That's where the news Petito just gave you comes in," Heather said. "What does it tell us that the killer froze Leeya?"

I considered. "That's mainly about timing. All along we thought she couldn't have been killed Friday night, but it's definitely possible. She could have even been killed before, if Lorraine lied about what she saw."

"Does it eliminate anybody?" Morgan asked. "You'd have to be pretty strong to shove someone in a freezer, wouldn't you?"

"Jenna, Quinn, and Trisha are all average size, so I wouldn't think it would be easy for them," I said. "But for all we know, they lift weights in their spare time."

"Or had help," Morgan said.

"Okay, but why?" Heather asked. "Why put her in the freezer?"

"Two reasons I can see," I said. "One, it's done a great job of messing up the timeline—we don't even know which alibis to check. But if Lorraine really saw someone attack Leeya Friday, the killer may have been suddenly faced with a dead body and cops at the door, with no time to figure out what else to do."

"If that's what happened, they had to return later," Heather said. "Put the body into the pickup, and drive it down to Leeya's studio."

"If that's what happened, it suggests they knew Leeya pretty well. Would someone like Kody Marcus have known where her studio was?" Morgan asked.

Heather shrugged. "Easy enough to follow her if he was planning on confronting her," Heather said.

"And he could've grabbed her keys so he could let himself back in later," I added.

"And at night, with the winter cold, all the killer'd have to do is wear a hoodie and they'd be unidentifiable when they left the scene," Heather said, then suddenly gasped. "And wait. Even if Lorraine is telling the truth, if Jenna or Trisha murdered Leeya earlier, they might have staged what Lorraine saw to make it purposefully look like Leeya was still alive when she wasn't that Friday, then snuck out!"

"Hmm," I said. "That could explain why they disappeared so quickly, if the part Lorraine saw was preplanned. Tricky to hope someone would see it, though."

"All of it's tricky," Morgan said. "Maybe Leeya was killed somewhere else entirely, and put in someone else's freezer."

"We also have to consider that Leeya was killed *later*, and just wasn't frozen completely. If that's the case, Lorraine must be lying." Heather slouched in her chair. "Ugh, I feel like a hamster on a wheel."

"Welcome to my purgatory." I swiped my napkin across my face. "The more people I talk to, the more confused I get. So, the question becomes, what's our next step?"

"We should start with something concrete," Morgan said. "We could take a stab at deciphering the code on the Min-Pan. Like you said, if we knew more about the object, that might tell us who's more likely to have taken it."

Heather perked back up. "Ooo, that sounds like fun."

I pushed my chair back to pull my laptop out of my bag. "No time like the present."

• • •

We found a cryptography-for-beginners site, which confirmed my initial starting approach—counting up the frequency of each number. "Not bad for something I haven't thought about since the 1980s." I laughed.

"There are about a hundred different kinds of ciphers shown here," Heather grunted. "Atbash, Caesar shift, Scitale cipher. Where do we start?"

"We can eliminate a lot of them," Morgan answered. "Scitale involves wrapping something around a cylinder, and that's obviously not relevant here. And we're looking for something that changes numbers into letters rather than letters into letters, so we can ignore ciphers like the Atbash."

"And we can ignore anything that's more modern than 1850," I said.

The criteria cut down our problem space considerably, but didn't yield any useful results. After two hours of trying every substitution cipher we could come up with, Morgan finally pushed her stack of papers away in frustration.

"There are so few numbers, there must be some sort of key we need," she said. "Without that we have no way of knowing what we're looking at."

"If it's even a cipher at all. It may just be a string of numbers that has nothing to do with hidden treasure." I stood and stretched my lower back. "No, before we waste any more time spinning our wheels, I should talk to someone who can at least confirm the artifact is from the right time period. I'll call my experts tomorrow."

"It would also be good if we could narrow down exactly when it went missing from her mantel," Heather said. "You checked her social media, but what about pictures on her phone?"

"I'll ask Petito to double-check for me." As I tapped out the text, another idea came to me. "But we all have thousands of pictures on our cameras these days. Maybe Zach or someone in the family has a more recent shot on their camera roll."

Morgan yawned as I sent a round of texts. "How did it get to be past midnight?"

Heather popped up like she'd been cattle-prodded. "I better get moving. Rose is gonna have a conniption."

We scrambled to give hugs and get on the road, and I finished the texts at stoplights on the way home, hoping at least one of my brain flares would bear fruit.

SF KILLER CRIME TOURS

The Financial District

San Francisco's financial district is built—literally—atop what was once the Barbary Coast. That's no coincidence; money equals power, and from the day gold was found at Sutter's Mill, the merchants who capitalized on the forty-niners had the largest financial interest in San Francisco's prosperity. When disastrous fires raged through the cove's boats, the city's merchants provided the firefighters who put them out; when the coastline had to be filled in, the merchants funded the process, redesigning the coast and determining who prospered. When crime on the Barbary Coast benefitted them, they turned a blind eye—but when it threatened their status quo, they took action that blurred the lines between murderers and murderees.

In 1851, the city's leading merchants, annoyed that official court justice was time-consuming and sometimes let guilty men go free, formed a "Committee of Vigilance" to quash the criminal element. On June 10, after conducting a "trial" that found John Jenkins guilty of stealing a safe, the committee hanged the man. On July 11, James Stuart was similarly hanged without due process for a handful of illegal acts. By August, two supposed associates of Stuart, Samuel Whittaker and Robert McKenzie, also came under suspicion by the committee for a smattering of supposed malfeasance—but by this time, the official police force were forewarned, and in an attempt to make sure Whittaker and McKenzie were given proper trials, the police took them into protective custody. The vigilante committee members didn't care for being thwarted—in *response, they stormed the jail and kidnapped the suspects, then hanged them without a trial. It would take five years and another round of due-process-free executions before the Vigilance Committee ceased to be a force in San Francisco's political landscape.

In the meantime, the Committee's pursuit of vigilante justice against James Stuart had an accidental positive consequence for the legal system: it led to one of the earliest Innocence Project–type exonerations in San Francisco's history. One of the crimes Stuart was hanged for was the murder of Sheriff Charles Moore, but several months before Stuart's hanging, the police had mistakenly arrested Thomas Berdue, a Stuart doppelganger, for that crime. Not coincidentally, the day before Berdue's arrest, a dry-goods merchant named Charles Jansen had been robbed and beaten by a man whose description matched up to Stuart's, so when Berdue—who police now believed was Stuart—was taken into custody, the police asked Jansen whether Berdue was his attacker. Jansen said he was, and Berdue was sentenced to fourteen years in prison for the attack—as James Stuart. Because of the outstanding warrant for the murder of Sheriff Moore, Berdue was then turned over to Marysville, California, to stand trial for that crime as James Stuart; he continued to protest both his innocence and identity but, in a time before DNA or even fingerprinting, was unable to convince the jury he wasn't Stuart. They rapidly sentenced him to hang.

When the real James Stuart was apprehended by the Vigilance Committee, he confessed to both the murder of Sheriff Moore and the attack on Jansen. Once Stuart was hanged, Marysville released Berdue and returned him to San Francisco, where the governor pardoned him for the Jansen assault, and* *the Vigilance Committee took up a collection to help Berdue start a new life.*

Not surprisingly, Berdue decided he'd spent quite enough time in the Golden State. He took the GoFundMe money, jumped on a boat to Australia, and never returned.

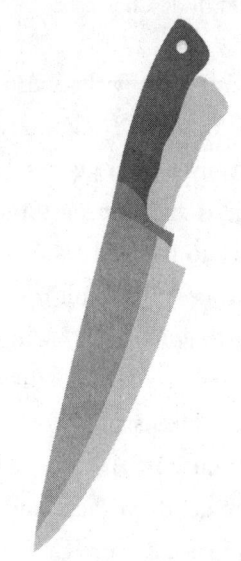

Chapter Twenty-Three

When I woke the next morning, the barrage of texts I'd sent before crashing into bed the night before had borne two juicy pieces of fruit. First, Trisha texted back saying she'd "never been the picture-taking type," but that Jenna most certainly was, and had taken "scads" of pictures at the "adorable little champagne soirée" Leeya had thrown to celebrate a successful gallery exhibit. I was excited to hear that Jenna's love of photography didn't just extend to her art, and completely unsurprised to see Jenna hadn't responded to my request for pictures.

"If I didn't know better," I said aloud to myself, "I'd be taking this personally."

Of course, taking things personally never got anybody anything other than high blood pressure—but I'd already watched a little informal social control from her mother work wonders on Jenna's cooperation. So I created a group text that included both Trisha and Jenna, recapped what Trisha had told me about Jenna's picture taking at Leeya's house, and let the pressure of having to explain any inaction to her mother kick on in.

In the meantime, I turned to the second text I'd received and set up a meeting with Arthur Lawler, a San Francisco history expert friend of mine. I might know more than the average San Franciscan about my city in general and true crime specifically, but there are a hundred and one subtopics I need to familiarize myself with to give quality tours, and I'm obsessive about getting the answers right. In the process I've built up an extensive web of cool people who know everything worth knowing about the City by the Bay, including Art, a trained archaeologist who specializes in San Francisco's maritime history. He usually works out of the Maritime Museum, and I love any excuse to visit him there—the building itself, purposely shaped like an art-deco yacht and containing a slew of restored Depression-era murals, is worth a visit all on its own. But Arthur couldn't meet at the museum because he was out archaeologist-ing at an excavation site in the Financial District. Normally an outsider wouldn't be welcome on an active site, but he'd been so excited about the picture of the Min-Pan I texted him that he'd extended me a rare and precious opportunity to visit him there.

A text from Petito came through as I made my way out to the meeting: *Looking forward to that glass of wine tonight.*

Me, too, I texted back, then caught a glimpse in the rearview of the goofy smile creeping over my face. I quickly wiped it off and refocused on the matter at hand.

The site extended around and under a stretch of several office buildings situated over what used to be the waters of Yerba Buena Cove. Arthur's directions took me to a courtyard between two of them, closed off by a huge canvas-covered fence plastered with a generic-sounding construction company name on every ten-by-ten panel. I found one with gatelike attachments and pushed at it; it swung partly open into a security checkpoint where a bored-looking man gave me an indiscreet up-and-down.

"Help you?" he grumbled.

"Capri!" Art's voice called from across the space behind the guard, and I spotted him a second later crossing over to me. He finished jotting something on a clipboard as he walked, then wrapped me in a huge hug once he reached me. "Thanks for coming out here."

"Are you kidding? I'm stoked about the chance to see an actual excavation site." But as I glanced around, I didn't try to hide my confusion. Art had told me they were excavating two of San Francisco's buried ships, ships that had become part of the city's landfill after the Gold Rush, but this site looked nothing like the pictures I'd seen of previous such attempts. On those other sites, large rectangular lots of land had been dug away, leaving the large wooden timber of the ship's hull peeking out like a brown skeleton from the mud. But this area was mostly still landscaped and untouched, except for the small, backmost area where two holes slightly larger than traditional manhole covers were cordoned off. Elsewhere the site was dotted with only mechanical equipment, temporary storage sheds, and worktables. "It's nothing like what I expected."

"Two reasons for that. One is, officially we're on a temporary hiatus. We did some initial work to get the lay of the land, to make sure at least one ship was truly accessible, but had to stop for approval. Right now we're doing prep work to start again next week. And the second is, we've never excavated ships using this method before." His eyes twinkled as he pointed to the two holes. "Previous ships have been found when buildings were being torn down, so the excavators had easy access. And those excavators weren't archaeologists in most cases, so they went about it very differently than we'd do it. For this site, and a sister site we have about a mile away for the whaler *Mariah*, the buildings aren't being torn down, they just need improvements to their seismic retrofitting. Based on our research, we believe there are at least two ships at this location, the *Nantucket* and the *Sarah*

Anne, and possibly one more, *Renegade*. We've been given approval to piggyback onto the retrofitting to excavate them, but since we can't compromise the structural integrity of the buildings, we have to excavate via shafts down to the ships."

"Oh, wow." I leaned forward for a closer look at the nearest hole. "You're tunneling in?"

"In essence. We're putting in support structures as we go."

"Like a series of mining tunnels?"

"Similar, in principle." He leaned closer to me. "This isn't public knowledge, so please keep it quiet. Our hope is to keep the ships in place and turn the area into an underground museum where people can see them where they lay. But about a hundred things have to go right before we can make that happen."

My imagination took off running. "So cool! I visited a museum like that in Paris, underneath Notre Dame. They called it an archaeological crypt, I think, and you could see all sorts of stuff. Ancient wharfs and city walls and even the remnants of Roman baths."

"Yes!" His smile burst across his face. "That's the model we presented to the committee. This wouldn't be nearly as extensive as that, but it would have tremendous significance for understanding San Francisco's past and the growth of the city."

His enthusiasm was infectious, painting pictures in my mind of exhibits going back through the Gold Rush to Alta Mexican establishments, then to Ohlone settlements. "What an incredible educational tool. Hopefully the city sees the potential."

"The city's in favor of the project, but we have to convince them it's physically possible and financially feasible. You know how complicated landfill and earthquake safety codes are."

I did. While the sand and detritus used to extend San Francisco's original waterfront was an excellent way to create more land for a rapidly growing city, it was a disaster for structural integrity: when earthquakes hit, landfill shifts, shaking down everything built on top of it. We learned this the hard way in 1906 and again in 1989, so seismic safety was an ongoing top priority for the city.

"And that must make it even harder to excavate," I said as the pieces came together. "You're not excavating solid ground under the buildings."

"Exactly right, and it's far more complicated than you'd think." He sprang toward the shaft, gesturing me to follow. "For example, did you know that the bay tide still rises and falls daily *within* the landfill itself?"

"I heard something about that once, but I've never understood how it's possible." The six-foot-wide hole looked impossibly small and fragile, with cables of some sort threading down a riblike support structure that delineated the space.

Arthur pointed to a yellow door about a third of the way down the shaft, then to its twin at the bottom. "Those are safety doors we've put in to structurally prop up the site entrances. We access two levels through this shaft, and the third, halfway between these two, via the other shaft."

"With only that ladder?" I pointed skeptically to the portable fire-escape ladder made of ropes with rods strung at intervals.

"That's actually the safest option given what we're doing. We can roll and unroll it as needed, and it's resistant to the bay waters and other environmental factors."

"Like the tides you mentioned?" I prompted.

His head bobbed furiously. "Because landfill is made up of debris and sand, it's porous. Water seeps into it as the tides rise, and back out when it ebbs. So when you dig shafts like these, the now-empty space fills with water as the tide rises. We have to pump it back out using a sump pump when we need to work."

"So when you let it fill back up, doesn't that flood the dig?"

"That's part of why we have those doors that look like prison cells set into the sides, to prevent that."

I nodded. "I can see how the cost skyrockets even before you get inside."

"Just so." His face dropped as something occurred to him. "But I'm going on and on about all this when you're here to talk to me about the artifact you found. Or, rather, didn't find."

"Oh, believe me, I could listen to you all day." But I switched gears and caught him up on what I'd read online about the Min-Pan. "I know only having a picture makes it hard to vet the object conclusively, but I figured you'd be able to spot any obvious red flags that it can't be from the Gold Rush era. I also figured if anybody had heard of the Min-Pan or anything related to it, it would be you. And if there is someone out there who stole the object and is trying to figure out where it leads, they'd have to seek out expert help, too, so you or one of your colleagues might have heard rumblings."

His eyes widened. "You're thinking that whoever stole this murdered the woman?"

I wagged my head. "It may not be related. But it's the only solid lead I have."

He recentered the glasses onto his nose and stared down at the picture I'd sent him. "I'm not seeing anything that rules it out as potentially from the time period; everything I can glean from this fits. And I've heard of this artifact before, but not for quite some time. I'll do some research into it, see what I can find out. And I'll put out a few feelers, see if anyone I know has been asked about it or approached via the black market."

"I'd appreciate that," I said. "How long will that take?"

He shifted his glasses again. "Such matters don't stay secret for long. The community's small."

I held his eyes. "Please be careful. If someone killed to keep this quiet and you ask the wrong person about it, you might be next."

He shot me a glare. "Oh, don't worry, I know how to be discreet. Dodging knives is a crucial skill for academic success."

I laughed, assuming he was being sarcastic. "Right. Academia—the center of murder and mayhem."

His brows popped and the corners of his mouth drooped. "You've clearly never tried to get tenure."

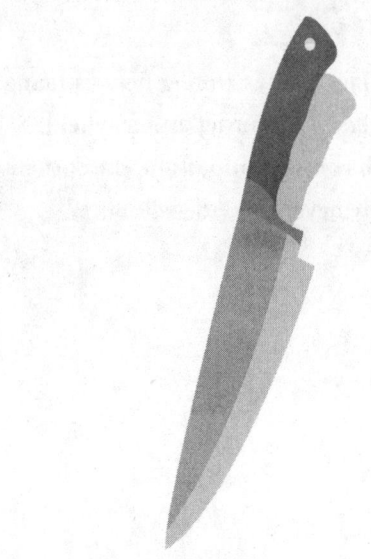

Chapter Twenty-Four

After another blissful hour at the excavation site learning inside secrets about archaeology, the ships buried under San Francisco, and the ugly side of the art antiquities market, I checked to see if my passive-aggressive guilt-o-gram had delivered its full punch to Jenna. Miracle of miracles, she'd texted me back, and when I called her from my car, she picked up.

But she wasn't happy about it. "How on earth could my pictures from Leeya's dinner party the other night be relevant to all this?"

I narrowed my eyes at the phone, trying to divine whether photographers were always so proprietary about their run-of-the-mill photos. "It's about that missing artifact I noticed. I'm trying to get a better sense of exactly when it disappeared, and your mother thinks those were the most recent pictures taken in Leeya's apartment."

"Oh, I see." Her tone shifted begrudgingly. "That shouldn't be a problem. I think I took about a hundred shots that night, maybe a few more. I'll send you all the ones I took from her living room."

"I'd appreciate seeing all of them, in case she moved the item to another spot in the apartment," I said.

She gave an annoyed tongue click. "That's too many to email easily. I have them in a Dropbox folder if that works for you?"

"That would be perfect. Thanks." I gave her my email address.

By the time I made it home and up into my office, the link was waiting in my inbox, and I hurried to get a look at the event. Given Trisha's penchant for drama, my imagination had downgraded the "soirée" Trisha described to a small gathering for drinks and dinner, but apparently even an overdramatic watch is right twice a day: everyone wore gowns and suits, while a waiter dressed in black passed flutes of champagne and canapés. Leeya's comfortable-but-artsy dining room had been decked out with fine china, silver, and crystal. Whatever gallery exhibit she'd been graced with must have been something special.

I made my way through the pictures slowly, both because I was scouring every inch for the Min-Pan and because the pictures themselves gave me the same sour note I'd detected in the photographs hanging in Jenna's apartment. Seeing Leeya's world through Jenna's perspective, I realized, gave everything an uncomfortable intimacy. Pictures of Trisha and Zach, each face burnished with pride as they beamed up at Leeya, were taken from just too tight an angle, demonstrating a shade too much focus on their reactions rather than Leeya's speech. Several captured Trisha and Roger's relationship; too close a shot of Roger's hand on the middle of Trisha's back, or of his hand stroking hers at dinner. And the pictures of Zach—his profile, his smile, close up, far back from tip to toe—all made me feel like I was looking at a Ken doll still wrapped in his package.

I shook my head to rid it of the flight of fancy and returned to checking for the Min-Pan. As Jenna's pictures walked me through the meal's courses I couldn't help but feel her distaste for Trisha's *ooh aah* expression at the caviar buffet, her amusement at Zach's intensity over his steak au poivre, and her dismissive scorn at Roger's pride in providing a stunning opera cake.

After the cake was sliced and coffee served back in the living room, I spotted the Min-Pan, in a picture of Trisha talking animatedly to Zach. It sat clearly on the mantel behind them.

With Roger bent over it, staring at it intensely.

My chest tightened as I zoomed in. Both the Min-Pan and Roger's face were out of focus since they weren't the intended target, but both were unmistakable. And Roger's gaze was undeniably pointed at the Min-Pan.

I thought back to my conversation with Roger, trying to recall his exact words. When I'd asked him if he knew what the object was, he said he didn't know, but hadn't denied having seen it before. Still, he also hadn't volunteered how interested he'd been in it, either, and that struck me as disingenuous. If I were helping the love of my life figure out who had murdered her daughter, I'd have tried to give whatever information about the object I could remember.

But, I told myself, maybe he'd only glanced at it for a second—maybe the picture just happened to catch the one moment when his eyes landed on it. I clicked to the next photo. Despite being taken from a slightly different angle, it also showed Roger staring at the Min-Pan.

That doesn't mean he stole it, the uber-cautious portion of my brain reminded me in a voice that sounded like Petito's.

But it sure as hell doesn't mean he didn't, the rest clapped back, sounding suspiciously like Heather.

I again shook off my thoughts and returned to the pictures. The next few shots captured everyone playing charades, while still dressed in their formal attire. After that, a visual chorus of hugs showed everyone departing one by one. The Min-Pan didn't appear again.

I went back through the last pictures once more, trying to read between the lines of the remaining pictures. But I had no idea how much time elapsed between each of them, so I couldn't tell if, under the guise of going to the restroom or the cover of someone else's departure, it was possible for him to snatch up the Min-Pan somehow. It wouldn't have proven anything, but it would have been nice to know if it had been possible or if I could rule it out.

Metadata, Ryan's voice in my brain whispered to me. Digital pictures contained metadata that could tell me when each picture had been taken. If I was remembering Ryan's lesson correctly, the simplest way to access it was to right-click on the picture itself. So I downloaded all the pictures to a folder on my hard drive, pulled over my Moleskine so I could note each time stamp, and hovered over to start clicking.

Almost instantly I realized several pictures were missing.

The file names were consecutive numbers: first DSC005698, then DSC005699, etc. But several numbers were missing—where had they disappeared to?

I grabbed my phone and tapped Jenna's contact.

"Hello?" She sounded even more annoyed.

I told her what I'd noticed.

"I probably deleted them." Her tone verbally shrugged. "I always get rid of blurry photos during my initial run-through of a set. Why?"

My hope deflated—until I remembered seeing several pictures that were blurry. "But why would you leave some of the blurry ones if that's what happened?"

"I wouldn't." Now she didn't just sound annoyed, she sounded pissed. "Hang on."

I heard shifting and thumping in the background, then what sounded like typing on her laptop. "Well, crap, you're right. There's no way I would have kept those blurry ones at the beginning but deleted the others."

My mind raced, and a possibility occurred to me. I glanced up at the top of my screen. Not only did I have permission to view, I also had permission to edit.

"Am I the only person you shared these with?" I asked.

"I sent the link to everyone, like I always do," she said.

"Who's everyone?"

"Everybody who was there?" She overemphasized the words, implying she was talking to an idiot.

But my brain was busy calculating. If the same link went out to everybody, they all had access to edit, too. Anybody who wanted to hide some form of suspicious behavior could have removed them.

"Do you remember what those missing pictures were of?" I asked.

"Let me look."

I listened as she clicked and tapped. "I mean—not specifically. The timeline looks right. I took pictures of everybody playing charades, after that we all went home."

"That's another thing. It didn't strike me as a very charades sort of event."

"Yeah, I think that's why Leeya did it," she said, her voice contracting. "Dad played games with us when we were little, but Mom hated them. Leeya knew Mom couldn't refuse on her special occasion. Vintage Leeya."

"Do you know if Leeya had any other gatherings at her house after that party?" I asked.

"I don't think so, but Zach would know better."

As we ended the call, I considered the pain I'd heard in her voice, and how it conflicted with the criticism of Leeya in her words. Human relationships were complex, especially family relationships—my relationship with my own father was proof enough of that. And when I closed my eyes and put myself in her situation, the emotions fit. If I had to answer questions in a murder investigation about a family member I had a strained relationship with, I'd be truthful, even if it put me in a bad light to admit our relationship had been rocky, because I'd want the police to find the truth. But that strain wouldn't mean I wasn't heartbroken to lose them—if I lost my father tomorrow,

I'd be infinitely sad not just about losing him, but about the tension that marred our relationship.

I remembered what Petito told me about different motivations presenting as the same emotion. It was also possible Jenna had stolen the Min-Pan and Leeya had confronted her—and the confrontation had turned deadly. Especially if it had been an accident, Jenna would feel guilt and regret, and that could be the emotion I was picking up.

As I clicked through the pictures, antsy at not having any way of knowing which of those explanations was right, Roger Prentiss caught my eye again.

The only thing I knew for certain was Roger Prentiss had been interested in the Min-Pan—and since I needed some sort of action-oriented way to channel my annoyance and frustration in a positive way, now was the perfect time to confront him about it.

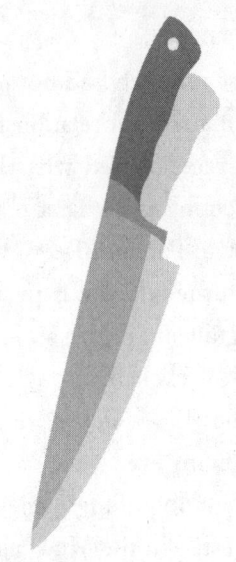

Chapter Twenty-Five

A little stealth reconnaissance—okay, a phone call to the bakery—confirmed for me that Roger was in-house working. I scored a parking space two blocks away, which allowed me a long moment to scope out the bakery as I approached by foot. I'm not sure exactly what I'd expected, but with a name like Holy Cannoli I sure hadn't expected much. Maybe tiny, kitschy, and filled with clashing colors and neon signs? But what I definitely *hadn't* expected was something that looked like the sort of upscale espresso bar Parisian cognoscenti visited after an evening at the opera. Everything was done in shades of brown, and everything that *could* be brass *was* brass. Pastries perched within glass-and-brass cases with recessed lighting that made them shine like jewels in a museum. Tall, tiny, chair-free tables dotted the perimeter, giving just enough space to chow down a pastry and chug an espresso, and the cream-colored boxes containing customers' purchases were secured with gold ribbon. An elegant gilded font made the name Holy Cannoli read as upscale cheeky rather than down-home tacky. And yet, to my astonishment, the prices listed on the board were surprisingly affordable. After buying a half dozen scones to take back to the Hub, I asked the smiling, efficient counter attendant if I could speak to the owner.

When he appeared, Roger's broad smile dented. "Ms. Sanzio. Do we have an appointment?"

"We don't. But I know you're eager to help me figure out what happened to Leeya."

"That I am." He glanced quickly around at the customers and employees pretending not to watch us. "Please, let's step into the office."

"You've perfected the feel of affordable luxury here," I said as I followed him. "I can see why you've been so successful."

As he motioned me into a small room, pride flashed over his face. "Thank you. When I was a little boy, my mother went to an upscale bakery on special occasions. We couldn't afford it except on Easter and Christmas and maybe a birthday, and she always lamented not being able to go more often."

The wave of nostalgia shaved years off his face, and for a brief second I sensed the child he'd once been. I sent another glance back toward the front of the shop—making the things he'd craved as a boy accessible to others was a far healthier way to fill his psychological voids than stealing to get them for himself.

"How can I help you?" he said as he took his seat across the spartan metal desk.

"That object that went missing from Leeya's apartment." I held up my phone, displaying the picture of him staring at the Min-Pan. "You led me to believe you'd never seen it."

Roger leaned back in his chair, jaw tight. "You didn't ask me if I'd ever seen it, you asked if I knew what it was. And I didn't."

Ah, word games! Challenge accepted. I leaned forward to take away the distance he'd put between us. "Based on how interested you look in that picture, it seems odd you didn't mention you'd noticed it."

His brows rose. "I don't see why. I've never visited Leeya's apartment without seeing half a dozen odd things that captured my attention one way or the other."

"Except this one went missing immediately after," I said.

A pink flush crawled up his neck. "Oh, I see. Since I have a criminal record, I must be the one who stole it."

I considered Petito's advice about using pressure points during an interrogation, along with an insidious technique my late mother-in-law used with me: whenever I'd get emotional, she'd respond by tilting her head at me and keeping her voice excruciatingly calm. It made me feel like a toddler and drove me absolutely insane, and I usually spiraled right into saying something I regretted. So I tilted my head at Roger and kept my voice calm.

"Everybody has secrets, Mr. Prentiss, and the vast majority of those secrets don't lead to murder. Leeya wanted to know what this object was, so if she saw you examining it, she might have been eager to talk to you about it. Maybe you offered to look into it for her and took the artifact with her full knowledge, but didn't want to admit to that after she turned up dead because you thought it would make you look guilty."

"I never so much as laid a finger on it." The pink on his neck turned to tomato red, and his hands gripped the arms of his chair. "Do you have any idea how exhausting it gets dealing with this type of prejudice every damned day? It's so fucking ironic. San Francisco is supposed to be the ultimate progressive bastion, but nobody here's willing to believe an ex-con can turn their life around."

I detected real pain behind the invective. "I'm just saying that if there's an innocent explanation, I'm listening. This object may have nothing at all to do with Leeya's death, and if that's the case, clearing it off the list would help me move forward."

He leaned toward me, hissing his words. "I don't know how to say this any more plain and simple. I. Didn't. Take. That. Thing." He slammed his hands on the desk and stood up. "I have a meeting soon. I think you'd better leave."

Chapter Twenty-Six

As I drove back to my house, I analyzed the conversation with Roger on an endless loop. There had been a ring of authenticity in his diatribe, but con men were by necessity experts at persuasion and believability—I'd seen more than one documentary that featured victims saying "but he's really a great guy at heart" about the person who'd bilked them out of thousands of dollars. I was still struggling with which side to land on when I arrived home, and had to force myself to shake off the push-and-pull between my emotional and logical responses so I could deliver my online Zodiac Killer tour.

I told myself the subject would be a good mental palate cleanser, since, as one of the few unsolved crimes I referenced in my tours, it engaged my brain in a way my other tours didn't. It defies all logic that Zodiac was never caught, for a slew of reasons: Two of his victims survived to provide detailed descriptions of him, but no identification was ever made. During the murder he committed in Pacific Heights, three witnesses called in the incident as it was occurring, and two patrol officers spotted a man they only later realized must have been the escaping killer. Zodiac also called the police to confess his crimes, once only blocks away from the Napa County sheriff's office—they quickly tracked his call to a phone booth where they were able to collect his palm print. In addition to all that evidence, Zodiac sent letters and cryptograms to area newspapers, one of which was solved almost immediately. He even included pieces of bloody cloth with the ciphers, but not even the advent of DNA testing has identified him.

As I discussed all of those frustrations with my guests and reached the point where I displayed Zodiac's ciphers, something clanked in my brain.

I didn't have time in the moment to think about why that was—I had to keep to a strict schedule in order to leave time for questions—so I jotted down a quick note into my Moleskine to remind myself to return to the relevant slide. When we got to the questions, several guests commented that since I'd solved the Overkill Bill case, I should try my hand at the Zodiac case, which caused my brain to momentarily seize up in a knot of imposter-syndrome self-doubt. I played it off by answering the remaining questions (including the steady stream coming in about Overkill Bill), then coyly fended off several people who wanted to know what was coming up next on the podcast.

"Heather's right," Ryan said once everyone else left the tour feed. "We need to strike while the iron's hot. Didn't you tell Leeya's mom that you'd put out a first episode about it ASAP?"

"I've been waiting to hear back from Lorraine so I could include an interview with her about it." I'd also been delaying because I was hoping I'd find a little more of a definite lead I could focus on. But he was right—the time had come for us to move forward, and I had to take the leap before I could talk myself out of it. Besides, while I was long on possible suspects, I was woefully short on ways to investigate them, and somebody somewhere out in the city might know something about the case. "Do you have time now? I can do it in the form of a conversation with you. It might help me to think things through, too."

His eyes lit up. "Let's do it."

The basic facts flowed far easier than I expected in the conversational format, and as I'd hoped, talking them through jostled loose a detail I'd forgotten. In the flurry of talking to everybody close to Leeya, I'd forgotten to follow up with Leeya's upstairs neighbor, Khalil Jackson, to see if he'd seen or heard anything useful about what was going on in Leeya's life.

But the note I'd jotted down in my Moleskine was also tugging relentlessly at me, so I clicked back through my slides to the section on the Zodiac's ciphers. I stared at every pixel on the screen, flipping back and forth between the relevant graphics, begging my brain to clue me in on what it was that had grabbed its attention. But whatever it was did its best greased-pig impression—the more I wrestled with it, the further it slipped out of my grasp.

After a revelation-free half hour, I pushed the laptop away and checked the time. It was late, but since Khalil was a night-shift security guard, he was more likely beginning his day than ending it. Since my other leads were all circling overhead in a holding pattern, it seemed like the perfect time to go find him.

• • •

I checked Khalil's apartment first. He wasn't home but Reynalda was, and she told me she'd seen him leave in his uniform. I figured that was a good indication I'd be able to track him down at work. I climbed back into my car and made my way to Union Square, the shopping hub of San Francisco, and hurried into Saks.

My eyes skipped across cosmetics, shoes, and mannequins before landing on a black-clad blond man with SECURITY blazoned across his burly chest. He watched me with a mildly bemused expression as I approached him, as though surprised I could see through his cloak of invisibility.

"Hey," I said by way of introduction. "I'm looking for Khalil Jackson. Do you know where I can find him?"

"He's down in the cage with a shoplifter."

That stopped me. "You have an actual jail here for shoplifters?"

He scrunched his forehead at me. "What do you think this is?"

I opened my mouth to respond that I thought it was a department store, not a penitentiary, but figured that observation wouldn't be appreciated. I decided it was best for all involved if I treated the question as rhetorical. "Can you direct me to it?"

He scrutinized my face but appeared to decide that if I were looking for trouble I'd be looking to stay away from the holding cell rather than waltz right up to it. "Elevator to the bottom floor. All the way back at the north end you'll see the security desk."

I thanked him and headed for the elevator while trying to figure out which way was north. I have a good set of mental maps—a crucial characteristic for a tour guide—but they don't work the same way most people's do. Mine rely on landmarks rather than an instinctive connection to cardinal directions, which means I can find my way around the city really well, but if you throw me into a department store basement I might as well be in a labyrinth. After asking twice for directions, relief surged through me when I caught a glimpse of the security office playing coy around a corner.

I swung the door open cautiously, half expecting to be told instantly I didn't belong there. A sixty-something Latina woman with a platinum-blonde shag of hair visually seized on me.

"You here for the kid?" she asked, looking hopeful.

The too-curious devil that perches behind my frontal lobes begged me to tell her that I was—but as satisfying as it would have been to delve into whatever drama was unfolding inside, I couldn't ruin my chance to talk with Khalil. I told her why I was there.

Her hope turned to annoyance and her eyes flicked to her computer—if I wasn't there to help her with her problem, I was dead to her. "You want to see him 'bout what?"

I considered and rejected several responses with lightning speed. No way was she going to accept "it's a personal matter," and I'd've bet money she was the sort who got joy from kicking journalists out on their asses. But I also got the sense that her brand of orneriness was born of boredom and lack of agency rather than a power trip or obsessive adherence to rules, so I leaned in and lowered my voice tantalizingly. "A murder."

The blood drained from her face—bored she might be, but she didn't need *that* kind of trouble in her life. She jutted a thumb toward the door behind her. "In there."

Inside, two more desks faced a row of plastic chairs lined against the far wall. A white, teenaged brunette bounced her skinny-jeans-clad leg in one of the chairs, resentfully eyeballing the two men who sat behind the desks. One periodically scanned a panel of CCTVs while the other filled out some sort of paperwork. They both glanced up at me.

"Khalil Jackson?" I asked.

The man behind the panel of monitors, tall and Black with warm brown eyes, turned an effortless smile on me. "You here to pick up the little lady?"

"No." I stepped past the young woman, closer to his desk. "I'd like to talk to you about Leeya Styles."

His smile dissolved, and he turned to the other man. "Rob, I'm gonna take my ten. You got this?"

Rob nodded and returned to his paperwork.

Khalil didn't say anything until he'd led me back into the hallway. "I already spoke to the police. I was working night shift both Friday and Saturday nights. I got witnesses, time cards, and security tape to back me up."

I hurried to reassure him, then gave him a quick explanation of why I was there. "So I'd just like to ask you about Leeya. Did you know her well?"

He shrugged, still wary. "We said hi to each other now and then. Exchanged mail when letters went in the wrong slot. That's about it."

"She never did anything to bug you? No late-night noise, no visitors coming and going at all hours, no conflict of any sort?"

His mouth tugged down. "She never had many visitors except her boyfriend, and Reynalda didn't let her do any noisy work at the house."

My hopes perked up. "You met her boyfriend?"

"A few times. And I met her mother twice." He shook his head as if in wonderment.

I zeroed in on the gesture. "You didn't like her?"

"She's the kind who wants to be her daughter's friend, not her mother. First time I met her she asked if I thought they were sisters." He raised his eyebrows and gave me a look. "Anybody took them for sisters needs LASIK pronto."

I laughed before I could stop myself. "What did you think of the boyfriend?"

He shrugged. "She could do better. She had a goal and worked hard for it. Brad was the typical bro who skated his way through life."

As I started to correct his use of "Brad" instead of "Zach," the *Pulp Fiction* reference hit me. "Check out the big brain on Brad?" I asked.

He smiled an insider smile. "Hundred percent, he knows the metric system. I wasn't at all surprised when she kicked him to the curb."

My jaw dropped. "She what now?"

His brows popped up, as if trying to lift my jaw back into place. "You didn't know they broke up?"

I tried to recover, since I really shouldn't have been surprised—after talking with Jenna, I'd decided Quinn's story was reliable, so it made sense that Leeya would have eventually realized it, too. But measure twice, cut once. "Are you sure? When?"

"Positive." His face turned somber. "I forget exactly when, but it was sometime last week. Had a ringside seat to the blowup. I couldn't hear her, 'cause she was never loud, but *him* I heard. Cycled through berating her to begging her and back again."

"What was the fight about?"

Anger flashed on his face. "He did her dirty."

"Cheated on her?"

He nodded. "When I ran into her the next day I told her she made the right choice, and if he made any trouble to just let me know."

I raked my teeth across my bottom lip. Zach had lied to me, but had the lie come from pride or something more nefarious? And why did everyone, including Leeya's mother and her sister, think they were still together?

"Just to make sure we're talking about the same guy," I asked. "Named Zach, tall, with black spiky hair?"

"That's the one."

"Maybe they got back together after the fight," I said, thinking aloud.

He threw me a skeptical look. "I didn't see him again."

My thoughts continued to seep out. "Do you know what made her decide Quinn was telling the truth? Did Zach say anything about that?"

Confusion washed over his face. "Quinn. Is that her sister? I thought her name was Jenna. Either way, Leeya saw it with her own eyes."

I stared at him in stunned silence while my brain tried to make sense of the words. "Let me make sure I'm getting this right. I was under the impression Leeya broke up with Zach because he hit on her *best friend*, Quinn?"

His confusion disappeared. "No. She broke up with Zach because she caught him banging her *sister*, Jenna."

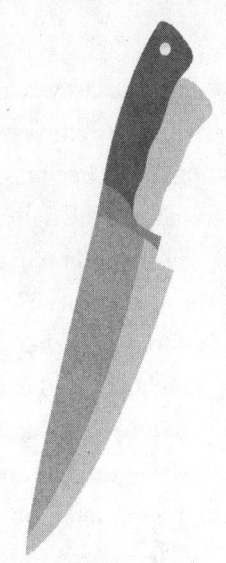

Chapter Twenty-Seven

I stumbled around for what felt like an hour trying to find the elevator again, my standard challenges with direction now amplified by my mental grappling with the implications of what Khalil had heard.

Zach had cheated with Jenna. Leeya caught them. How?

Leeya broke up with Zach because of it—and it hadn't gone well. That certainly explained why Jenna had dodged my call for as long as she did—she and Zach must have been figuring out what to tell everyone.

Khalil might be lying, the investigative part of my brain reminded me. But Khalil had no reason to lie, and he *did* have a rock-solid alibi for the entire weekend. And while I'd already come to the conclusion that Quinn was telling me the truth, this pulled together a number of the remaining threads I hadn't been sure what to do with. Like, why Jenna had told me Quinn wasn't trustworthy—because she needed to discredit the cheating story so I wouldn't examine Zach's fidelity too closely. And why Leeya hadn't gone to Zach rather than Roger about her difficulties with Kody Marcus—because they'd broken up. It also explained Leeya's abandoned birth-control pills, and why

Jenna hadn't been bothered by being single—it must have given her great satisfaction to know she was having sex with Zach in the face of Leeya's concern about her relationship status.

I grabbed out my phone as I walked and navigated to the pictures I'd downloaded from Jenna's link, looking them over again. At the time, I'd interpreted the too-intimate vibe of the pictures she'd taken of Zach as envy, but on second viewing I saw furtive amusement: an illicit lover indulging her secret directly under the nose of the person she was betraying.

"Excuse *me*, young lady."

My eyes snapped up from my phone—I'd almost barreled into an octogenarian walking with a cane. I apologized profusely, then dropped my mind back into playing everything out. Quinn had been worried that Zach's temper might have come out if Leeya tried to break up with him. Khalil had run into Leeya the day after the breakup and she'd been fine, but had Zach returned to try to convince her to reconcile and killed her when she refused? Or maybe, after breaking up with Zach, Leeya had confronted Jenna in turn, and *that* had ended badly? But how would that end up with *Leeya*, the injured party, dead? I could see how Jenna would have enjoyed taking something from Leeya so much she would have somehow arranged for Leeya to "accidentally" discover her with Zach, and I could see how amid the heightened emotions in a situation like that things might escalate out of control. But everybody had come out of that initial situation alive—Leeya hadn't broken up with Zach until later at her apartment, so heat-of-the-moment emotions weren't at play here. But—what if Leeya had threatened to tell their mother? The thought of falling even lower in her mother's eyes might have been too much for Jenna.

Speculation would only get me so far—I needed facts. But what approach would allow me to get to the truth? I could confront both of them about it at the same time without giving them time to get their stories straight—but they'd certainly already done that. Maybe it would be better to play them off each other? Maybe call Zach and tell him Jenna had confessed the affair to me, and implied he'd killed Leeya? That might prod him out of his silence and get him to say something incriminating. Or vice versa.

It was worth a shot, but I'd only get one. Who was more likely to crack? Jenna had been contained, even borderline icy, when we spoke. But Zach had seemed shaken during our conversation, and Quinn felt sure he had a short fuse. If so, he was far more likely to lose it and say something stupid.

I checked the time on my phone. Ambushing him at his house would give me the ability to see his face when I confronted him, but it would also give him the ability to unalive me if he so desired. Since my mama didn't raise a fool, if I was going to see him in person, I needed to trick him into meeting me somewhere public.

I dialed his number, which went to voicemail. I injected an edge of confusion into my voice after the beep. "Zach, it's Capri Sanzio. I just found out something really strange about Leeya and I need to talk to you about it. Can we meet up? I need to get some dinner anyway, maybe we could meet over pizza at Salerno's? Let me know."

I hung up the phone, then tapped to send him a text.

And was interrupted by a car backfiring impossibly loudly.

As I turned to locate the car, my brain registered the pain searing through my arm—then I fell to the ground.

SF KILLER CRIME TOURS

The Tenderloin

While the Barbary Coast was home to San Francisco's adult Disneyland during the Gold Rush, by 1913, Californians attempted to put the kibosh on the fleshier of these attractions by passing the Red Light Abatement Act. However, since it only garnered fifty-three percent of the vote, it would take more than shutting down the physical brothels to end mankind's supposedly oldest profession: the only real effect the law had was to force "ladies of the night" onto the streets, a situation that was far more dangerous for all involved and far harder to patrol.

One area that welcomed these sex workers with open arms was the Tenderloin (named after New York City's crime-riddled zone). A smallish area bordering Union Square and Nob Hill, the neighborhood was (and still is) replete with small, single-person dwellings that originally housed the workers who rebuilt the city after 1906's earthquake. A network of bars and gambling dens sprang up to help those men relax after their hard-working days with nights of not-so-wholesome fun. That's why when Prohibition hit a few years later, the Tenderloin was poised to respond with a vigorous hold my beer: the area's nightlife flourished into the Barbary Coast 2.0, sprouting a barrage of speakeasies, gambling dens, and other illegal entertainments.

Just like the original Barbary Coast, the Tenderloin has always attracted more than its share of crime. Perhaps the most well-known saga was the relationship that fatally flared between brothers Jim and Artie Mitchell, two of the most famous "porn kings" of San Francisco. The Mitchells battled police raids and court cases for decades over the definition of obscenity—employing a political-activist attorney who would go on to represent Timothy Leary and Cesar Chavez—as they built an adult-entertainment empire centered around the notorious O'Farrell Theatre in the Tenderloin. Their careers included popularizing close-contact lap dances and producing Marilyn Chambers's Behind the Green Door, which made more than fifty million dollars. Their collaboration ended when Jim shot Artie multiple times, killing him. Jim claimed the shooting was an accident caused by Artie's addiction to drugs and alcohol, while the prosecutor called it premeditated murder; the jury split the difference, sentencing Jim to six years for voluntary manslaughter.

But the Tenderloin is more than vice and crime. Also due to the high density of its single-room dwellings and its no-questions-asked vibe, the area has historically been a haven for anyone facing discrimination. The Tenderloin was the site of the Compton's Cafeteria riot in 1966, where transgender residents battled police harassment three years before New York's Stonewall Riot; it was also the precursor to San Francisco's Castro District. It's no coincidence that social justice movements ranging from civil rights to sex-worker protections to hydroponics for feeding the homeless were born here, forming the backbone of San Francisco's social-justice identity.

And so the Tenderloin evidences a beautiful yin-yang: by shining a light on universal aspects of the human condition that many would rather not see, the history of the Tenderloin celebrates the complexity of humanity itself.

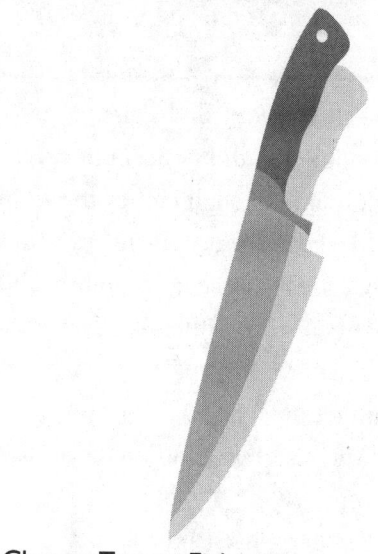

Chapter Twenty-Eight

"Mom. The doctor said you need rest. You've been *shot*." Morgan glared at me, one hand on her hip, one pointed out of the kitchen toward my bedroom.

I tamped down the grounds in my moka pot. "You're being dramatic, Morgan. It's a flesh wound. The bullet grazed my arm."

"*Bullet*, Mom. *Bullet* is the key word in that sentence. When you're hit by a *bullet*, that's called getting *shot*." She sent a pleading glance for help to Heather, who was busy pulling down every type of painkiller I had in my cabinet. "Whether it results in a flesh wound or a collapsed lung, getting shot is a stressful event. You've lost blood and you're in shock."

She wasn't wrong, and I knew it. But I also knew that if I thought about it too long, I'd never set foot outside my house again. And since that's exactly what whoever did this wanted—to scare me off investigating—that was exactly what I was *not* going to allow to happen. The very possibility made my heels automatically dig down deep.

You've always been stubborn, my father's voice whispered through my head, tinged with disgust.

"Stubborn" didn't begin to cover it, I was well aware of that. But I didn't have enough money to pay for the legion of psychologists it would take to figure out why my own brain could undermine my confidence in my investigative abilities, but that same brain only strengthened my resolve in the face of an assassination attempt.

"I'm fine, Morgan," I said. "For all we know, the bullet wasn't even meant for me."

"And that makes a difference to your blood pressure how?" she sputtered.

Heather closed the cabinet door and took stock of what she'd found. "Advil, Tylenol, Midol, baby aspirin that expired before the pandemic, and for reasons I'll leave between you and the universe, a tube of anti-itch cream. You sure you don't want me to run home and get my leftover Percocet?"

I pointed to the strip of gauze wound around my left forearm. "It's a *two-inch scrape* across my arm. They didn't even give me Percocet when I pushed a *seven-pound human* out of my vagina."

"Really?" Heather looked horrified. "One more reason to never have a child." Heather shrugged. "But it wouldn't hurt you to at least sit so we don't have to worry about picking you up when you faint."

"It absolutely *would* hurt me, because neither of you can make a decent cup of coffee to save your life. And I sat in that ER for three and a half hours. I came out of shock at least two hours ago, and my body has long since regenerated what little blood I lost. What I *need* is caffeine and sugar." I wrenched the bottom and top of the moka pot together with a furious twist, set it on the burner, then opened the refrigerator door and grabbed my jar of sweet pickles.

Heather jumped forward to wrench the jar from my hand. "No way.

You need real food. We'll order something." She pulled her phone out of her pocket. "I'll get an extra-large special from Salerno's."

I nodded assent, and she tapped at her screen. Then, my doorbell rang.

I froze. Nobody I knew came over without calling first.

But if I let Morgan see me shook, she'd never leave me alone again. So I did what I do best—deflected with mediocre humor. "Wow, that was fast. I know Salerno's is close, but that's just showing off."

Morgan blocked my path as I took a step forward. "No, Mom. You sit. I'll see what's going on."

I pointed at my phone on the far counter. "I was just going to check the security camera."

She swiped it up and tapped at it—we knew all of each other's passwords. "It's Inspector Petito."

My memory rushed back. "I forgot he was supposed to come by tonight. Don't either of you say a word to him about this. I'll tell him in my own way." I zigged past Morgan, trying to figure out which details would best be finessed.

But when I flung open the door, his eyes were a deep shade of midnight blue that reflected the gale-force storm on his face.

"They told you?" I grumbled. "I thought medical records were private."

"Hospitals are required to report all gunshot wounds." His eyes flashed to the gauze on my arm. "Why didn't you call me?"

As I stood there trying to come up with a less snarky answer than *I figured calling a man when you get shot is more of a fifth-date sort of milestone*, Morgan and Heather stepped into the room, Heather's hand tugging pointedly at Morgan's arm.

"Morgan and I are gonna head out," Heather said, then hurried on when Morgan opened her mouth to object. "Your namby-pamby excuses for painkillers are all lined up. If you decide you want something real, let me know." She leaned in to give me a quick hug.

Despite looking confused and annoyed, Morgan followed her lead. She also gave me a hug, then grabbed her coat from where she'd hung it. "I'll call when I get home to see how you're doing—"

Heather pulled her the rest of the way onto my porch and closed the door behind them.

Petito turned to me, eyes still intense. "What happened?"

"Okay, so, first of all, it's not really a gunshot." I raised my hand to cut off his objection. "It's just a scratch. A single stitch and a tetanus shot is the extent of it."

He took another step toward me and put a hand on the rolled-up bloody shirtsleeve I hadn't yet changed out of. "What. Happened."

"I don't know exactly, everything happened at once. I went to talk to Khalil Jackson at Saks and was walking down Mason back to the lot where I'd parked my car. I heard what I thought was a car backfire and looked up to see where—"

The muscles in his temple flexed and released. "Looked up?"

I winced mentally—that was exactly the sort of detail that would have been better off finessed. "From my phone. I was sending a text, and—"

"You were walking alone, after dark, *in the Tenderloin*, focused on your phone." Now the muscles in his jaw flexed and released.

I bristled. "It's *barely* in the Tenderloin, only a block away from Union Square! And I do tours in the Tenderloin all the time."

"Alone? After dark?"

No, Ryan was always with me after dark, but admitting that wasn't going to help my case. "The point is, it was a wrong-place-wrong-time scenario, and all's well that ends well. I'm sure it wasn't intended for me." I stared up into his eyes without blinking, looking to see if he'd buy it.

"Wrong place wrong time. Did you see who fired the shot?"

"I—no. But based on the angle I was shot, they must have been down that alley that makes an L through the block. Ellwood, I think?"

"If you didn't see them, how do you know the shot wasn't intended for you? You've been bouncing all over the city asking questions, letting everyone know exactly what you're thinking and why. And, just in case you managed to miss threatening the killer directly, you dropped a podcast episode about it all informing the rest of San Francisco about your interest."

Yep, that was pretty much word for word what my brain had been trying to whisper to me since the bullet whizzed past my forearm, and I was rapidly losing my ability to ignore it. I straightened up as tall as I could. "Okay, fine, I don't know for certain it wasn't intended for me. But it doesn't matter if it was, because there's no way in hell I'm going to let someone intimidate me away from finding the truth."

His annoyance morphed and shifted, and I could tell he was having difficulty keeping his emotions under control. "We need to talk. And I don't know about you, but I have a feeling I'm gonna need the wine we talked about to get me through the conversation."

• • •

While Petito grabbed glasses and a bottle out of my prized stash of Ravenswood zinfandels, I changed my bloody shirt. When we met back at the couch Petito poured the wine, his face still cycling through expressions.

When he finished, he reached for the gauze on my forearm. "Let's back up a step. Can I take a look?"

I pulled the gauze back. "The doctor said I could just put two Band-Aids over it after I showered."

"You weren't kidding. A single stitch," he said, gently turning my arm for a better view.

The feel of his skin on mine sent a rush of emotion over me. Tingles, of course, but also a sudden desire to bury my head in his shoulder and cry. Quickly followed by a rush of shame, because I'd worked hard to be the sort of woman who didn't need a man to protect her.

So, I shrugged instead. "I told you, no big deal."

His hand slipped down to clasp mine. "Two inches back and he'd have shot you in the side."

I reached for my wine. "I've been trying extremely hard not to think about that. And it's also why I think it was a scare tactic. We're only talking about a few yards here. If the shooter wanted me dead, I'd be dead."

"Maybe. But either way, we can't afford to not think about it. For two reasons. One, because you and I are straying into murky ethical water here."

I bristled. "Is there some rule against inspectors dating journalists who are looking into a case?"

His jaw flexed again. "No. But if someone on a case I'm investigating shoots the woman I'm dating, that gets complicated."

"Interesting. So all a criminal has to do to get an inspector thrown off a case is to shoot at their significant other?" I slid my raised brows into a glare. "And we just agreed we couldn't know for sure I was the intended target. So is this just a convenient excuse for you to pressure me to stop investigating Leeya's murder?"

He threw up a hand. "I only said it was complicated. You have to admit that much."

I nodded reluctantly. "But I'm not going to stop investigating this case."

He matched my nod. "Then we move on to the second point. I need you to walk me through everything you did today, however small."

I took a deep breath to stroke my hackles back into place. "That's easy, because I've been keeping you up to date as I go. The only thing you don't know about is my conversation with Khalil." I gave him a recap.

He sipped as he listened. "Did you tell anyone you were going to talk to him?"

"No. I didn't know myself until after my tour."

"Then someone must have followed you to Saks and waited. I'll need to check to see who has an alibi for the time you were shot. When exactly did it happen?"

I gave him the specifics and cast my mind back to the scene. "I don't remember seeing or hearing anyone running or anything like that. People mostly just froze in place and stared. Disconcerting, really." I shifted gears. "At that point, nobody knew I'd found out about Jenna and Zach, so that couldn't have been the impetus."

He shook his head. "You can't be sure. If Jenna killed Leeya, she's already on the lookout for any sign you've found out, and even asking for those pictures would have alerted her that you're getting too close. You said there were some missing from the ones she linked you to?"

My mind leaped along with the logic. "She might have deleted something that gave away her relationship with Zach. She told me she shared the link with the whole family, so it makes sense she'd have deleted anything too revealing." I paused to down the rest of my half-filled glass. "Or their relationship may be irrelevant and something I did struck a nerve with someone else."

Petito's eyes followed my now-empty glass back to the coffee table. He reached over to thread his fingers through mine. "It's okay to admit this has you rattled. I know it has *me* rattled."

I shook my head. "I have no problem admitting it."

He squinted dubiously at me. "Then what was that whole line about 'wrong place wrong time'?"

I sighed. "Oh, my brain wove a whole tapestry of BS while I had nothing else to do in the ER. I do think it's possible this has nothing to do with Leeya, but I also know that's not likely."

He softened his voice and stroked the back of my hand with his thumb. "So why put on the front?"

The smart thing to do would have been to zip my lip tight, but that's never been a particular strength of mine. "Because I really don't need a lecture."

His thumb froze. "A lecture?"

A laugh burst out of me. "You know, like the one about me being in the Tenderloin by myself after dark?"

He stiffened. "That's not a lecture, that's just good sense."

I removed my hand from his grasp. "I'm a single woman with responsibilities. I don't have time to wait around for an escort every time the sun goes down."

"How about the part where you were paying attention to your phone instead of your surroundings?"

Part of my brain wanted to throw down, but the rest of me was too tired to fight the obvious. "Yeah. Maybe not my finest moment."

"Thank you." His shoulders relaxed but his eyes intensified, back to their deep-midnight incarnation. He reclaimed my hand and squeezed it gently. "I know we've only been on one date, but my lungs stopped working when I heard you'd been shot."

Gazing into his eyes felt like I'd slipped into a warm bath, with every inch of me nestled into soothing water. I'd forgotten what it was like to have someone invested in me romantically; it felt strange but familiar all at the same time, like eating a dish you've never tried before only to discover it's your favorite. I hated feeling weak, but after the terror of being shot and the tension of knowing I couldn't afford to be intimidated, what I wanted more than anything was to allow myself to feel safe, if only for an evening.

I leaned forward and, moving slowly enough to give him time to bolt if he so desired, placed my lips lightly on his.

It was all the encouragement he needed. As he deepened the kiss, his hands slid up my arms and down my sides, and with one hand he pulled me up onto his lap. I ran my hands up his chest, then around to the back of his neck; he moaned and slid one hand up to cup my breast.

Then he broke the kiss, and his eyes pierced mine with an unspoken question. When I smiled, he slipped his hands under me and he stood in one fluid motion, lifting me from the couch and carrying me across the living room.

When he reached the hall, he froze.

"What's wrong?" I asked, praying he wasn't having second thoughts.

His dimple popped. "Which one's the bedroom?"

I laughed a huge burst of relief. "Second door on the right."

• • •

I've always believed I do my best thinking in the shower—but as it turns out, my brain gets a postcoital power boost that puts my shower thinking cap to shame.

Not that I realized that right away—at first I was far too caught up sinking into Petito's arms. My mind may have forgotten what sex was like, but my body sure hadn't—it came alive as he kissed and caressed and stroked every part of me, like a low electrical current flowing from his lips to my skin, innervating me inch by inch. And, as it also turns out, muscle memory is real; as soon as I felt him inside me, all sorts of long-neglected skills roared back to life, much to my delight—and to my relief. I was also pleased to discover I was in better shape than I'd feared—hiking up and around San Francisco's mountainous topography had kept me fit enough to go not just once, not just twice, but three times before slipping into his arms and falling into a deep sleep with my head on his chest.

It was then, while my body slept, that the investigator portion of my brain freed up to chug efficiently away. I dreamed the Zodiac Killer showed up at my door waving copies of the letters he'd sent to the police in my face, yelling, "You'll never be a good journalist if you can't see what's right in front of you." I snatched them out of his hands and tried to read them, but the ciphers shifted and morphed like a watercolor painting in the rain.

I woke and sat bolt upright, now fully aware of what had been bothering me during my Zodiac Killer tour. Despite eluding my conscious mind, my endorphin-packed cortex had identified it lickety-split: I'd been trying to decode the *wrong part* of the Min-Pan.

The Zodiac had used strange symbols for his cipher—arrows and circles with lines through them and boxes with dots—not so very different from the tribal-type symbols decorating the pan portion of the Min-Pan.

The cipher wasn't the numbers etched onto the tools—it was the tribal-pattern symbols etched onto the background.

Moving carefully so as not to wake Petito, I snaked over my phone and pulled up the picture of the Min-Pan, zooming in as much as I could. Sure enough, rather than a predictably repeating pattern, there was an irregularity to how the lines and dots related to each other. Sometimes the lines formed a box with four sides; sometimes one or more of the sides was missing. Sometimes there was one dot, sometimes more; sometimes the dots were in the center of the symbol, sometimes outside the lines. What if each symbol corresponded to a different letter?

I needed to test it out as a possible cipher, and to do that I needed my notebook. I slipped my legs out of bed and grimaced as my bare feet touched the cold hardwood floor.

"Hey. Where're you going?" Petito's sexy rumble halted me in my tracks and threw me into a tar pit of indecision. On the one hand, I desperately wanted to test my new cipher theory . . . but literally on the other hand his fingers were stroking me, and half his chest and one leg were peeking out from under the sheet, giving me glimpses of muscle tauter than any fifty-something had a right to possess. As the two priorities threw on gloves and prepared to duke it out, a shifting shape at the top of his leg swelled, and I figured if the previous evening's activities had sharpened my wits enough to help me stumble on the right code, another round would surely help me parse the cipher that much more effectively.

Half an hour later, I found myself lying on my back trying to catch my breath. "Coffee?" I panted.

"Mmm. And I'm starving. How about I scrounge up some breakfast for us before I head out to work while you make a pot?" He reached for his phone.

"No need to order anything. I'm pretty sure I have eggs and a smattering of vegetables I can turn into an omelet," I said.

"Only if you let me make it," he said.

"You mean in addition to the trick you do with your index finger, you also cook?"

He waggled his brows at me. "Oh, that's just the tip of my iceberg."

I widened my eyes comically as I grabbed my robe. "If that's only the tip, I'm in big trouble."

As he began chopping veggies, I checked my phone to see if Zach had called me back yet. He hadn't, not surprising since he was hiding something pretty darned big, but it meant I'd need to track him down. Then I called Morgan to update her on my conversation with Petito about the case, and to warn her to take safety precautions. Despite my thick vein of denial the night before, I needed to be realistic—if the killer was coming after me, it wouldn't take them long to figure out my daughter was my Achilles' heel, so she'd need to be careful. Then I made coffee and he sautéed, chatting as we worked, easy and smooth like we'd prepped a thousand meals together in that kitchen before.

As I finished the last bite of my tomato-and-onion omelet and got up to stash our plates in the washing machine, I remembered my earlier revelation. "I forgot to tell you. I have a new theory about the cipher on the Min-Pan."

His brows rose over his mug. "Do tell."

I recounted my Zodiac Killer dream for him, pretending I didn't notice he was trying not to laugh. Then, when I pulled up the picture of the Min-Pan and explained my thinking, his eyes brightened and I watched his own mental gears start to turn.

"Hang on, I'll grab my notebook." I snatched my Moleskine from the office and hurried back. "The first thing I need to do is copy it all out in linear form, then make a chart to help me count which symbols occur most frequently."

"Have you searched the internet for these symbols yet?" he asked.

"No, something distracted me when I tried to get out of bed. But the blog I read about the Min-Pan said the code on it was created by Winston Phelps, the guy who made the Min-Pan, when he and his brother were kids. So I'm not sure we can count on finding it."

"Might as well give it a shot while I'm finishing my coffee. You continue on with that."

I transcribed and counted while he clicked and scrolled. When I was about halfway through my count, he leaned over and kissed my neck. "Normal couples do crosswords over breakfast."

"*Normal.*" I grimaced. "Normal is highly overrated."

Then Petito's phone rang, making me jump in my chair.

"Petito." His face went rigid almost immediately as he listened. His eyes met mine for the briefest moment, then glanced away. "You're sure about the identification?"

Tiny knives sliced into my abdomen.

"I'll be right there." He hung up, then met my eyes again. "Waste Management found Lorraine Kostricka dead in the bottom of a dumpster."

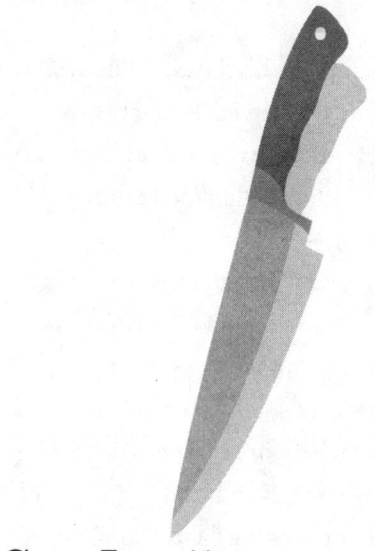

Chapter Twenty-Nine

"Lorraine's dead?" Adrenaline radiated out of my chest to my limbs, negating the need for my second cup of coffee. I grabbed it anyway and followed Petito into the bedroom. "Where? How?"

Petito stuck his legs into his pants and pulled them up over his boxer briefs. "In an alley off Bush, near Union Square. Waste Management was emptying a dumpster, and one of the guys was standing outside the truck talking to one of the tenants. When the front loader emptied the contents into the truck, the guy saw a body he said was too 'floppy' to be a mannequin."

"And they're sure it's Lorraine?"

He patted his pockets, checking the contents. "Her purse was there, too, with her credit cards and ID. But they'll need to confirm."

That circled around my head for a moment before the implication hit. "Her ID wasn't enough? Was she . . ."

He cleared his throat. "Decomp."

Another jolt of adrenaline speared through my system. Decomposition meant she'd been there for a while. "How long?"

He shook his head. "The ME will have to determine that, but Carlton, the detective they dispatched, thinks at least two days."

"Her hotel was right off Bush. That can't be a coincidence." I followed him as he left the bedroom and headed for his coat hanging by the door.

"I agree. That doesn't seem likely." He zipped up the coat.

I extended my coffee out to him. "Take this. I'll make myself another cup and meet you over there."

His eyes snapped up to mine as he took the cup. "You'll what?"

I reached for my own jacket. "I figured it makes more sense for me to drive myself so I can—"

He threw up a hand. "You need to stay put. I'll call you as soon as I know anything."

My hackles flew up like a frilled-neck dragon-lizard's collar. "Like hell I'm staying put. How can you even ask me that?"

He started to clap back, but caught himself and made an effort to soften his expression. "Capri. Someone tried to kill you last night—"

I stabbed my arms into my jacket. "And you think they're going to try again out in the open at a crime scene crawling with cops and witnesses?"

His tone took on an underlying rumble. "They could follow you back to your car, or off to your next lead. And I'd really appreciate being able to go focus all my attention on this crime scene without having to worry someone's gunning you down somewhere."

I pulled up the zipper with a ferocious snap. "So what am I supposed to do, never leave the house again? You're aware I make my living by walking the streets of San Francisco, right? And yes, *I'm* aware that came out wrong, but you know what I mean. And I have a tour in a few hours. Am I just supposed to not go to that, too?"

He set the mug of coffee down on my hallway table. "Given the circumstances, a few vacation days might be a good idea. You said Ryan's eager for more responsibility—"

I took a step back from him. "So I'm supposed to live in fear? Let this killer intimidate me into dropping the investigation? How can I claim I'm serious about being an investigative reporter if I turn tail and run the first time someone throws me a mean look?"

His jaw tensed. "Someone shooting you is a little more than throwing you a mean look. And I didn't say drop the investigation, I'm just saying there are ways to be smarter about it. I can keep you informed, and don't you want to get that cipher figured out anyway?"

I narrowed my eyes at him. "Nice try, but I'm not a child you can distract with a piece of candy. Lorraine needs me *now*, and you have no right to ask me to back off just because we're having sex."

"'*Having sex*.'" His jaw snapped shut.

I instantly regretted the clinical choice of words. "I didn't mean that the way it came out. But you have to understand. Twenty-odd years ago I put my chosen profession aside before it even started to become a wife and a mother. And I don't regret making sure Morgan had an amazing upbringing, but I now understand I didn't have to sacrifice that part of myself to give her one. I've been given a second chance, and I can't ever again allow myself to be less than I'm supposed to be. Especially for my partner."

"And I just want you to be safe." He took a deep breath and sent a desperate glance back into my house. "If you're going to be putting yourself into dangerous situations, you should at least be able to protect yourself. Do you have a firearm?"

I felt my eyes widen. "You mean like a gun?"

His eyes narrowed. "Since a crossbow isn't worth the hassle, yes, let's stick with a gun."

"I— No," I stammered. I'd never even considered owning a gun. "I have Mace, and I've taken self-defense."

"Martial arts?" he asked.

I shifted my weight to my other foot. "One of those three-class deals down at the community center."

"The ones where they teach you to yell 'no' if you think you're about to be raped, and to put your keys between your fingers?"

I threw my hands onto my hips. "That's solid advice."

"It is, for a wide range of situations. But if you're going to keep angering murderers, you'll need something more substantial."

I didn't like the ring of truth circling my head. "But aren't people who own a gun more likely to shoot themselves than anyone else?"

He took in a deep breath. "You're not quoting the right statistic. But the answer to your general point is that if you're going to own a gun, you have to know how to handle it safely."

"Which I don't know how to do—"

"I have a list of firearm safety courses I can refer you to, and you'd need to pass a firearm safety certificate and apply to carry concealed."

Holy crap—he was serious. "Or I could just get a Taser," I squeaked.

"That would be an improvement over what you have until you can go through the proper training for a firearm." He stared down at me, waiting for an answer.

"I, um—I'll think about it."

I got the sense he was going to object, but then he looked at his watch.

I seized the opportunity. "Exactly right. We both better get moving."

● ● ●

As soon as Petito was out the door, I threw the remainder of my coffee into a travel mug and tucked my Moleskine deep into my cross-body bag, all while trying not to think too much about how someone could be at that very moment plotting how to take another shot at me. I did very briefly consider taking an Uber—that way I didn't have to walk from whatever godforsaken place I'd need to park to whatever godforsaken place they'd found Lorraine's body—but since I had no idea where I'd have to go after visiting the crime scene, I said a prayer that broad daylight and police presence really would make the danger minimal.

The crime scene was immediately visible on Bush Street thanks to both police cars and caution tape blocking an alley next to a smoke-shop-slash-souvenir-store. I hunted down a space and trotted back quickly, leaving my phone deep in my bag and my eyes firmly scanning my surroundings while the stitch on my arm pulsed out a warning to turn back while I still could. I chastised myself for being dramatic, but made a mental note to buy a Taser on the way home.

I couldn't quite see to the end of the alley what with the people crowded around it and the law-enforcement officials inside, but I was able to make out two dumpsters looming at the end. I pulled out my phone, hoping that if I lifted it over my head I'd be able to get a decent picture or two.

"You gotta give us more than that," a tall, thirty-something blond guy a few feet from me said to the officer guarding the perimeter.

"I don't gotta give you anything," the officer responded. "When I get something more, I'll let you know."

"Don't give me that BS. The ME's been in there for almost half an hour, and I saw Petito sneak in. Why's another homicide cop suddenly showing up when a team's already in there? This must be linked to something else."

I was impressed, and by "impressed" I mean smacked hard in the face with hot-out-of-the-oven humble pie. This guy knew all the detectives by sight, by unit, and by who usually teamed with who. If I was going to be serious about putting local crimes on the podcast, I had a metric crap ton of homework I needed to do.

As several other reporters peppered the officer with questions he refused to answer, a forty-something woman with a messy bun of too-red-to-be-natural curls pushed her way up to the blond with two Starbucks cups strategically aimed in front of her.

"Oh, thank God," Blondie said. "My hands are half-frozen."

"It's fifty degrees, you crybaby," Red said. "What'd you find out?"

"Middle-aged woman, strangled."

Strangled, just like Leeya had been.

"Hooker?" Red asked.

"Maybe." Blondie shrugged again, then sipped his coffee.

"They know how long she's been there?" she asked.

"They won't say. But I talked to one of the boutique employees, and she said the woman didn't look 'fresh,'" Blondie said.

"What the hell does fresh look like when it's at the bottom of a damned dumpster?" Red asked.

I snorted agreement before I could stop myself. Red turned and lasered in on me. I figured it was a good time to make myself scarce.

"Who's the newbie picking at your scraps?" she asked as I slipped away between the lookie-loos.

Once I made it to the other side of the smoke shop, I stopped to orient myself. As I did, I spotted the Vincennes in the distance and headed toward it. I located the front entrance of the hotel and snapped several pictures of the area. I tried to think back on what little I knew about Lorraine's stay after my tour. She'd mentioned that the whole weekend was booked other than the time she'd spent on my tour and some shopping time, so she should have been out with her friends until late Saturday night, whatever "late" was for a fifth-grade teacher. And Petito said the hotel confirmed she'd checked out Sunday, so the most likely scenario was that she'd asked if she could keep her car parked and went off shopping on foot before heading back out to Roseville.

Except, a voice in the back of my brain whispered, *how would you pull someone into an alley in broad daylight without being noticed?*

It was an interesting point, but not conclusive. Stranger things had happened, and from what I could see from the pictures I took, there were no security cameras in the alley.

Except, the voice continued on as I turned back down the steps and surveyed the area, *the alley was in exactly the wrong direction, a block opposite from the way she'd have walked to Union Square.*

I peered around again—why would Lorraine have gone that direction? I couldn't imagine Lorraine going into the smoke shop, since she hadn't smelled of tobacco or any other inhale-ables, and since she only lived a couple of hours away, I didn't see her sprouting a burning desire for an I ♥ SAN FRANCISCO T-shirt. But as my eyes swept over the stores on the block, my mind flashed to Lorraine clutching her Starbucks cup during my tour like it was an extension of her soul. I understood that sort of bond with caffeine, and its consequences—the first thing I always did while traveling was locate the nearest source of liquid gold to my hotel. Sure enough, the Kahunamaya Café, three doors down from the alley, was the closest coffee to the Vincennes.

I jogged back across the street and entered the café. Only a few patrons lingered inside, probably because people were trying to either avoid the crime scene or were down at the alley scoping it out. Either way, the three employees I saw behind the counter looked pale and distracted, their gazes periodically flicking in the general direction of the alley as though they could see what was happening there if they just tried hard enough.

I found a picture of Lorraine on her Instagram account, then walked up and ordered a nonfat mocha. "Do you remember seeing this woman anytime within the past couple of days?"

The twenty-something, purple-pigtailed barista wagged her head indecisively. "Maybe?"

One of her colleagues, a slightly older man with long brown hair, instantly alerted to her confused expression. "Hey, Maddie," he called to the third employee. "Isn't that the woman who made you remake her caramel macchiato twice?"

Space-bunned Maddie jumped to attention and leaned in to render judgment. "Yep, that's her. First too little caramel, then too much. I mean, seriously—is there any such thing as too much caramel?"

"Do you remember when that was?" I asked.

"Friday morning, around seven maybe?"

It fit; Lorraine told me she and her friends had arrived late Thursday so they could have all of Friday and Saturday in the city. "Is that the only time you saw her?"

"Yep, thank God."

"I saw her again," the guy said. "When I spotted her I took over her drink so we wouldn't have another situation on our hands."

"When was that?" I asked.

He stared up at the ceiling, trying to remember. "The day after the caramel macchiato situation, and that happened on Friday. So I'm pretty sure it was Saturday. Might have been Sunday, though."

That was the kind of specificity that got innocent men hanged. "You don't happen to remember what time of day it was?"

He nodded, happy to have a concrete answer. "Pretty late. I know because she surprised me by asking for drip, and she wanted decaf. I had to make a fresh pot, but she said she didn't mind waiting because she was meeting someone."

My mind did a stutter-step. "Wouldn't you get *more* requests for decaf at night?"

"You'd think that, wouldn't you?" Space-buns said with an eye roll.

She didn't clarify, so I mentally shook my head and moved on. "She and her girlfriends must have stopped by for coffee before heading back to the hotel."

The guy's brow creased at me. "No, like I said, she came to meet someone. And it wasn't a girlfriend, it was a man."

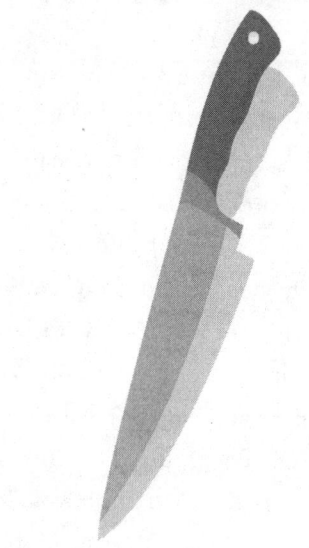

Chapter Thirty

I blinked as my mind wrapped itself around what the barista had just said. "A *man*? You're sure it wasn't a woman?"

He shrugged. "If they were AFAB, they were masculine-presenting. I didn't get a close enough look to say."

That wasn't exactly what I meant, but it raised an important point: I shouldn't assume anything. "Were they bigger than her, or smaller?"

"Couldn't really tell, because I only saw the one sitting down."

I pulled up a picture of Zach. "Was this them?"

He shrugged again. "No idea. Only saw them from the back, and they had a hat on."

"Did they leave together?"

"I didn't see."

"And you're positive it wasn't Sunday morning?"

"It might have been Sunday, but it was right before closing time."

I thanked the trio, stuffed a twenty into the tip jar, then hurried out to text Petito about what I'd just learned.

Who was the mystery person—most likely but not necessarily a man—that Lorraine met, and when exactly had she met them? If it was late Saturday, why would she be meeting with someone after hanging out with her friends? Right before midnight closing didn't really seem like a great time to casually catch up with a friend, or have some sort of date.

My brain split into two factions. The one reminded me that I had to be open to the possibility that the meeting had nothing to do with her death, or with Leeya's. But the other laughed hysterically in response—the notion that Lorraine met with a mysterious stranger and coincidentally ended up dead in the neighboring alley stretched credulity. The only question left as far as I was concerned was whether Lorraine was killed because she'd seen something she shouldn't have, or because she was involved and whoever involved her couldn't risk keeping around someone who knew too much.

If it was a man, and the barista seemed to think it was, Zach was a possibility. He'd lied to me, and cheated on Leeya. For all I knew, he was a former student of Lorraine's, and he brought her in to create an alibi for him. But as I considered the possibility, something about it seemed wrong—there'd have to be more than a fond teacher-student relationship to motivate something like that.

Roger, with his history as a con man before dating Leeya's mother, was a more plausible possibility. Maybe he'd known Lorraine during his con-man phase; maybe she'd even been in on the cons with him. That would explain the house she shouldn't be able to afford, if she had a little ill-gotten nest egg stashed away somewhere. And it would make sense he'd call in someone he knew he could trust if he'd realized the Min-Pan might be a treasure map.

But my mind kept flying to Kody Marcus. Maybe it was just easy for me to picture him waiting for her in a café, fuming over how Leeya'd sicced a collection agency on him, because the setting was similar to where I'd met him. But that stack of Gold Rush books indicated he was cramming Gold Rush lore, and if he'd seen the Min-Pan while visiting Leeya, it was very possible he could have arranged for Lorraine to come into town and pretend to see someone attack her. That could have been the perfect cover if Leeya had caught him stealing it and he'd had to kill her to keep her quiet a day or so before. And if Lorraine needed money for some reason, say for a mortgage payment she was struggling to make, a few extra dollars for a few hours' work might be very welcome. I needed to dive back into both his and her social media accounts and see if I could cross-reference any friends of friends that might show me how they could be connected, or what connection she had to anybody else in Leeya's life.

As I texted a condensed version of that stream of consciousness to Petito, a strange feeling came over me, like I was being watched. My head snapped up—again I'd managed to completely ignore my surroundings—and I searched for anyone staring at me or anything out of the ordinary.

But there was nothing. I was either too slow, or I was losing my mind.

I couldn't afford to let the paranoia get to me. "Stop it," I said sternly to myself as I stuck my phone back in my purse.

A woman walking toward me zagged as far from me as possible as she passed, watching me out of the corner of her eye.

I tapped my empty ears. "Earbuds."

She sped up.

Pull yourself together, I said, internally this time. If I was alarming a San Franciscan pedestrian, a breed of city dweller who routinely saw far more than six strange things before breakfast, it was time to rethink my mental state. Yes, fine, okay, I was more afraid of being attacked again than I wanted to admit, even to myself. And no, there was no way I was going to drop this case. But Petito was right, I didn't have to be stupid about it. And I probably shouldn't go around unarmed.

I hurried the rest of the way to my car, and once I was safely locked inside, I went onto Amazon and searched for a Taser. As I was scanning through the disconcertingly abundant results, my phone shrilled at me, causing me to jump so high I hit my head on the roof of my car.

I rubbed my scalp as I tapped to connect Heather's call.

"Hey, how are you feeling today?" Her voice was tentative, something that happened rarely and only in the face of unpleasantness.

I instantly felt horrible—I'd forgotten to call her, and her mind was probably running crazy with visions of me going septic in the middle of the night. "I'm so sorry I didn't call sooner. I'm fine, I swear. I need to call Morgan and let her know, too."

Her voice perked up. "That's my girl, straight outta Chumbawamba. Takes more than shots fired to knock you down."

"Yeah, well," I said, my stomach doing flips. "Petito thinks I should get a gun."

Instead of the sharp intake of shocked breath I expected, she made a pensive clicking sound with her tongue. "He's not wrong."

My brain raced immediately away from the topic, and I blurted out another. "They found Lorraine murdered."

Again I was surprised by her lack of surprise. "I had a feeling. What happened?"

I caught her up on what I'd learned, easing out into traffic as I did.

"You think the guy she met with was the murderer?"

"I think we have to consider that possibility. I'm sure Petito will check any security footage they have, but it might be deleted already. Maybe I can put out an appeal on the podcast to anybody who was in the café that night."

Heather took in a slow, deliberate breath. "About that. Maybe we should wait a little bit before dropping another episode."

"What?" I said in a voice that stopped just short of being a screech. "You were the one telling me how I had to strike while the iron was hot, and how we had a moral obligation to help this family find Leeya's killer!"

She cleared her throat. "I know I did. But that was before someone took a shot at you. Morgan and I were talking last night after we left, and—"

I slammed on my brakes for a red light as a thousand conflicting thoughts slammed together in my brain. "You and Morgan? You sat down over dinner and had a little conversation about how I should live my life?"

"Capri." Heather's voice took on the sort of slow, steady quality used to calm a toddler. "We just love you and want you to be safe."

My mind reeled. "So what am I supposed to do, Heather? Just walk away from this? It's too late now even if I wanted to, which I don't. You wanted an investigative podcast, and asking questions people don't want to answer is part of that."

"I'm not saying stop completely," she said. "Maybe lie low for a little while until the police catch the guy. Ryan and I can take over your tours. I can even be your boots on the ground for the interviewing if you want."

I narrowed my eyes dangerously at my dashboard. "Have you been talking to Petito?"

"Of course not."

I struggled to keep my voice calm and collected. "Okay, cool then—just one thing. Tell me that if it were you, *you'd* be willing to sit home and cross-stitch while other people went after the killer."

She sighed. "No, I wouldn't be. That's why I said you should get a gun. I've been thinking about getting one myself. My cousin says he can teach me to shoot."

As I struggled to put together a coherent response, another call beeped at me. "I have to go."

"'Kay. Just think about it." She hung up.

I connected the other call. "Capri?"

I winced at the sound of my ex-husband's voice. "Todd. Now's not really a good time, can I—"

"Oh, I bet it's not a good time. Just like it wasn't a good time when Morgan ambushed me."

My heart sank into my ankles, and pain seared through my temples. "About what?"

"Really, Capri? You told her I'm trying to get the Hayes Valley house? You know, there've been plenty of times I didn't agree with something you said or did, but I never once trash-talked you to our daughter."

For a moment, guilt washed over me—but then anger and indignation grabbed it by the neck and throttled it. "Don't you dare, Todd. I just told her about our conversation. As one of your business partners, she has a right to know if you're having problems that could hurt her future."

His voice rose, and took on a dangerous quality. "How dare *I*? Whatever issues I'm having in my life, I'm not the one someone *shot at* last night, am I? What if Morgan had been walking next to you, and she'd ended up dead? Before you start throwing stones, clean up your own damned side of the damned glass house."

With that, he hung up.

• • •

I have no idea how long I spent sputtering and gasping at my windshield. I only know if some guy in a Miata hadn't leaned on his horn, I'd have never realized the light was green. As it was, I'd allowed the calls to distract me, and I was now running late for my Alcatraz tour. I floored the gas pedal and ran a couple of orange lights—that felt a little too cathartic—but still almost missed the ferry out to the island, something that has never happened in the ten years I'd been giving tours.

As I settled into a seat, I tried to take myself by the mental lapels and give my brain a good shake. But my brain proved annoyingly resistant, and throughout the entire tour kept diving back into a spinning spiral of self-doubt. Sure, Petito had told me I should back off, but he'd been telling me that since the day he met me. For Heather to say it was an ice bucket right to my face. Since we were kids, Heather had been riding the sidecar of my life decisions by unabashedly encouraging me to take risks, whether that meant smart ones like starting my own business or stupid ones like wearing four-inch heels to a dead-of-winter frat party. No path was too rocky and no sandals were too strappy. For her to balk at *anything* was a huge red flag.

But if I was honest with myself, what had really burrowed its way deep into my cortex was the visual of Morgan being shot instead of me. It was one thing for me to be bold and brave when it came to my own safety, but the line began and ended with my daughter. Todd was right—I was dragging her into danger. I was being even more irresponsible than he was.

By the time I finished the tour and returned home, my spiral had turned into a cyclone. I trudged into my bedroom, dropped my bag and jacket onto the floor in a heap, then dropped myself onto the bed in the fetal position. What had I been thinking poking my nose into all of this? Sure, I'd managed to solve Sylvia's murder and the Overkill Bill murders, but I hadn't had any choice—either Morgan or I—or both—had been headed to jail. And I'd almost gotten myself killed in the process. Now here I was sticking my nose into something that had nothing to do with us because of some misguided delusion that I might be able to become the twenty-first century's answer to Nellie Bly.

My phone pealed from deep inside my purse. I was tempted to ignore it—I wasn't in any fit state to talk to anybody—but I'd already been irresponsible enough. I was a mother and a business owner, and I didn't have the luxury of drowning in a vat of self-pity amid my responsibilities. So I dug out the phone and checked to see who was calling.

My mother.

Fear stabbed through me. "Ma. Is everything okay?"

"Yes, honey, everything's fine," she said. "But *you* don't sound okay."

Her voice spun me back through the years and I was a child again, tiny and scared, wanting nothing more than to crawl inside my mother's embrace for comfort. Sobs ripped through me, and as the tears poured down my face, all the thoughts that had been swirling around my head poured over the phone. She listened in near silence, making soothing sounds until I ran out of steam.

"Well," she said when I finished. "You've had a trying few days."

"I don't know what I was thinking, I really don't. When am I going to learn to look before I leap?"

She cleared her throat. "Would you like to hear why I called you?"

My thoughts screeched to an abrupt halt. It wasn't like my mother to push aside someone else's emotion, no matter how important the reasons—invalidating someone else's feelings was a sin on par with murder, or bras with underwires. Something was *very* wrong.

"I'm sorry. Yes, of course."

She cleared her throat again. "I read over the sample chapters you sent from the Overkill Bill book."

Okay, now it made sense. Like everyone else, she'd called to tell me my brief flirtation with investigative journalism was a huge mistake, and my breakdown forced her to find a more gentle way to tell me so she wasn't just piling on. "It's okay, Ma. You can be honest."

"I was calling to tell you how powerful your writing is, Capri. You made me care about the victims, and you made me care about the suspects. With every word it's clear how important each and every one of them is to you, and how much you need their truth to be known. This book is important, Capri. I'm so proud of you for writing it."

I sat, stunned, looking for words that wouldn't come until some dark corner of my brain spewed out, "Of course you think that. You're my mother."

"I've never been the sort of mother who lies to spare her children's feelings. Do you really think I'd encourage you to keep writing a book if it wasn't any good, especially one that was so upsetting for your father?"

It was a valid point. My insistence on writing the Overkill Bill book had put her in a very awkward position. She'd gone out on a limb to help me while knowing it was going to upset my father, all because she believed in me and that I was doing the right thing. If I was dropping the ball, she'd surely let me know. "No, I don't."

"The universe put you in this place for a reason—there's a job here only you can do. You were meant to investigate Sylvia and Overkill Bill. And after hearing everything you just told me, I believe you're meant to help this other family, too."

As an adolescent, I'd routinely rolled my eyes whenever my mother started in with her woo-woo hippie Age of Aquarius *the universe planned this* ramblings, and that portion of my brain picked this moment to rear up again. "Petito would tell you in no uncertain terms that it's the police's job, Ma. All I'm doing is risking my life and my daughter's life."

"No, that's exactly wrong. What the police do is not the same, and investigative reporting is just as important as what they do. Like Bob Woodward and Carl Bernstein. They saved this country, Capri. Somebody has to keep an eye on the people in power."

It was a song I'd heard my mother sing countless times before—how she'd watched every moment of the Watergate hearings with Leo on her hip and me in her belly, and she'd forced us both to watch *All the President's Men* at least once a year since I was born. "That was government corruption, Ma. The Overkill Bill case was a set of local murders that the police worked hard to solve."

"And that makes it even more important that someone like *you* was there to take a second look and find the truth. I've been listening to some true-crime podcasts since you started yours, you know, because

I want to understand the whole phenomenon. You all do more than just report. You're investigative watchdogs that keep interest alive and eyes on cases. The stories need to be told."

"I agree with all of that. But that doesn't mean I'm the one who should be telling them. In just a couple of days I've managed to get myself shot."

Her voice took on an edge of steel. "I know I instilled in you the importance of standing up for what's right, even if it's dangerous. You know I went to jail more times than I can count for protesting, and you know all those protesters risked their lives."

"But Todd was right. If Morgan had been—"

"What Todd said was manipulative, because he needed to pull attention away from his bad behavior." There was a rare, angry crispness to her words. "On any given day, any of us could get hit by a bus or carjacked or a million other things. Life isn't guaranteed, and the best we can hope for is to make ours *matter*. I've never known you to be the sort of person who allows fear to control her decisions. If you walk away from Leeya and her family, what lesson would *that* teach Morgan?"

Her words finally sank down into my brain, past the fear and the guilt and the frustration. Just like my mother had raised me to be willing to sacrifice for what was right, I'd tried to raise Morgan the same way. "A coward dies a thousand deaths, but the brave only die once." I grumbled the paraphrase as I reached for a tissue to swipe across my face. "Actions speak louder than words."

"That they do, my dear daughter." I could hear the smile in her voice, and the pride. "So what action are you going to take today?"

There wasn't even a question. The only choice was to fight.

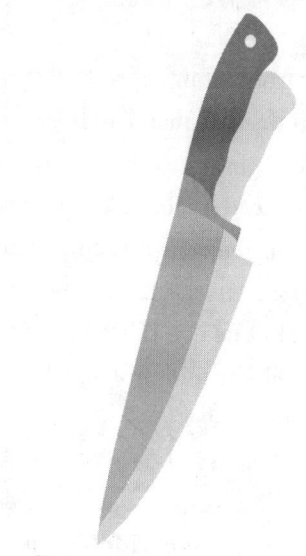

Chapter Thirty-One

Armed with a freshly brewed pot of coffee, I perched myself in front of my whiteboard and started from the beginning.

Kody Marcus went up first, because he was the only person with admitted and clear animosity toward Leeya—not one but three possible motives, between the collection agency she'd set after him, the Min-Pan, and his dislike for women who refused his advances. Any of those could have led to an altercation with Leeya, and ended with him stuffing her into her own freezer, then grabbing her keys so he could come back and get rid of her body once he established an alibi. For all I knew he was an old friend of Lorraine's, and they'd been in cahoots to create an alibi for him. I jotted a note making a search for connections between Lorraine and the suspects my top priority.

Next up was Jenna. Her jealousy for Leeya was even more serious than I'd first suspected, since she'd slept with Leeya's boyfriend. True, it was usually the cheaters who ended up dead, not the cheat*ees*. But jealousies and resentments between siblings could run deep, and such tensions could bubble and erupt in unpredictable ways during a confrontation. Especially if realizing Leeya had stumbled on a Gold Rush treasure map had been a final straw for Jenna.

And yet, if overboiling emotion was the motive, it seemed to me Zach was the more likely culprit. I'd never seen any evidence of violence in Jenna, but Quinn told me he had a temper, and Khalil had witnessed it in action. Sure, Leeya had walked away from their initial fight, but he could have easily returned. Since he was known around the building and probably had a spare key, the logistics of it all would have been easy.

As much as I didn't think she was a serious suspect, I had to consider Quinn. Just because I'd confirmed Zach was a cheater, that didn't mean she hadn't been angry at Leeya for ending their friendship. Or maybe, in her anger at being friend-dumped, she'd helped herself to the Min-Pan on the way out of Leeya's life.

Then there was Roger. As much as I hated to buy into stereotypes about criminals, past behavior was the best predictor of future behavior. That made him the most likely person to have stolen the Min-Pan, despite his protestations of loving Trisha. I didn't doubt he loved her—his emotion toward her had seemed very genuine to me, even touching. But how many humans in the course of history had discovered that love wasn't enough to keep them away from bad behavior? Old habits might have kicked in and been overwhelming, and he may have found himself in a situation where the only way out was murder.

Last was Trisha. As a mother, my gut resisted the idea she'd killed her own daughter. But she'd proven herself to be clueless at best when it came to her daughter—she didn't know half of what was going on in Leeya's life—and dishonest at worst. Either way, they weren't as close as Trisha wanted to claim, and when Leeya refused to give her more money, that may have been one bridge too far. Trisha wasn't going to live the high life on the money Leeya left for her, but it was nothing to sneeze at, either.

I looked over the list, and rank ordered them. Kody and Roger seemed to be the most likely suspects, with Zach and Jenna coming in next. Trisha was last, and Quinn got an honorable mention.

With all of that sorted out in my head, I made myself another huge cup of coffee and set to work on phase two. First I left another message for Zach, walking a careful line between sounding urgent enough to hook him into returning my call, but not so urgent that he'd guess I'd figured out what had happened between him and Jenna. Once that was done, I dug into any connections between Lorraine and the suspects. It was time-consuming, arduous work, but it had to be done—yes, Petito would get access to her email and phone, but if Lorraine had been up to something illegal with someone, she would have been careful to cover those sorts of tracks. She most likely would have communicated via burner phones or some such, and that wouldn't show up the easy way.

The job started off simple enough, with a series of Google searches pairing Lorraine's details with the names and details of each suspect, then hoping some article would pop up showing that Lorraine had come in contact with one of them in the course of her teaching or some other arena. When I came up with nothing, I switched to social media, which was infinitely more time-consuming and arduous. Since there were no first-degree connections I could find, that meant I had to cross-reference all the people Lorraine followed and who followed her with the followers and followees of each of the suspects. That meant compiling lists, scrolling endlessly, and plugging name after name after name into search bars. Thankfully, Lorraine's list of followers was on the shorter side, both on Instagram and Facebook, or it would have taken me a week to do even a cursory search. Only after I came up short and was working the kinks out of a nasty neckache did it occur to me that Ryan probably knew of some sort of program that could have searched it all for me in a few minutes. I chose to believe that wasn't the case for the sake of my sanity, then moved on.

Phase three involved pulling up the names of all the fellow

employees at her school and at the nonprofit, then quickly checking them against the lists I'd made. I also did a quick scan of their social media accounts. While I didn't turn up anything directly relevant, the process helped identify several women who were reasonably close friends; I sent DMs out to them telling them who I was and asking them to call me. Then I rounded off my efforts by going onto Craigslist and Fiverr to see if I could find any old ads looking to hire an actor to play a role in San Francisco this past Friday night. I couldn't, but for all I knew the relevant ad had been taken down, or a side deal had been made on the back of some other sort of deal.

I sighed, took a mental step back, and regrouped to consider my options. As far as I could see, I had three avenues of attack. One was to go ambush Zach. The second was to head over to Lorraine's house in Roseville and get into some hardcore sleuthing—interviewing neighbors, staking out houses—but that long drive would have to wait for my next day off, since I only had about two hours before my last online tour of the day. The last option was to dive back into figuring out the cipher on the Min-Pan. I did a quick calculation both of my time and my priorities, and figured Zach probably wouldn't want to talk to me for long, so if I hurried, I could try to catch him at his house.

• • •

After sending texts to both Petito and Heather letting them know where I was going, I headed out. Zach's apartment turned out to be in a dirty dusty-rose Victorian-esque apartment building in the lower Haight, the kind with an entryway lobby housing one panel of mail slots and another with intercoms to each apartment. Zach's was listed as #1B, and sure enough, when I hit the button, I heard a vague buzzer on the same level off to my left. The building was already quiet when I entered, but somehow after I buzzed the apartment, it went a notch quieter, and I got the odd impression I was being watched. I glanced up and around the enclave for a security camera. I couldn't see one, but that didn't mean there wasn't one hidden somewhere. I caught myself holding my breath as I listened for any sound—but none came. I buzzed again, but again there was no response.

I pulled out my phone and called Zach's number. Sure enough, a tiny cell phone ring floated across the air from my left.

Just as I was reaching out to push the buzzer again, Zach's voice crackled over the intercom. "Hello? Is someone there?"

I modulated my voice carefully, putting on the slightest edge of desperate nervousness. "Zach? It's Capri Sanzio. I've been trying to reach you. I really need to talk to you."

"Right. Come on in." I heard a thunk in the door to the left.

I pushed through the door into a miniature hallway that contained another door across the way and a staircase up to the next floor. The door swung open to reveal Zach's spiky black hair.

"Sorry about that," he said as I entered the apartment. "I was in the bathroom when the buzzer rang."

Sure, that was one way it could have happened. Or maybe he'd seen me coming up the street and tried to play possum, but knowing I could hear his cell phone shook him out of his tree.

"Not a problem." I put on a nervous half smile. "I'm just glad I caught you in. I really need to talk to you."

"Right, that's what you said on the phone. I just got home from work. I was about to call you back."

I had no doubt. "That's okay, this works better anyway."

He looked around uncomfortably. "Would you like to sit?"

I really didn't; I wanted to stay as close to the door as possible. But I also didn't want to set off any alarms, so I moved forward toward the couch. My eyes skimmed over the room—part living area, part office with a messy desk overlooking the bay window—as I shifted in. The furniture was generic and functional, of decent quality, but nothing with any style of note. I'd seen apartments like this before, most often school friends of Morgan's who spent nineteen out of twenty waking hours working. I perched myself carefully on the edge of the gray couch closest to the front door.

He sat in the chair across from me, in between me and the door. "What's going on? Have you found out something about who killed Leeya?"

I slipped my hand onto the top of my bag, painfully aware of the Taser that hadn't yet arrived from Amazon. I took a mental deep breath and forced myself to get on with it before I lost my nerve. "I had a conversation with Khalil Jackson last night. Leeya's neighbor. He told me that a few days before Leeya was killed, she broke up with you."

Fear flashed across his face for a quick moment. Then he covered with a downcast glance and a wave of his hand. "Our relationship was always a little fiery. We broke up and got back together more times than I could count."

I continued to watch his face carefully. "Khalil said you broke up because Leeya caught you having sex with Jenna."

His eyes snapped up at me, and this time he didn't bother to hide the emotion on his face. His hands tightened into fists, and I braced to run.

Then his face crumpled.

"I know how this looks. If the police knew she caught me cheating with Jenna, they'd use it as a motive to say I killed her. But you have to believe me, I'd never hurt a hair on her head." He stared directly into my eyes. "Yes, I did a shitty thing. A real shitty thing. But I didn't kill her."

"Khalil said you were angry when she broke up with you," I pushed.

Anger flashed across his face. "Of course I was angry—at myself. I loved Leeya." He must have caught the look on my face, because his brows puckered together. "I did love her. But I've always had this—

weakness, I guess, when it comes to women, and Jenna just kept coming for me. And Leeya couldn't forgive me."

A tangential thought occurred to me. "The pictures that Jenna took at Leeya's celebration dinner. Did you delete some of them because you thought Leeya would see them and realize you were having an affair with Jenna?"

He looked confused. "Pictures? I didn't delete any of Jenna's pictures. And she didn't take any that gave anything away because I never would have allowed that to happen. I'm not stupid."

I'd have to trust him on that. "Leeya realized the story Quinn had told her was true, though, didn't she?"

He nodded. "She asked me if I lied. I came clean and told her I did. She started to cry, and said she'd destroyed the only real friendship she ever had because of me. I told her I'd fix it, that I'd talk to Quinn. But she just kept shaking her head and saying she never wanted to see me again."

I put on a sympathetic voice. "So you got angry, and things got out of control. You didn't want it to happen, but—"

"No, it wasn't like that." Tears sprang up in his eyes. "I swear it wasn't. When she told me to leave, I left."

I decided to roll the dice. "But you came back later."

"What? No! I never saw her after that. If that neighbor guy says I came back, he's lying." He popped up out of his chair and reached for his phone on the coffee table. "I need to talk to the police and straighten this out. I wanted to tell them the truth right away, but Jenna told me it would land us both in jail for no reason because they'd never find out otherwise. But they need to know. I'll take a polygraph, whatever they want. They need to know I didn't do this."

There was a desperation in his eyes that cut to my core. I knew what it was like to be suspected of murder, and I knew the terror of thinking I had no way to clear myself. My gut told me he was telling the truth—but then, I'd been played before. I couldn't take any chances, especially of Jenna getting back into his head.

"You should call now. The sooner they hear from you, the better." I nodded at the phone in his hand. "I'll give you Inspector Petito's direct line."

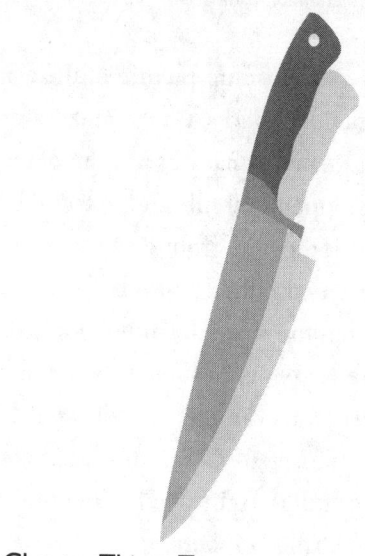

Chapter Thirty-Two

I stayed with Zach until he reached Petito, then listened to him repeat the story he'd told me. He agreed to go down to be interviewed, and I watched him head off in an Uber. As I headed back home, I tried to sort through the implications of it all and determine my next move. Zach was right, just because he cheated on Leeya didn't mean he killed her, but it didn't mean he hadn't, either. Still, I couldn't see how else I could follow up until I heard what he told Petito. Besides, I only had just over an hour before my next tour—but if I hurried, I might just have a few minutes to take another stab at turning myself into San Francisco's answer to Bletchley Park.

Once back home, I pulled up the transcription I'd made on the Min-Pan of the background patterns and double-checked it for accuracy. Then I tabulated the frequency of each symbol in my notebook and pulled up a site that listed out exactly how frequent each letter was in English. I plugged in the options as best I could, but that turned out to be frustratingly little—I was fairly confident which symbol stood for E, but that was about it.

After finishing up my online code, I decided to try another tack: I cropped a close-up picture of the symbols and did an image search. Google identified several similar codes, but try as I might, I couldn't adapt them to what was in front of me.

I stopped to think, and to take a long sip of my most recent cup of coffee. If the background symbols were the code, each of the symbols represented either a number or a letter. I counted up twenty symbols, ten too many for numbers, so I had to be dealing with letters. There were lots of substitution ciphers that worked in a predictable pattern, for example, substituting Z for A, Y for B, etc. So I made some guesses about how the numbers of lines and dots might indicate order, and used the one I'd identified as E for a starting point to plug in established ciphers.

Every one gave me strings of gobbledygook.

I pushed away from the desk and paced around the room, fearing I was barking up the wrong tree, but fully aware I was far too stubborn to give up in the face of overwhelming evidence. "How has someone not invented some program that can decipher any code imaginable?" I muttered aloud, then instantly stiffened as my brain heard what I'd said. Because of course someone probably had—at least one good enough to crack something created by two kids in the mid-1800s.

I hurried back to my laptop and plugged in *program for deciphering code*. Several sites popped up—but they all used letters as input. There was no way to enter my strange symbols.

So change the code, my brain whispered to me. *Assign each symbol a letter and plug* that *in. If there's an underlying pattern, the program should be able to identify it from that. The* pattern *is what matters, not the exact symbols.*

Was that true? Would it work? I wasn't sure, but it was worth a shot, especially since I'd just assigned a bunch of possible ciphers to the symbols. So I typed in the first string of gobbledygook into the program, and held my breath.

The program spit out a series of letters:

Seconddeckaftendleftmostcabinetremoveleftsideinternalboardsearchbetweenyourribbing

Words jumped out at me. I hurried to put spaces in between them:

Second deck aft end leftmost cabinet remove left-side internal board search between your ribbing

Little prickles of excitement tingled up and down my arms. These were definitely instructions to find a hiding place—and since it mentioned things like "aft" and "ribbing" and planes didn't exist in 1850, boats were the only possible source of those things.

The only problem was it didn't specify which boat.

I raked my teeth over my bottom lip and flipped my Pilot Precise back and forth as I looked for a logical next step. If Winston Phelps had hidden his stash of gold on a ship in San Francisco in 1850, three possible things could have happened to that ship. One, it could have left San Francisco and, since no boat lasts forever, eventually been demolished. If so, the treasure was long ago discovered or destroyed. Two, it could have been demolished right in San Francisco, with the same effect. Or three, the ship might still be in San Francisco—or rather, buried underneath it. At that time Winston would have been able to access some of the landlocked ships, and he'd have been reasonably confident such a ship would stay put for a while.

My phone chimed, reminding me about my online tour. I shifted gears into giving a top-notch quality tour, then switched back into decoding mode as soon as it was over.

But before I could start, my phone rang, and my pulse sped when I saw Petito's name. "Hey," I said.

"Hey. I'm about to turn onto your street. Are you at home? Do you have time for an update?"

"I am and I do. I have news for you, too."

• • •

As I crossed through the house to open the door, I couldn't tell if the flutters in my tummy were because I was excited to see him again, still angry with his overprotective BS, or scared of what might be contained in his update. When I opened the door, I read a similar mix of emotions on his face.

He leaned in to kiss me gently. "How are you holding up?"

"It's been an emotional day," I admitted. "How did it go with Zach? Can I get you a glass of wine?"

"I'd appreciate that." He pointed down onto the porch. "There's a package here for you."

"Wow, that was fast." I stepped out to grab it. "I ordered a stun gun from Amazon."

"Glad to hear it." His face remained tense.

I tossed the package on my entryway table, then led him to the kitchen to grab a bottle of wine. "What did he say?"

"Not much more than he told you, despite us making him retell the story of their confrontation five times. She broke up with him, he left, he never saw her again. Swears he has no idea who Lorraine is. His friends claim they were out together but so far we haven't been able to find any confirmation other than their word."

I poured out two glasses of wine. "Anything you can share about Lorraine?"

One hand ran through his hair with a fierce swipe. "The ME confirmed she's been dead at least two days, more likely three. And her hotel now says she never checked out Sunday morning."

"Wait." I felt my face pucker in confusion. "They changed their minds?"

"She had an automatic checkout set up, the kind where you don't have to show up at the front desk, you just leave the keys on the bed and be on your way. When housekeeping went to clean the room for the next guest, all her belongings were still there, untouched. But when I called that hadn't happened yet."

I nodded as I poured the wine. In large hotels like the Vincennes where they juggled at least several hundred rooms, you often couldn't check in until three or four in the afternoon because the rooms weren't ready. "But they didn't call you when they figured it out?"

Annoyance flashed across his face. "By the time they realized, the manager I spoke with was gone for the day. The one who took over figured Lorraine just decided to extend her stay, and since they had her card on file, didn't worry about it."

"And nobody noticed for *three days*?" I wrapped my arms around my chest against the specter of disappearing without anybody noticing.

His jaw flexed—he wasn't pleased, either, and I suspected he'd let that be known. "It's off-season. They're not full and didn't need the room. And the housekeeping staff rotates, so nobody noticed nothing had been touched."

"Right," I said. "It would have looked like every other room where the guest is out for the day. But that can't be legal."

"Mistakes were made." He rubbed his chin.

"What about her friends? Have you been able to find them?" I took a generous swig from my glass. "I found a few potential names during my searches."

"Give me the names. The hotel is working on a list for us of everyone who checked in on Thursday. That should identify them."

"If they even exist," I grumbled. "And the whole story wasn't just an invention for me."

He seamlessly followed my leap in logic. "Excellent catch on the café—crucial, in fact. The café footage is long gone, but we checked

Lorraine's phone records and she received a text at ten Saturday night, from someone claiming to be 'Craig Fredricks' of the *Examiner*. The phone it came from turned out to be a burner, and you won't be surprised to find out there's no Craig Fredricks employed at the *Examiner*."

I set my glass down. "And if she never checked out, she most likely never made it back to the hotel. So smart money says Craig Fredricks is our killer."

Petito nodded. "Sure seems that way."

My brain churned over the new facts, trying to make sense out of them. "But unless they were using some sort of predetermined code, that means Craig Fredricks lied to get her to the café. Why would he have to pretend to be from the *Examiner* if she was working with him to create an alibi by pretending to see Leeya attacked Friday night?"

"I don't buy that it was predetermined code. If she knew the person, something simple would have sufficed. They wouldn't have wanted to leave something so obvious on her phone for us to find."

I leaned against the counter. "It fits better if the killer saw her interview in the *Chronicle* and was worried Lorraine saw more than she realized. What better way to lure her out to kill her than pretending to work for another paper, since she'd signaled she was willing to talk to the press?"

Petito's jaw clenched again, and his eyes bounced around the room. "I don't suppose knowing our killer is getting rid of witnesses will convince you to back off until we catch him?"

My mind flew back to my conversation with my mother. "Not a chance."

He sighed, scratching his chin with this thumbnail. "Have you given any more thought to getting a gun?"

I'd prepped for this. "I wouldn't be able to get one and learn how to use it fast enough. That's why I ordered the stun gun."

His eyes met mine, and the set of his jaw made clear both that he recognized my sidestepping for what it was, and that he intended to revisit the topic in the future. "True. So, given this killer's agenda, I'd feel better if you keep me apprised of your movements until we bring him in. And yes, I'm aware it's a sketchy request to make of a woman I'm in a relationship with."

I smiled to acknowledge he wasn't just being controlling. "I can do that."

He continued to hold my eyes. "And I need to hear you say out loud that you'll leave the dangerous moves to me and my team."

"Believe you me, I have no desire to seek out danger." I picked my glass up again and gestured it toward my office. "But since we're on the subject of updating you, I think I solved the cipher."

For the first time since he arrived, I saw some of the tension retreat from his posture and new life come into his eyes. "Show me."

I gave a brief explanation as we crossed into the room. "So I'm thinking the only way the treasure still exists is if it's on one of the ships under the city."

"Strange that Winston didn't specify which ship. That seems like a big piece of information you wouldn't want lost."

"Yeah, that's been bugging me, too. I suppose it's possible Winston included that information in whatever letter he sent with the Min-Pan originally, and now it's lost to time." I leaned in, examining the decoded words. "But something else is bothering me about it, too."

"What's that?"

"Bear with me because I know this is going to sound crazy. But I really don't like the word 'your' at the end of the instructions. Maybe I've just been writing so much lately I'm inordinately obsessing about words, but . . ."

He leaned in and read the sentence aloud. "*Second deck aft end leftmost cabinet remove left-side internal board search between your ribbing.* You're right—wouldn't it be *the ship's* ribbing or just *the* ribbing?"

In that moment I learned my brain finds nothing sexier than a man who can level-peg me when it comes to hyper-parsing words within an inch of their lives.

"Yes, but it's more than that." I pointed to the beginning of the sentence. "He's used a telegraphic style, including only what he has to for the sake of brevity, right? So 'second deck aft end' rather than 'on the second deck, at the aft end.' He pulls out any unnecessary words—so why leave in 'your'?"

He scratched his chin. "What's your theory?"

My excitement deflated. "No idea. But when I look at it, it tugs at my inner editor like a piece of spinach in someone's teeth."

He half smiled, popping out his single dimple. "You're sexy when you're obsessive."

"Funny, I was just thinking something very similar about you."

He slipped his arms around me and looked down into my eyes. "You know what would be even sexier?"

I pressed myself up against him. "What?"

He raised one eyebrow at me. "Pulling out that stun gun you bought and making sure it's fully charged before you set foot outside this house again."

A laugh burst out of me despite myself. "Fair enough."

I slid one hand into his and led him back out to the entryway. I grabbed the box off the table, glancing down at the address label. "Huh, that's weird. Normally you only get same-day delivery when it's directly from an Amazon center. But this looks like it's from a third-party vendor."

His hand shot out to pin my arm in place. "Put it down."

One look at his stony expression was all I needed. I replaced the box and raised both hands off it.

He dug into the pocket of his jacket, now hanging on my coat tree, and extracted two nitrile gloves. He snapped them into place on his hands, and then reached for the package.

"Is it safe for you to do that? Shouldn't we call somebody if you think it's a bomb?"

"We all go through an ATF course on detecting explosives. But you should be in the other room while I make the assessment."

I did as he instructed but kept him in my line of sight. He examined the package's labels and the loosely taped seams, then leaned over to sniff it. "No signs that it contains a possible incendiary device. Do you have a box cutter?"

I hurriedly retrieved it from my utility room.

"Back out." He gestured me out of the entryway.

"You just said there was no bomb." I kept my voice low.

"Most likely there isn't. But there are other ways it might be dangerous," he replied.

I quickly stepped back, visions of anthrax-laden envelopes dancing through my head.

He slit the tape on first one side, then the other. He reached for the flaps and my eyes squeezed shut reflexively.

"You have to be kidding me," he blurted.

I started forward, alarmed. "What's wrong?"

He held up the box so I could see the contents.

Tucked inside was the Min-Pan.

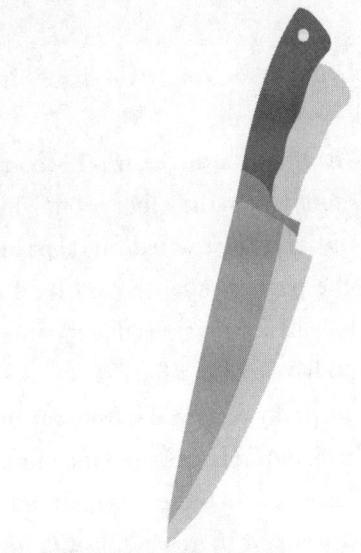

Chapter Thirty-Three

"Somebody has quite the sense of humor." Petito's eyes narrowed as he set the box back on the table.

My eyes flicked back and forth between the Min-Pan and Petito's face. I found it far more chilling than humorous—the fact that the killer had followed me and figured out where I lived freaked me out more than the shot they'd taken at me. "What the actual hell?"

"Well said." Petito peeled off the gloves he'd used while opening the package and set them on the table. "I need to bag this up and have it tested. I have collection kits in my car. Don't touch anything."

"Of course not."

I stared at the Min-Pan while Petito dashed outside, half expecting it to burst into flames at any minute. Then my brain took itself off pause and I ran to grab my phone, then snapped pictures from every angle I could without touching it.

"Any chance you could let me see the back side of the pan?" I asked when he returned.

He pulled on a new set of gloves and carefully picked up the artifact, turning it so I could see. I snapped a picture, not that it mattered—there was nothing on it. "Dammit."

"You were hoping the name of the ship would be etched on the back?" he said.

I shot him a look, but he wasn't making fun. "Yes. My brain doesn't like leaving things like that unfinished."

"Couldn't agree more." He put the Min-Pan back in the box and slipped the whole thing into an evidence bag. "Good thing I didn't finish that glass of wine. I'm going to run this down to be processed right now. Hopefully something here will identify our killer. I'll call you tomorrow."

After Petito drove away, I sent a text to Art Lawler telling him I potentially had some news about the Min-Pan and asking if he had time to talk. Then I went through the motions of my bedtime routine and tried to go to sleep, but my logic circuits continued to whir at full speed. Why the hell would the murderer send the Min-Pan *to me*? If they didn't want to risk being caught with it, the far more sensible answer would be to pitch it into the Bay or Lake Merced or some dumpster on the other side of town. The police would be able to track where the package had been sent from, and possibly where the label had been generated. There was also a high likelihood of physical evidence in or on the package in the form of fingerprints or DNA, or even an errant hair. The sender wouldn't take that sort of risk just to get rid of the artifact—there had to be some solid reason why they wanted it to reach *me*.

My mind flashed back to the Zodiac Killer's letters. The prevailing theory was he sent them because he enjoyed toying with the police, that it gave him a sense of superiority to lord something over them they couldn't figure out. Another theory was he wanted to spread fear. Was that what this killer was doing? Was he just trying to mess with my mind?

I wracked my brain for any other case that might be a closer fit. It pulled up Matthew Muller, who'd pleaded no contest to kidnapping Denise Huskins in 2015. He'd sent communications to a journalist rather than the police, including an audio recording proving Denise was alive when the police accused her boyfriend of killing her. When Muller released Denise and the police then decided the whole thing was a hoax, Muller sent further emails to convince the police the kidnapping was real, not a hoax. Could something like that be the reason I'd been sent the Min-Pan? I couldn't see how, since me having it didn't really clear anybody or prove anything. Just sending me the Min-Pan didn't negate the murder committed to obtain it.

Unless, I realized—unless the theft of the Min-Pan *wasn't related to the murder*.

Everyone knew I'd been asking about the Min-Pan, so maybe the thief was afraid my fixation on it would keep me and the police away from the real reason Leeya had been killed. Maybe sending it to me was a clear statement they didn't want anything to do with money connected to a murdered woman.

Or maybe they just wanted me to think that. Maybe they'd already solved the cipher, and had obtained the treasure—after all, if I could solve the cipher, someone else could, too. Except if I was right and the treasure was buried under the city of San Francisco, there was no way to obtain it without a professional excavation team. So maybe when they realized that, they decided sending the Min-Pan to me was the best way to thwart a no-win situation.

I threw back my covers and got out of bed. Whatever the truth was, I couldn't help but feel like I was missing something, and I needed something to relax and kick my subconscious into gear.

I padded into the kitchen, downed half a bottle of sweet pickles, drained the rest of the wine I'd left in my glass, then crawled back into bed hoping the pieces would work their way together while I slept.

• • •

Although I woke in the morning with no more clarity, I did have a text from Art telling me to call him whenever it was convenient for me. But Thursday was one of my busiest days—I had a slate of four nearly back-to-back tours filling up my day. So I spent the day fending off questions from tourists about Overkill Bill during the tours, ignoring hints from Ryan and Heather about when I was going to put together an actual Overkill Bill tour, and checking my phone obsessively hoping for updates from Petito. By the time I had enough time to reach out to Art, the sun had set and evening was upon us.

Hey, do you have a few minutes now? I texted him.

He responded almost immediately: *Was just about to text you. I heard from one of my contacts with some information about the Min-Pan.*

Tingles of excitement danced up and down my arms as I texted a quick response. *What did you hear?*

Somebody's been asking about it. The person thinks the treasure is on the Mariah, the whaler I mentioned at the other excavation site.

The tingles of excitement shifted to prickles of fear. After the decoded message on the Min-Pan pointed to one of San Francisco's buried ships, I figured that put the kibosh on anyone searching for it since you'd need an excavation team to reach it. But, if an excavation team was already in the process of doing that hard work, that opened up a world of possibility for a potential thief.

Why do they think that? I asked.

My source says they were oddly cagey about why. And he got the sense that time was of the essence.

Neither my brain nor my fingers could handle any more texting—I tapped the contact to put through a call to him.

He answered right away. "Hey, Capri. Probably best to talk, anyway. I don't like how reticent my contact was. He didn't want to put anything into writing."

I pushed back against the alarm creeping up my spine. "That sounds ominous. Is he in the Triads, the Russian mob, or the LCN?" The addition of the last signaled I was trying to be funny, since San Francisco's branch of La Cosa Nostra had been quiet since before I started college.

And yet, he didn't laugh. "*He's* not. But I wouldn't be at all surprised to find out whoever he's talking to is. Or worse."

What was worse than organized crime? The very thought deflated all my sass. "But—you're an academic. You work for the Maritime Museum. How are your sources getting mixed up with someone like that? Isn't there some law making it illegal to mess around with antiquities?"

His volume dropped. "The UNESCO convention, as well-meaning an attempt as it was to make sure antiquities stopped being stolen from their home countries, only succeeded in pushing the trade into the black market. Any curator who claims they've never been approached by an unsavory type is lying. Badly."

I rubbed my eyes and reminded myself that people were people and money was money. "Got it. I'm guessing that means you can't tell me who your source is?"

"I cannot, but I *can* tell you I trust him." His voice tensed. "You said you had news. Does it relate to the *Mariah*?"

I caught him up on what I'd decoded from the Min-Pan. "So yes, it looks like the treasure is on a ship, but I don't know which one. Do you have any guess about why your source thought the *Mariah* was the ship in question, or why it felt to him like time was of the essence?"

"He wouldn't specify."

"How about if the person was male or female?"

"No. I'm not even sure he knows."

"When exactly did this person reach out to him?"

"Initially, I don't know. But they spoke most recently this morning."

This morning—*after* the Min-Pan had been sent to me. "Didn't you say you were about to start up the excavations again sometime soon?"

"We just got the go-ahead to start tomorrow. We're doing some final prep."

The pricks of fear turned to full-on daggers slicing into my stomach. "That might be why time is of the essence. Who knows about your timeline?"

"It's a matter of public record. Anybody following the excavation efforts can find out in minutes."

"Dammit," I said. "If the killer has a theory about the ship, they must have figured out the code. And if you're starting the excavation up again tomorrow, that means they only have tonight to try to get at it themselves before the dig site is monitored twenty-four seven. How likely do you think it is that your source is right about which ship is at issue?"

"How likely is it if I mention cement-filled barrels in Golden Gate Park you'll know which serial killer I'm talking about?"

"Anthony Sully. Former cop. Active in the eighties."

"And would you know where to find his crime scenes?"

"All the same scene. He tortured and raped women in a hangar in Burlingame before bringing them here to dump them."

"You see my point. We know more about these ships than anyone on the planet. Even the smallest hint will tell us something nobody else will see."

I did see his point. Any colleague of Art's knew his stuff, and that meant the killer was likely on his way to recovering the treasure. And once they found it, they'd be on the next plane to a non-extradition country.

We had to move, and fast.

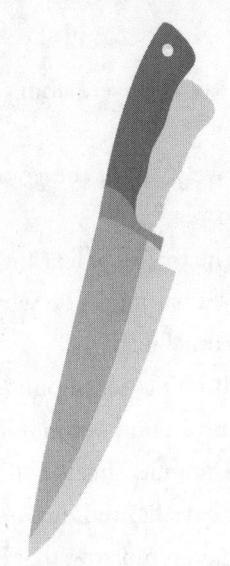

Chapter Thirty-Four

I texted Petito immediately about the potential danger to the *Mariah*. I expected him to be skeptical given the vagueness of Art's information, but he jumped instantly—apparently dirty money really did flow through the antiquities black market like a flash-flooding river through the desert. Within the hour he had a team in place surveilling the site of the *Mariah*, ready to grab anybody who put a single hair through its safety gates.

Of course I asked if I could be there. Of course he refused to allow a civilian to be in a situation that involved potential danger. Of course I objected and made a fuss and argued with him for a good half an hour. Of course nothing I said made any difference, and he stuck by his decision.

That turned out to be one of the biggest mistakes he'd ever made.

I tried to resign myself to waiting at home, reminding myself I should just be proud I'd done my part—there was no way I'd be able to get near the site, and even just trying could give away the ambush the police were trying to set up. Besides, with any luck, it would all be over soon; the killer would be caught red-handed trying to steal money from an archaeological site, and that would almost certainly allow the police to gather the evidence they'd need to convict the perpetrator of Leeya's and Lorraine's murders. So, to keep myself from obsessing about it all, I turned my attention to the podcast episode I needed to record and the Overkill Bill chapters I needed to write.

I've often been amusedly frustrated by how getting the human brain to work is like wrestling a greased pig: the harder you try to make something come to you, the faster the little piglet squirts out of your hands, leaving only a nasty stain on your shirt and some stinging scratches from their little cloven hooves. But as soon as you give up, the piggy leaps directly into your arms—and as soon as I was writing the next chapter about my grandfather's trial, the solution to my ciphering problems popped right into my mind, clear as day.

The numbers on the Min-Pan that I'd thought were useless were anything but: they were a code within the other code.

During all my arcane research on ciphers, I'd seen numerous examples of ciphers that used an orienting key to direct the decoder to which items were relevant; for example, a hidden message might be contained on the page of a book, and a simple list of numbers could direct you to which words or letters should be picked out of that page. Maybe, just maybe, the numbers on the Min-Pan tools were a key, directing me to which symbols to pull out of the background cipher.

I snatched up my Moleskine and flipped back to the page where I'd jotted the original numbers—81 56 5 48 74 63 10 39 31—then flipped to the code I'd deciphered from the background symbols.

I counted to the eighty-first symbol: N.

My heart sank—there was no *N* in *Mariah*. My theory must have been wrong.

I pulled out the fifty-sixth symbol, followed by the fifth. A, then another N.

My crushed hopes deflated further, and I almost stopped. But my borderline obsessive-compulsive tendencies prodded me to continue, so I counted out the rest of the numbers on the list.

T. U. C. K. E. T.

The word jumped out at me like a rabid raccoon: *Nantucket*—one of the ships currently being excavated at the site I'd visited with Art. That's why the initial code contained the extra word "your" that didn't fit with the rest of the grammar—Winston needed a *U* to spell out the name *Nantucket*, but there wasn't one in the rest of the message.

I did a celebratory fist pump and laughed out loud—the killer had gotten it wrong. He must not have figured out the last part of the cipher and had used some other criterion to decide on the *Mariah*. Either way, he was looking in the wrong place, and the only thing he was going to find was the police stakeout waiting for him. The irony was so delicious I decided I'd earned myself a little reward, and trotted off into the kitchen to pull down the tin of amaretti cookies I kept stashed for special occasions.

I was on my third cookie, still giggling and self-congratulating, when the back corner of my brain raised its hand.

I ignored it, too happy with my win to allow it to ruin my good time.

It cleared its throat and started speaking without my permission. *Maybe the killer didn't get it wrong. They know you're on their trail. What if they put out a red herring to Art's colleague to throw you off the scent?*

Every cell in my body turned to ice. Because if that were true, the police were waiting in the wrong place—and the murderer might be making off with the gold that very minute.

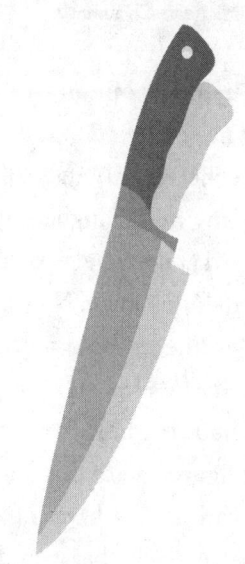

Chapter Thirty-Five

I sprang up and paced my office, trying to convince myself the simpler explanation was the right one, that the killer had just failed to decode both halves of the cipher. But I couldn't be sure, and if the killer managed to find the gold, they'd likely be across the border to a non-extradition country before the sun came up, and any chance of getting justice for Leeya and Lorraine would be gone with them.

I grabbed my phone and stabbed at Petito's contact. When the call went to voicemail, I literally growled at the phone in frustration, then tried again—and again it went to voicemail. Had they put their phones on silent or something to avoid giving away their position? Surely they'd heard of putting them on vibrate?

I continued to pace like a cat trapped in an elevator as I considered my options. For one, I could go down to the *Mariah* excavation site myself and find Petito. But if they were hidden away, I wouldn't be able to find them without breaking in myself, which would involve several felonies and considerable property damage, and possibly getting shot.

The other option was to go to the *Nantucket* site and catch the killer myself.

At the very thought of doing something that stupid, the majority of my brain laughed hysterically, slapped its knee, and rightfully shouted at me that every horror movie ever made was fueled by similarly deluded logic. No way was I gonna be *that* girl.

But, the intrepid journalist portion of my brain screamed back, *you have the element of surprise.*

I had to admit that was true. The killer wasn't expecting me to have figured all of this out. If I was smart about it, if I brought someone with me so I wasn't alone and we brought weapons to protect ourselves, well, that would be a very different type of movie.

I called Todd first. He was tall and strong and despite our recent kerfuffle, I was sure he'd want to keep me safe. Unfortunately, he didn't pick up. I left a quick message, then moved on to Heather and Ryan. They also didn't pick up.

You can leave messages telling everyone where you're going, the intrepid journalist part of my brain wheedled. *That'll keep you safe.*

All that'll do is ensure they know where to find your body, the sensible part snapped back.

In this case, I had to side with my sensible half—we were veering too far back into horror-movie territory, and I was well aware of my weaknesses. Going alone and with no gun was suicide, plain and simple. Even the stun gun I'd ordered wouldn't have been enough—it wasn't the kind that shot darts, so you had to be in reach of your target to use it. Since this killer had successfully strangled two women already, I had to assume they'd be able to overpower me, too.

I dropped into my chair, deflated but convinced I was doing the smart thing. Even if it meant the killer got away scot-free to live a life of pisco sours on a beach in Argentina, there was a fine line between boss-bitch journalist and corpse-in-waiting, and I wasn't willing to go this close up to it.

So much so that, when Heather returned my call, I reached for my phone fully prepared to tell her to disregard my message. Two unarmed women probably weren't a whole lot better than one, and all us going together would accomplish was putting us both in danger.

I tapped to answer the call. "Hey, girlie. Thanks for calling me back, but I don't think it'd be smart for us—"

"Capri." The icy fear in her voice silenced me.

"What's wrong?" I said.

"I need you to come right away to the *Nantucket* excavation site." She overpronounced the words like she was reading them off a screen. "Come alone, unarmed, and don't call the police if you want to see me alive again. You have half an hour."

The call disconnected, leaving me in terrifying silence.

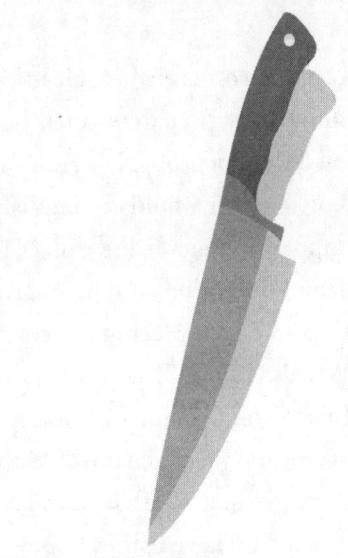

Chapter Thirty-Six

For the first time in my life, I would have given anything to own a gun.

Icy panic tightened my chest as my brain quickly tabulated the results of countless true-crime cases I'd read over the years, trying to determine whether calling the police or not was more likely to keep Heather alive. Neither option had a good outcome. The lizard portion of my brain screamed at me to *follow directions*, but the newly primed-and-pumped rational portion pointed out I'd already told the police where I was going, regardless. So I called Petito again and left him another message, then called Kumar and Garcia, his homicide detective partners, to be extra certain. I briefly considered calling 911, but the associated flashing lights and blaring sirens were guaranteed to seal Heather's fate.

I stared at the time. I only had half an hour to get to the site, and it would take me at least ten minutes, possibly more if traffic was jacked up. My best bet was to keep calling Petito on my way, hoping beyond hope that he picked up before I arrived, or that some other solution would present itself.

But by the time I screeched into a red zone a block away from the excavation site, I was still solution-free. I turned the corner onto the side street containing the entrance to the site and quickly scanned the environs. The large fence surrounding the site loomed up impossibly high in front of me—my intermittent yoga practice wouldn't come close to helping me here. I'd need to hope for one of those bursts of adrenaline that helps mothers lift cars off their babies. But—surprise, surprise—the nearest streetlight was out, and as I approached, I only narrowly avoided the shards of glass scattered around. The killer had taken out the light; hopefully whatever they'd done to break into the site would still be available to me, too. Sure enough, near the gated area a long, clean slice bisected the fence covering. I cautiously pulled the canvas forward to peek in; the chain-link fence behind it had been snipped through. I stepped through the opening, then gently replaced it behind me.

Once inside, I stood motionless. The darkness was a double-edged sword, providing me cover so I could orient myself and hatch a plan, but hiding God-only-knew-what horrors awaiting me. The muffled, distant street sounds harshly foregrounded the immediate silence and murky shadows, as though I were surrounded by a forest of mute, watching eyes. A shiver tightened my muscles, and I forced myself to assign labels to the lumps of gray slowly emerging from the landscape as best I could from memory of my earlier trip. Was there something I could use as a weapon, or for some other sort of advantage? The storage sheds were easy to pick out, but the darkness distorted the relative dimensions of the space so I couldn't get my mental map to track.

But I didn't have the luxury of time to sort it out—at least another five minutes had elapsed since I'd parked the car, leaving me only ten minutes more to reach Heather. I pulled out the small flashlight I'd been hoping I could do without. Nobody was waiting for me—which meant Heather and the killer were most likely down in the excavation space looking for the treasure.

I was going to have to climb down one of the shafts.

The memory of that temporary ladder, dangerous enough in the full light of day, sent icy dread down into my legs and broke me into a clammy, nauseated sweat. I forced myself forward, strafing the area with the flashlight, certain someone would jump out and attack at any minute. The shaft loomed up in front of me far faster than I'd thought it would, and I sent a desperate flash of the light around for any last-minute makeshift weapons. But the sheds were locked, there were no other entrances, and nobody had left any random crowbars lying around.

I peered over the side. About twenty feet down, light glinted off a moving surface. My mind flew back to Art's lesson about the tides that washed through the landfill twice a day; with the sump pump off, the water had seeped halfway up the shaft. Thankfully the top platform was still above the level of the water—the minutes were ticking quickly, and I had less than five minutes to find Heather.

I took a deep breath, shoved the flashlight into my mouth, and threw one leg over the side of the ladder. My body swayed and my foot shook as it searched for the next rod down. I stretched further, foot flapping around in empty air—and just as I started to panic about plunging into the water below, my foot grazed the solid, semi-flat tube. I gingerly tested my weight on it, expecting it to slip out from under me, but the ridged tread was surprisingly stable. But my arms refused to believe this and refused to let go of the ladder with even one hand—so I slowly slipped first one hand, then the other, down the side ropes as far as I could manage. Only then could I convince my foot to lower onto the next rung.

Lather, rinse, repeat, I chanted internally, forcing myself to continue down. *Nothing scary here. No reason to look down. Easy-peasy.*

Finally my foot clanked against the more substantial surface of the small entrance platform. I grasped at the cold metal of the safety railing, securing both hands before allowing myself to release the ladder from under my feet. My knees wobbled as I stepped through the open door into the packed-dirt tunnel, fully expecting a gun to jab into my side.

The space was far more claustrophobic than I'd anticipated. Wooden planks stretched out almost immediately in front of me, delineating a ship's deck from the surrounding mud. Every few feet support beams dotted the space and joists crossed above, too low for my full five-eight height. I moved forward slowly, waving the light in front of me, feeling like I was creeping through an ancient set of air-conditioning ducts.

Within a few short yards, I hit a wall of dirt.

"Capri," Heather's voice trickled up from below me. "Down here."

My stomach clenched violently as I searched the floor—and spotted a rectangle cut into the deck to my left. A second temporary ladder hung down from it. "I'm coming," I called out, keeping my voice as calm as possible.

I shoved the flashlight back into my mouth and dropped onto my butt so I could swing my legs down onto the rungs. I expected to climb down this ladder the same way as the first, but this ladder didn't have a wall of dirt directly behind it. I flew out awkwardly, then slid—and grasped desperately to stop myself from plunging down.

When the dim flashlight beam hit the floor, I realized I was only inches from the ground. The lower space was even more cramped than the deck above—I could have jumped directly down without hurting myself.

A mammoth beam of light suddenly blinded me.

"Stay where you are," a voice rang out. "Put your hands where I can see them."

Chapter Thirty-Seven

The voice sent a wave of ice through my limbs, and the flashlight dropped from my mouth. "Roger?" I said.

"Please don't act like you didn't expect me." He shifted, moving the beam of his headlamp out of my eyes, revealing a glimpse of his enraged face. Heather sat about six feet from him, eyes wide and face stiff, legs folded under her, arms behind her back. In all our years of friendship, I couldn't once remember seeing her look so terrified.

"I didn't. I believed your story about how much you loved Trisha."

"It wasn't *a story*, I do love her. But I read your suspicion all over your face, and I knew nobody would ever believe I had nothing to do with the Min-Pan." He waved one hand, holding a gun, toward Heather. "Untie her feet, then her hands."

I scrambled over to her and pulled frantically at the knot securing her ankles. My fingers were suddenly made of putty, slipping and sliding ineffectually. I gasped with relief when the ropes finally shifted, then moved on to her wrists. Roger checked his phone periodically while I worked.

When I finished, he jutted his head toward the ladder I'd just come down. "Now both of you back up the ladder."

I gawked up at it—why lure me down here just to send us back up? "But the treasure's down here—"

His eyes blazed at me. "I told you, I don't give a *rat's ass* about the treasure."

My mind raced to make sense of what was happening. "If you don't care about the treasure, why are we inside a buried ship?"

"Because I knew you were convinced I'd stolen the damn Min-Pan, and I had no idea how many other people you'd also convinced of that. The only way to throw suspicion off me was to throw it onto you, so I had to figure out how to use everyone's obsession with the Min-Pan to my advantage. I've always been good at code breaking, so that part was easy. And yes, because of my past, I have shady connections I was able to call on. When I put out feelers, I found out you'd been making inquiries. So I leaked information that would play into your certainty that Leeya was killed for the Min-Pan and the killer was searching for the treasure."

Daggers stabbed into my abdomen, almost distracting me from the huge hole in his logic. "But the information you leaked was about the *Mariah*, not the *Nantucket*."

"That's right," he said with a singsong intonation like he was talking to a child. "That way the homicide detective you had that bang session with Tuesday night would go look *there*, not *here*, when you went missing."

"But then how did you know I'd decipher the part about the Nantucket and show up here?" I sputtered.

He narrowed his eyes at me like I was having a breakdown. "What do you mean?"

"You leaked information about the *Mariah*, but—" I stopped abruptly as my memory kicked in. He hadn't waited for me to decode the part about the *Nantucket*—Heather had directed me specifically to the *Nantucket* when she called. "You didn't figure out all of the cipher, did you? You didn't know the treasure is on the *Nantucket*. You just came here because it's the only other excavation site besides the *Mariah*, so it was your only other option. You just picked one and once you made sure the cops were watching the wrong place, you kidnapped Heather and had her tell me to come to the other."

He tapped a finger onto his nose sarcastically, then gestured the gun toward the ladder. "Now move."

As I reached for the ladder, I struggled for some way to stall until Petito got my messages. "But the treasure *is* here. Shouldn't we at least look for it? You won't be able to come back after this."

His face twisted again with rage. "I told you *I don't want the damned treasure*. I'm about to make millions off the franchise rights for Holy Cannoli, and that's on top of the profits we're already making. Whatever piddly bullshit is hidden here, it's not worth the trouble. What I *want* is to get you off my ass so I can get back to the honest life I've built up for myself. So get up that ladder." His voice rose on the last few words.

As my brain searched frantically amid my confusion for something to say, I put one foot on the bottom rung. "But if you didn't steal the Min-Pan and you didn't kill Leeya, why are we all here?"

He shook his head. "That's what I'm trying to tell you. I didn't kill Leeya *for the Min-Pan*. I never *took* the Min-Pan, and I never *wanted* the Min-Pan."

The words he emphasized finally penetrated my brain. "You *did* kill Leeya—but you did it for another reason."

He pointed to the ladder. "Up."

I lifted my other foot off the floor, but immediately swung forward and found myself clinging helplessly to the ladder like I was back in gym class with the stupid knot-filled rope.

"Steady her." He gestured Heather toward me with the gun.

When she stepped in front of me to brace the ladder, my eyes met hers. While they were still wide with fear, her mouth was now drawn into a taut, stubborn line. I'd only seen the combination on her once before, when she'd come out to her father and he'd kicked her out of the house. That had nearly killed her—and I was damned if I was going to let this do the same. Hoping she could see my expression in the shadow, I narrowed my eyes and gave a sharp nod.

Then I climbed, trying to keep him talking. "So if you didn't steal the Min-Pan, how did you decode the cipher—oh, right, from the picture just like I did. But if you didn't steal it, why did you kill her? Because she told Trisha about your past?"

"You're just as bad as Leeya was—you'll never let that go," he exploded at me. "I killed Leeya because she threatened *to lie to Trisha, telling her* I stole it."

The words clanged through my head—something wasn't right here. Had Roger lost touch with reality? Had I? If he hadn't stolen the Min-Pan, how could Leeya possibly tell her mother that he had?

"That confusion?" he said, reading my face. "That's exactly how I felt, too, when she first accused me of stealing it. So I went to her apartment to talk some sense into her. But as soon as I started trying to talk to her, I realized the whole thing was a setup."

I continued scrambling to follow his logic. "A setup?"

His tone ramped up an octave. "What would *you* call it when someone frames you for a theft you didn't commit in order to destroy your romantic relationship? She'd been trying to get her mother to dump me from the beginning, and I was stupid enough to think when she saw we really loved each other she'd come around. I never in a million years thought she'd make up a vicious accusation when the truth wasn't enough."

Again the claim clanged in my head. The false accusation didn't fit with what I knew of Leeya—she'd verified her facts about Roger before going to her mother with them, and she'd refused to believe Quinn when Zach's character was in question until she got proof.

So what the hell was Roger talking about? Unless—unless he was trying to daze and confuse me, because that's what con men did. They said whatever they needed to say to convince you they were the good guys.

But good guys don't hold guns to your best friend's head.

"No, sorry," I said. "I saw Jenna's picture of you staring at the Min-Pan with my own eyes. You *did* steal the Min-Pan."

"Everybody stared at the Min-Pan that night! Leeya wouldn't shut up about how she was sure it was some sort of hidden Gold Rush treasure map, even though it was clear everybody was humoring her like we always did when she found some new piece of junk she was obsessed with." His voice shook with frustration. "See, that's the fucked-up thing about our world. People like to talk about paying your debt to society and deserving a second chance, but when push comes to shove nobody actually believes it. If there's a potential treasure map, of course the ex-con can't resist stealing it, right? But why would I risk losing the love of my life and my lucrative businesses for something that probably wasn't even real?"

"The hunt itself," I blurted, trying to ignore the ring of truth echoing in the back of my mind. "The pride of solving the puzzle. People on the sites go nuts."

"If that's what I wanted, I could have just *helped Leeya* find it," he snarled. "For fuck's sake, think it through. Who would've been the first suspect when the Min-Pan went missing? Me, of course. There was no way I'd be able to liquidate whatever I found."

The ring of truth turned into an air-raid siren. I'd seen Holy Cannoli myself, and Petito had verified both that the business was lucrative and that a franchise deal was in the works. Whatever treasure was buried on this ship was worth a few hundred thousand dollars at most—a huge amount for someone like me, but nothing compared to Holy Cannoli. And that was *before* factoring in the woman he loved—and while assuming the treasure really did exist, something that was far from certain. "So you killed Leeya to keep her from destroying your relationship with Trisha?"

"What else could I do?" he roared. "I was protecting myself. Leeya was the one who created the situation, not me."

"Trisha believed you before," I said. "You could have told her the truth."

"How do you prove a negative? If her daughter showed up saying I'd stolen from her—that kernel of doubt would have eventually destroyed us."

He was right about that, too. But the idea of a setup kept bouncing off my brain like a deflected satellite signal—I just couldn't get it to fit my picture of who Leeya was. If she really believed Roger had stolen the Min-Pan, that was one thing—but to set him up? "That doesn't fit with Leeya's character. She just wanted her mother to be safe and happy, and she'd started to trust you. Why else would she ask your advice about Kody Marcus? She wouldn't have made up something she knew wasn't true."

"That's what I thought, too, and that's why I didn't realize at first she was framing me. I thought she really believed I'd stolen it. But when I talked to her, she got downright devious."

More alarm bells went off in my head. "What do you mean, devious?"

"When I realized she was framing me, I told her she could drop the act because we both knew I hadn't taken it. Then she got all weird and her face changed and she accused me of 'gaslighting' her. That's when I realized she wasn't going to stop at *anything*, not even claiming abuse—when your gaslighter accuses you of gaslighting, there's nowhere left to go." He shook his head bitterly. "Talk about irony. The first time in my life I couldn't get someone to believe something, couldn't get her to believe I loved her mother, and it was the *absolute truth*." He extended the gun several inches closer to Heather's head. "Now get up that ladder, or I'll shoot your friend."

I jumped to scramble up onto the deck, then peered back down. Roger stepped over to the ladder. "I'm keeping my gun pointed right at her head while I climb up. If you try anything, she's dead instantly."

I froze in place, but hurried to keep him talking. "I don't understand how it all went down. She just called you up and invited you over?"

He climbed one-handed, impressively dexterous, gun trained on Heather's head as his gaze flipped back and forth between the two of us. "She called and said she needed to talk to me alone. When I got there, she confronted me with Jenna's pictures. She said she knew I'd stolen the Min-Pan, and told me I could keep it if I broke things off with her mother and left town. Said I could tell Trisha whatever I wanted to, but that if I ever came back, she'd show Trish the pictures."

Heather chimed in from below. "But why bother to pretend she really thought you stole it? Why not just tell you she was going to sabotage you if you didn't make your excuses and go?"

He pulled himself onto the deck. "That's what I mean about devious. It wasn't enough to get rid of me, she wanted to screw with my head. That's when I knew I had no options left."

My brain whirred and clicked—something still didn't fit. "So you murdered her on the spur of the moment. Then why put her in the freezer? Why not just leave her there to be found?"

He pointed the gun at me, then gestured Heather up. "I had to buy myself time to figure out how to cover it all up. Making sure the police couldn't tell when she was killed was the only way I could think of to give myself an alibi after the fact." His voice hardened again. "My original plan was to return later that night, but when I slipped out the back way, I saw the cop car and realized somebody must have seen or heard something. I had to figure out what exactly, but didn't know how. Thank God Lorraine spewed everything to the *Chronicle*."

"So you pretended to be a journalist and lured her out to the café to be sure she couldn't identify you," I said.

"Who knows what she might have remembered down the line? But if she hadn't been such an attention seeker, I'd've never been able to find her."

Attention seeker? She'd been trying to help a woman in distress. "And then you tried to get rid of me by shooting me, but you missed."

"What the hell are you talking about?" he said. "I never shot at you."

I felt reality shift under me again. "Tuesday night, in the Tenderloin. Near the alley."

He barked a laugh. "Wasn't me. I guess you have more enemies than you know what to do with." He turned the gun back on Heather as she pulled herself up, then slipped his phone out of his pocket and quickly glanced at it. "Killing you that way wouldn't have solved the problem, anyway. What I need is to introduce doubt, to make the police or at least a potential jury think *you* were the one hunting for the treasure. But at this point I'd be happy to shoot you both if you try anything." He pointed toward the exit out to the shaft. "Now go."

He was going to kill us anyway, that much seemed certain. "So after you killed Lorraine on Saturday night, you went back to Leeya's and pulled her out of the freezer. Why not just leave her there?" I glanced around for anything I could use as a last-ditch weapon.

"If Trisha hadn't heard from her by the next morning, she'd have called the police and they'd have done a more thorough search. If they found Leeya at home with no forced entry, they'd have gone right back to the police report you made, which would have pegged her time of death back to when my alibi wasn't solid. So I dumped her at the studio hoping the police would think it was a random attack Saturday night."

Once we reached the platform, Roger gestured the gun toward the ladder leading down into the water below. "Pull that up."

I exchanged glances with Heather, trying to glean whether she knew what he was planning. But she looked just as confused as I felt, so I pulled up the ladder, ice-cold and dripping from the water below.

"Drop it down onto the platform."

Once I did, he toed at it, trying to pull it toward himself. The wet ropes and metal slipped and slid like a recalcitrant bowl of spaghetti, and I fought back the hysteria-edged laughter that bubbled up in response to the futility.

He finally abandoned the effort. "Throw your phones over the side."

A fresh wave of fear stabbed a thousand knives into me—time had run out. I tossed my phone over the side, praying Heather had something in mind. But, once mine splashed, she tossed her own.

"Now," he said. "Jump into the water."

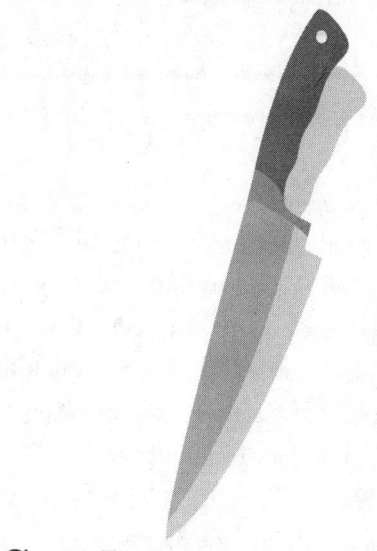

Chapter Thirty-Eight

I gaped at him as the meaning of his words hit me. "Jump in the water? Why not just shoot us here?"

He shrugged. "Your choice, but I'd rather not have to worry about somebody calling the cops when they hear gunshots. This way is cleaner—you jump into the water, and I climb up and out without anyone being the wiser." He read the reaction on my face and continued. "Don't get your hopes up. I'll be surprised if you can tread water for more than ten minutes, but even if you can, hypothermia sets in quickly when you're immersed in cold water. No way you're going to survive, I'll hang out long enough to make sure of that. And when the work crew gets here tomorrow, they'll assume you diverted attention to the *Mariah* so you could search for the treasure yourself, but slipped and drowned."

"You think she was stupid enough not to leave—" Heather started, but caught herself when she saw the look on my face desperately trying to get her to shut up.

He slipped his phone out of his pocket and waved it at her. "Do *you* think *I'm* stupid enough to not put a cell-signal jammer at the excavation site to make sure no calls made it through to the cops? And to not have cameras watching to make sure they didn't leave the site?"

My mind flew back to Roger repeatedly checking his phone—he must have been monitoring the camera he'd planted watching over the *Mariah*'s excavation site.

He continued. "But even if she left a message behind for them, they'll never be able to prove who lured you, even if they suspect." He gestured at Heather. "You first, spider monkey, while I've still got my gun on Kinsey Millhone here."

Heather caught my eyes, and I gave a tiny nod. She turned and stepped off into the darkness, landing with a gentle, graceful splash.

It was true, nobody would ever mistake me for the spider monkey of us two. But having the grace of an elephant had its own set of benefits—like making people underestimate you.

I took a tentative step toward the edge then leaped back away. "I—I can't do it—"

With a swift single motion, Roger shoved me over the side.

What he didn't know was when I'd leaped back, I'd stuck one foot squarely under the top section of the ladder, hooking it so it fell over the side with me.

What *I* didn't know was one of *Roger's* feet was also hooked into the ladder—and just before I hit the water, the ladder went taut, anchored to him on the platform.

But my momentum was too much for him. When the ladder went taut, it knocked Roger off-balance. He tried to catch himself—but swayed and fell over the side.

I hit first, and a thousand daggers of near-freezing water expelled all the breath from my lungs. A second later he landed on top of me, pushing me under just as I was gasping for breath.

Turns out, my automatic response to potentially drowning is to grab whatever I can reach like it's a life raft—in this case, what I could reach was Roger. I instinctively tried to climb up him, in the process pushing him down into the water. He must have reacted in kind, because I then felt myself being dragged back down. By then I was in full panic, all flailing legs and clinging arms, and neither of us could gain any purchase.

Suddenly something yanked us, and Roger went still.

I tried to stabilize myself against him, but we both sank. Heather pulled me toward the side of the shaft—I put out one hand and steadied myself enough to start treading water. "What happened?" I gasped.

"I reached for the headlamp because I knew it was attached to his head. Then I swung it into the wall of the shaft, and his head tragically followed."

I looked down at him. "Is he dead?"

Heather tilted her head at me. "Do you care?"

"I do. Because if he isn't, he could wake up at any minute." I flipped him over. "Where's the gun?"

We scrambled to find his arms while keeping ourselves afloat, but both were empty.

"He must have dropped it," Heather said. "And with no gun, he won't be able to overpower us."

"Hopefully." I glanced up at the platform, eerily illuminated by Roger's headlamp, which now seemed a thousand miles above us. "I kicked the ladder down thinking maybe we could throw it back up and catch at least one of the hooks on the platform, but . . ."

Heather followed my gaze up. "Yeah, not likely. Please tell me you called Petito before you came out here."

"I did, but you heard what he said about the cell-signal jammer. And Roger wasn't wrong about treading this water. My hands and feet are already going numb. We'll be dead before the police get here regardless."

Heather's eyes darted around the shaft. "What about this support structure holding everything in place? We should be able to climb up that."

We tried our best, and if the water level had been even a foot higher, we might have been able to manage it. But the vertical metal support bars that ran down the sides of the shaft were only intermittently ringed by horizontal supports, and the closest one was too high for either of us to reach. The vertical bars were too small and too flush with the shaft to allow us enough purchase to climb.

"Maybe if we scream someone will hear us?" Even as the words came out I knew it would never work. We were at least fifteen feet below ground, surrounded by buildings with nobody in them. If by some miracle our cries made it out past the site, they'd be so faint nobody'd take them seriously. In the meantime, we'd both started shivering so hard our teeth were chattering. I reached for the rope ladder still attached to Roger's foot. "I th-think the ladder's our only h-hope."

She navigated back toward me and helped me pull up the rest of it, a far more challenging task than it should have been since we were still treading water. But after what felt like an hour, we managed to retrieve it all, piling it up on Roger's either-dead-or-sleeping abdomen as we went along.

"You're the spider m-monkey," I said once we'd finished.

"That d-doesn't mean I can throw worth a d-damn," she said.

"You were on the softball t-team."

"You're t-taller than I am," I said.

"Not when we're in the w-water," she replied.

"Fine. We'll t-take t-turns." I lifted the end with the hooks on it, held the top rung like a javelin, and threw it up as hard as I could manage.

The rung went farther than I thought it would, I'll give myself that. But it still only rose about two-thirds of the way to the platform above us. Heather tried, but her throw was actually a bit lower than mine. I tried again and so did she, but our reach didn't improve.

"There must be something else we can d-do." Heather cast around desperately. "Maybe we could d-dig out foot holes in the sides and climb our way up?"

"We'll be d-dead long before we can d-dig out enough holes," I said.

"No, we only need to d-dig out a couple and then we won't have to t-tread water anymore. After two more, we'll be out and won't be l-losing body heat into the water."

Little bursts of hope fireworked through my chest. "It's worth a sh-shot."

Her arms disappeared under the surface and her face twisted with concentration. I followed her lead, reaching as far down as I could while treading water. But the dirt was packed together far harder than I'd expected and my half-frozen fingers were useless against it.

"Wh-what is this, b-bedrock?" I asked, checking to see if I had any skin left on my fingers.

She grimaced at me. "How would a ship get b-buried in b-bedrock?"

I glared at her. "It w-was a hypothetical question."

She glared back. "Us d-dying isn't hypothetical."

My growing panic finally smothered my fledgling hope. But my hope's death rattle woke my anger, and with as fierce a scream as I could wrench from my shivering lungs, I chucked the ladder up as hard as I was able—and sent it flying far higher than it had on my other attempts.

It still stopped short of the platform.

But, because of my chaotic throw, it hit the side of the shaft at a strange angle, then slid down the side—and one of the hooks caught on a horizontal support ring.

"Holy sh-shit," Heather said. "You couldn't d-do that again if your life d-depended on it."

I didn't think mentioning that our lives did in fact depend on it would be helpful, so instead I crossed over and tugged tentatively on the end of the ladder. Not only did it hold, the hook lodged more firmly between the ring and the dirt. "F-fat lot of good it d-does us," I said. "It only r-reaches halfway up."

She swam toward me, still staring up. "If I c-climb to the top of the l-ladder, I m-might be able to pull up the other end and th-throw it the rest of the way to the p-platform. There's h-hooks on both ends, r-right?"

"Yes, I th-think it's reversible." I stared up, judging the feasibility of what she was suggesting. "C-can you balance and th-throw at the same time?"

"Won't know until I t-try," she said.

I shifted so she could reach the rope. It held as she started up, but since the ladder was holding on by one hook only, the rungs hung lopsided and formed loose triangles rather than rectangles; she slipped her hand into the highest one she could reach, then stared down at the water while fishing with her foot.

"G-good news is, if I f-fall, it'll just be back into the w-water." She tugged again and rose almost completely above the surface.

My pancreas leaped into my chest as she reached for the next triangle, then the next. She moved carefully but still fluidly. She slipped—but recovered, and continued on.

When she got to the top, she tucked both feet into the highest rung she could reach, then pulled up the ladder from below her with one hand. I hurried to lift the submerged section from the water—she didn't need any extra drag making things harder. Slowly, inch by inch, she hiked up the rope, looping each section over her other arm as she went. Before long both arms and legs were visibly shaking from the effort.

"Take a b-break," I called up.

"No way. This is nothing next to doing plank during Pilates," she said.

Despite the false bravado and the no-longer-chattering teeth, I saw her eyes close for a few long seconds as she blew out a deep breath. Then she arranged her hand around the bottom rung, lifted it, and took careful aim.

It flew through the air. I tensed, readying myself to catch it. The rung hit with a clang—but didn't hold, and slipped back over the platform to the edge. My chest contracted with desperate frustration.

But as it reached the last piece of lattice work, one of the hooks latched on. With a sharp clang, the second one slipped into place beside it.

"Hell yeah!" I shouted.

"Damn straight!" Heather responded.

"Can you c-climb up?" I asked.

She tugged again, testing. "There's some slack, but I think I can make it."

"I b-believe in you," I said, hoping my fear wasn't as audible to her ears as it was to mine.

She pulled and adjusted, reeling in as much of the slack as she could, then seemed to make up her mind. "Ladies and gentleman—I give you the woman on the flying trapeze."

She shifted one foot to a rung on the now-upper part of the ladder, then brought her other foot alongside it. She gripped several rungs above that with her one hand, then, with another big exhale, let go of the now-bottom section she'd been hanging on to.

The ladder swung away from the wall, sending her rolling. Her body tensed into a straight rod, and one of her feet slipped off. Time seemed to stop as the rest of her fell along with it.

But her right hand refused to let go.

She hung there by one arm, legs flailing to locate a rung. She found a lower one, and it was enough. She pulled herself back onto the ladder, then continued up to the platform.

My heart started beating again and my lungs resumed drawing breath. She pulled up the ladder to dislodge the hook caught on the support ring, and once it was free, dropped it down so I could reach it.

It took me twice as long to climb up a fully functional ladder as it took her to navigate the makeshift slip-and-slide; I blame that on how badly my legs and arms were shaking with relief. Whatever the reason was, once she helped me up onto the platform, we wrapped each other in a huge, clingy hug.

After a few seconds we separated. "C-come on," I said. "We need to get to a ph-phone ASAP. Roger may still be alive, and I want him to stay that way so I can w-watch them cart him off to j-jail."

Once we reached the top, we hurried around to the main street as fast as our cramped, frozen legs would take us. My car keys were missing—they must have slipped out of my pocket during my scramble in the water. So we accosted the first people we spotted, a pair of selfie-taking tourists, and begged them to call 911. At the sight and sound of our shaking, they insisted we take their jackets while we waited for the police, and within minutes a small crowd of other do-gooders formed around us, contributing whatever outer layers they could spare.

Once the pile of coats had stopped my shivering, Heather narrowed her eyes at me. "Now. Please explain why I had to hear from *a homicidal maniac* that you slept with Petito on Tuesday night."

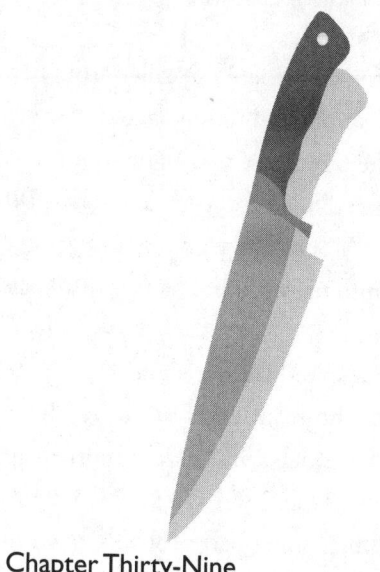

Chapter Thirty-Nine

"Mom. This time I'm putting my foot down. You need to rest." Morgan stood, one hand perched on her hip, the other pointing toward my bedroom.

"There's no point." I settled further into my kitchen chair. "The doctor said I'm fine and Petito said he'd call as soon as he's finished with everything. But I'll take a refill on the chamomile tea. And some pickles, because they said I could have extra sugar." I held up my cup.

She puffed air out her nose as she plucked it from my hand. "It's almost midnight!"

I pointed toward her old bedroom. "So go to sleep!"

She glared at me, silent and unmoving.

"Aw, you're so cute when you try to use my own Jedi mind stare against me. And you've almost got it right, but the ability to instill terror with a single glance doesn't fully kick in until you're a mother." I smiled. "I'm pretty sure it has something to do with the hormones."

She made a disgusted noise at me and turned away.

I rolled my eyes at her retreating back, then stood and started to tiptoe across the kitchen.

"No caffeine!" she called from her room.

I scrunched up my face in her general direction, then slunk back to the table. She was right about that—once the adrenaline wore off, I'd need to sleep. And as much as I'd never admit it because I didn't want Morgan to worry, a strange soreness from the cold water had set into my muscles, along with a nasty headache and a light case of nausea.

Despite Heather's and my insistence that we were fine, the officers who responded to the call had insisted we be seen by medical professionals. Since we'd both struggled to get warm after being in the water and didn't know whether that was due to shock or hypothermia, going had probably been the right move. The officers took our statements as we waited for treatment in the ER, and while they assured us they'd been in contact with Petito, they wouldn't give me any other information.

I listened with a tremendous sense of guilt as Heather recounted what had happened to her. Apparently Roger had lain in wait outside the Hub for Heather to leave, and when she did, he'd intercepted her with his gun. He'd forced her into his car, onto the dig site, and down into the ship. I'd been so worried about him going after Morgan, I never considered that if he followed me for any length of time, the person he'd see me with most often was Heather.

As I sighed and tried to push aside the guilt, Morgan reappeared. But instead of watching me with an eagle eye, her face was resigned. She slid into the chair next to me and folded her hands in her lap. Something was coming, and I had a feeling I wasn't going to like it.

"Mom. I know about the call Dad made to you." She met my eyes. "He didn't know it, but I was in the next room and I heard everything he said."

My first instinct was to reassure her, to take the burden off her shoulders the way I'd done her entire life. But Heather's advice came back to me, reminding me that I was at the part of our mother-daughter journey where I had to trust her to handle her own business. So I pushed down my instincts and simply said, "Okay."

"I confronted him afterward about it. I told him that if we were going to be in business together, he needed to treat me like an equal, not like a daughter. And I asked him what was going on."

I nodded, not trusting myself to speak.

"He dodged and weaved and wouldn't look me in the eye, and when I didn't give up he got angry."

From the expression on her face, I expected her eyes to fill up with tears at any moment, but they didn't. After a pause, she continued.

"He told me I needed to remember that I was the daughter and he was the father, and to treat him accordingly."

A thousand responses flew through my head as my angry mama bear reared up, bringing with them all the parallels to Leeya's dynamic with her mother. But, I held my expression steady.

"I told him if that's how he felt, it was best that we sell The Chateau. I'm not willing to be in a business where I don't know everything that's going on, and I'm not allowed to ask questions."

My brows popped before I could stop them. "What did he say?"

"He apologized and said he didn't want that. I suggested we take a few days to think through how we want this to work, and then make a decision. I've told the renters they can't move in until next week. If he can give me a reasonable explanation of why he asked to put his name back on this house and we can agree to some basic guidelines about the business, I'll consider moving forward. Otherwise, I'll put The Chateau up on the market."

I'd never before experienced my heart breaking and bursting with pride at the same time, and it took me a moment to gather my words. Thankfully, she was just as patient with me as I'd been with her.

"I'm so sorry you're having to deal with this, honey," I finally said, and slipped my hand over hers. "I know how much The Chateau means to you, and that couldn't have been an easy choice to make. But I couldn't be prouder of you for taking care of yourself."

"At the end of the day, it's just a house." She squeezed my thumb. "What matters is my relationship with my parents. If I get caught in some sort of shady situation because of him, it will be impossible for me to respect him. I'd rather lose The Chateau and preserve my relationship with him than the other way around." She took a deep breath, stood up, and leaned over to kiss my cheek. "Anyway. I know you well enough to know what he said to you got into your head, so I wanted to kick it right back out so we could both sleep better. 'Night."

I kissed her back. "Good night, honey. Sleep tight."

I watched her walk back down the hallway, then stared at the spot where she disappeared for several minutes. If I knew my ex-husband—and I was pretty sure I did—the situation wasn't going to be as clear-cut as Morgan wanted it to be. But, somewhere, somehow, I'd done something right with her, even if for the life of me I had no clue what. I needed to trust in that.

While watching him every second, of course.

I sighed, forced myself to put the issue aside, then stared down at Morgan's phone, which she was allowing me to use until I could get a replacement for my own. Why hadn't Petito called to update me yet? But as the obsessive portion of my brain tried to use telepathy to make it ring, the sensible portion reminded me that just like a watched pot does not boil, an obsessed-over phone does not ring. So, to distract myself, I went into my office to distill everything I could remember about the night's events into a podcast episode, an activity that turned out to be deeply cathartic.

About midway through the episode, my doorbell rang—Petito had skipped the phone call and come directly to the house. I squeezed my eyes shut for a moment and rubbed my brow for courage. Because it would have been so much easier to defend the evening's choices over the phone, *without* having to stare directly into those blue eyes.

But when I opened the door, his eyes weren't steely with judgment, they were smoldering with worry. As soon as the door closed behind him, he pulled me to him and kissed me with an intensity that made my muscle soreness melt away and my headache retreat.

"Hey, you," he said when he finally pulled back.

I exhaled slowly. "Thank goodness. I thought you'd be angry with me."

"Let's not get ahead of ourselves, I never said I wasn't. I have to get back down to homicide so I can't stay for long, but you'll have to defend your questionable decision-making skills to me tomorrow."

I bristled. "Great, I look forward to it. Because I called you multiple times for help, and I wasn't going to let my best friend be murdered because of me."

His jaw clenched and unclenched, but in the end he didn't take the bait. "I have news. I don't suppose you have any coffee made?"

"I was just about to make a pot." I threw a guilty glance toward Morgan's bedroom. "Is Roger alive?"

"That's the news. He didn't make it. And no, the impact and head injury didn't kill him, hypothermia did."

A strange mix of emotions rushed through me, all underlaid by an aching sadness to hear that he was dead. And not just because he wouldn't face justice—some other strange little corner in the back of my mind tugged at me, and my heart panged in my chest.

Petito's eyes scoured my face. "What?"

I took in a deep breath, then exhaled it slowly. "It's just . . . I don't know. I feel like something isn't right. I know he tried to kill me, but . . ."

He nodded, then waited for me to continue.

"I just can't make it make sense. Maybe I'm just flat-out wrong about who Leeya was, maybe she had no issue framing him to get him out of her mother's life. But why would she pretend to Roger that she really did think he'd stolen it? I can't make it fit."

"Maybe she really did believe he'd stolen it." He watched my reaction, judging my judgment.

"But that doesn't fit her character. Before she talked to her mother about him the first time, she'd done her research and had all the receipts. And she didn't believe Quinn about Zach's bad behavior without proof. She didn't accuse people without hard evidence." I shook my head and pointed toward my entryway. "And the other thing is, who sent me the Min-Pan, and why?"

He stood and crossed as the last bit of coffee sputtered through. "Roger told you he wanted it to look like you were the one after the treasure. Maybe that was part of the attempt?"

"So how did he get hold of it if he didn't steal it? And even if he did steal it, wouldn't it make more sense to leave the Min-Pan with us at the excavation site in that case, to frame me?" I dragged my teeth over my lip. "I don't know, maybe I'm overthinking it. Maybe it really is just that someone else stole the Min-Pan and when Leeya turned up dead they needed to get it out of their hands."

He poured two mugs and handed me one. "But you don't think so."

I shook my head as I gulped my coffee. "And Roger was adamant that he didn't shoot me. Why bother to deny that when he'd admitted to two murders and had a gun pointed at us?"

His brows shot up. "Maybe you were right all along. Maybe it was a stray bullet never meant for you."

I searched his face, weighing whether he was just playing devil's advocate. "Any one of those things might be a coincidence. But all together? I can't shake the feeling I'm missing something. And I get the sense you agree."

"One of my personal guiding principles is to never ignore loose ends. I've solved more than a few cases by pulling at them." He downed his coffee, then set the mug in my sink. "Hopefully the lab will find something on the package you received that gives us a name. But let me know if your gut comes up with a theory before then."

• • •

You'd think with everything I went through that night, I'd've slept like a baby. And to be fair, as soon as Petito left and my head hit the pillow, I did fall asleep, despite the coffee and Morgan's snores tearing through the wall between us. I'd barely finished making a mental note to tell her to get checked for sleep apnea before I was out like I'd been drugged.

But I woke less than an hour later, heart pounding and throat completely dry, convinced I was back in the shaft treading water. I got myself a glass of water and tried to shake it off, but when I snaked back under the covers, a slew of memories paraded through my head: Soul-chilling cold water stabbing every inch of my body. Roger's face as he held the gun to Heather's head. The desperation that sheared through me each time the ladder had bounced back from a throw like a hellscape boomerang.

I tried reading a book.
I tried listening to a guided meditation.
I tried half a glass of wine and a Tylenol PM.
None of it worked.

So I turned my head back to the loose ends. I went through the list of every person associated with Leeya and played out alternate scenarios and motives to see if I could come up with anything that plugged the holes in Roger's story. Maybe Trisha took the Min-Pan because she needed money, or Zach took it because he was angry at Leeya for breaking up with him, or Jenna took it because she was jealous of everything Leeya had, or Kody took it because he had no ethics when it came to money. Even Quinn—I only had her word for it that she hadn't been in Leeya's house for a month. Maybe she'd come to try to rekindle the friendship, and had stolen the Min-Pan then.

Does it really matter? my father's voice whispered in the back of my mind. *Roger admitted he was the murderer. He's dead now, and justice has been served. If the murder had nothing to do with the Min-Pan, do you really need to know who stole it?*

Yes—I very much did need to know. The horrible flashbacks to my evening in the shaft made it clear I'd never be able to find peace until every loose end was tied up tight. And, more importantly, I couldn't be sure justice truly had been served until all the pieces fit into place.

I slipped out of bed and retrieved my Moleskine, then went page by page through every step I'd taken investigating the case. I replayed everything in my head, looking for any remaining anomalies I hadn't been able to explain.

There was only one I could come up with: the deleted pictures from Leeya's dinner party.

Even at the time I hadn't believed it was a coincidence or a mistake. I'd assumed Jenna had taken a picture of something the murderer didn't want me to see, something to do with the Min-Pan, and the murderer had deleted it. Once I found out about Jenna and Zach, I figured Jenna had just deleted some compromising pictures she'd taken of him, but when he told me he never would have allowed her to take pictures like that, I went back to my Min-Pan-murderer theory. But what if that wasn't what happened at all? If the theft of the Min-Pan wasn't committed by the murderer, there would have to be some other reason why some of the pictures Jenna had taken that night would have to be deleted . . .

And as I rethought it all from that perspective, the remaining pieces fell into place, forming a theory that fit every strange anomaly. I hoped desperately it wasn't true—but as I planned out how to determine that once and for all, I feel into a deep, healing sleep.

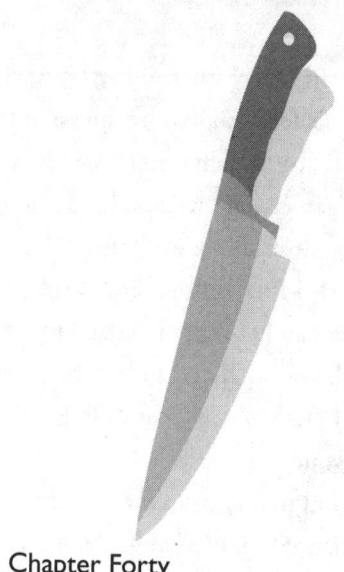

Chapter Forty

After a check-in with Petito the next morning to tell him that my gut had in fact come up with a theory, I made a not-so-quick trip to get a replacement phone, then made a series of phone calls to Jenna, Zach, and Quinn giving a simplified update about Roger and asking if I could speak to them for purposes of the podcast. They all said yes, and I said a little prayer I could pull off what I needed to pull off.

When Jenna answered the door, her eyes were again rimmed with red. "I'm so relieved you figured out who killed Leeya." She pointed me toward her couch, then dropped into her chair with a look of shock and confusion. "She was right the whole time about Roger. I never would have believed he could do something like this."

Once seated, I pulled out the contents of my bag and set them beside my leg. "Do you mind if I record this? It'll be great to have some clips of your actual voice for the podcast."

She waved the question away. "Sure."

I told her I wanted to start with the background, asking her to tell me again about her father and what it was like for the family to lose him. Her previous expression returned, and I had zero doubt she'd loved him with every fiber of her being; losing him had broken her. When she finished, I shifted her into a description of the family's life after his death. She took her time—nearly half an hour recounting it all—and I didn't rush her. I wanted her to have a safe space, just two people having a conversation, everything else forgotten and set to the side.

Then I transitioned to Roger. "Your sister was protective of your mother and took it on herself to research Roger's history."

She nodded and lit her third cigarette. "'Protective' isn't the right word. Leeya was controlling. She thought she knew better than everyone."

"But in this case, she was right." I put a sad twist into my tone.

"Ironic," Jenna said solemnly.

I walked her through Leeya's confrontation with her mother about Roger. Then I said, "It's weird, though, isn't it, that Roger stole the Min-Pan? You'd think you'd steer clear of stealing from someone you knew had already ratted you out."

Her eyes widened. "He must have figured Leeya would never have the guts to go to Mother again with her suspicions."

I shook my head like I agreed. "You know, it's funny. He admitted to killing Leeya and Lorraine, but he swore up and down he never stole the Min-Pan."

"Really?" She blinked at me, face blank. "Bizarre."

"It is. Especially since Roger was about to make several million selling franchise rights for the bakery. Stupid to risk that over some treasure that might be nonexistent."

She shrugged. "I guess it's like an addiction. Once you get a taste of money, especially free money, it just becomes impossible to turn away. Con men are psychopaths, right?"

I wagged my head. "I suppose that's one possibility. But if he did steal it, why deny it when he admitted everything else? Leeya wasn't stupid enough to accuse him with no proof."

She shrugged again. "She did have proof. You saw the picture of him looking at it yourself."

I pursed my brow. "I don't think she would have risked alienating your mother based just on that—it's too easy to explain away. I think there was at least one other picture that showed something far more damning. And I think it was one of the pictures deleted from the folder."

Her eyes widened. "And that's why he deleted it? But I can't for the life of me remember anything that would have been so damning."

I took a deep breath. "I don't think *he* deleted it. I think *you* did."

Her cigarette froze in midair. "Why would I do that?"

"I think you slipped the Min-Pan off the mantel and put it somewhere that incriminated him. Like the pocket of his overcoat, which I saw in another picture lying on her bed. Then you 'accidentally' took a picture containing that damning evidence." I put the word into finger quotes and held eye contact. "You framed him. You made it look like he stole the Min-Pan."

She burst out laughing. "You must be crazy, or stupid. Because if *I* was the one who confronted him, *I'd* be the one dead, not Leeya."

"I never said you confronted him. That wouldn't have accomplished what you wanted."

She shook her head confusedly at me. "That makes even less sense."

"Roger said Leeya was talking to everyone about the Min-Pan at the party. You knew that, and you stole the Min-Pan knowing Leeya would notice it missing almost immediately. When she started asking about it, you 'discovered' the pictures you'd faked and brought them to her."

"Why on earth would I do something like that?"

"Because you wanted to create a permanent rift between her and your mother. You knew she'd have to tell your mother, and your mother had already drawn a line in the sand. Getting Leeya to cross it would create a nice little space for you to slip in as Mommy's favorite."

She blinked at me, but remained silent.

"The only problem was, Leeya didn't go to your mother. She knew as well as you did she was skating on thin ice with your mother, so this time she decided to go directly to Roger. She gave him what she thought would be a compassionate way out for everyone—she told him he could keep the Min-Pan if he'd just go away and leave your mother alone. She told him to give her whatever excuse he wanted to save face."

Red blotches crept up her neck. "You never even met her, but you want to believe she was that noble."

I ignored the potshot and kept my eyes lasered in on her expression. "You didn't count on her approaching Roger. You also didn't count on the fact that Roger loved your mother so much he'd kill Leeya for trying to break them up. The realization that he was going to lose the only woman he'd ever loved over something he didn't do was more than he could handle."

I mentally tabulated the chain of expressions that paraded across her face: guilt, desperation, anger, fear, pride.

She stubbed out her cigarette. "That's the craziest thing I've ever heard in my life. There's no way you'll get anybody to even listen to it as a possibility."

I didn't blink. "I have proof."

"You can't have proof of something that never happened." She rolled her eyes, but I caught a small quiver at the corner of her mouth.

"Another thing that bothered me about it all was why Roger would send the Min-Pan to my house. The far smarter thing would be to dump it into the Bay."

"People do stupid things."

"They really do." I nodded my head vigorously. "Have you heard of touch DNA?"

She laughed. "Of course my DNA is on the stupid thing! I'm sure I touched it when she showed it to me. That doesn't prove anything."

I tilted my head. "That's not true, actually. Touch DNA usually identifies the last person who touched an object, not those who touched it previously. But the police wouldn't need to make that argument anyway. Because if you didn't send the Min-Pan, your DNA shouldn't be on the package I received. And it definitely shouldn't be on the *label* or adhesive attached to the package."

"See, now I know you're full of shit because I wore gloves the whole—" She froze and stopped abruptly.

"You wore gloves when you assembled the package?" I finished for her.

Her jaw clamped shut, and a vein popped out at her temple. "I didn't do any of that," she finally said. "But so what if I had? There's nothing illegal about it."

I shook my head. "You stole the Min-Pan from Leeya's house. That's theft."

Her eyes blazed. "Maybe she loaned it to me."

"If she loaned it to you, why would you need to take a picture with Roger's coat?"

"You mean the picture you're *speculating* exists based on missing file numbers?"

I kept my eyes pasted to her. "You sent a copy of that picture to Leeya. The police found it on her phone this morning after I asked them to look for it."

She opened her mouth to object, most likely to tell me I couldn't prove the picture had come from her—but she knew as well as I did they could trace the metadata. "It's a nearly worthless object. It would be a misdemeanor at best."

"It's a period artifact, so it's worth quite a lot. But the really damning part is that obstruction of justice is a felony offense in California. Once you found out the police were looking for the Min-Pan and you chose to get cute by sending it anonymously to me rather than them, you obstructed justice."

She shook her head. "Like I said. There's no DNA evidence on that package. And there's only your word I ever said anything about gloves."

I reached down to the side of my leg and held up my phone again. "Except I've been recording this entire conversation. You gave me explicit permission to do so at the beginning of our interview."

She stared at me for another moment—then lunged directly for my throat. "You fucking bitch! I'll fucking kill you!"

But I was ready for her. I'd also placed the stun gun that had been delivered that morning next to my leg, and in one quick move, I zapped her. She collapsed to the ground, jerking in pain.

I picked up my phone and called Petito in from where he was waiting outside.

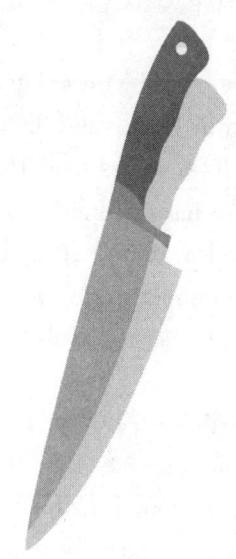

Chapter Forty-One

It took a little over a week to sort everything out with Jenna, a time frame that felt like a snail's pace to my impatient little heart, but which I was learning was lightning fast in the world of police procedure. After several days of nothing new, Petito finally told me he had news to catch me up on over the dinner we'd scheduled for that night. He'd wanted to take me out somewhere, but I'd insisted on making him my famous chicken scallopini—not at all because it would be a far easier journey to my bedroom from my kitchen than from a restaurant.

I blared my P!nk playlist as I pounded my chicken breasts into oblivion, then formed my little assembly line—cutlets, egg, seasoned flour. I gave myself the same prep pep talk I'd been giving myself since age ten about the wet-hand-dry-hand dredging method my mother had drilled into me—one hand touches only the wet ingredients while the other touches only the dry—and promised myself this would be the time I finally got it right. As usual, the first cutlet went perfectly, but I'd been fooled by the false confidence of success before, so I carefully maintained focus while grabbing the second one. Chanting "wet-hand-dry-hand" and moving with deliberate slowness, I managed to get the second cutlet breaded with one hand still fully dry. I was so excited I mentally high-fived myself—and grabbed the next wet cutlet with my supposed-to-be-dry hand. Then, as I released my traditional torrent of cutlet-related profanity at my pair of dripping hands, my phone picked that moment to ring.

I hurried to scrub off the salmonella goop, then stabbed at my phone.

Art's voice poured over the line. "Capri! Is this a good time?"

I shot a nasty glare at my recalcitrant chicken—an archaeological update about the Min-Pan's gold would be a most excellent excuse to pause. "Couldn't be more perfect. What's up?"

"We found it, Capri."

My pulse spun out and I grabbed the counter. "You found the treasure?"

"We did. The directions you deciphered were perfect, and since we'd started the excavation at the aft end of the ship it didn't take too much work to get us there."

I could barely breathe. "Was it actual gold?"

"Indeed it was. Three-quarters of a million dollars' worth, in fact. And since Winston Phelps has no living descendants, the money belongs to the city. And we're going to lobby to have it go to help fund the subterranean museum."

I couldn't help but break into a smile. "I'm so glad to hear that! If I can help with the lobbying, just let me know where to show up and I'm there."

"Actually, that's part of the reason I'm calling," he said with a tentative edge on his excitement.

My mind brought up images of city council meetings filled with graphs and charts and signed petitions. "Not a problem. It'll give me an excuse to buy a nice new business suit and get out of my tour-guide jeans and trainers."

He cleared his throat. "No need for that. We were thinking along slightly different lines. We were wondering if you'd do a podcast or two about it all."

I hadn't been expecting that. "A podcast?"

"Since you're the one who identified the artifact and deciphered the code, it would be enlightening to hear what process you used." His words tumbled out like he was afraid I'd say no before he could finish. "Then we could talk about how we uncovered the actual treasure, because we took video and audio of it all. You're the expert and you'll know how to do it best, but we think it would be an excellent way to raise public awareness about what we're finding at the excavation, and why it's important."

I picked up the line of his logic. "And that could help persuade the city to allow you to move forward with the museum, and use part of the gold to fund it."

He laughed sheepishly. "We certainly wouldn't complain if that ended up as a side benefit."

"I think it's an incredible idea. I'm annoyed I didn't think of it myself." My doorbell rang. "But I have to go. Can I call you tomorrow to work out the details?"

After we said our goodbyes, I hurried to let Petito in. As soon as the door closed behind him, he set down the wine he was carrying and wrapped me into a long, languorous kiss.

"Hey, you," he said when he eventually pulled back. "I brought wine. I noticed you have a penchant for zinfandel."

"I do. I'm also partial to pinot noir and Syrah."

"Interesting." His hand continued to caress my waist.

I dropped my hand to his. "Keep that up and we'll never eat."

He grinned. "Don't threaten me with a good time."

"Oooohhh no," I said with a laugh, and tugged him toward the kitchen. "I've been waiting a week for news. And as it turns out, I have some for you, too." I caught him up on my conversation with Art as he poured the wine, then set him to slicing mushrooms as I finished dredging my chicken and heated up my skillet.

"That's great news." He smiled, but then his expression turned dark.

I narrowed my eyes at him. "Tell that to your face."

He took a deep breath. "My news is more of a mixed bag."

My heart did a thunk-thud. I picked up my wine and took a swig. "Hit me with it."

"First off, some good news. We solved the mystery of Lorraine's house. She inherited a home from an aunt who passed away and used the sale's proceeds to upgrade her own living arrangements."

I nodded. "Once Roger confessed, we knew she wasn't involved anyway."

"Next up, we sat Jenna down with the picture of the Min-Pan in Roger's pocket we found on Leeya's phone, along with your recording. She took a plea deal."

My heart added a clank to the thunks and thuds. "Please tell me she's not just getting probation."

He returned to the mushrooms. "No, she's going to jail for five years on the second-degree attempted murder charge for attacking you when you confronted her. But she didn't admit to everything."

"What did she not admit to?" I slid my dredged chicken in the skillet, relishing the boisterous hiss as it sank into the melted garlic butter.

"She's adamant her intention was for Leeya to go to their mother. She never considered Leeya would go to Roger, and she never thought Roger would get violent," he said.

I nodded, still watching the sizzle and pop. "I think that's true. What she wanted was to alienate Leeya from their mother."

"I have a feeling a jury will agree with you," Petito said, and set the knife next to the finished mushrooms. "And so does the assistant DA. She's not confident she can make a charge of negligent homicide for Leeya's death stick."

An inconsistency struck me. "What about when she shot at me in the Tenderloin? That wasn't second-degree, that was a planned attempt."

"That's the other thing she didn't admit to. Shooting you." He took another sip of wine.

"Of course she's not going to admit to it," I said, and flipped my chicken. "But then, I can see how it would be impossible to convince a jury it was her who shot me when there's reasonable doubt about Roger."

When he didn't respond, I looked up from the frying chicken. His expression had turned even darker.

"There's something you aren't telling me," I said, watching him closely.

His face didn't move. "How much longer until the chicken's done?"

I threw a hand up. "Don't do that. Don't change the subject."

He raised a brow. "I'm not. But you'll want to give this your full attention, and that smells too good to let burn."

I pushed the pan off the fire. "Tell me."

He rubbed his chin. "We arrested a guy for armed robbery three days ago."

I stared at him, not blinking.

"We had him dead to rights, and it wasn't his first offense. So he offered information in exchange for a lighter sentence."

I didn't like where this was headed. "What information?"

"Information about a man who'd been hired to take a shot at Todd Clement's ex-wife."

I leaned against the counter as my stomach plunged into my knees, but refused to let my voice quaver. "Someone hired a man to kill me. Please tell me it wasn't Todd." I couldn't believe he'd do something like that—but then, two weeks ago I never would have believed he'd ask to be put back on the house.

He held my eyes. "We're working on finding out who hired him. I don't think it was Todd, because from what our offender said it's more likely someone who wanted to scare Todd, or scare you into signing the papers. The informant was very clear you weren't supposed to be hurt, it was just supposed to send a message."

I reached down and covered the scab on my arm. "A message? How many guys care if their ex-wife gets shot? It sounds more like Todd's trying to intimidate me into putting his name back on the house."

He reached for my hand. "These are the type who do their research. They'd know you're the closest connection he has now that his mother and father are gone. It's also possible he was stupid enough to tell them you'd refused to put his name back on the house, which would have tipped them off to you as a pressure point."

That definitely sounded like Todd's brand of stupid. "And if Todd was the one behind it, it makes no sense for him to call me and accuse me of putting myself in danger by recklessly investigating Leeya's death. He'd have tried to use it to leverage his name onto the house."

He nodded. "An excellent point."

But another thought occurred to me, and this time my voice did quaver. "I'm not his closest connection, Morgan is." I held his eyes. "Is this one of those mafia-don't-go-after-children things?"

He shook his head. "That's a myth. But you're right, it tells us something that they went after you rather than Morgan."

My mind flew back to something he'd said. "You said you're working on finding out who's behind it. But you know the identity of the person who shot at me, so you must have some idea."

He watched me carefully. "If our information is good, it's a guy who does grunt work for Shawn Malger."

I knew the name. Back when I was looking into my ex-mother-in-law's business affairs, I'd identified Shawn Malger as someone involved with several dirty business deals. "So the guy who was involved with my mother-in-law's investment companies is also somehow involved with Todd?"

"Allegedly. It's all still under investigation."

"But that's an awfully big coincidence if they're trying to get money out of Todd. And it would make sense why they wouldn't go after Morgan, if they know the house is their only chance of getting money out of him. Going after Morgan wouldn't get that for them."

"All true," he said. "And that's why we need to talk about your role as an investigative journalist."

My hands sprang to my hips. "I thought we talked about—"

He threw his hands up. "Let me finish. Yes, we did talk about it, and what you said about needing a partner who's not going to ask you to be less than you are? That's a big part of the reason my first marriage broke up. She couldn't handle me being a cop and wanted me to quit the force. So I get wanting to be with someone who loves you for who you are, not *despite* who you are. And the truth is, your tenacity and your intelligence and your need to fight for justice, those things are all what attracted me to you in the first place. So how could I justify cutting them out from under you?" He stared down at me, his eyes shifting into their deep, midnight-blue incarnation.

"Thank you," I said, dropping my hands off my hips and onto his.

He held up a finger. "Still not done, because we need to talk about the flip side of it. If that's how things are going to be, I have the right to expect you to take proper precautions. There's a reason private investigators apply to carry concealed, and if you're bound and determined to walk that line, you should, too."

"Would you suggest that for every investigative reporter?"

"Not every one, no."

I wanted to go on the defensive again, launch into how little sense it made for me to become a gun owner. But as I stared up at his face, I was struck by his expression. This was a man who knew more about the dark side of human nature in general and San Francisco specifically than I could even imagine—and that was saying something given the decades I'd spent pouring true-crime cases into my skull. Given everything he saw on a daily basis, he understood the dangers of gun ownership better than anyone, and the challenges of investigating murders. My mind flew back to Roger's face, and the water in the excavation shaft.

"It wouldn't hurt to look into my options," I said.

A relieved smile spread over his face, and he pulled me into his arms. "That was a lot easier than I thought it was going to be."

"Yeah, well. It's the only way you're gonna let me finish making my chicken."

He leaned down, so close I could feel the warmth of his wine-scented breath. "Funny, I'd forgotten all about the chicken."

And when his lips met mine, I forgot about it, too.

Acknowledgments

Hey there! If you're reading this far, you definitely deserve the biggest thanks of all—I can't thank you enough for choosing to spend time with me and Capri. Without you I wouldn't get to spend my days researching the city I love and making up cool stories about it, so thank you thank you thank you!

Once again, my editor, Madeline Houpt, was vital in helping me make this book what it is. Not just because she believed in the voice and in Capri, but because she took time to talk out plot ideas with me, had patience with me during the editing process, and poked and prodded at me to make it all the best it could be. It's so much easier to let my mind run free and try cool things when I know I have the most amazing safety net watching my back.

Two agents at my agency have played a role in this book. First, Lynnette Novak, who believed in the concept and secured the contract for me. Nicole Resciniti has picked up where she left off, and both have been there whenever I needed them, every step of the way. Thank you for believing in me and helping me carve out a path for my career!

I can't say enough amazing things about the incredible team at Minotaur. My cover designers, Rowen Davis and David Baldeosingh Rotstein, have again created a fun, happy cover that captures the essence of the book's soul. My copyeditor, Janine Barlow, is amazing—she knows my stories better than I do, and she keeps me on track so that when all is said and done it looks like I actually know how to use commas and hyphens. (Which I do, I swear—I just forget sometimes. That's my story and I'm sticking to it, and with Janine's help, you'll never be able to prove otherwise.) Hector DeJean, Emma Paige West, Drew Kilman, Mac Nicholas, and Stephen Erickson have been the best publicity and marketing team any book could ever ask for—not only did they get people to notice the series, they did it while answering a slew of annoying questions from me. To say marketing is not my strong point is the height of understatement, and their patience and expertise have been everything. They haven't just helped me, they've also helped me to learn to help myself. Elishia Merricks did an amazing job with the audiobook version in every possible way, not the least of which was bringing on the incredibly talented Stephanie Nemeth Parker to narrate. There's something indescribable about the joy you feel when you hear someone who really understands your characters and your world bring them to life.

I'm surrounded by an amazing group of writers who lift me up, and who lifted up this series. Catriona McPherson, Laurie R. King, Michelle Gagnon, and Jesse Q. Sutanto all took the time to read and endorse the first book in the series, helping ensure this second one made it into print. Adam Plantinga helped me sort out all kinds of things regarding the SFPD—any mistakes or liberties are completely my own! Others who helped prop me up on a daily basis include D. K. Dailey, Laurie Sheehan, Tammy Qualls, Mysti and Dale Berry, Vera Chan, Daisy Bateman, Erika Anderson-Bolden, Christina Flores, Dianna Fernandez-Nichols, Katy Corbeil, and Anna Jorgensen. SinC NorCal and MWA NorCal also play a crucial role in everything I do, from write-ins to get-togethers, to talks and workshops and research resources.

The absolute best thing about writing this series is it gives me an excuse to spend as much time as possible wandering around San Francisco, the coolest city in the world. Special thanks to San Francisco City Guides tours—I've learned so much from them. Their tours are free—if you come to San Francisco, you should take one!

Then there's my endlessly patient husband. He walks along foggy streets with me and pretends to be interested as I prattle on about why the fire hydrants in San Francisco are different colors, why the sidewalks have the street names stamped into them, and how the tides rise under the buildings. He entertains himself for hours as I go down research rabbit holes about historical places and people that will likely never make it into one of my books. He pretends he's not at all disturbed by my obsession with true-crime podcasts and documentaries. What more can you ask for in terms of a life partner?

And last but not least, I have three cats and a dog that keep me on task—the cats sit on my lap so I can't stop writing and the dog demands walks that give my brain a chance to sift through plot points. One of these days I'll find a way to insert a fur baby into Capri's life. . . .

About the Author

Michelle Chouinard is the author of the Serial Killer Guide to San Francisco Mysteries, and, under M.M. Chouinard, the *USA Today* and *Publishers Weekly* bestselling author of nine previous mysteries. Michelle has a PhD in developmental psychology from Stanford University and was one of UC Merced's founding faculty members. She lives in the Bay Area and enjoys caffeine in all forms, amateur genealogy, baking, and anything to do with Halloween or the zombie apocalypse.